CúChulainn of Eirú

Book I
The Isle of Shadows

By

Richard Roche & Derek Fennell

CúChulainn of Eirú - Book I: The Isle of Shadows
by Richard Roche and Derek Fennell

Cover and Maps by Mark Hill.

eBook ISBN: 978-1-3999-1105-4
Paperback ISBN: 978-1-3999-1106-1

First Edition

Dedication

For our parents,
Dick & Mary Roche
and
Mick & Mary Fennell.

Acknowledgements

The authors extend their deepest gratitude to the many friends and supporters for their feedback on drafts, inspiration and encouragement on this (almost) twenty-year journey to publication; we are in your debt. Thanks also to Mark Hill for his beautiful artwork, and to Donal O'Connor for early visualisations. We also thank Colmán Ó Raghallaigh of Cló Mhaigh Eo, Lissa Oliver of the Irish Writers' Union and Brian Langan for their insight and sage advice. Finally, our sincere thanks to Sophia Hadef for her belief in the power of myth and dark adventure.

iv

Foreword

The following is a modern reimagining of the ancient Celtic myths that comprise the Ulster Cycle of Irish Mythology. Whenever possible, this telling of the myth has remained as close as possible to the original stories and tales as they are reported in such sources as the Yellow Book of Lecan, the *Táin Bó Cuailgne* and others of the manuscripts written and illuminated by early Irish monks, as well as modern translations such as that of The *Táin* by Thomas Kinsella. However, there are a number of problems associated with a heavy reliance on these texts which have played a major part in the form of the current text. Primary among the problems with the original texts is the fact that they themselves are retellings of stories which had existed for generations in the form of an oral tradition and as such, they are subject to contamination for two reasons; firstly, due to the nature of the oral tradition of storytelling in the *seanchaí* style, certain elements of the stories will have been exaggerated to almost absurd proportions, while other aspects of the stories will be nonsensical, as in the example of the warrior who is slain in one part of the tale of the First Battle of Moytura only to be revived and slain again in a later part of the tale. Through such 'Chinese Whispers' have many elements of the original stories been rendered baffling to the reader, which in many cases is to the detriment of the storyline (although it should be noted that the preservation of the storyline was not always the primary purpose of the storytelling process for the seanchaí).

    The second problem with the early manuscripts is that they were written and illuminated by Christian monks who replaced many pagan elements and parts of the tales with biblical references, as can be seen in the sheer number of references to the Deluge of Noah and other biblical characters and locations in the early cycles of stories; the monks sought to make the Christian God more accessible and appealing by intermingling these stories with biblical themes and figures. For both of these reasons, we have felt justified in making whatever changes and alterations were necessary in the interests of telling the story. It is hoped - and perhaps it is not entirely implausible - that the stories as they are now told here come closer to the original storyline.

The dramatic potential of the Ulster (*Uladh*) Cycle has never been in any doubt; such tales as the boyhood deeds of CúChulainn, the Combat of Ferdia and CúChulainn, the Exile of the Sons of Uisliú, the Cattle Raid of Cooley (*Táin Bó Cuailgne*) and the Death of CúChulainn contain many moments of high dramatic content and stirring battles which are the fodder of the epic saga. The problem has always been that the stories have never been anything more than a collection of disjointed vignettes linked only by the characters involved in them. This fact is probably due to the reasons stated above, as well as the poor quality of many of the original manuscripts resulting in many sections and passages being lost forever. What we have done here is attempt to link these vignettes by means of a coherent plotline that simultaneously links the characters and events of the classical stories, and also tells the story in a manner that would be entertaining to a contemporary audience, while still doing justice to the themes of the original stories; themes of Magic (*Draíocht*), Trickery, Romance and Conflict. We have therefore written a story with a coherent framework which explains the motives of the various characters and links the vignettes. This proved to be no easy feat. We believe that in so doing, we have remained true to these themes and the traditions of the stories while also presenting the characters and situations in a less cartoonish manner than the treatment usually given them in the texts.

Here, we tell the stories of the Ulster Cycle (*an Sraith Ultach*), in three books. Book I, **The Isle of Shadows**, tells of the conception and boyhood deeds of CúChulainn, as well as the resistance of the men of Uladh to the second invasion of the Fomorians. Book II, **Seeds of Ruin**, will tell of the subsequent events including the combat of CúChulainn and his son. Finally, Book III, **Gods' End**, will tell of the *Táin Bó Cuailgne*, the

Cattle Raid of Cooley, which is the most famous story in the entire Irish mythology.

When asked about the relationship of Middle Earth to our world, JRR Tolkien famously described his Middle Earth as the world we live in, but at "a different stage of imagination". Similarly, we present Eirú as a version of early Ireland at such a different stage of imagination; one in which magic and sorcery rub shoulders with feudal rivalries, where the veil between the worlds of the living and of the *Sídhe* is thin in places, and absent in others. This difference is reflected in our maps of Eirú – this is Ireland, but not as we know it. It is rather a *version* of ancient Ireland, one that has been nudged two or three degrees off the axis of reality.

We have written this story with one intention – that it would become the story of CúChulainn as we would like to see it told. For those purists who would claim that to deviate from, or change aspects of, the original stories is to somehow corrupt or diminish them, we can merely state that what we are doing here is no different to what each and every *seanchaí* of the ancient oral tradition has done for generations: to make the story more accessible and entertaining for the audience who hears it. We hope we have succeeded.

Richard Roche & Derek Fennell,
October 2021

About the Authors

Richard Roche is an Associate Professor at the Department of Psychology, Maynooth University, where he lectures in neuroscience and neuropsychology. His areas of research include memory, dementia, synaesthesia and neuroaesthetics. To date he has published three academic books and 36 research papers, as well as several short stories, but this will be his first novel. His other interests include mythology, art and science communication, and has taken part in many outreach and engagement events.

Derek Fennell once put porridge on his table working as a sports writer in his native Co. Kildare and later Dublin. Chronically vulnerable to romance, adventure and literature, he threw caution to the wind and moved to Paris in 2006 where he constantly gets up to no good, keeping cheese in his larder as a language trainer, translator and interpreter. A deep fascination for Irish mythology has burned within him all his life, colouring and inspiring the fantastical short stories he amuses himself by writing. He describes working on this book as a labour of shared love - with his co-author - for the unique folklore of his home country and a monument to a friendship.

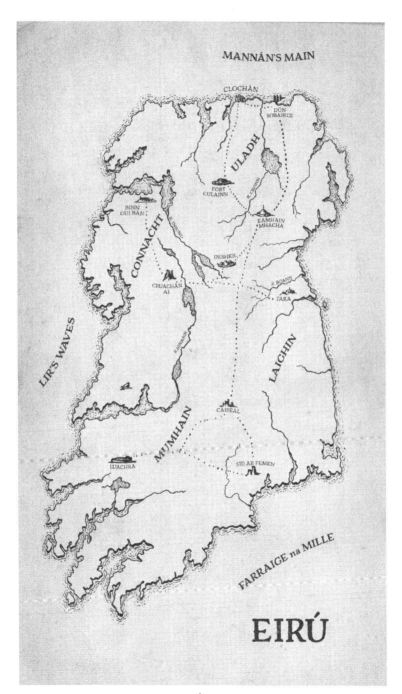

MANNÁN'S MAIN

CLOCHÁN

DÚN SOBAIRCE

ULADH

FORT CULAINN

BINN GULBÁN

EAMHAIN MHACHA

CONNACHT

DESHKIL

CRUACHÁN AI

TARA

LIR'S WAVES

LAICHIN

MUMHAIN

CÁISEAL

LUACHRA

SÍD AR FEMEN

FARRAIGE na MILLE

EIRÚ

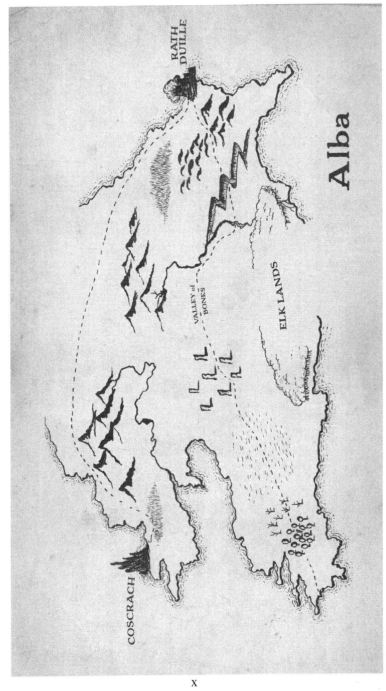

Prologue

I can only relate the tales as they were given to me to tell.

And if they seem more fantastic, or incredible, or somehow different to the ones you have heard yourself, then I say to you that this is just the way of tales.

They are alive, and never twice the same, nor should they be.

Every age brings freshness only to those legends that have strength enough to endure.

They change, and stay powerful.

What remains of truth, you might wonder? That thing we call truth concerns me little. There are certain truths which can cripple and harm and make weakness in men, and certain lies which can lend force and justice to actions.

In any case, I seek not to recount you histories, but stories; tales of renown as they have been passed down to me. They are the purest truth, because they have survived in our hearts.

So harken, if you will, to the deeds of a hero you thought you knew, but forgot.

But I have not forgotten, for I am Amergin, the Binder of Fates, and through me all is soon told....

*****

It began in the Ancient Times.

The days of the Tuatha Dé Dannan, the ancient race of powerful beings who dwelt in the raths and the secret places, were finished.

For millennia they had lived and reigned, weaving their magick, shaping what now remains.

But at length those Mighty Ones had chosen to slip out of our world and dwell elsewhere. Men, the newcomers, had emerged to forge their own destiny and inherit the earth.

But just as the Sun casts a shadow, there were those of the old race who resisted relinquishing their grasp on this earthly domain.

Some who found great nourishment from the souls of men.

And so these wicked powers had to be dragged by force into the nether realms, or imprisoned in the Sidhe, when the wise Dananns judged their fate.

But one lingered.

She was too wily, hiding herself from their thoughts, lying dormant and still as an ancient grave, so that in their final reckoning, the Dananns overlooked her.

And so it came to pass that The Morrigan, who whispered in men's ears, inciting them to combat so she might feast on their battle-slain souls, was left free reign on this earth.

Unchecked. Unopposed.

Or so she thought. For there was one of the Tuatha Dé Danann whose mind shone as brightly as the Sun itself. Long had he hunted The Morrigan and thwarted her evil designs. He alone was not deceived by her cunning.

Lugh of the Long Arms, SunGod of the Eternal Light, bent his great will to her undoing. Never would he ascend to the distant stars to dwell with his kindred gods while the people he had grown to love – the Gaels – were in danger from her.

His task was not easy, but he did all that he could. Finally he came to realise the shocking error of his strategy at the great conflict known as the Second Battle of Moytura.

Balor of the Evil Eye, that loathsome and deranged Fomorian king, had led his twisted people from the cold deeps of the sea on a campaign of slaughter against the land dwellers.

Balor's orgy of havoc threatened to consume the land until it was finally opposed by the League of Lugh – men of valour who chose to fight alongside the SunGod himself. The battle was long and brutal – the Fomorian horde vastly outnumbered the brave few who stood against them, yet resist them they did, and with much honour. But the sheer weight of numbers could not be overcome, and steadily they fell.

The songs tell of Balor's great rage that day as he cut down wave after wave of noble warriors until he stood untouched and triumphant upon a hill of bloodied corpses. The flower of Lugh's army lay shattered.

Hope had faded, and all seemed lost, until a shaft of light penetrated the looming clouds, reflecting on the golden armour worn by Lugh as he advanced on his bedazzled foe.

Balor howled in rage and beckoned the SunGod to a duel.

With unerring thrusts of his spear, Lugh quickly crippled his opponent. Then in a flash of light, he unsheathed his great sword Freagartach, The Answerer, and sundered Balor's monstrous head from his body.

Thus ended the fighting on Moytura Plain that day, but the battle would become known for what immediately followed.

For as Lugh stood over Balor's fallen corpse, his heart broken at the sight of the dead and dying strewn all around him, the dreaded Crow of Battle, The Morrigan, swooped down from the stormy clouds and began to mock him.

'Do you feel victorious, then?' she croaked maliciously.

'The Fomors are broken. They won't return to foul this land again,' Lugh proclaimed, but already he was wary of the other's triumphant tone.

Many times he had tried to capture The Morrigan, and yet here she was openly displaying herself to him. He sensed trickery, but advanced on the crow nonetheless.

From her perch on an upright sword-hilt, the goddess of death continued.

'The bodies of the greatest of your League lie dead beneath me, Lugh of the Many Deeds. The mighty souls of all who have met eternity in this carnage are my prize. I grow fat from your tribute!'

And it was then that Lugh realised that the Morrigan drew her power from the souls of those slain in battle. There was no way to overcome her now; her strength was too great after so many deaths.

In frustration he cursed her.

'The day will dawn, Fell Spirit, when there will no longer be a Morrigan to feast on the spoils of death. I will find a way to vanquish you. You will wither to nothing. This I vow.'

But the Morrigan merely laughed her coarse crow-laugh and took off into the heavens.

'Even the God of the Sun will have burned cold before such a day! Death is the one constant. Wars will be waged. Men will perish in wickedness; my table will never be bare!'

Then the legends tell how the Morrigan drew around her dark clouds that churned and span with lightning. Those who were left living that day told of the souls rising like a mist from those slain upon the field of battle; Man and Fomor alike were dragged in terror into that obscene vortex.

And the sound. Some say those departing souls screamed. Others swear they heard them weeping, for the eternity of torment that now lay ahead of them.

Lugh knew then he could never defeat her. How could he, in battle, vanquish that which was death itself?

This was a fight he could never win.

No, Lugh would not be the one....

Part I

The Naming of CúChulainn

The Lay of the Land

The story that I tell unfolds in the last Age of Heroes.

After the disappearance of the Tuatha Dé Danann, power over the land was disputed by those mighty men of valour whose deeds live on in tales that blend and change, but never fade as long as hearts can soar and lips can speak.

At this time there were ranged against one another two principal forces. Firstly, that of King Conchobar MacNeasa, who ruled from the great hill fort of Eamhain Mhacha in the northern lands of Uladh, and to whom I was counsellor, and friend.

Strong and stubborn, his victories in battle were numerous and decisive. But his ways were harsh; opposing chieftains would be killed and replaced by one of his own trusted men, but it cannot be said that people did not live well under his rule. I saw his growing power and chose to stay beside him to temper the fury that would crush his enemies into extinction, and to guide his burning ambitions. This, I knew, was the duty the fates had planned for me.

Among the fearsome and cunning warriors who swore fealty to Conchobar was Fergus MacRoth. Fergus of the Flinted Fist, Wielder of Heaven's Call, the Axe of Singing Sorrow, Fergus the Hundred-Slayer, commander of one half of Conchobar's army, the Ruddy Boars. Many were the names they had for him, and his very presence on the battlefield caused enemies to suddenly lose grip upon their weapons and weep like infants.

And there was Forgall Manach, the general of the Second Sword, who led the other half of Conchobar's army, the Wolf Horde. When it was required, the two forces would merge into one mighty battle host. It was thus that Conchobar kept his enemies off-balance. A wily and unpredictable tactician was Manach; he could see into a man's heart and know his ways.
The only other power in the land that could truly oppose the primacy of Eamhain lay in the West, in Connacht, where dwelled the armies of Queen Medb, the untamable BattleDame of Cruachán Ai.

The province of Connacht was wild and proud, just like its people, and the Queen was no ordinary woman, for she was of the Tuatha Dé Danann. How this came to be is a tale I may tell another time...

The powers of the Danann kind confounded even the best-conceived plans of Forgall Manach and the valour of Fergus MacRoth, so that no invasion of Connacht ever came to fruition. For their part, Medb's forces laboured in vain to find a way to counter the expansion of Conchobar's dominion.

Our story unfolds at a time when Queen Medb had allied her forces with those of King Ailill of the Steady Hand, whose forts controlled the great lakes and rivers at the heart of the land, thus putting further forces between Conchobar and her territory. And not long after this pact was consecrated in Medb's bedchamber at the great castle of Cruachán.

And so this was how the land lay before these events of great renown took place.

And they are soon told.

1.

The Red Branch

Sunlight bathed the Great Plain of Muirtheimne in the province of Uladh, though there was no heat in it. This place had seen much death in the past, but with the coming of the season of Imbolc came new life – the first delicate shoots and buds hinted at the rebirth to come. Before the Ogham Stone knelt Fergus MacRoth, the great champion of Eamhain Mhacha. As he meditated, head bowed, his hand travelled slowly down the edge of the rough-hewn surface, his lips moving in silent incantation as he deciphered each word with his fingers.

The silence was broken by a voice from behind him, but Fergus felt no shame at being found deep in prayer, even if such practices were largely mocked these days; rather it was his failure to detect the approach of the stranger that disturbed him. It was no easy thing to creep up on Fergus MacRoth by foot, and this intruder was on horseback. The voice that greeted him was little more than a whisper, and sounded out of breath. Fergus attributed this to the portly stature of its owner.

'Begging your pardon, my lord, I did not mean to interrupt you,' it wheezed.

'Begging your own, but you *have*,' retorted Fergus gruffly, getting to his feet and regarding the newcomer suspiciously. 'Draw back your hood, stranger. I can see much of you, for there is much to you, but I would look upon your face if I am to speak with you.'

The face the rider revealed was not a fair one; his cheeks were as fat as his belly was large, and an array of sores were dotted across his unhandsome features. Fergus relaxed slightly. In his experience, assassins tended to be leaner, and kept in better health by their retainers.

'Well? What business have you with me? It does not please me to be disturbed while at prayer on such a day as this. Particularly here, at the site of the Second Battle of Moytura where Lugh slew Balor of the Evil Eye.

'Aye, 'tis true, the SunGod blesses us today. Though I fear the days of His influence are drawing to their end.' He shook his head slowly, though his eyes never left Fergus.

'Another one who dishonours the Gods!' muttered Fergus, his hostility toward the stranger rising again. 'I ask you again, what is your business here? Your face, foul though it is, is not known to me and your accent is hard to place. How came you so quietly along the road that I heard no approach?'

By this point, he had moved his hand onto the handle of the great axe tucked between his tunic and belt, as if ready to draw the weapon.

'Peace, my friend, I mean no disrespect. I would be in your debt if you would but lead me to Eamhain Mhacha and its King Conchobar. It's a perilous road these days, I hear, and I'd feel much the safer if I were accompanied by one of renown such as you.'

Fergus stared at him for a moment. 'Eamhain Mhacha is wary of strangers at this time. What business have you there?'

'I am just a wandering bard,' continued the stranger, 'hoping to seek the protection of the king's walls in return for my services. There are not many other places in this land safe for the likes of me now... But I'm told that Conchobar is just.'

Fergus found it difficult to imagine much musical talent emanating from such stubby fingers or breathless lungs. Yet he felt a sort of pity for the stranger, a pity that was beginning to replace his initial mistrust.

'You have heard true enough, Conchobar MacNeasa is a fair King. Very well, fat bard, you don't seem a likely brigand or warrior. Come with Fergus now and you will see how unhindered an Uladh champion moves in his own country. What is your name, traveller?' he asked as he mounted his own horse and made to lead the bard along the road to the great citadel of Eamhain Mhacha.

The newcomer paused for a moment, staring at the Ogham Stone as if lost in thought. Then he turned to Fergus. 'Ah, I have many names, though the one that seems to attach itself to me most often is *Ramhar*...'

Fergus laughed aloud at this. 'And little wonder, fat bard, I can see that you are well rewarded for your craft, though it seems to me that such payment comes mostly in cooked form! Come then, Ramhar, Eamhain lies yonder.'

As the pair trotted away across the plain, it seemed to Fergus that the sun's light gradually grew a little warmer on his neck.

*****

The two men journeyed side by side following an unmarked trail through the woodlands that Fergus seemed to know by heart, and as they rode, the bard asked many questions of the champion: of the kingdom, its people, and their customs. All of these things seemed to interest the newcomer greatly, though Fergus saw no reason to keep information from him; he was growing increasingly fond of this 'Ramhar' as they made their way across the countryside.

'I know too little of Conchobar,' said the bard. 'How came he to his throne – has his line ruled here for generations as in other lands?'

Fergus looked askance at him as they rode.

'How can you expect to earn your keep at Eamhain Mhacha if you do not know the story of its king?'

They rode on in silence for a few moments. An almost imperceptible smile formed on Ramhar's lips.

'Would you tell it to me, champion? I have travelled far, and am always in search of tales to tell, and stories to sing.'

'Very well, bard, the tale will pass the hours. He is the son of a king, though his ascent to the throne was far from bloodless.

'It was twenty-four summers past, and the kingdom of Eamhain Mhacha faced a grave threat. The sons of the dying king Fachtna Fatach were squabbling amongst one another for the right to proclaim themselves the new ruler.

'The eldest, Eochu, would have been the uncontested choice to take his father's place, but he was opposed by the second son, Feidlech, who could never bear his brother's greater prominence.

'Wise Amergin, the renowned sage, was summoned by the king. Naturally he pronounced in favour of the eldest son Eochu, who seemed a just and promising leader, whilst Feidlech's manner caused grave concern.

'It had seemed that Amergin's judgement had been accepted by all: the two brothers embraced before the court and, the problem of his succession solved, old Fachtna died peacefully that night.

'The funeral feast lasted a week and as it came to an end Feidlech invited Eochu to hunt with him on the day before his coronation so that, through the ritual of the chase, they could seal the covenant of their loyalty to one another.

'Alone the brothers set off into the forest to find a stag worthy of their father's memory. It wasn't long before Eochu spotted a fine beast and took chase. Feidlech followed him, but just as Eochu pulled back his arm to

10

hurl his spear his horse reared and crumpled beneath him - struck in the flank by Feidlech's lance. Eochu fell hard to the ground, his horse falling upon him, crushing his right arm and leg. Feidlech could see his brother lived yet, and raised his sword high to deliver the killing blow.

'But he noticed a woodsman appear from the trees and, not wanting to be seen committing murder, shouted to the newcomer "Ho, come quick, the new King of Uladh has fallen from his horse. Help me bring him back to Eamhain Mhacha, for his wounds look grave!"

'The woodsman nodded and together they gently lay the groaning Eochu upon his brother's horse and brought him back to Eamhain.

'There at the court Amergin examined Eochu's wounds, and sadly announced that nevermore would he walk with two firm legs and that his arm had thrown its last lance. At the news Feidlech pronounced that according to the law, it was impossible for a king to be blemished in this way, so it now fell to him to rule Eamhain Mhacha.

'It was then that the woodsman who had helped bring the wounded Eochu to the court pushed his way forward and declared:

'"No! Feidlech should not become king! He is a rogue and full of deceit. I saw him in the woods strike down the horse of Eochu, causing these wounds. I saw him raise his sword to kill his brother, and he would have done so if he had not realised I was there to witness the villainy!"

'"Who are you, peasant, to make such vicious claims?" shrieked Feidlech.

'"I am Conchobar MacNeasa, the son of Ness Fian who laid down with King Fachtna Fatach during the summer when the great king defeated the army of Eochaind Salbruide!"

'Feidlech knew then that this man, a direct son of Fachtna and thus eligible to the throne, could ruin all his schemes. He roared that he was born to rule and that the newcomer should be put to death immediately for such an affront.

'But Conchobar challenged: "I swear that what I say is true, and I will prove its truth by putting a *geis* upon you! If I can defeat you unarmed whilst you yourself can use any weapon you wish, then my words cannot be unheeded."

'"Very well!" cried Feidlech, seeing that the advantage was so heavily stacked in his favour.

'He seized his father's sword from where it lay upon the throne and swung it with all his treacherous rage.

'But Conchobar ducked beneath the blow and quickly came up behind Feidlech; before anyone could draw another breath, he seized the young pretender's neck and snapped it like a dry twig.

'"The truth of my words is before you," cried the victor.

'"I tell you again, I am Conchobar MacNeasa, son also of Fachtna Fatach, and I've lived long enough in hiding with my sister in the woods. Am I fit to be king?"

'Those in attendance roared their fierce agreement, for along with the *geis*-bound deed which had taken place in front of their eyes, the warrior before them bore a strong resemblance to his father.'

*****

When Fergus had finished his fine tale the bard cheered heartily and, the mood becoming more confortable, they began to speak more freely as they rode. Ramhar enquired much about the current state of the province of Uladh: and was told how it was at war with the western land of Connacht and that her borders were constantly under threat; how danger came from the seas, whence the hideous Fomorian creatures were occasionally known to attack the outlying lands in small raiding parties.

'Do not expect the air to be light in Eamhain Mhacha at present. Though the Fomor remnant has been fought back for now and the wars in the West are going well, the king is still laid low over the loss of his sister, the lady Dechtire.'

Fergus's face grew dark as he broached this subject.

'Whatever became of her?'

'Taken in some dark manner from the very banquet table of Conchobar's Great Hall.' It still troubled him that all of the great warriors, himself included, should have been so powerless to prevent the abduction.

'Some fools think it was the strong sun and the ferocity with which the champions took to the mead that day that laid us low. But I tell you, there was some magick surely at play that made us as drowsy as milked cows. When we came to our senses again, Dechtire was gone. No one knows whither.'

'Tell me more of these Fomorians. You say they are enemies of old?'

'At one bleak time,' Fergus began, 'the Fomorians almost had this country under their sway. Some say that they were men once, cruel, wicked men who dishonoured the Gods with their vile, blasphemous acts, so the Dananns banished them to the seas for all time, their bodies ruined and misshapen that they might suffer life in the abyss. But even the Gods, it seems, cannot foresee all. The sea could not contain such evil; they learned to control the creatures of the deep, even bred with some of them, it is said. They formed crude craft that allowed them return to these lands and their rampages began afresh. Initially they merely controlled the coasts. But eventually they grew more aggressive and pillaged inwards. They sought to destroy our way of life, to enslave us.'

Fergus's disgust was evident as he recounted these events, but his voice grew proud yet reverential when he began to speak of the Danann folk.

'But they could not stand against the mighty charge of Lugh of the Long Arms! No warrior was ever better equipped than he. He rode the steed of Mannán Mac Lir, Enbarr of the Flowing Mane, which ran so swiftly no adversary could catch it. He wore Mannán's armour and breastplate, which no weapon could pierce, and he wielded a great sword, Freagartach the Answerer, which cut through flesh like butter, creating wounds that no physician could ever hope to heal. Lugh came against the Fomorian horde in all his might and scattered them like frightened cattle. Nine alone survived, to bear the story of his deeds back to the Fomor people.'

His words had a strange effect on Ramhar. Unseen by Fergus, a pure golden light flickered in the eyes of the bard at the mention of the Sun God's great deeds. It burned for a moment, then faded and was gone. When he spoke next, his voice was weary.

'But now you tell me the Fomorians are gathering strength again. Lugh did not complete his task...'

'The men of Uladh are stronger now. We could repel them. But even if we could not, Lugh would return. The Sun God always rises to banish the dark of night.'

Ramhar looked at Fergus for a moment. 'Your faith impresses me, my friend. I only hope that the Gods are deserving of your devotion.'

Fergus was about to say something in response to this when the pair crested a hill and found themselves looking down at the great fortress of Eamhain Mhacha. Even after many years, the sight of the capital was still enough to steal the breath from him. To call Eamhain a fort seemed somehow inadequate, for it was in truth much more than that – part ring-fortress, part crannóg, with high walls of piled stone supported by massive

13

oak logs upon which forbidding wooden battlements were perched. The stronghold was host to countless huts, bowers, workshops, stables and other dwellings of man and beast. Within these great defences, aside from the buildings, lay green fields of produce, grazing land for herds of livestock, a small wooded grove through which ran a narrow river that widened into two small lakes at points, and even playing fields. Towards the rear rose a great hill, shielded behind further defensive walls, at whose crest shone the magnificent Great Hall, golden against the dark foothills of the Twelve Peaks beyond. This was Eamhain Mhacha, the heart of Uladh, the centre of civilisation in this dangerous land.

As they entered through the defences and into the main expanse of the fortress, signs of everyday life unfurled all around them. People came and went with cattle or pigs, leading them to and from pens and enclosures for milking or butchering. Growers toiled in the earth and gathered vegetables. Craftsmen and women wove, stitched, hammered and forged in their huts. Children ran amuck with wooden swords and shields; others batted a *sliotar* to and fro with crude *camáns*. Inside the safety of these great walls, thought the bard, life can go about its business in peace. He turned to look at the fortified hilltop, which was crowned by the Great Hall, seat of King Conchobar MacNeasa's court.

'There's an inn over yonder which may have use for a bard such as yourself,' said Fergus, gesturing toward a long, dimly lit hut across the courtyard. Ramhar seemed puzzled by this, and his response came in a voice that was firm and steady.

'I am here to see Conchobar.'

Fergus shook his head. 'I told you, the king is not in the mood for merriment, so you'll have more luck over...'

Ramhar transfixed him with a stare. 'Bring me to Conchobar, man. He will see me.'

Fergus blinked, wavered, then regained himself. For a moment he sought to bring words of dismissal to his lips, but was suddenly soothed as he regarded the inoffensive, flabby face of the other man.

'Come then!' he grunted finally. 'I will enjoy watching the sport he makes of you.'

Fergus rode off up the heavily guarded hillside, his fat companion trotting behind on his straining mount. The gates swung open unbidden at Fergus's approach.

*****

14

Conchobar shifted uneasily in his throne while Forgall Manach, his most senior general, made his report. The king's displeasure was obvious to most of the assembled warriors, courtiers and wise men; it seemed to Conchobar that even the servants were uneasy around him. And with good cause, he thought sourly to himself. He watched as Forgall moved around the great wooden map of the land that took up a sizeable area before the throne, driving flag-bearing spears into key locations to indicate success on the battlefield and ground gained from defeated enemies. Such news should lift a king's heart, as well he knew, but matters were grave in the court of MacNeasa.

'Coupled with your own victories on the eastern coast, my King, our claiming of the land around these ancient *sídhe* will ensure the neighbouring chieftains see the sense in your becoming High King of All Eirú.'

Forgall paused and glanced around at the other Uladh warriors attending this council.

'Few could argue against a king who is uniting the old lands of the Dé Danann for the first time since the struggles in the Age of Plagues? Their druids will see the wisdom of it. You *are* High King, in all but name now. Even Ailill of Connacht is said to whisper this in his own court.'

Silence lingered in the high-vaulted hall for some moments as all eyes turned to Conchobar. At length, he spoke with a weary tone.

'All this I know, Forgall, for I myself have planned these events with you. And 'tis true that such proclamations hearten the men, most of all when so little Uladh blood has been spilled. But I am more eager for you to tell me of other pressing matters.

'The fact that you have not already delivered good news of her bodes surely that my heart is soon to grow heavier yet.'

The general looked to the floor.

'The lady Dechtíre is... not in Connacht, my King.'

He steeled himself for the response. Conchobar had risen to his feet, drawing himself up to his full, impressive, height. His booming voice shook the Great Hall, causing the golden apples on the ornate silver bough that adorned the wall behind his throne to chime with the vibration.

'By the tears of Danú! Who else but Ailill could have taken her? He seeks to destroy this fledgling unity before it can threaten him, so he takes my

15

sister from under my very roof to attribute weakness to me in the eyes of the petty kings!'

His face flushed crimson; his fists clenched. None dared move until a gnarled, ancient hand reached gently for the king's arm. Amergin, the wise sage of the court, brought his bald, dark-skinned head close to the king's ear.

'We do not know this, O King. Be not so quick with your accusations. We are far from the young king Ailill's influence here at Eamhain.'

Conchobar seemed lost in thought for a moment, but then he shook his head and sat back down heavily.

'The Fomors could not have done it, for they always leave their trace on the land. Perhaps she simply...'

His musing was suddenly cut short by a great clamour as the huge doors of the hall were swung open. Fergus strode in, followed close behind by the shuffling figure of Ramhar. The king's spirits rose visibly.

'Fergus! What news? Come, my brother, and bring cheer to your sullen friend. Tell me, you have some news of Dechtire. And who is your fat companion? You know that strangers may not enter here...'

Fergus came to a stop and stood silent in the middle of the Great Hall, swaying slightly. When he finally spoke his words came slowly, as those of a man waking from a dream.

'Who? He is... the one... who must speak with you... I...'

Forgall was the first to react. 'He has been tricked! 'Tis an assassin!' he roared. Drawing his blade, he leapt between his king and the uninvited guest who Fergus had brought before them. But before his stroke could fall, he found himself frozen by a strange sight unfolding before him. Unnatural light appeared to be shining out from the hood and the cuffs of Ramhar's cloak, and as the gathering looked on stupefied, it appeared to them that the figure grew larger and larger. The glow grew more intense, like sunlight breaking through mottled clouds, casting beams of gold around the hall.

The cloak rose higher into the air, appearing to hover unsupported while the now blinding light continued to escape from beneath its folds. Finally, the garment was shaken off, fluttering softly to the floor. Now in the centre of the hall stood a great pillar of light, almost twice the height of a man, dazzling to look upon. All stood aghast but Conchobar was the only one to summon a response to these strange events.

16

'By Danú,' he breathed.

'By that name indeed!' uttered a booming, resonant voice from the midst of the nimbus, and as the intensity of the light faded, a form became discernible. Feet clad in golden boots, a shimmering ochre breastplate upon which were engraved three swans in flight, a helm the colour of the rising sun, a flowing crimson cape. The giant figure took a step forward and all could now see, and knew in their hearts without any words needing to be uttered, that Lugh Samildánach, Lugh of the Long Arms, the SunGod himself, had returned to Uladh.

And not alone.

As he advanced, Lugh drew back his great cape to reveal a woman, dazed and heavily pregnant, his arm held protectively around her shoulder. Conchobar was so moved by the sight of his sister that he momentarily abandoned his reverence at the reappearance of Lugh and rushed across the floor to catch her as she wavered.

'Dechtíre! What has become of you?' he gasped.

'It was no enemy, Conchobar MacNeasa, that took your sister. She came to dance with Lugh, and did so willingly.' A broad smile creased the great bearded face of the giant, and it was as if the sun had broken out inside the walls of the great hall. All who were present later recounted a slightly different description of the apparition, no doubt some magick of the Faerie Folk; but each to a man would agree about the compassion and warmth which they found in his lined face, the great troughs of wrinkle etched across his brow, and the reassuring light that shone from those golden eyes. It was a moment that none present would ever forget. The Sun God continued:

'Pay heed now, doughty Uladhmen. Though now triumphant in your victories, I tell you there is much darkness ahead. In less than a score of years, the greatest test of your people will be upon you. It will overcome you and sweep you aside, of that there is no doubt. The waning spirit of your kind has weakened the strength of mine. But fear not! To counter this we shall be linked again as we were linked in the past.'

Confused looks were exchanged around the hall. Murmurs of concern were quickly silenced by Amergin, the ancient sage commanding silence with a sweeping gesture of his hand.

'Your king's sister will soon be breached... *by my son*. He alone will have the strength to leap into the maw of the beast. As Lugh was before him, he will be a warrior without equal. You will name him Setanta. He will be the

17

last slender hope for men in the face of the coming storm. The task of his teaching, however, falls to you.'

He looked around the court and each one present felt the sudden weight of responsibility carried with those words. Conchobar, having seen to his sister and seated her on his throne, stepped forward, bowing low before Lugh.

'You honour us, Lugh of the Great Deeds. But who among us men could teach a God the divine knowledge as befitting your son. We are not prepared for this.' Shaking his head slowly, he looked to his sage for support. Amergin, his brow furrowed deep in thought, raised his knotted hands in supplication.

'My knowledge is as nought before that of the gods.'

'He will not be fully divine; he'll also be a flesh and blood man,' Lugh went on. 'His mind and body will be as a rough rock that you shall hew to perfection. It is for you, Conchobar, to raise the child, for he is next of kin to you. Let Sencha the Poet instruct him in speech and oratory; let Fergus the Warrior hold him on his knees; let Forgall the Tactician instruct him in strategy; and let Amergin the Sage be his tutor.

'The child will be praised by all, by chariot drivers and soldiers; by kings and seers. He will avenge your wrongs; he will defend your fords; he will fight your battles. Here in this hall, where flourishes the bloodlines of those who fought alongside the Tuatha Dé Danann when we were at our greatest need at the Second Battle of Moytura, *here* will I leave my legacy.'

From the folds of his crimson cape, Lugh then produced a golden staff. As he held it aloft, it began to glimmer with a ruby glow, as if veins of scarlet were spreading along the length of the shaft. Twirling it deftly in the air, he suddenly and effortlessly planted the end of it into the floor of the hall, smashing through the flagstones and into the earth beneath.

'Behold! You are forever under the protection of Lugh Samildánach and to this branch, pruned by my own hand from the last Quicken Tree, will your destiny ever be tied.'

With this, he released his grip on the staff, which then began to take root in the floor, metamorphosing from a smooth length of pared wood into a shape more akin to a burgeoning sapling. The young tree, still red and gold, began to grow and reach toward the rafters of the great hall.

'This branch will be your symbol and your namesake. You must protect it always. For when the darkest hour is upon you, then will it be your final salvation. I charge you now with these two tasks, Knights of the Red

18

Branch. The success of the one depends upon the survival of the other. They are as powerfully linked as Lugh is to his People. One day, all this will be made manifest and on that day will my debt to your kind be repaid.'

Raising his arms aloft, he spoke one final time.

'Raise him well, Uladhmen.'

With that, he bowed low to Conchobar, then to the Branch, and at last he turned slowly and strode towards the great oak doors of the hall. Pushing them back as though they were no heavier than calfskin curtains, he disappeared into a sudden surge of afternoon sunlight that momentarily dazzled all those inside, and was seen no more.

A heavy silence deadened the air in the chamber. Some were still gaping in awe at the strange red-golden branch that still showed tiny signs of growth and movement. Others looked to Dechtire; Conchobar had returned to her side and was hovering anxiously as Amergin tended to her. She was returning to her senses, and showed no signs of distress or ill-treatment. The sage turned to his king with a wan smile.

'I do not know what is most fitting at this hour, to rejoice or to despair.' 'It is a murky sentence the Sun God has passed on us.'

Conchobar nodded. 'He has brought life - that cannot be ill.'

'Time will tell, my King,' said Amergin, and despite the strange events there was a warmth and humour to his voice. 'One way or another, we'll be kept busy for the next twenty years or so it seems!'

The Great Hall of Eamhain Mhacha, which from that day forward was to be known as *An Craobh Ruadh*, the Hall of the Red Branch, then rang with a sound it had not heard for many months – the laughter of the king. Such was his relief and joy at his sister's return that the golden apples above the throne chimed with his delight. The sound shook the other warriors from their trance before the Branch and slowly they made their way back towards the throne. Rising, Conchobar addressed them.

'Then let us fill those years with worthy deeds, and make fertile soil in which this great lad may flourish. For if he is to be our final defence against what is to come, then we had best make sure he is well-constructed.'

So it was that while the Hall of the Red Branch rumbled with sounds of preparation and bustle, the people of Eamhain assembled outside the inner gates as word of the divine visitation began to spread. No-one noticed the small, squat, hooded figure that slipped silently through the crowded citadel, weaving his way towards the exterior defences. No-one except

Fergus, who, staring from the door of the Great Hall, followed the fat man's movements as he slipped past the guards who appeared not to even see him. Then, the portly bard looked back for a moment and caught his eye, before moving off past the gates and into the countryside beyond.

Fergus could see that the sun's rays followed him as he went.

*****

And so it came to pass that, three days after the visitation of Lugh, Dechtíre delivered the promised child into this age of strife.

And she named him *Setanta*.

Bringing to bear all the knowledge of divination handed down to him by his order, Amergin the sage foresaw that the boy would become the champion of champions, and that his life would be the torch of hope in a time of darkness.

But his vision was also clear on one thing.

Though all the skills of the greatest Uladh heroes were his to learn, together with the abilities natural to his Danann blood, they would not be enough to secure him a great age.

His life-path was short. Like many legendary warriors, Setanta would die mighty and die young. But he would live beyond most men's capabilities.

As Setanta grew out of childhood, his skills in the art of war became a source of wonder at Eamhain Mhacha.

All of the women of Uladh loved him for his strength, his handsome features and his fine way of speaking. They also admired his wisdom, his prudence in battle and his gifts of prophecy and judgement.

Indeed they could only find three faults in him: that he was too young, too brave and too beautiful.

And while none doubted that he would grow into the warrior upon whom all hope would one day rest, few imagined that day would arrive so soon. But such is prophecy – it has a way of making fools of those who purport to understand it.

And so it was that, before the end of his nineteenth year of life, Setanta would face the first of his many great challenges.

The Red Branch Knights

Everything changed at Eamhain Mhacha from the day of Lugh's appearance and the return of the king's sister Dechtíre.

The great branch the Sun God struck into the ground grew thick and tall, until it finally reached out from the roof. Its topmost parts, spreading towards the heavens, could be seen proudly from anywhere in Eamhain. And the chamber of the King came to be known as An Craobh Ruadh, in honour of the red branch.

Those soldiers who that day bore witness to the event took the russet-skinned tree as their emblem. Conchobar was in agreement that from then on it would adorn his standard alongside his own sigil – a bloody spearhead – for Conchobar was fiercely devoted to Lugh, the Celestial Warrior.

Then some days later, the king visited me and told me of the dreams that had come to him since that auspicious day.

He dreamt, said he, that the Red Branch spoke to him and the voice said that its will was one and the same as the will of Lugh in what it had to reveal.

It told of terrible trials ahead and the need for great valour in the future. The son of Dechtíre would do a thousand great deeds, but in the convulsions to come he would have equal need of the best soldiers of Eamhain Mhacha.

The Red Branch told that it would know which among Conchobar's warriors were fit to face the ultimate challenges and sacrifices that lay ahead.

Visions of heroic tasks came to Conchobar, and he put it to his soldiers to accomplish these feats if they desired to join his new order of elite fighting men - the Red Branch Knights.

Those that proved their mettle in this series of trials were allowed to carve away a sliver of the red-golden bark from the mighty branch and attach it to their gauntlet as a sign of their undying fealty and readiness to defend Eamhain Mhacha to the last drop of their blood.

It was well that they were so-willing, for soon there would be grave need of them, these stout battle-brothers of Uladh…

21

2.

The Garden of Lugh

It had rained heavily enough that morning.

And from the look of the eastern clouds, Emer felt sure it would rain again before the evening drew in. But at this moment Luglochta Lóga, the Garden of Lugh, was filled with sun. The pine-ringed gardens behind the south wall of Eamhain Mhacha had a curious way of capturing and channelling the light so that any who reflected on time spent there would be filled with memories of sunshine and warmth.

The Garden of Lugh was Emer Manach's favourite place in the world, as much as she knew of it, which was considerable enough, given that she was the daughter of Forgall Manach, the far-riding war-planner of Eamhain Mhacha.

But war was a long way from her mind now as she sat on one of the wooden benches that formed a ring in the garden, encircled by five other well-born girls of Eamhain. For it was here that poets and storytellers came to weave tales when the days were suited.

Today was a day for needle-work instruction. It was one of her duties to ensure that young Mhachan girls could seam and repair both finery and leather armour alike. Grace and battle went hand in hand at Eamhain Mhacha.

Pausing from her demonstration and regarding the skies, she began to think it strange, even in this garden, that the light would shine so intensely today.

'That's a faerie sky if ever I saw it,' she declared.

'Why do you say that, Emer?' asked one of her companions, Saidbh, the spear-maker's daughter.

'Look at the sky above us. A hole in the clouds, it seems, where the sun comes in to bathe us here in the garden. See the clouds move around it? They don't dare cover the hole, they go around. The master of Luglochta Lóga has play in his heart today.'

'He doesn't seem to be the only one,' whispered Saidbh and Emer saw her eyes fix on a point behind where she was sitting, her face a little flushed.

Then a voice from behind her spoke her name - a voice Emer Manach had spent her whole life trying to resist. But for how much longer, she often wondered.

It was a voice full of honey and danger; to Emer it was the very sound of love in all its frightfulness.

'If the men of Uladh could wield a blade half as skilfully as Emer does her needle, then there would be no need for war, for all our enemies would cower from us!'

Emer turned to face the speaker, but for a moment could not reply as the sun's rays shone onto the figure, surrounding him in a dazzling glow playing on his wild mane of hair, the colour of ripe barley. When she she put a hand to her brow there he was in full, an off-kilter grin adorning that otherwise perfect face, impertinence incarnate flashing from his sky-blue eyes.

That damned Setanta!

She ignored the shameful giggling of the other maidens, turning to face the young man she had known all her life yet felt she could never know, and met his grin with a sharp smile of her own.

And in that moment Emer began to realize something of the power that she alone held over the great hope of her land.

She stepped close to him and wielded that power with exquisite deftness.

'And if the celebrated Setanta could only handle his sword as well as some people say, then we'd all have nothing to fear,' she breathed into his face before turning quickly away, her blossom-laced hair casting a fragrance as it spun, causing Setanta to blink despite himself.

'Swordsmanship, is it?' he began, feeling a curious mixture of humiliation and burning desire.

'Well, let me...' he stopped short, his hand confusedly patting his empty scabbard.

The young girls around him laughed when Emer turned back, revealing his sword, newly adorned with daisy chains around the hilt.

Then, her voice thick with gentle mockery, she goaded the blushing Setanta further.

'Come, mighty warrior, and relieve the poor maiden of this heavy thing before her dainty arms break off!'

But, somewhat to her irritation, the lopsided grin wasn't long absent from Setanta's face. He accepted the sword from her gracefully then twirled it impressively around in dizzying circles before placing it back in his scabbard, keeping the daisy chains in place.

Typical! Trying to win back the crowd! Emer thought.

'See what happens, children, when you try to pay a compliment to a champion's daughter?' Setanta asked the handmaidens, theatrically. 'She has fighting blood, so it will make a fine battle of wooing her!'

There was no way Emer was going to let him get away with that one.

'There are other daughters of other champions in this fair country who would fall easily to your 'attacks', Setanta. But not I,' she snapped, yet her retort didn't come out strong enough for her liking. *Damn it.* What was wrong with her?

Setanta had stepped closer now, and his eyes moved slowly from her face, down her neckline and below...

'*That* is a fair country,' he said quietly. 'And how I might wish to wander there.'

Shocked at this temerity, Emer was at a loss for words until Setanta touched her cheek with two fingers and began tracing a line downward. She snatched those fingers and grasped them tightly before they could even travel past her jaw.

'No man may travel there unless he can prove that he actually is a man. And there are few enough around here; only boys who think their big mouths and fists make up for their hollow heads and...' - Emer wrinkled her nose in feigned disgust – '...lack of charm.'

To her delight, his grin had disappeared and showed no sign of returning. The proud Setanta was enraged; he stood speechless, staring at her with his hard eyes. She was so close to him close to him, she could actually feel the heat of his fury radiating from his body!

'*Setanta!*' a voice called from beyond the conifer trees. Emer recognised it as Conall Cearnach, one of Setanta's vagabond friends.

'Tear yourself from your needlework practice! The hunt awaits and I wish to revenge myself on you, you dog!'

24

Somewhat relieved by this interruption, Emer turned sharply and walked back to her maidens, offering a final few words to Setanta without turning her head.

'Away with you now, Setanta. I hope you can pursue an animal with more guile than you do a woman, or the king won't dine well tonight.'

As hard as she tired, she could not keep the smirk from her face, and the giggling reaction of her maidens on seeing it was enough to tell Setanta of its presence. Although she would scold herself for it later, she was relieved that he would know her harsh tone was in jest.

'Come on then, Conall! How eager you are to be shamed!' he called. Then Emer heard him charging back through the trees.

And she heard also that the anger had passed from his voice.

The voice she already missed.

3.

Prey

Setanta breathed in long and deep, drawing the scent of the forest into his lungs. Bracken, lichen, moss, leaf-litter, earthy and fresh! How he revelled in nature and all the richness it brought to his senses. The morning's rain had left the leaves moist and dripping, cooling the air slightly, but now that Lugh's disc had returned to the skies, bringing warmth with it, the puddles lay steaming in the sunlight and the trees seemed to be stretching their limbs upward in ecstasy. Truly the final days of Imbolc were a fine time for a hunt!

The party was small; Setanta and Conall, having arrived late, joined a group of three others, all of similar age to the two friends. Diarmuid, the hunt leader for today, was well known to Setanta from their childhood encounters on the playing field – their clashes had been robust but honourable, and as with any who dared to challenge him for dominance, Setanta had immediately decided that he liked him. The party of five trotted through the dense woods, dappled light falling on their faces, as the hounds ruffled and sniffed the undergrowth in search of a scent.

This *is* a fair land, he thought; a fairness reflected by that curious creature Emer. He smiled, his thoughts returning to their earlier exchange. *What strange spell did she weave upon me, to nestle in my memory so?* His contemplation was broken by the voice of the hunt leader. Diarmuid was displeased.

'The hounds are addled. There's too much of the scent of the fawning season. We won't track our quarry in this manner.' Some of the others agreed glumly; they had been roaming the Great Forest to the west of Eamhain Mhacha – which some called the Venery Forest for its rich hunting grounds – for close to an hour, and as yet nothing had stirred the hounds into pursuit. Reluctantly, Diarmuid voiced the suggestion that the others had hesitated to raise – that they relocate the hunt to the smaller, more manageable woods on the fort's south aspect. The hunting was easier there, though the quarry tended to be smaller, and less tender. It was, in effect, the training ground for Machra youngsters learning to hunt; the Venery Forest was where the menfolk of Eamhain sought their prey.

Conall objected immediately. The majority of the Wolf Horde of Eamhain was on campaign at the western border, but they were to return in a matter of days and a healthy supply of boar and deer was required to meet their needs. Failure to provide adequately for the great feast would cast shame on the young warriors. The others accepted his point, but were already swayed by Diarmuid's pessimism. And he was, after all, the hunt leader;

the decision was his to make. Then Setanta, who had remained silent until now, spoke.

'We need not be slaves to the dogs' noses. A hunted beast flees like a thrown spear, straight and violent. The skilled warrior can judge its flight, positioning himself so that the quarry comes to *him*.'

Diarmuid, more exasperated than annoyed, for he was used to his friend's contrariness and playful jibes, quickly countered:

'You're a great man for the words, Setanta, but even your fine pronouncements won't catch you a decent-sized boar here. On with us,' he called to the others as he spurred his mount around and started back in the direction of Eamhain. Setanta remained motionless on his horse.

'I choose to follow my own lead on this. When I see you again at the fort we shall compare what prizes I bring back with what you manage to catch in the nursery wood.'

Diarmuid smiled involuntarily at this. He had no option now, the challenge was set.

'Aye, so be it, Setanta. But the hounds come with me!'

This brought not a flicker of annoyance from the grinning Setanta. 'It's them who'll lose out! You'll hunt with me, Conall?' Conall had already pulled his mount over to join his friend. He knew him long enough to pay heed to the steel in his voice which belied the nonchalance of his smirk.

As the hunting party split, Conall was visited by a feeling which he had often encountered in childhood. A feeling of confidence. A strange sort of premonition that victory was somehow assured. It was a feeling that he always had when Setanta had lined up, *camán* in his steady hand, alongside him on the playing field.

It was the feeling that he was on the winning side already.

*****

Setanta's plan, as Conall had anticipated, was brutally simple – hitch up the horses, move downwind on foot, crouch in some bushes within view of a stream, and wait. Having found a suitable position, amongst the branches of a gorse bush, they hunkered down as the sounds of the forest of high Imbolc clamoured all around them. Small birds fretted in the boughs above, the gentle wind brought a sighing rustle from the oak and beech leaves in some distant part of the wood, the stream continued its babbled discourse with itself. At one point, a scuffling of the leaf litter drew the hunters' attention, but it was nothing more than a hedgehog in search of a morsel. As the day wore on, their limbs began to ache for want of movement, and still the forest would yield no sign of their quarry. True to form, Conall was the quicker to give in to boredom.

'This does not seem like hunting to me,' he whispered. 'I feel more like a shivering rabbit up here, cowering from the...'

'Shh!, *Look.*' Setanta was gesturing toward the stream, his eyes aglow. 'On the far bank. Courage has returned to our prey.' True enough, a large male boar had shuffled cautiously to the opposite bank of the brook, its head bent low to drink from the bright waters. Conall steeled himself for the worst – there would be no living with his friend after this petty victory. He was pleasantly surprised to find that Setanta was too gripped with excitement to bother with gloating, though he was not content to let the moment pass completely uncommented.

'For your patience and faith in my tactics, Conall, I will let you strike it down.'

'*Let* me, is it?' Conall began, but he quickly abandoned his retort as pointless; Setanta was already beaming and looking elsewhere about the trees as Conall readied his sling for the strike. He was a skilled shot, his movements fluid and requiring no thought: his eyes remained fixed on his prey as his hand moved lightly to the small pile of rocks he had placed within reach earlier. He loaded the rock, weighed it and began to swing the weapon, slowly at first, then steadily increasing in speed. In a moment, he would deftly spring to his feet, release the shot and the prize would be theirs.

Setanta listened with satisfaction to the soft '*whup whup*' of Conall's sling. He did not mind surrendering the killing shot to his friend, and he had no doubts about the accuracy of his arm. He gazed happily at the patterns of sparkling sunlight falling on the running waters, then over at a yellowhammer as it hopped from one branch of a chestnut tree to another. He enjoyed the unpredictability of its furtive movements, and was about to turn his gaze back to the boar when a pinprick of light from the bushes beyond the hopping bird captured his attention. Something bright and shiny and... almost, but not quite, like... metal.

In an instant he was on his feet and had broken cover, his head thrust in the direction of the glint of light. This had two effects on the actors of the drama unfolding around him: it caused the boar to instantly take to its stubby hocks and disappear into the thick greenery. It also caused Conall to miss his shot completely, his stone sailing harmlessly wide of where the boar had been. He was about to vent his rage upon Setanta when he caught sight of the curious twinkling that was holding his hunting-mate in thrall. The two of them crept silently across the forest floor.

The first thing to reach them, before they even drew near the thicket, was the smell. Foetid, rotting, putrefying; as if some great, yet invisible, creature had been expectorated from the underground faerie realms only to expire on the very earth they now walked upon. By the time they had come within a few feet of the bushes, both Conall and Setanta were struggling to overcome the urge to gag as the unspeakable stench of foulness seemed to intensify with each passing moment. One thing was becoming apparent – whatever lay ahead of them was something ghastly and unwholesome.

Reaching the shelter of the bramble, they crouched low and peered through the tangle of briar and leaves. Beyond, the forest sloped downward into a deep hollow. What they saw first filled Setanta with shock, but this feeling was quickly replaced by anger. For on the far rim of the hollow, a war band was assembling. Its size was more than enough to overwhelm Eamhain's currently depleted defence forces. A glimmer of light came from the sun falling on their weird scabrous, yet iridescent armour, and their wicked coral-forged machines of battle. Setanta could see over a dozen chariots, strangely shaped and pulled by angered bulls. There were also battering rams and instruments of pain whose purpose he could scarcely guess, nor did he wish to. For this was not an army of men.

'I'd swear these are Fomorians,' Setanta hissed. 'See how they try to keep under the canopy of the trees until the sun has set, Conall? Lugh has shown to us who the true prey is this day.'

'Their timing could not be worse for us!' Conall said, his voice choking with mounting dread. 'The main force of Eamhain's army is absent in the west and the Ruddy Boars are recuperating at Fort Culainn. But how could invaders know this? The word has gone out from our emissaries that we are at full strength. Someone has betrayed the strategies of our king!'

Setanta nodded. 'Whatever the score on that, Eamhain Mhacha sits ignorant of the threat. We must bring word to the king swiftly; this may be the making of us yet. Away with us!'

The two crawled backward to the stream where the boar had evaded them, sprinting through the woods to the small clearing where the horses remained grazing. Mounting with a great leap, Setanta spurred his steed fiercely and galloped away in the direction of Eamhain Mhacha. Conall, barely managing to keep pace with him, rode furiously after.

'A fine prize you've found to set against Diarmuid's, Setanta! I hope his catch is tastier than the word of impending doom!' he called grimly.

29

Yet even at so grave a moment as this, Setanta would not be outdone. Shouting back over his shoulder and with hint of his customary humour, he yelled:

'Well, you're the one who let the boar escape.'

Conall cursed him silently, then instantly scolded himself for doing so. That was Setanta – impossible, irrepressible, indomitable. That was why Conall loved him dearly. That was why he would follow him to the gates of death if he asked him to.

4.

Lord Nardul

The Deepwatch were Lord Nardul's personal bodyguard. Far larger and more vicious than the fearsome and cruel Fomorian raider that made up the bulk of Nardul's army, they remained eternally stationed around their commander's battle palanquin.

They were the very key to Nardul's rise to power, for these nine-foot paladins of combat were the remnants of a powerful aquatic race, the Halosa, who were conquered by the Fomorians in the time of Balor – he of the Evil Eye. He had used his formidable powers of insight to discover the Halosan hatching grounds and wipe out the future generations of those potent enemies by slashing or devouring the egg sacs that lined their undersea grotto. This had all taken place while the mainstay of the Halosan army fought those Fomorians who had feinted back to their own regions, luring their enemies further from their strongholds and leaving the spawning caves unprotected.

Balor had intuited that the Halosan's minds were linked in some way to their kin, and the psychic shockwave from the slaughter in the hatching cave caused their warriors to clutch their heads and fall to their knees in agony. Having lost all will to live, they were hacked down by the triumphant Fomorian forces, who then went on to butcher their females and spawn with great cruelty.

But Nardul, then one of Balor's most trusted nobles who had been present in the hatching grounds, was charged with overseeing the final destruction of any remaining eggs while Balor went forth to enjoy personally crushing the helplessly stunned leaders of the Halosan army. But, the possibility of advancement quickly conquering his fear that Balor might discover his treachery, from that defiled nursery Nardul stole away with him several Halosan eggs.

Nardul's blubbery lips retracted into an obscene mockery of a smile at the thought of this ancient betrayal, of his fear, and of his ultimate success. He of the Evil Eye had been blind after all! He had lacked the vision to grasp how to truly dominate and control the old enemy. The fool had deserved his brutal fate and the ensuing power vacuum had been a great gift to Nardul.

In nurturing his hatchlings, he had taken supreme advantage of the one Halosan weakness known to him – their undying parental loyalty. They grew, in their infancy, utterly devoted to their 'father' Nardul. With the passing of years they became mighty sons and daughters who fought and

31

lived and coupled - according to Nardul's wishes - with the stoutest of his own followers. Soon he had at his disposal a race of hybrid monstrosities, unstoppable in battle and unswerving in their devotion to him.

These became known as the Deepwatch, and their superiority in warfare changed the history of the Fomorian race.

Thus all other pretenders to Balor's position as High Warlord fell and, one after another, their cleanly sea-eaten skulls were attached to Nardul's battle palanquin. He had already been undefeated under Balor's legendary rule, and since the Evil One's defeat, Nardul had remained all-conquering. In his four hundred and eighteen years, he had never once come even close to losing a skirmish, let alone a campaign. His Horn of Prestige, a jagged forehead protrusion that grew psychically in Fomorian leaders according to the awe and reverence they received from their kin, was long, thick and proud.

Nardul and his Deepwatch were - quite simply – invincible, and ruled with absolute authority over all the under-realms.

Now it was time to take the realms above.

Before him, two of the Deepwatch moved aside and allowed a scout to flounder towards the base of the palanquin, splaying out his arms in wet reverence to the High Warlord.

'The defences are not weak, Lord Nardul' it gurgled. 'But against our greater number they are as vulnerable as the open clam!'

Nardul glared down at the scout. His small size and keen eyes made for a good tracker, but ultimately what was the point of this creature's life? He seemed empty of all ambition. He would serve and die without any personal glory just to avoid the uncertainty of living outside the Warlord's graces. This kind served through fear. The thought disgusted him in equal measure to his satisfaction of having the wit to use such runts to gain valuable tactical advantage.

The report was nonetheless pleasing to his vicious mind.

'Ahh, Eamhain Mhacha' he growled softly. 'King Conchobar's pride in his meagre conquests has exposed his stupidity in leaving such a prize unguarded. Let me drink to my victory!'

Nardul extended a brawny arm that glistened moistly in the narrow rays of sunlight that pierced their way through the thick foliage overhead. Into his waiting hand a servant placed his favoured goblet - a loathsome thing fabricated from the cranial case of his final enemy before the seas were totally conquered.

He drew the vessel toward his lips... but no further; an unseen force interrupted the motion, sloppong some of the deep-green fermented algae liquor onto his chest plate.

A painfully hoarse and echo-less voice came to him.

'Now is the time for attack, Nardul... not for celebration.'

The Warlord's features twisted into a blasphemous expression. He cocked his head slowly and made out the thin, cowled figure standing, slight and un-nerving, between two Deepwatch who remained unaware of the intruder.

The Morrigan!

'This is not a battle that requires caution and siege,' continued the dark one.

'But victory will not be assured if you delay and allow reinforcements to arrive.' She raised a long clawed hand and pointed it towards where the hill fort lay.

'Strike *now*!'

Nardul pondered this for a moment, then heaved himself forward on the palanquin and stared squarely at the strange apparition with whom he had forged a pact at the start of this campaign.

'What salvation could there possibly be, Deathless One?', his guttural voice managing to lend ironic tones to his discourse, '...when you have assured me that no word of Conchobar's plight has left this place? All would-be reinforcements are too distant to aid him now, said you.'

'I am not the only power in the heavens and on earth, Nardul,' hissed the Morrigan. 'There may be other forces at play against our designs. Do not be surprised if the Gods of Men deign to interfere.'

Nardul's hand began to fidget and worry at the hilt of his great sword, Doomwave, which lay sheathed in a special socket upon the shell-encrusted battle-litter.

'You promised a victory ripe for the taking, a battle we could not lose! Are you sending us to filthy earthen graves, O Twisted One? I tell you now –

you will grow weak from lack of sundered human souls provided by the war-making of my race if Nardul should fall here to treachery!

The Morrigan moved closer to the Fomorian leader. He could discern hints of her deathly hideousness from deep within her darkly-wrapped head and felt the uncomfortable numbness of her touch as she gripped his upper arm.

'I brought you to the prize and here it stands before you, quaking in fear. Aaahh... I can taste already their dread of death! My eagerness for attack is born from my hunger for the souls of those therein. There is but little chance of reinforcement, Nardul - but attack now to be certain.'

More to be free of her unsettling presence than anything else, Nardul nodded and, pulling his arm from her grip, raised it over his head then splayed his webbed fingers and roared:

'We march on Eamhain Mhacha... *Now*!'

'This fortress will be the first capital of the new Fomorian empire above the sea, and I will have Conchobar's head as my drinking vessel... but not before he witnesses the full agonies we mete out upon his females and spawn!!'

With another flick of his upheld arm, he then motioned for his palanquin bearers to hoist him high and into the battle march. In only moments the great host of Fomor began trudging out of the woods and in the direction where, not far off at all, lay the vulnerable capital of Uladh.

As for the Morrigan, she had already taken to the skies, her dark spirit filled with excited lust.

5.

Ramparts

On days such as this, thought Conchobar MacNeasa, *Lugh surely smiles on his chosen people.*

For his face was indeed bathed with the warm afternoon sun - a thing not overly common in his realm in recent years. The morning had started cloudy and overcast when Conchobar had begun his tour of the defensive walls of his fort Eamhain Mhacha, but had soon cleared up from the east. This clement weather reassured him that his strategies of late were just and bound to be fruitful.

Now if only Amergin too could share Conchobar's confidence, then perhaps his enigmatic councillor would give him some peace to enjoy the rest of this blessed day.

'Your boldness leaves me ill at ease, my king,' the curiously dark-skinned sage was saying with those small, disapproving shakes of the head that generally irked MacNeasa. 'You stretch your power too far too quickly.'

Conchobar was far too full of confidence after a satisfactory inspection of the solid ramparts to allow Amergin's questionings to weary him, so he strode on briskly a few paces before answering with a certain level of distraction.

'Since when was boldness not considered a virtue?'

'When it turns to folly. Beware sire; the fish that breaks water too often in order to catch the dragonfly may leap into the mouth of the heron.'

Damned druid and his cryptic parables! He turned and squarely faced Amergin, who stopped and regarded the king with his piercing brown eyes.

'For sixteen years I've followed this course, o sage, and until now you've never bemoaned my tactics. Uniting these lands under my banner will not remain dream for much longer. Soon we will even triumph over the forces of Ailill and his troublesome concubine Queen Medb. But only if we stay truc to the path! No great prize was ever gained without risk. How many times have I heard you say that?'

'What I fear, Conchobar, is that you count too many of your defeated foes as toothless. A beaten and collared wolf knows when its captor's grip loosens.'

35

'Allay those fears!' shouted the king with a dismissive wave of an arm. 'You fray at my nerves with them. Fergus and the Ruddy Boars will be back from Fort Culainn in a matter of days in any event...'

Suddenly the air was filled with bellowed warnings. The king and the sage turned to face the south gate where two young riders had erupted into the courtyard. Conchobar saw that it was Setanta and young Conall Cearnach.

'Warband! Warband!' they cried.

Setanta must have noticed the king despite his haste to make it to the Red Branch Hall, for he turned back his horse, then leaped from the mount to stand directly in front of Conchobar and delivered his news.

'Fiends of war from the east approach. A strong and armoured band.'

Conchobar thought he would never cease to admire this lad. No preamble, no overwrought courtesy. Straight to the point, and he wasn't even out of breath.

'The east? How many strong are they?'

'Too many to resist, my king.' Then, stepping even closer as if discussing strategy with an equal in both experience and rank, he added 'The Branch Knights here should prepare themselves. For the moment let us young bloods - myself, Conall and the like - let us fly and meet them. We'll stall them, with bloody sacrifice if necessary, and by then you'll have the time to...'

'Hold on, boy.' Conchobar's admiration would only grant Setanta free reign up to a certain point. He was still a stripling after all, and, despite his qualities, knew nothing of caution. But who were these attackers? It could not be Connacht men... that meant... He glanced at Amergin - the sage had one eye closed, his head tilted up. Long experience had taught him that the gesture meant it was time to heed the old druid's opinion. He turned back to the boy, who was visibly trembling with excitement and eagerness to be heard.

'How far?'

'Their power forces them to trundle slowly. There is maybe a day and a half at most to make ready.'

A day and a half! A grim estimate.
Conchobar would have preferred if Conall had said it, at least then there might have been room to hope for more time, but Setanta was too accurate, all the time.

'No talk of sacrifices yet, brave lad,' he said, a calming hand firmly on the boy's shoulder.

'To the hall!'

*****

The sparrowhawk had flown in from one the high windows of the Craobh Ruadh, encircling the mighty limb that dominated the chamber before coming to perch on Amergin's outstretched arm.

Setanta was in awe. He had seen many falconers call hunting birds to them, but to summon an animal from the exterior to the interior without seeming to make a sound... There was, it seemed to the young warrior, no end to the mystery of Amergin. Despite trying every day to learn as much as he could of secret lore in their long talks, he felt that there were simply some things the sage thought best not to impart. But Setanta also had the conviction that in time he *would* know all.

Because, after all, he *was* Setanta.

'Four thousand is the number that marches on Eamhain Mhacha,' Amergin pronounced to the king and the hastily assembled knights and Youngbloods of the Red Branch.

Silence reigned for a long moment. Red Branch Knights were trained hard to never show any fear. But this news was truly fearsome and Setanta could sense that those around him were either waiting for someone to risk speaking with a voice that might betray their anxiety, or they were formulating something fittingly heroic to say

In the end it was Conall who cracked.

'We will not stall four thousand men for long, no matter how bravely we take to the fight,' he said with quiet honesty.

'Not men,' responded Amergin with foreboding. 'The approaching army is, as the boy Setanta surmised, *Fomorian*, my lord.'

The tension rose to an unbearable degree inside Setanta. The mixture of stress and battle eagerness he felt in the room made his hair stand on end and his muscles clench. So it *was* the Fomorians! What sort of fighters would they be, these savages from the depths? And in such number! Was this how his life would end? Slaughtered against all hope? He searched himself for fear; there was none. Only excitement.

The king rose to his feet.

'So... the Fomors rise once more. And a more timely attack they could not have contrived.'

Suddenly, in a flush of realization Setanta blurted: 'So we are betrayed! How could the twisted ones know to launch an assault if not privy to our war plans?'

'That is a question that we will seek to answer another time,' replied Conchobar, addressing all assembled. 'For now the main task is to make sure that we survive to *see* another time.

'The Wolf Horde of Forgall, battling for ground in the west, is too distant to aid us and many of our best fighting men are part of that brave band. We cannot stand against the Fomorians so depleted: all of you are war-wrought enough to know the truth of that.

'But there is hope. The Ruddy Boars of Fergus are on their way back from the northern battles.'

Conchobar stepped forward and plucked the spear from the oaken battle map, then drove it back into the carved surface some distance north west of Eamhain Mhacha.

'Just now they are resting at Fort Culainn, here.'

A bitter sound – somewhere between a snort and laughter – caused heads to turn in Diarmuid's direction.

'We will all be cold and broken before they return this far south,' said he darkly.

'The legendary hospitality of the Forgemaster will waylay them for days. My father won't be sober till well after the crows clean my skull.'

Setanta knew that Diarmuid had no fear of dying, but he *did* fear not dying at his father's side in battle. Nevertheless, he could not stand to hear him so despondent, and so he grabbed the other young warrior by the shoulder.

'He will be proud, Diarmuid! As will all our kinsmen when they see how savagely we fought for our king. Their vengeance upon the raiders will be terrible, unmatched by any tale, and we will be satisfied in our graves!'

'Noble words, Setanta, and I'm glad to hear them,' said Conchobar. 'But know this - you will not be taking the fight to the invaders.'

Setanta's fury was rising. Amergin had warned him about the rage that had sometimes compromised what would have been perfect execution of his warrior feats, but still he could not master himself. He pondered the king's meaning for a moment, then his eyes widened with outrage at the perceived implication.

'We cannot be flying Eamhain Mhacha! We cannot just let the foul sea spawn sunder your throne without a fight! We could not move all our people in time, in any event. No! I will not let one man, woman or child of Uladh die un-fought for!'

Conchobar remained calm against this tide of passion.

'If you are as worthy as we all hope, young Setanta, then not one shall die at all. It is my command that you ride out to Fort Culainn this very moment. Using that skill of horsemanship of which you are so proud, you should make it there 'ere the night falls. Alert Fergus of our peril: instruct him to bring his men. We shall hold them until then, slowing the filth on the open field. Here is my marker.'

The king removed the gauntlet from his left wrist, the one upon which was fixed his strip of bark from the Red Branch - the emblem of a proven Knight. His was the largest piece ever taken and the most ornately carved.

Once Setanta took hold of the gauntlet, he felt destiny circle in upon him in ever-tightening rings of certainty. Conchobar was right, yet his warrior's heart railed against this solution. He placed the gauntlet on his naked right wrist. Would he live long enough to become a Red Branch Knight and earn his own strip of bark?

'It is a fair plan, I concede... yet I feel nothing but cowardice! My sword arm is better than my swiftness...'

'That is another reason why it must be you,' insisted Conchobar, drawing himself to his considerable height to loom over the confused young warrior. 'Surely you cannot have forgotten. *The Hound.*'

Setanta felt his pulse quicken at the word; yes, he knew the tales of Culainn's vicious nocturnal protector. And he had nothing but admiration for it: its ferocity, its loyalty, its legend. The tale went that several years past, the ForgeMaster Culainn came upon a strange, delicate creature lying prone by a rock pool. Culainn swears still that it was a nymph, a child of the Sidhe, normally never seen by human eyes. On the night before there had been a terrible storm and one of her fine gossamer wings had been broken.

39

The nymph called to Culainn in his head, 'Stout hero,' said she in a voice like chiming bells 'I will only ask once, then you will see me no more - please give me some of your strength for my shattered wing. If you do this, I will protect you forever.'

Of the tale, Setanta knew no more, only that Culainn returned to his home weary and stricken, and lay ill for weeks. On the final day of his recovery, Culainn walked painfully back to the rock pool and there, under a full moon, the earth shook and from the ground emerged an incredible hound, swathed in blood and soil. It approached Culainn and bowed its head and spoke for the first and only time.

'Sleep soundly evermore, Culainn, for I shall protect your nights until the end of our times.'

And so it proved, and no more powerful guardian a fort could ever have.

Setanta's mind came back to the present, his reverie unnoticed by those around. Conchobar continued.

'Should you not reach Fort Culainn by nightfall, then all will be lost. You have proven yourself the most able of our young strategists. If your speed should fail you, then you will have need of all your war-craft and guile to prevail against the Hound.'

'Tis true,' admitted Conall beside him. 'And you won't find any quarrel among us, though each of us would gladly take the task if given.'

Setanta hesitated no further. The excitement and pride of this duty surged maddeningly into his heart, his head, almost blinding him with a lust for adventure.

'Say no more. I will return with the army of Fergus. I swear it, or may the great worm tear my soul asunder!' With that he turned and tore off out of the Craobh Ruadh to a roar of encouragement from the assembled youths and Knights.

'Go, lad!' Conchobar added to the din. 'As for the rest of you, make ready! If Setanta should fail, the Fomorians shall still find a most painful welcome at my door!'

As the great hall emptied, the king turned to Amergin. 'I would hear your ideas on how to harry the enemy now, my friend.'

'And I yours,' the sage replied.

Both men laughed, but only briefly.

6.

Riders

Hooves thundered across the great plain of Muirtheimne, scattering a small herd of red deer that had been grazing idly in the afternoon light. With wild shouts of encouragement and urgent nudging of his heels, Setanta drove his powerful steed onwards, towards the fort of Culainn, the Forgemaster.

Normally a day's ride north-west from Eamhain Mhacha, the task had fallen to Setanta to reach the fort in less than six hours, before the sun set and the fort's unique, but formidable, defence was set loose. As was his way, he had set about his task with intelligence and wisdom. Conchobar had spoken true, he was indeed the swiftest rider in the kingdom, but Setanta knew that it would count for little if he sat atop the wrong horse. He had rushed immediately to Laegaire, master charioteer and horse-breeder of Eamhain to seek his advice on the fastest mount to take. They had settled on a raven-black colt named *Fréamh* (meaning *root*, after the dark and knotted appearance of his muscular flanks), as he was the horse of choice for the king's messengers when they were sent on an errand of highest import. He was of good stock, a carefully bred line of superior mounts that were long of leg and shiny of coat. When Setanta enquired about the animal's temperament, Laegaire had replied wryly:

'Oh ye'll get on fine; he's headstrong, stubborn and fiery – a four-legged version of yourself!'

So far the choice had proven wise; Fréamh loved to run, loved to be pushed and tested. So far, they had traversed the lush plains of Uladh, upon which horses enjoy stretching their legs, in fine time; but next would come the Venery Forest and later, the Barrier Wood. Dense and thick, these huge woods covered most of the expanse between the River Cronn and Fort Culainn, and travel through them necessitated slower going. Setanta's strategy was a simple one – make haste across the flat, open ground, for any advantage they made there would surely be lost once they met the tree line.

But for now, with the sun high in the heavens, their progress had been heartening.

And so, from the plain into the green and dappled light of the Venery Forest they plunged, the pace slowing considerably to allow the many obstacles to be safely navigated. Setanta wondered how long he would be able to avoid taking the chance of speeding up once more; his need was great, but was it worth risking an injury to Fréamh? A fallen log, an unstable footing, a concealed rock and the price of a suddenly lame horse would be felt all the more keenly by his brethren back at Eamhain. Its price would be paid in blood.

So, despite his instincts, Setanta maintained his sensible - if maddeningly slow - pace through the forest, passing deeper and deeper into the clutter of trees as they changed from oak and chestnut to beech and ash. He could tell from a change in the exterior light which managed to filter through the leaves that the afternoon was wearing on, and the moment was fast approaching when he would have to abandon caution and ride at full pelt once more.

Suddenly the tranquillity of the woods was rent asunder by an agonised scream which seemed to come from somewhere nearby. Setanta was inclined to press on, but there was something in the quality and timbre of the cry that gave him pause; it had sounded human. But here? So deep inside the Venery Forest? Another ear-splitting scream from the undergrowth left no doubt – a human, a *female* voice, in great distress. Cursing the timing, and the oath of honour he had sworn as a lad to never knowingly turn his back on a person in need, he pulled Fréamh around, allowing the horse to nimbly pick his way through the thicker forest growth toward the source of the commotion.

Drawing close to a dense briar, he called ahead 'Hai! Of what help can I be?' and stretching forth his sword, still sheathed, to part the bramble a great fluttering of wings, and a third piercing screech, burst out from the bushes. A large crow, producing that human-sounding scream, flapped and pecked at Setanta's face as he struggled to bat the bird away whilst simultaneously endeavouring to prevent Fréamh from bolting. The crow eventually took to its wide black wings and disappeared into the canopy of leaves overhead.

Setanta was still staring after it, cursing its mischief and ruefully wondering how much time this may have cost him, when he was assailed from behind. His first thought was that the crow had returned, but dismissed the idea immediately – an arm was quickly wrapped around his neck, stout and sinewy and... scaly. Fomorian! Setanta instinctively reached around with his right arm, searching for the creature's head, when three more of the foul grey-skinned and barbel-faced raiders emerged from the dankness and hastened toward him. Fréamh reared up, thrashing at the nearest Fomorian with his hooves, and as he rose up on his hind legs, Setanta and his attacker were toppled from the mount. They landed hard, but Setanta was on his feet faster, his sword now unsheathed. The Fomorian groped awkwardly for his own weapon, a jagged and cruel scimitar of some black substance – but his sluggishness was his undoing, for Setanta struck with terrifying speed, splitting the creature's torso with a powerful strike. He had little time to savour this success, however, as his sword was suddenly wrested from his grasp by a new attack – a great bony club, wielded by the second of his foes, came down hard on his forearm. Now unarmed, Setanta lunged straight at the club-swinging warrior, driving thunderous punches into the cold skin of the Fomorian's chest and abdomen. His foe reeled back, but as Setanta stepped forward to take full advantage, a hard blow to his lower back brought him to his knees. Setanta could hear the panicked clamour of Fréamh still rearing and kicking his hooves at one of the Fomorians, as he felt the strong arms of the third Fomorian clasping his own, pinning them to his sides and holding him in place as the club-bearer regained his senses and loomed closer for a killing strike.

Setanta tried pushing backward with his legs, but could achieve no purchase on the loose leaves and detritus that covered the forest earth. And anyway, the creature behind him felt extremely powerful – the largest of the group, he guessed, which meant that courageous Fréamh must be doing battle with the runt, a stunted creature with a spear. For Setanta that was all he ever needed. As the great club was swung powerfully downwards, he pitched himself forward, almost into the swing. The sudden change of direction caught his restrainer off guard, and the huge Fomorian toppled forward with him. Using his knees as a lever, Setanta strained forward and down, so that the Fomorian was stretched across his back, almost flat. The creature looked up in surprise as his comrade's club came down brutally, reducing his head to pulp. Moving swiftly, Setanta now scrambled forward on all fours and retrieved his sword, he then sprung to his feet and lopped the club-bearing arm from the brandisher's body, weapon and member falling together. The vile being howled in pain, but his screams were cut short as Setanta's blade next found his throat, slicing though scale, tendon and bone with a wet crunch. Greenish black blood oozed from his sword while the creature gurgled into death.

One left, he thought to himself, but he noticed a silence once more in the wood – Fréamh must be as good a fighter as he is at a gallop! Setanta turned, expecting to see his dark mount awaiting the resumption of their journey, then fell to his knees once more. The smallest Fomorian lay dead, his head cleaved and flattened by Fréamh's strong hooves, but poor Fréamh lay lifeless opposite, the cruel Fomorian spear driven through the animal's neck.

'Ah, no...' sighed Setanta, his bodily aches now wholly insignificant. He looked toward the sun, or what trace of it he could see through the leaves and branches. The lower edge of the bright disc had begun to show a tint of orange. Dusk was coming. He took a deep breath, stretched himself and then whispered a short prayer:

'Great Danú, lend strength to these legs. I must not fail.' Suddenly a vision of desecration flashed through his mind that made him gasp in horror. He could see that holiest of places for him, Luglochta Lóga, full of misshapen Fomorian creatures: they were setting fire to the pine trees and staggering about drunkenly among the shrines. And burning intensely in his mind was the face of his mother, Dechtíre, a golden halo of light about her brow. He could hear her gentle voice in his head - was it a memory? Was it a message? He didn't know but the words were clear.

To despair is to fail, my sweet Setanta. Never despair and you will never fail.

The words of his mother, who now rested in the arms of Danu. With that, he snapped open his eyes and took off running in the direction of Fort Culainn. As he raced away from that place of death and betrayal, silence returned once more.

All save the sounds of a lone crow that sat perched on a limb. Sounds which any listener might have taken for cruel laughter.

*****

Panting, gasping, muscles burning, mind racing, lungs screaming for air, Setanta raced on across the countryside. From his glances at the sky he reckoned that this was his second hour of unbroken running, and in that time he had cleared the northern parts of the Great Forests of Uladh, entered a sloping plain, thence into a river valley and now he was bearing down on another large woodland. The sun was declining steadily closer and closer to the line of blue hills to the west – he somehow could always tell the exact location of Lugh's Disc, even without seeing it – and the horizon had taken on the grey and smoky quality that usually precedes a sunset.

Into the wooded glade he plunged, his route becoming more meandering as his strides became wayward from sheer exhaustion. Then, on sighting a freshly running stream, he pitched himself onto his knees and drank deep of the cool, clear waters.

'*Uisce*!' he proclaimed, as he doused his face and neck, then rubbed some of the cooling liquid onto his throbbing legs, trying to coax some further effort from them. The air had cooled now, which was to his liking – better conditions for running. He was in the process of readying himself – both physically and mentally – for another bout of sprinting when his attention was captured by the sound of approaching hooves. Never one to be caught unawares twice in one day, Setanta unsheathed his weapon and crept silently behind the large trunk of an oak tree.

44

Through the cover of leaves he could discern the form of a single rider, hooded and seemingly in no great hurry. Fomorian scout, he surmised, then dismissed the idea – the sea-creatures did not employ horses, as all land animals were instinctively repulsed by their foul odour. This was why only harshly-whipped bulls were forced to drag their chariots. Bandit, then? More likely, given that the approaching figure clearly wanted his identity kept hidden. Setanta was ready for action – a swift blow to the head with his sword hilt would incapacitate the vagabond, and Setanta would be on horseback once again, perhaps – just perhaps – in enough time to reach Fort Culainn before nightfall.

Setanta set himself, dug his toes into the earth and sprung forward as horse and rider drew close. With the pommel of his sword already beginning its arc toward the rider's hooded head, the figure suddenly looked up and Setanta was startled to recognise... Emer! Too late to change direction, all he could do was release his grip on the sword, which spun harmlessly away, and crash straight into the young maiden. As the pair tumbled through the air, Setanta managed to position himself so that it was his own back that took the brunt of the landing, depositing Emer on top of him.

'Well! What a capture this is! A horse and a lady!' he exclaimed, doing his best to overcome his embarrassment with bravado. 'Though I only have time now to mount *one* of these fine creatures!'

Emer gave him a withering look that warned him not to test her. 'Idiot!' she growled as she peeled herself off him. Setanta picked himself up meekly, and thought it best not to employ any more of his disarming charm at this time.

'My apologies Emer,' he began. 'I took you for a bandit, and...'

'Do I *look* like a filthy robber?' she snapped as she inspected her cloak and hood for damage. His flustered explanations were cut short as she made her way after her horse, which was now grazing on some scrub grass.

'So this is the famous refined manner of Setanta that flusters the tavern girls of Eamhain? I'm not impressed!' she called back.

Setanta's mission returned to his mind. His need was still great, and Emer's forgiveness could be sought later, if either of them survived.

'My horse has fallen. I need to take yours,' he said simply.

Emer was indeed unimpressed. 'You warriors are all the same. You think your comings and goings are so much more important than a woman's that you can just take her horse without question? Forget it. Laitha stays with me.'

A flash of anger, then a thought suddenly occurred to Setanta.

'Emer, when did you depart Eamhain Mhacha?'

'Just after you left on your merry hunt this morning, what of it?'

'Then I have overtaken you.' The realisation that Emer was totally unaware of the threat facing Eamhain hit him like a blow from a stallion's hoof. His tone now became urgent and serious, the jousting and banter abandoned.

'Emer, I *need* your horse. A Fomorian army now bears down on Eamhain Mhacha bent on its destruction. I have been charged with mustering Fergus and his company from Fort Culainn so that they may ride out to protect our people. I was ambushed and my steed killed. If I do not reach the Fort before nightfall then all might be lost.'

She scanned his face, his eyes – those strange, bright, sapphire eyes – for traces of further mischief, and finding none, her own eyes widened in horror.

'You are speaking the truth!' Then, suddenly resolute, she nodded, and in that moment Setanta saw the other side to Emer: the general's daughter, the warrior woman that she was surely destined to become.

'Laitha responds only to me, so you will have to ride up behind me. Besides, I am heading to the Fort myself, though I had planned not to arrive until the morn.'

Setanta was looking appraisingly at Laitha and nodding. He had heard of Emer's treasured steed, and he knew how such animals could be particular about who they allowed at the reins.

'It is well, then, but we must try and get there sooner. Before sunset, or all will be in vain. You ride, Emer, as swiftly as you might. Perhaps Lugh will smile on us today and move more slowly through the heavens.'

Emer mounted gracefully, and Setanta leapt up behind her, taking the opportunity to squeeze her firmly about the hips.

'It's a lucky thing indeed that I found you, Emer. These lands are wild. All manner of danger could leap from the trees and attack you. You need my protection!'

He heard a loud 'Tsk!' from Emer, followed quickly by another razor-sharp retort. 'The only protection I need is from the likes of you!'

Setanta allowed himself a broad smile, then his face hardened as he caught sight of the sun sinking ever lower. He squeezed Emer again, but this time to encourage her to spur Laitha on faster.

'Come on, Emer! Let's ride!'

7.

The Deepening Gloom

From their position on the battlements of Eamhain Mhacha, Conchobar and Amergin could just about make out the distant glow of campfires in the dusk below the ridge of the low hills; they were still far off yet - a good night and day's march from the fort.

Not many fires. Not nearly enough for an attacking force of the size Setanta had claimed. The king had begun to ponder the meaning of this during one of Amergin's long, silent moments of reflection when the creaking of the ladder that served this turret took his attention.

The eternally-tussled head of Conall Cearnach appeared at the top of the thick wall and forgetting, as always, to display the proper courtesy, the youth gave his report there and then.

'My King!' he shouted gracelessly. 'The Fomors are well armed. They have nine chariots and all seem like seasoned warriors, the curs!'

Conchobar had to smile at that to himself, the lad was a rough stone alright but he was hardy; in view of their current situation, he needed all of his young bloods to be of that nature.

'Our harrying attacks have not met with much success. Five of our outriders have been taken. The enemy's vision seems to improve in the deepening gloom.'

'Naturally,' responded Amergin. 'More accustomed are these peoples to the murk of the sea-bed than the light of Lugh.'

Conchobar remembered shivering at a winter season's fireside to horrible tales of the Fomorians when he himself was just a lad. But he had never before heard them called a 'people'. Monsters, devils, lurking demons from the hellish canyons below the waves – thusly were they always described.

'Harry them no further, Conall,' he said. 'It would only be a waste of life. Better to have as many able bodies here to defend to the last 'ere Setanta returns with Fergus and his army.'

'Yes, my King!' replied the young warrior with un-tempered enthusiasm. 'They will not cross our gates!'

Once the boy had slid back down the ladder to re-join the defenders, Conchobar turned to Amergin who wore a troubled expression on his dark, many-lined face.

'With all my soul I pray that your gambit proves worthy in this, Conchobar,' he said quietly. Our treatment at the hands of the Fomorians when they storm this place will not be tender.'

'Nor will their reception be tranquil,' the king retorted firmly. He then squinted for a moment into the gathering darkness at the dimly glowing hills. 'Tell me sage, a thing I have never understood, if these creatures need not light to see or warm themselves, then why do they raise fires so.'

'Two reasons my King,' replied Amergin. 'Firstly to instil fear in the hearts of our warriors to weaken their appetite for battle...'

'Bah!' interjected Conchobar 'Do they not know that knights of the Red Branch have no dealings with fear? It is an un-informed enemy we face. All the better.'

'Secondly,' continued Amergin. 'The fires are no doubt being used to torture those we have sent to spy on them. They have an unnatural lust for the agony of others, and flames are a novelty to them; they never cease in their search for new ways of using this exotic element to inflict pain.'

Conchobar's bearded face darkened with disgust.

'Then it will please me all the more to cleanse this world of them when Fergus returns. Setanta has no doubt already reached his ear.'

Amergin offered no reply but remained staring at the fires, as Conchobar fancied he heard agonised screams reach him faintly on the wind from those terrible pyres.

*****

Laitha proved to be a horse of incredible endurance. Free as he was from the duty of guiding the animal, Setanta had plenty of time to gauge the strength of Emer's fine grey steed. There wasn't a fleck of foam under her legs and her stride was as long and steady now, as they neared Fort Culainn, as it was when they had set out.

They spoke not at all during the first few hours' course, hurtling through steadily darkening woods, though this was not for lack of initiative on the part of Setanta. Thrice already he had tried to ignite a conversation, but Emer had hardly responded. Was it the dread of the impending attack on

Eamhain, or was there another preoccupation that made her hold her thoughts to herself he wondered.

Setanta detested silence. He adored life and laughter; every emotion from joy to anger was a source of excitement. But lack of dialogue was repellant to him, even if this gave him time to appreciate Emer's long black hair so close to his face, her fresh, clean scent in his nostrils, and the shape of her waist under his encircling forearms. But the silence was killing him.

Leaning closer to Emer, he spoke loudly enough to be heard over Laitha's relentless hoof beats

'Though I am grateful of it, I must wonder what foolishness has you travelling alone through these lands, Emer? Forgall would be displeased to hear of the peril wherein his daughter boldly places herself.'

Setanta thought that she was continuing to ignore him, but then she angled her head slightly, enough to make herself heard to his keen ears.

'My business is my own,' she glowered. 'And be sure my father does not hear of it, Setanta, or things will go badly for you.'

At this, Setanta knew that some game was afoot and he could spar at leisure with his alluring opponent.

'Oho! So that's how it is!' he goaded. 'It is my experience that when a girl seeks to conceal her movements from her father, it is often because she feels that he would disapprove of he with whom she might secretly be savouring the moonlight.'

'And of what concern of that is yours?' replied Emer hotly.

'Ah, let's see if I can figure it out. Warriors are not to Emer's taste, allegedly. Yet here she steals off to a keep full of such men! Though admittedly there are one or two other types there as well. Judging by her temperament, it is likely to me that the fortunate man is either... hmm... a bard or a scholar.'

Setanta felt that he had struck home with his probing, but ignoring his comments, Emer changed the flow of the conversation.

'We will never make it before the night falls, and I despair of the hope that Conchobar put in you.'

'We just need to get there soon,' replied Setanta, but he wasn't going to let her evade him as easily as that. Having Emer so close to him, however, was beginning to get the better of his self-control; he'd have to keep himself in check.

Suddenly he clicked his fingers loudly at her ear.

'Donagh MacLabhrás is a bard! And lives not far from your father's house, as I recall.'

'Indeed I think he might be at Fort Culainn this very night! Were you and he not great friends, Emer?'

'Very well, Setanta,' she answered evenly. 'Perhaps Donagh and I are more than that. And though he may be no warrior, he is true and kind. And he does not bother me to distraction as you do.'

Setanta tightened his grip around Emer's slender waist and leaned further into her.

'Ah Emer, it is not my fault that you become distracted around me. Many are the women who complain of these ailments in my company!'

It seemed from the stiffening muscles in her back that Emer was about to launch another verbal assault. But then, to his surprise, the tension eased and she merely shook her head and said nothing. Confronted with that annoying silence, Setanta finally grew weary of the game. And as they rode on into the darkening evening, Emer was surprised at her own small smile; a smile that she was glad went unseen.

8.

The Tenebrous Tide

Conchobar Mac Neasa knelt reverently before the simple wooden altar in his private chamber. Upon it lay three small squares of pottery flanked by two thick beeswax candles. On the first plaque there was a handful of dried silt from the nearby river, on the second an acorn, on the third a sprig of Lily of the Valley. His forehead was pressed to the hilt of his faithful, and many-notched, heavy iron broadsword *Gan Trua*.

Normally it would be enough for a warrior of Eamhain Mhacha to offer his prayers and oaths to the Red Branch, and Conchobar had already done this, in plain view of his men. Nevertheless, now he wished to utter words that might have seemed like signs of apprehension or even weakness to some of the younger, more inexperienced fighters who would very soon be putting their lives at risk defending these walls.

But his prayers had nothing to do with weakness, rather that he wished to have every possible force, every conceivable advantage – human or otherwise – working in his favour during the coming conflict.

He was not ignorant of the overwhelming odds against them and their likelihood of prevailing against this untimely tide.

And so he whispered –

Great Dagda, lend force to my blows this night,
Oh Lugh, grant strength to my heart,
Sweet Danú embrace my people tonight,
Should I fail and they bloody the earth.

Noticing the sound of shuffling leather slippers behind him, Conchobar turned around and saw Amergin moving back the deerskin drape that cut off his chamber from the great hall.

The druid stood for a moment and scrutinized the kneeling king with a skeptically arched eyebrow.

'Forgive my sharp hearing, my friend, but that is the first time in a long while that I have heard uncertainty in the battle prayer of the mighty King Conchobar.'

The chieftain stared sourly at his counselor for a few moments, then stood, dusting off his knees and, having kissed the hilt of his sword he placed it within its well-worn scabbard.

'No uncertainty, Amergin. We will win this battle. In so far as we will keep the enemy away from this place until my knights arrive. It is unwise however to scorn the gods before a fight. It was not uncertainty you heard in my rites, it was custom.'

The druid smiled.

'You are a dogged warrior, my friend, and a fine king. If ever there was one who could lead so few to victory against so many it would be you.'

'Aye,' said the king somewhat absently. Then he nodded, seemingly reluctant to say something, but then deciding to do so quickly.

'But you will not be here to witness it, Amergin. It is time for you to leave.'

'Oh?' said the druid in an intrigued tone.

'Should the dark will of the foetid Fomorian gods somehow undo us I will not have the names and deeds of this hall forgotten. You will carry the news of such a calamity across the land and bring the terrible wrath of the Red Branch to bear on the tainted ones. Go now, and do this thing for me. For Eamhain Mhacha.'

Amergin raised his empty hands and shook his head sadly.

'I would sooner stay here so that I might be in the measure of giving a true account of the day when all is done. If I am struck down then that is the way of it.'

The pair stood their ground, glaring unblinkingly at one another. Conchobar did not like to be defied but if there was someone who did so with the most regularity it was Amergin. Suddenly, the deerskin curtain was torn hastily aside and Conall Cearnach blustered in.

'The wave of filth is come!' he shouted.

'How do you know it?' Conchobar asked.

'As you know, the enemy fires disappeared many hours ago. Now war horns, or something of that ilk, loudly blow out from the darkness.'

Conchobar realised he could indeed make out the sound of some distant pealing. The sound was alien, but any warrior knew it meant attack.

'Let us take the fight to them!' he intoned. 'They will not darken the threshold of this hall!'

Conchobar quickly clasped a hand on Amergin's shoulder.

'I'll expect to hear you fled, old friend.'

Then, before the druid had a chance to reply, he turned and stalked out to join his men at the battle-line.

Conchobar followed Conall through the hall, down the hill from the Craobh Ruadh and out to the scaffolding which accessed the inner-battlements.

From there they walked across a recently constructed wooden platform of stakes and planks that took them high above and across the outer courts where below the townsfolk rushed to and fro preparing for the battle. This was the Heroes' Walkway and its purpose was to display the king, and the greatest champions of the Red Branch to the people of Eamhain as they strode out to face down their enemies.

Below him Conchobar saw the townspeople of Eamhain rushing to and fro, preparing their homesteads for the coming battle. If the walls should fall he knew they would fight to the last soul. Even now he could see a band of youngsters who, having escaped their parents' sight, were now dividing out wooden swords, slings and rock-headed clubs from a reed bag. They too wished to join in the defence, so deeply ingrained was the honour of battle in the minds of Eamhain folk.

As he continued past some troops that were filing towards the outer fortifications, shouts of Conchobar's name went up, followed by cheers and bellowed declarations of loyalty.

Finally they reached the outer walls where they descended another ladder and came down outside the massive stakes that ringed the fort to join the rest of the waiting army.

Then the wooden platform across which they had reached the outer fortifications was pulled down and dismantled by workers from within the walls. Conchobar glanced over to see that the main gates of Eamhain Mhacha were blocked by many heavy lengths of wood layered down by large stones. Finally, the ladder they had just used was winched back over the wall and into the town.

For the assembled warriors there was no way in or out of the fort now.

They would fight and either prevail or die. They would not be holed-up by a siege, for such a thing was not the way of a Red Branch Knight.

And if they were wiped out then the townsfolk could, if they chose, flee by the north gate whose weakness was well concealed from the enemy and which could swiftly be pulled down from within.

Conchobar knew that the great strategist Forgall Manach would not have agreed with this decision. But Forgall was far from here, and Conchobar would not allow himself to enter into the tales as the first king to allow Eamhain to be besieged.

It would be bloody, maybe even foolish. But it would be in the spirit of the Red Branch.

Conchobar and Conall made their way to the front of the ranks where a grizzled Red Branch Knight was walking up and down, hobbling slightly and yelling orders and profanities at the rows of fighters.

The man, Eochaid, was a veteran, but one who had given up the sword to work in his orchard two seasons ago. Yet Conchobar also remembered well his mighty deeds of the past.

Eochaid was holding the reigns of the king's horse, and when he saw Conchobar approach he beat his breast with his left fist and called out Mac Neasa's name for all to hear.

'Mighty Eochaid,' said Conchobar, taking the reins of the chestnut stallion.

'I am glad that twisted hoof of yours has kept you away from the battle lines and you are here by my side this night. It is my hope that we all fight as bravely now as you have done for me these many years.'

Eochaid looked back at the assembled warriors with a winning smile.

'They're a hardy bunch, my King. Some of them may look like beardless skelps but they'll take some beating before they lay down and that's a fact.'

The king gazed along the lines of warriors. They were a mixed bag to be sure - mostly young boys freshly out of the Machra with nary a mark of warfare on their faces. Too few broken noses he thought. But there were a contingent of older fighters too, some missing hands or eyes from past combats. Conchobar recognised them and remembered the tales of their former acts of valour from the time of his own father. Among them too were some hardy artisans, smithies, carpenters and the like who he knew would also sell their blood dearly to protect their families.

On seeing all this, his pride and love for the people of Eamhain Mhacha and their unbreakable resolve sent his spirit soaring.

Then Conchobar peered hard out into the deep blackness beyond the torches that ringed the hill-fort. He could see nothing. A heavy blanket of cloud blotted out the stars and the moon was in her dark cycle. Nothing could be seen, yet an evil whiff came along the wind from the impenetrable darkness.

'The horns have stopped,' said the king pensively.

'Aye. They should be on their way.' Eochaid said.

'Though I have never seen such a large army advance in total darkness before.'

Conchobar growled unhappily.

'Amergin said they don't need any light to guide them. So they could be upon us at any moment. Let's have everyone sharp.'

Beside them, young Conall Cearnach, who had seemed unwilling to leave the king's side - despite Eochaid having earlier placed him two lines further back – had moved forward out toward the ring of torches and was staring off into the gloom.

'Look at that out there! Did you ever see the like of it?' he called back over his shoulder.

Conchobar, though irritated by this lack of discipline, followed the young fool's gaze and to his consternation discerned many reddish pinpricks of light moving about in the distance at the point Conall was indicating.

'Could that be faeries then? Or maybe 'tis only glowflies?' Conall continued seemingly unaware that he was breaking all battle protocol and privilege of rank with his unrestrained jabber.

'No insects are they,' said Eochaid grimly.

'Indeed they are not,' Conchobar added. For he could see, as could the other warriors as they squinted into the darkness, that the glowing red pinpricks were jostling towards them now, floating along in tight pairs.

'They... they are eyes!' Conall spluttered. 'The sea-demons are truly that!'

While Eochaid mounted up and began to bark his orders at the troops, Conchobar wheeled around in his horse to face them. He wrenched forth

Gan Trua from its scabbard, and before the sight of all, he drew its sharp edge across his fore-arm, releasing rivulets of his regal blood.

'Hear me defenders of Eamhain Mhacha!' he shouted.

'If my blade should have its final drink in this battle, then I will let it remember the taste of a true warrior's blood before gorging on whatever foul muck runs in Fomorian veins!'

Eochaid and Conall looked on in approval at this gesture, then without hesitation followed suit - as did all the Uladh warriors standing proudly before the walls of their homes that night.

'Defenders of Eamhain Mhacha!' Conchobar repeated, rearing up his horse and pointing his blood-stained sword at the oncoming Fomorian army who now could be seen in their entirety. Squat muscular creatures with oily grayish skin bearing glistening weapons of bizarre marine origin. The glowing red eyes were surrounded by dark blue or purple shell-like helmets. There were huge numbers of them, three times as many as the defenders. They advanced forward in a strangely menacing skipping motion, their weapons whickering through the cool night air.

'Carve lumps from them! Leave no limb unpruned! Plough furrows in their heads! ONWARD!' cried the king.

Then every fighting man the fort could offer bellowed their most vociferous oaths and charged headlong at the hurtling horde of inhuman invaders.

9.

The Hound

Laitha charged up a branch–strewn incline and came to the top of a small hill, just in time to behold the rim of the sun sink below the horizon. They watched as the orange glow retreated from the straw-topped buildings of Fort Culainn down below and the darkness quickly gathered around them.

The settlement was huge – almost an equal to Eamhain Mhacha. It consisted of a sizeable expanse of land populated mostly by small farm holdings, dwellings and workshops, dotted with gorse bushes and some trees, all encircled by a huge wooden fence. There was ample grazing land and some large areas where vegetables were grown. Setanta could even make out what looked like a playing field for the youngsters of the fort to practice their hurling. Within that outer fence, toward the centre of the settlement, a moat ringed another inner stone wall which encircled the stronghold itself, a great stone keep surrounded by outhouses, stables and other huts. It was at the corner of this further barrier that Setanta first caught his glimpse of the beast.

No sooner had the light failed than his keen eyes saw great heaps of soil erupting from the earth as a monstrous shape pushed itself up from some unimaginable realm hidden below the world of men. The immense sloping shadow that emerged snarling and steaming from the rupture blocked off the edge of the inner wall with its bulk; it shook itself, reddish matter flying in all directions, then trotted off and was lost behind a copse of trees.

The young warrior swore softly, but not from fear of what he saw: rather because he had failed to reach the fort in time. But, then, a tremble of excitement coursed up through his legs and his arms, and ignited within him like a flaming torch.

This would be a challenge, and how he loved that!

Suddenly a blood-curdling bellow tore into the clear night and Emer, too, realised they were too late. The cry was composed of three horrific ululations, the likes of which no single animal could possibly have released. It was more like the symphony of a baying pack of horrors, alien and obscene; yet both Emer and Setanta recognised it, for they had heard it before – but then they had been safely behind the walls of Fort Culainn.

'*An Cú* is loose. We will not be in the company of Culainn or Fergus this night,' she said with deep dismay.

'Or Donagh' added Setanta, to Emer's consternation.

'Were you not so headstrong, Setanta, and had let me go alone, Laitha would have gathered enough speed to deliver word of the plight of Eamhain Mhacha. Your arrogance has seen the ruination of our home.'

'The task fell to me!' cried Setanta. 'And I will complete it - do not doubt that, sweet Emer! Night may have fallen but there is still time to muster those stout warriors inside to the defence of our king.'

Emer's shoulders sagged as she sighed, shaking her head.

'The Hound roams the land beyond that fence until sunrise. Anyone foolish enough to enter is ripped apart in its jaws. You know the stories as well as I. It is a dog of the Aeder Worlds, gifted to the ForgeMaster by Danann folk long ago. An invincible guardian.'

Of course they both knew this, thought Setanta, for it was only a few years back that they had both attended a feast at Culainn's fort when Conchobar and Forgall had brought them along for Samhain's Eve. As children they had thrilled to listen for the howling of the Hound when the sun had sank; and they had not been disappointed, though frightened enough to run screaming happily back to the feast hall, teasing and shoving one another.

Did Emer remember those joyful times as clearly as he did, he wondered?

The mood was not so light now. There were heavy stakes at play. Setanta seized Emer by the shoulders and turned her to face him. Laitha trotted back and forth uneasily at this but both being expert riders, they kept their posture nevertheless.

'We can make it, Emer!' he urged. 'With this fine horse we can! Since when have you heard of a dog that can outpace a horse at long pelt?'

Emer was about to answer when another loud howl reverberated through the freshly fallen night. They both looked towards the source of the sound and simultaneously saw the shadow of the Hound coming from behind the copse of trees and begin rambling towards them. Surely it hadn't spotted them in the darkness? Maybe it could scent them...

'Such a dog as that could,' Emer replied coldly. 'Neither I nor this horse will pass through those gates this night, Setanta. We would better serve our king by delivering the call to arms at dawn. At the very least we could assure our people swift revenge.'

Setanta nodded once. His mind was set.

'Tis a fair sized dog, to be sure. But I'll not let a mere beast prevent me from fulfilling my word. Good luck to you, Emer.'

With that he leaped from the horse and began to walk down the slope towards the outer wall.

'I'll see you again before long, when the war-band of Fergus rides out those gates.'

'Setanta!' Emer hissed. 'You cannot hope to pass by the beast once inside!'

Setanta turned without breaking his stride and put his finger to his lips, continuing to walk backwards towards the gate. 'Shhh, Emer. If he spots me then I promise I will go easy on him.'

'Setanta!!'

He was off, his warrior's heart pumping with anticipation of the coming trial, his restless mind searching for a feasible way past the hellish sentinel. Emer could only look on with misgiving as Setanta reached the thick-posted wooden barricade and climbed gingerly atop it. He crouched upon it for a moment, surveying the land, and noticed that the Hound had wandered off in the other direction, perhaps after some other animal offering a more alluring scent. As soon as he sensed that the great beast was a sufficiently safe distance away, he rose and ran lithely across the top of the wooden posts, almost covering half the circumference of the wall, then, finally leaping down to the inner side, tumbling and rolling behind a clump of bushes. The sparse patches of gorse offered very little cover but by sprinting silently between them Setanta managed to elude the Hound's attention until he was almost within the shadow of the innermost wall of the fort.

Peering from his hiding place under a patch of dense thorny foliage, Setanta could see now why the great dog had not scented him. The huge animal was near the further wall, tearing apart a clump of sinewy matter. Then he remembered that the guards left an offering of meat each evening to nourish the beast, though he had also heard that Culainn was known to leave murderers, thieves and other miscreants to their fate outside the gates. Whatever it was eating now, remains of man or side of pig, it was keeping the Hound occupied.

Calling on all his hunting prowess, Setanta picked his way under the dense brambles, getting ever closer to the inner wall. There was another empty stretch of land ahead; he would have to time the last part precisely when the Hound was definitely facing away. Now, there before him, at the end of a small bridge across the moat, he could see the portal in the wall which led into a kind of rough courtyard. Beyond that would be the very innermost gates - hopefully from there he could gain access to the fortress itself. He shuffled forward again on his knees and forearms... when suddenly a piercing cry rent the night air.

Setanta looked up to see a huge rook shrieking and flapping above his hiding place.

'Crom Cruach take you, damned crow!' he swore, then grasping a nearby stick he swung at the hateful bird. But it wheeled up and away from him and, circling his bramble bush, it continued to caw noisily.

Setanta turned to see if the Hound would take heed of this disturbance and saw that the beast had swung its ruddy-tinted head around in his direction, ears pricked up and mouth closed tightly in an expression of potential violence.

It trotted towards his position and then Setanta saw the flare of nostrils, a yellowish mist seeming to billow from them for a second; it had scented him and its pace quickened. The young warrior knew that to stay cowering where he was would be to invite certain death - the beast would simply root him out like a cornered rabbit and rend him to pieces. So, brandishing his stick, he stood up from the bushes and, in clear sight of the encroaching Hound, roared at the top of his lungs.

'Lay on then, Hound! Come here to me!'

He hoped this bravado would confuse the beast, no doubt more used to seeing its prey either flee screaming or paralyzed with terror.

And now that Setanta beheld the hulking animal in more detail, he felt sure that that some of those unfortunates had simply collapsed in petrified horror at the sight. For *an Cú* was a fearsome thing to see. Its eyes were on the same level as Setanta's -, baleful ochre pits without an ounce of pity. From its strangely steaming body, rivulets of reddish, earth-like material seemed to fall from the black shaggy hair. Setanta recalled long talks with Amergin about elemental creatures from fire, from the earth, from the winds, and from the seas. *An Cú* seemed not to be fixed to the mortal world, with every step it took the very air and ground protested at its presence, generating these unnatural effects.

Still advancing, the Hound pulled back its upper lips revealing thick yellowed fangs. The hair on its head and back sprang to attention, standing straight up like spears, lending even more height and awe to its forbidding form. Setanta swung the stick twice around his head then flung it far to the right of him, just across the Hound's field of vision. Without moving, *An Cú* snapped its head to track the flight of the stick. It then slowly turned

61

its attention back to Setanta and glared at him askance, a low dangerous growl in its throat.

Setanta winced.

'Alright then. Let's get this going.' And with that he turned on his heel and pelted towards the nearest wooded area which stood between him and the inner gates. There was nobody at Eamhain Mhacha, or indeed all the great land itself, who could come close to matching Setanta in a foot race. And it was this that brought him to the cover of the trees before the Great Hound could pounce upon him. However, the trees could not afford that much cover and though Setanta moved like quicksilver - ducking under branches, leaping over logs, hurtling between narrow gaps in trees - the Hound bellowed as it crashed after him and closed the distance with ease.

Sensing the inevitability of battle, Setanta took his sword in hand and turned to regard his monstrous pursuer – but there was not even enough time to complete this motion, as he was instantly disarmed, falling under the weight of the leaping Hound, and fighting desperately to keep its jaws away from his face.

He called upon all his strength to hold a firm grasp on its maw, the hairs on its face, its cheeks, its ears, anything. But it shook its great head free easily each time and plunged again and again in search of a mortal bite. A combination of thick, ropey saliva, hot steam and filthy red matter rained down upon Setanta, but, undaunted, he seized the jugular of the beast with one arm, and then propelled his other fist directly up and into its lower jaw with a force that would have reduced a strong man's mandible to powder.

The Hound yelped in surprise, then shook its massive head violently from side to side. Setanta tried to squirm out from under the creature but its filthy paws were tearing great gashes in his chest and stomach, and the pain seized hold of his mind for several moments.

The beast recovered first and once again lunged its fangs forward; Setanta ducked aside and received them deeply in his shoulder and neck. Through the pain his eyes found his sword lying within reach. He seized the blade and drove it into the flank of the Hound.

This time the great dog reared up and roared its deafening triple-toned cry to the impassive moon. Setanta knew he must move or perish now. Refusing to acknowledge the pain, he rose up and punched the Hound's muzzle several times with both fists until it slipped back on its hind legs. Momentarily ignoring the raging warrior, the Hound reached its head around to try and pull at the sword buried in its side.

Seeing the feeble effect his blows were having, Setanta turned and, drawing upon all his energy, he ran towards the Fort, thinking the dog would be preoccupied in trying to dislodge the sword.

Rushing through the inner gates and the outer courtyard, he was shoved violently to the ground once more for the Hound was already upon him again and he only barely managed to turn from his stomach to his back in time to hold off the slavering jaws.

'The paws!' he thought. He couldn't allow them to continue to wound his torso, so he seized one forepaw and shoved it into the Hound's own maw. Now, it could not bite down upon itself and, clutching its opposite ear, Setanta launched kick after kick of his mighty legs into the belly of the beast. It reared off him and stalked curiously, almost casually, away for a few steps then turned and stood still, staring at the warrior, seeming to evaluate his strength. Setanta pulled himself to his feet and despite the agony began to hop from foot to foot, nonchalantly beckoning.

'You didn't like that so much now did you? Let's be having you, hound!'

The Hound roared and leaped at Setanta with astonishing speed, but he just managed to sidestep the Hound and landed home a powerful blow to the side of its head. He followed this with a kick to the temple and, as it buckled and crashed into a hay cart, Setanta took off running once again.

Before him lay an arch in a stone wall, and beyond that a grill of iron - could he call for someone to open the gate from there? With *An Cú* at his heels again, Setanta began to feel dizzy and had a strange sensation in his stomach; he began to wonder if this was what it was like to feel fear, but when he looked down he realised a more likely explanation lay with the fact the deep wounds in his belly were leaking dark blood.

From behind him the Hound took Setanta's elbow in its jaws and swung him against a stone pillar, then dashed him to the ground. Loud cracks detonated in his mind as his bones splintered.

An Cú straddled him once again.

'If you're to be the death of me, then I'll be damned if I'm letting you off unharmed!' Setanta roared, then pulled himself from its grasp, leaving most of the flesh of his left tricep in the creature's jaws. Then he pummelled with all his might at the relentless face of death.

Suddenly the weight of *an Cú* was off him, but it had less to do with Setanta's weakening blows than the force of the two horse hooves that had pounded directly into its flank. Setanta saw Laitha twist and position herself for another kick, with Emer aloft, her expression grave and terribly beautiful.

'Run to the gate! It is opening, Fergus is there!' she called as Laitha kicked backwards again at the enraged Hound who, far from injured, seemed to be weighing up just which morsel to attack.

Setanta saw his blood on the stones below him, and in its colour the Red Branch of Eamhain Mhacha. By all the *sídhe*, he would not sleep under the earth tonight!

And so he ran, and indeed the gate was opening before him. He was conscious also of the pounding of Laitha's hooves behind him as Emer too bolted for safety.

But the terrible howl of the Hound rang out again and it soared over Setanta with a mighty leap to land before him, turning to bay angrily at Fergus and the guards, who could but fall back.

Setanta spied a cart beside him with wooden weapon handles visible beneath a covering. A sword! He wouldn't lose this one so foolishly! He seized one then stared with disbelief; there was no blade - it was a *camán*, a hurling stick!

The Hound turned to face him and, opening its jaws, shifted its weight to its hind legs; there was such a scalding anger to its gaze that Setanta had to smile despite everything.

What a guardian - never would he suffer to let me pass!

Setanta seized a rock from the ground and, feeling the world tightening around him and ghostly voices whispering names and words from the Aeder Worlds in his head, he saw the Hound leap through the air towards him, its countenance a vision of pure death.

In a heartbeat he hefted the rock into the air and struck it squarely with the *camán*. He ducked forward immediately as *an Cú* crashed to the ground on the spot where he was standing. The rock had flown true with incredible speed into the demon's mouth, crushing the throat within.

Setanta's blurring vision suddenly cleared for a moment as he beheld the Hound struggling to regain its feet. It clawed and tore at its own throat, ripping apart the jugular. Then it stood to attention on its hind legs and, with a gurgled yelping noise of protest, the yellow vapours lifted from its body and into the night air, the red material cascaded away into the earth, and what then remained of *an Cú* fell back wetly as nothing but a mass of hair and loose flesh.

Having finally opened the gate, Fergus dashed to Setanta, who had fallen to his knees, and took the bloodied young warrior by the shoulders.

Tentatively, the other guards walked around the vague mound of matter that was once the Hound, and behind them came a brawny, barrel-chested figure with a gaze of steel and a bearded face like blackened iron. Culainn the Forgemaster surveyed the scene, then walked over to take hold of Laitha's reins as Emer dismounted. She too ran to Setanta.

'Who killed my dog?' the big-boned chieftain yelled gruffly at the newcomers.

Setanta propped himself onto Fergus's broad shoulder and responded as steadily as he could despite the perilous state of his body.

'My apologies, Culainn. But if I did not... your mourning would soon be a thousand-fold stronger. I bring... grim news.'

Setanta held up his arm feebly and the two men recognised Conchobar's Red Branch gauntlet.

'Eamhain Mhacha is in peril. She needs her champions,' said the boy straining for breath.

His strength left him then, and he sagged against his old battle tutor.

'Bring him inside,' the chieftain said to his men. 'Tend to his wounds.'

After they had done so, Culainn took a moment to look down once again at where the Hound had fallen, though by now there was nothing much left to see. The flesh seemed to have poured away into the soil with only a blackened outline to mark where his faithful guardian had been struck down.

He looked then into the night at his now unprotected lands and beyond, toward where Eamhain Mhacha lay. Biting his lower lip, he quickly followed the others inside.

*****

The great hearth fire was blazing forcefully inside what the denizens of Fort Culainn called the 'Big House'. It was here in this tar-lined and smoke-blackened wood lodge that the Forgemaster held the famous banquets that were at the heart of scores of far-fetched tales of drinking and questing.

There were drunken remnants of revelry still going on in some parts of the hall - it was clear a great feast had been interrupted by Setanta's entrance. A sojourn at Fort Culainn was only earned after two full seasons of warfare. It was here the hardy battle veterans of Eamhain came to drench away the rigours of combat and try to forget the faces of death for a time.

Apart from that, the Fort was, of course, Eamhain's principal supplier of weaponry and items of metalworking; Culainn had been a brother-in-arms and great friend to Conchobar's father. This unbreakable bond continued to his heir so that economic protection, trade security and the finest boar was always afforded from the Red Branch in return for the superb blades and spearheads that were forged in Culainn's fires.

Setanta sat slumped now at a large table that had been only recently used for festivities; still littered with fat-splattered bowls and mugs of mead. He tried as best he could to tolerate the women who were attempting to clean his injuries, but finally he pushed them aside as gently as he could. Standing unsteadily, he saw Fergus approach.

The massive, red-bearded warrior steeped forward, clasping him strongly yet warmly by the shoulder and back of the neck and looking hard into Setanta's eyes.

'So now: how far from Eamhain Mhacha are these spineless curs?'

Setanta could smell the mead on Fergus's breath; he must have been drinking like there was no tomorrow. So must have all of the men. But they would have no time to sober up, he feared, for Eamhain needed them straight away.

'Too near to call far, Fergus. We must ride out this moment if we are to join the fray in time.'

Fergus gave a little smile and held back a belch with the back of his fist. 'Good man, Setanta! You have done well.' Then he turned and shouted to those warriors around the hall who were, at best, searching for their equipment or, at worst, heaving themselves from the floor.

'Heed me, men! Shake the mead from your heads! Our king and home need the steady sword arms of their champions. To the stables at once! There is battle promised for the morning light.'

Just then Culainn emerged behind Fergus – the Forgemaster had insisted on raising an ogham marker where *an Cú* had fallen and had remained muttering silent prayers for some time.

'My house will also take part in this fray,' he affirmed gruffly. 'Never let it be said that Conchobar could not count on old friends when fortune betrays him. Fomorians will die for the cost of my hound.'

For the two veterans no further discussion was needed, and so with a nod to Setanta they turned and made to leave. The younger warrior stumbled after them but Fergus turned and hefted him back to his seat as though lifting a small child.

'Ease, Setanta,' he murmured. 'Your part in this is done. Rest here and take care of your wounds.'

'There is fight yet in me!' protested Setanta.

'Other battles lie ahead on your path, Setanta. That you raised the alarm at all is a mighty deed.'

'Fergus, do not...'

But he could speak no more for Fergus had cupped one mighty paw over the youth's mouth. He shoved him back down onto the wooden bench nodded to the women who began once again to bind the vicious-looking wounds. Fergus pointed a stern finger at Setanta's face. A gesture the young warrior and many others had grown to respect and fear over the long years of training in the Machra.

'Do not waste what little time our people have with arguments. Now *stay*!'

Fergus turned and hurried to the door of the Big House and the stables.

'I can ride!' shouted Setanta, but his voice was strangled in pain.

'You would only slow us,' called the other, without turning around.

Setanta sagged back for a moment and almost closed his eyes against the pain and weariness. But then he bolted them open again and once more struggled against his exasperated nurses. He noticed that a pretty young one was smiling adoringly at him and even in this state he could not resist returning an appreciative glance.

But then his eye was caught by something that was to him far more stunning standing behind the blushing young maiden. Something beautiful but with a look of pure desolation on its features. Her gaze was distant and aimed somewhere over Setanta's head.

'Emer!' he gasped, wincing now and denying to himself that his wounds were grave. 'You have to help me talk to Fergus... get him to let me go with them. I need a woman's guile, by Danú!'

Emer simply shook her head slowly, then covered her face with her hands and began to breathe deeply, seemingly trying to control her emotions.

'Emer...?'

'Donagh... is dead,' she replied flatly dropping her hands to her sides. 'He is in the Arms of Danú now. I've just been told. He was out hunting with Fergus and his men. There was a surprise attack on their camp during the night by some Connacht men. They stuck when Donagh was telling a tale at the campfire. A cowardly spear flew out from the night and down he fell... into... the fire...'

Their gaze met for a moment, then Setanta closed his eyes and lowered his head. At that Emer walked off, in a numbed trance and was lost among the noisy throng of warriors.

'Emer!' called Setanta and he struggled up after her, but his pace was slow and he was jostled by the brusque traffic of assembling warriors about him. Determination and fatigue collided mightily inside his body but Setanta pushed on regardless. Gritting his teeth all the while, he managed to hobble his way out of the Big House and towards the stables, where he came upon Fergus and Culainn preparing to mount up and lead the battle horde to Eamhain's aid. The Forgemaster seemed the very symbol of consternation as some of his warriors were unsteadily trying to mount their steeds.

'Too lavish, perhaps, are the comforts of my hall these days,' Setanta heard him say. 'The blame may yet fall to me if we meet with defeat from these invaders. Your men are now less able than when they first returned from battle.'

'Worry not, Culainn,' replied Fergus. 'The night air and their oaths will soon sharpen their wits. The Fomorians will learn that an Uladhman with drink in him is an even more dangerous enemy. And virtually indestructible!'

As he uttered this, one of the more inebriated warriors tumbled off the side of his horse with a coarse yell and a stream of slurred oaths.

Culainn took in the sight with a heavy sigh.

'Aye, indeed. Let us tarry no longer. We will speak again when the battle is won.'

68

The two grizzled warriors clasped hands, then Culainn strode off to where his men were gathered with his horse at the ready.

Fergus mounted his own steed, then noticed with a look of annoyance that Setanta had managed to stagger this far, and was badgering the horse-handler.

'No horse for that one! All horses should carry an able man.'

Setanta took a few pain-wracked steps towards the mounted Red Branch Knight.

'Even so mauled I am more able than these mead-soaked warriors!' he cried hoarsely.

'Your bravery is not in question, lad. But I recognise the wounds that rob strength from a fighter. Horses are scant. Take one and I will not be pleased.'

A warrior that he recognised as Fiachu, Diarmaid's father, pushed past Setanta and leaped upon the horse he had been trying to wrangle - the last that now remained in the stable.

From the entrance Culainn appeared on his steed, still securing his great battle-hammer, *Emberling*, to the side of his saddle.

'Away, Fergus?' he bellowed with impatience.

Setanta looked hard at his old battle master.

'I could have fought by morning, and well you know it.'

'This is not your time, lad,' said the other simply, then turned his horse to the entrance. He trotted out into the night to join the mustering battle horde that wasted no further time and charged out of the gates of Fort Culainn.

'Away, ye Ruddy Boars!' Setanta heard Fergus yell, as he was left standing despondently in the flickering torches of the stable. And by that light he saw Emer Manach approach.

'Emer...' he began as she moved to where he stood. 'I am ashamed of my earlier remarks. I am sorry that Donagh did not live to see your fair face once more.'

69

'I cannot stay in this place,' she replied, with her strength having returned. 'He is here neither in body nor memory. I would ride and die where his name is known. In Eamhain Mhacha.'

Setanta shook his head sadly.

'If they had not taken all the horses I would go with you.'

'There is one horse they could not ride,' said Emer.

Despite his exhaustion, Setanta's eyes suddenly lit up with a fierce blaze.

A short time later, Laitha thundered from the gates of Fort Culainn, Emer riding with a face of steel and heart of stone, and the unsteady shape of Setanta gripping on as best he could behind her.

10.

Battle at Eamhain

They rode just as vehemently all through the night as they had done in their wild dash to Fort Culainn, and the pain in Emer's arms and back were about the only thing stopping her from losing her grip and being thrown from the saddle in weariness. Finally, even the seemingly inexhaustible Laitha could go no further, and so Emer carefully brought the suffering and steaming horse to a stumbling halt in a copse of silver birches, then dismounted and set about taking Setanta down from his unsteady perch.

The badly mauled young warrior seemed to be slipping in and out of consciousness. Crimson patches were evident, and growing, under the hasty dressings.

Emer looked in utter sadness at Setanta's growing pallor and knew this change for what it was; for she had seen it before on her cousin, her aunt and also upon many warriors as they lay whimpering on barrows when on their return from battle. It was the grey complexion of death.

'Lay down here, Setanta,' she whispered, pulling her shawl around his shoulders and gently helping him onto the grass. 'Better your chances in the wild than riding into battle with closed eyes.' For his eyes were indeed closed, his head turned, and he seemed far from this world's worries.

'May Danú keep you safe,' Emer managed to breathe, but as she made a move to stand, Setanta's arm came to life and he seized her wrist The grip was not strong, and far from warm. His right eyelid opened a fraction and he spoke.

'Emer... I know what you would do... and I thank you for it... but... I need your help.'

'Shhh. Take to the woods, Setanta,' Emer soothed, fearing this last battle against his stubborn pride. 'Find solace in the earth mother. Die peacefully in her embrace as a reward for your efforts, your bravery here.'

'No,' Setanta urged, and to Emer's amazement he began to haul himself back up to a sitting position. Just grant me one favour. Bring me up out of this wood... to a high place. Let me clothe myself in the light of Lugh... *please*, Emer...'

He strove to stand but could not, and in helping him do so, Emer slipped and they both tumbled sideways. With their heads side by side she saw the intensity in his eyes and she lost herself within them yet again before they closed and he muttered.

'...Take me out... of the dark.'

Distraught and drained she looked from the handsome, pained face to the reddening sky above.

A long night was coming to an end.

*****

Fergus MacRoth had already been the greatest fighter of Uladh when Conchobar strode into Eamhain Mhacha and took his rightful place on the throne. He had not yet pledged allegiance to the king, and was known in the region as a myth and a legend; a name that inspired and terrified in equal measure.

So many things were said of him.

That he could throw a spear through a stag, lifting it off its feet.

That when drunk and roused, swords and javelins were no good against him and it was better for whole villages to be abandoned for six days and nights until he calmed.

That he wooed the raging maiden Dornolla of the Big Fist, and put manners upon her.

That once an entire army became unmanned, wept, pulled out their hair and fled, never again in their lives to take up arms, on learning that he would be among their enemies.

On hearing all these tales Conchobar, who would suffer no rivals, summoned Fergus to Eamhain Mhacha so that he might estimate this mighty warrior himself. When MacRoth caught wind of this and arrived at the court, all held their breath as they prepared for a mighty combat, for it was also said that Fergus had long harboured thoughts of becoming king.

But the ruddy warrior merely stared at Conchobar for a long moment, then inclined his head and said:

'This is a man worth putting my shoulder against. My axe will swing for you if you need it, MacNeasa. Your enemies will be my own - and more's the pity for them.'

The king had presented him with an army of his own to command, the more unpredictable of Eamhain's warriors, and they became known as the Ruddy Boars after their tempestuous leader. From that time onwards MacRoth was no more known as the Terror of Uladh, but rather as the First Champion of Eamhain Mhacha.

Conchobar thought of Fergus' oath as he led the fight against the Fomorians that bloody night. The First Champion's axe and his Ruddy Boars were sorely missed.

The king and his men had made four forays against the frontlines of the enemy throughout the early part of the night, rushing in and chopping down the skittering creatures, then pulling back and looping towards another section of their lines. He and Eochaid were directing his fighters against the enemy like a lethally turning wheel, scraping and scathing away at the attacking forces. At first the sea raider army were hesitant in the face of these tactics and foolishly allowed many of their number to be slain needlessly, including the loss of most of their chariots which could not turn or cope with the lightning assaults, until some sharper military mind urged them forward at each end of the line. Finally, Conchobar's forces were cornered between the two prongs of the vastly superior force. They had no choice then but to drive as deeply as they could into the mass of the enemy horde. They had charged in a sudden and somewhat unexpectedly powerful surge into the heart of the enemy ranks, which had once again destabilised the Fomorians for a time, but they had now regrouped and the men of Eamhain found themselves trying to resist wave after wave of frenzied attacker from all sides. Conall Cearnach was not least among them in courage, and from his mount he wielded his long-handled cudgel, *Lámhtapaidh*, to sweep away weapons from wet Fomor grasps or crack and scoop brain matter from exposed greenish heads.

But the sheer numbers of the invading horde were too great for such precision tactics to pay dividends for long, and his horse - speared and hacked at - fell tumbling beneath him. Conall quickly launched himself from the dying beast before it was engulfed under the attackers. He dealt two killing strokes before landing on his feet and cleaving a vicious path towards Conchobar and a group of the most stalwart warriors encircling the king.

Pulling free his shorter handled mace, the young-blood warrior battered a series of gibbering Fomorian faces until he managed to reach the command group, but there he noticed with dismay that they were being relentlessly swamped.

Eochaid and Diarmuid stood fiercely behind Conchobar, turning away with screams of rage any Fomorian seeking to blindside the king. Conchobar, for his part, was halving attacker after attacker with a stony, terrible expression wrought upon his face.

For a long stretch there was nothing but the hideous cries of cloven Fomorian warriors and gouts of dark green blood as a fearsome stalemate held sway. But slowly, inexorably, their strokes lost speed and they huddled ever closer in a tight protective knot. Suddenly a mournful pealing sound was heard over the clamour of battle and the attackers hesitated, then stepped back from the flagging Red Branch warriors.

Conchobar looked with suspicion at the attackers directly in front of him, who warily moved back a few steps. Then a baleful sound rang out again and from behind the massed ranks of marauders a hideous sight hove into view.

A huge litter was carried forward upon the shoulders of four gigantic Fomorians. Even with their peculiar hunched posture they stood nine feet at least, and their hard grey skin was stretched over an awesome muscular frame. Their smooth heads were split from one side to the other by a wide sharp-toothed mouth and their eyes were barely visible black points under craggy brow bones. Monstrous as they were, however, they struck less dread in the defenders' hearts than the thing sitting aloft the palanquin, blasting a damnable bass note from a massive conch.

Like the palanquin he perched upon, Lord Nardul was draped in long, dark sinuous garments that seemed fashioned from deep sea vegetation. Upon his head he bore a great leathery helm, and jutting proudly through an opening on the forehead was a stout yellow horn more magnificent and prominent than those of any of the other Fomorians on the battlefield.

Removing the conch from his lips, he sneered down at the rise where Conchobar stood some distance away, then he brought it back and spoke through the shell, which amplified his guttural voice.

'Ahh Conchobar! Is that all you could muster? Here ends your pitiful saga. But worry not; this place will never again see such a poor defence as this – but that will be under *my* rulership! Lord Nardul Gol-Guir, First Fomor, Steersman of Destiny!'

With that he blew once more through the conch and the hideous squalling sound caused heads to drop and eyes to close in sorrow and utter desolation amongst the ragged defenders and the folk huddled behind the walls of Eamhain.

But as the hideous note died down and Conchobar readied himself to sell his life dearly in Fomorian blood, another note blared into the morning air.

This note was clear, sonorous and beautiful, and it sang out in mighty defiance.

To the exhausted fighters, that sound was a glorious response to Nardul's foetid blast - it was the hunting horn of Fergus MacRoth! Conchobar knew then that Culainn and Fergus had come to their aid and that Setanta had accomplished a wonder.

Next they heard the battle cry and thundering hooves of an approaching host from just beyond the wooded hills to the west. Immediately, the king launched himself at the enemy and, with Conall and the younger warriors following suit, hacked and slashed with renewed vigour and belief.

'Rain hard and harsh upon them!' shouted the king. 'Bring sorrow and woe to their worlds!'

Then the first rays of the morning sun touched the western hills and glinted from the armour of Culainn's forces as they came cascading down from the crest of the hill to charge directly into the flank of the Fomorian forces, cutting their way in to meet the defenders.

Conchobar took a moment to shout to his saviours as his warriors battled on around him.

'Culainn you old rogue! Keeping my men in their cups while there's battle to be fought! Shame on you!'

The Forgemaster took heed and manoeuvred his horse around Conchobar, clearing away foes with great swings of his war-hammer.

'My apologies, young lad!' he roared at his old friend. 'I didn't think someone as clever as you would get himself into a tangle of this kind. How would you say it's going?'

'Ah, fair to middling!' Conchobar answered between killing strokes. 'Tell you what, blacksmith! Help me to corpse up a few hundred of these fiends and we'll call it even!'

'Fair enough!' yelled Culainn as he reared his horse to trample a few more suicidal Fomorians

The arrival of Culainn and Fergus with the troop altered the course of the battle significantly. The men of Eamhain were still outnumbered but their skill was far greater than the disorganised rabble of Fomorians. Soon the invaders had no chariots left for the bulls that pulled them had been skewered by the Uladh fighters. Further back from the epicentre of the fight, Lord Nardul watched from his palanquin as Fergus hewed down enemies like wheat beneath his axe.

'Curse the bitch crow! She has played us false!' he snarled, then reached forward and seized his subaltern by the throat. 'Send forth the Deepwatch!'

Nardul shoved the servant from the litter, then stood and gave another blast of his conch, yelling at the brutes around him, who were already lowering the palanquin.

Now unburdened, the tough skinned giants lumbered together in a phalanx, joining up with others of their kind who up until now had been held back from the battle; Nardul had wished to keep their energy in reserve for an eventual siege but now his hand had been forced.

While his elite guard slogged towards the enemy, Nardul pulled Doomwave from the socket in his throne and followed them, waving the elaborate blade in strange patterns. Those unfortunate warriors who happened to be close by as Nardul entered the field of combat swore afterwards that they thought they heard the keening of ocean storms as his sword cut the air.

*****

Emer couldn't believe what she was doing. It seemed as though she were dreaming, her footsteps both weary and light as she walked alongside Laitha up a grassy hillock towards she knew not what. How had she allowed Setanta to convince her to hoist him upon the horse?

It was madness, but she found she was unable to resist him when he had pleaded with her to help him do... whatever it was he was intending.

When they reached the top of the knoll, Emer was surprised to find a stone plinth standing before her. She knew these woods around Eamhain well, but never before had she seen such a dolmen.

How could it just have appeared like that? Suddenly Setanta slid from his perch, and would have landed heavily on the ground had Emer not grasped him on the way down. But, amazingly, he kept his footing and began to stumble towards the table-like dolmen.

With Emer's help he dragged himself up onto the cold stone and lay on his back, his arms outstretched. Emer could only stare in numb puzzlement at her friend's strange behaviour, then the misty morning air brought a sound to her ears: cries and the cacophony of warfare.

She turned and, as the mists parted, she saw below her that a terrible battle was raging. Hordes of hideous creatures were swarming around the Red Branch Knights. She watched as a group of huge lumbering forms cut their way towards the king's battle standard, blithely killing their own kind in order to hasten their arrival. Emer had never before witnessed such horror; she sank to her knees and despair seized hold of her mind.

'Many are the cairns that will be required for our kin tomorrow... if any were to be left alive to raise them' she whispered, her heart a painful knot in her chest.

Beside her Setanta began to mutter. 'Come, come, healing sun. Fill me with your light as oft before – never have I needed you more than now... I am your vessel...'

It is maybe well that he has gone mad, so that he does not see this woeful sight, Emer thought dimly.

At that moment, Emer was suddenly dazzled as the morning sun's rays found the peak of the hill; she shielded her eyes with her hand for a moment. Then she stood wearily up and began to move back towards Laitha, dark resolution in her thoughts.

'I must go now, Setanta, to lend what little skill...'

Emer gasped in astonishment as she beheld the miasma appearing around the body of Setanta.

'In the name of the Goddess!'

The young warrior was aglow with a yellow and golden luminescence, loops and tendrils of light entwining and caressing his limbs and his head. The wounds he bore seemed to fill up with the light and when it dimmed again they were gone, healed. His whole body seemed to expand and brim with a tangible aura of power.

*****

Even with the timely reinforcements of Fergus and his knights along with the worthy men of Fort Culainn, the defenders of Eamhain Mhacha were hard pressed against the seemingly endless numbers of Fomorian invaders. And now that the Deepwatch had entered the fray, any hopes of victory dwindled even further. The original defenders were fatigued and the hurried journey to join the fight had sapped the strength from the newcomers.

Culainn himself had been unseated from his horse as he attacked one of the Deepwatch. Initially intending to trample it down under-hoof, the vile creature had slashed its serrated, chitinous weapon through the horse's belly, tearing out its viscera. Culainn had then been bludgeoned from his saddle by a sweeping blow from a shield edge. Now he found himself fighting back to back with Conchobar. They were beating off their attackers, but only just. There seemed to be no human left unwounded. Even though a huge mound of Fomorian corpses was building up around them, the forecast was grim.

Elsewhere, Conall and Diarmuid had decided to tackle a particularly brutish Deepwatch. Their weapons were finding their mark now and again, but the dense grey skin resisted most of the blows, and no blood flowed from the scant wounds. Diarmuid ducked under the Deepwatch's weapon and riposted, smashing his sword against the giant's side with all his might, but to little effect other than a grunt expelled from the wide, fang-filled mouth. But the warrior had no time to feel disheartened as, suddenly, a smaller, lithe Fomorian creature leaped on his back, a black knife in its grasp. Diarmuid's head was severed free a second later and the raider leaped back and onto the shoulders of its companions, the dripping crimson prize held aloft in triumph.

Conall Cearnach witnessed all of this but the force of his rage was focused on just keeping him alive under the hail of blows. Many of his fellow young bloods were dying, and the certainty that he would join them fueled his attacks for a further few heartbeats at least.

To his right he saw a sight that quailed him more than the decapitation of his friend – Fergus MacRoth, the mighty and ruddy Fergus of the Flinted Fist, had been toppled from his horse.

To his left he saw Eochaid of the Twisted Hoof lose his weapon as he was impaled by a Deepwatch. The monster flung aside the dying elder warrior and strode towards Conall.

Meanwhile Lord Nardul stalked ever closer towards the invincible pairing of Conchobar and Culainn, almost nonchalantly gliding through the men who dared bar his path. As the evil blade Doomwave swept and gouged and stabbed, a swift corrosion raced from its disastrous wounds causing men to turn black an instant before their bodies crumpled to pieces like parched strips of seaweed which then scattered to the winds.

*****

Setanta rose to stand upon the dolmen; the halo of light was still playing around his body, circling his waist, snaking around his arms, pulling his hair straight up from his head.

The Hero-Light is upon his brow, thought Emer, without really knowing what it truly meant. The words seemed to ring in her mind, but they weren't fully hers. She had the impression that other voices were around her, coming from the wind, the sky, the trees, the grass beneath her. Was she in a place of the *sidhe*?

Setanta spoke to her then, his voice hale and strong. And beautiful to her ears.

'I'm indebted to you, fairest Emer.'

Then he gazed down at the battle taking place below.

'We can't have this!'

*****

Another Fomorian head exploded with a powerful blow from Culainn's hammer. The old warhorse then turned quickly, on instinct, to see Nardul wielding his huge black sword with lightning speed. The Forgemaster managed to block the heavy blow using the haft of his hammer but even he, renowned for his great strength, felt his calves buckle under the strain.

Nardul lashed out with a thrusting kick that blasted the air from Culainn's body, sending him toppling back to the ground. A mob of lesser Fomorians was on him in seconds.

Conchobar noticed the absence of his friend's reassuring presence at his back. He had no need to glance around to guess the turn of events; there were none more experienced in battle than Conchobar MacNeasa. He crouched and suddenly spun about, his hefty blade crunching into the side of the Fomorian Lord's knee.

Nardul roared in shock and outrage, then struck the king with a backhand swipe of his barnacle-studded gauntlet. It was a blow that would shatter a tree. Conchobar rolled with the impact but, as he attempted to rise again, his body realised the force of the strike. The world darkened, and his legs gave out from under him.

Mere yards from this, but obscured by a wall of bodies, Fergus was unleashing the full extent of his battle fury. He swung his fearsome axe, *Heaven's Call,* again and again at the Deepwatch who opposed him, and the nearby Fomorians were shocked to see how, with the sheer force of his blows, he pulped the giant's hands so that it could no longer grip its weapon. Thereupon Fergus hefted the great axe around again and left the creature trying to clutch at the gash in its throat with a crushed stump of a hand.

But even as he did so, he spied another of the juggernauts lurching towards him bearing a triple-forked lance. Without hesitation, Fergus rushed towards the titan, his axe swinging in windmill arcs, his roar terrible to hear.

But as he advanced toward his enemy, he suddenly skidded to a halt some way short of the snarling sea beast, and stared gawp-mouthed at something over its head. Bodies were being flung high into the air. Fomorian bodies. *Dozens* of them. Twisted, halved and wrecked, freshly cleaved Fomorian corpses being threshed into the sky.

What was this new madness?

The Deepwatch before him, psychically linked to his brethren, turned its large smooth head and beheld the spectacle. And, as the lower portions of one of its kin fell upon him, he witnessed a strangely possessed warrior, fire playing about his hair, wading through the now thinning ranks of Fomors with no weapons but his fists, smashing them aside, chanting strange hymns of destruction.

Fergus smiled, his heart bursting with joy and pride, then swung his great axe once more, cutting down the confused creature at the waist.

Then Setanta was there before him, standing a full arm's length taller than his mentor and... glowing! But more than that, shimmering as if with the light of a dozen suns, pulsating with strange energy, muscles strained, veins tracing haphazard routes across his arms and neck. Hideous in its beauty, it was a ghastly, glorious sight.

MacRoth never allowed himself to be too impressed by folk, no matter who they were or what they did.

'How is it you never do what I tell you, boy?' he grunted sternly.

'If you feel up to it later, Fergus, you can try and punish me!' said Setanta. A rich music seemed to embellish his words, lending weight and conviction to them.

The Hero's Voice thought Fergus. *His roars could deaden the fish in the sea.*

MacRoth bellowed a hearty laugh. 'Come on! Let's carve our way to the heart of this scum!'

80

Setanta grinned savagely, then with a nod the pair launched themselves back into the enemy. The Knights of Eamhain, heartened by this turn of events, lent their roars to their kinsmen's battle cries and charged after them.

Setanta made his way directly to a mound of Fomorians who were scrabbling over a downed figure, something that still had some fight left in it.

He dashed forward and wrenched the creatures from their quarry, flinging them high in the air as though they were men of straw. Below he saw Culainn, wounded but alive, dagger in hand and eyes ablaze in wonder and frenzy.

Setanta seized a spear-like Fomorian weapon from the ground and swung it around twice, cutting the heads off four more raiders. Then he addressed the shocked Forgemaster.

'Where is the king?'

'Over yon', grunted Culainn, getting to his feet and pointing towards another part of the battle to Setanta's right. 'With the leader of the sea-swine.'

Setanta narrowed his eyes slightly. 'Come, Fergus!' he cried, then immediately sped towards Conchobar, batting away any foe unfortunate enough to find itself in his path.

Seconds later they spied the king struggling against a huge single-horned warrior; the pair were trading powerful blows, yet the enemy lord was cackling, toying with his opponent, despite Conchobar's great skill. They also noticed two Deepwatch encroaching behind the king, and another to his left, their bizarre nacred blades ready to deal death.

'Fergus!' shouted Setanta again, and pointed with his spear towards the grey-skinned brutes. Then he flung the weapon with such force that it embedded itself in the chests of the two further Deepwatch, one behind the other. With a surprised groan they tried to extract the lance but being skewered together they only succeeded in toppling one another over.

The third Deepwatch glanced in surprise at this development but was even more stunned when Fergus and his axe crashed into him at full pelt; the tough carapace resisted the strike and they both went toppling down a bank of freshly sundered bodies.

Nardul saw all this and for the first time noticed the impact Setanta was having on the battle. The glowing warrior was stalking towards him, slaying his wiliest horde-leaders with casual ease - never before had the Fomorian warlord seen such ferocity. His astonishment pulled his focus away from the failing Conchobar and, before he could bellow a challenge to the newcomer, his head reeled back from the shock of a powerful blow. A shock that tore open his mind for several seconds, igniting a psychic fire that threatened to claim his consciousness.

He staggered back away from Conchobar and the fearsome newcomer, then raised his hand to his helm and found that the horn that grew from his forehead had been sliced off! With a single well-aimed swing, Conchobar had taken the Horn of Prestige from him!

In supreme horror Nardul turned and retreated back to where his final file of warriors still held sway, trying to hold his diminished head away from view. But it was useless - many of the Fomors nearby had already seen, with alarm, the sight of the stump, now pumping greenish dark blood, and they fled. The Horn was not just the ultimate symbol of power in their culture, but represented the health and confidence of the entire race. The shock rippled quickly through the dark army. The loss was sudden and utter, and the raiders took flight almost as one like a frightened school of fish. The Deepwatch, being of another race, were slower to realise the magnitude of this event, and found themselves outnumbered by the remaining Red Branch Knights. Some finally heard the conch calls of their handlers and scattered off away from the fighting. Several of the men of Eamhain gave chase, delighting in being able to reverse the fortune of their would-be destroyers.

Before he disappeared from sight into the woods, Nardul turned and snarled one final time at Conchobar, his bladdery cloak pulled up over his head, his mind ruptured by searing agony and shame.

The king was too exhausted to give chase to his enemy. Panting heavily, he leaned down and plucked up the severed horn. Nardul in his stunned horror had not seen where it had fallen. Conchobar slowly and painfully ascended a nearby rock littered with corpses and slick with clotted Fomorian blood. Holding aloft the horn he uttered a wordless cry of triumph.

Those around him echoed his cry of victory as the final Fomors disappeared into the morning shadows of the woods. Fergus clambered up to the rock to join his king; he was already tying a length of gut through the eyes of a severed Deepwatch head. He had no words to exchange with Conchobar, but they clasped hands in silent thanksgiving.

They turned to see Setanta and Culainn coming towards them, the younger warrior bearing half of the weight of the old Forgemaster under his arm.

'Well!' called Fergus. 'That was a decent ruck, anyway.'

'It seems unreal,' said Culainn. 'I can scarcely believe we yet live. How did we prevail against such odds?'

Conchobar turned then and walked down towards his old friend and the boy he had raised as if he were his own son.

'There is but one reason for it,' he said, smiling. 'Setanta'.

Before him the young warrior had begun breathing heavily. His head was bowed and the glow lessened by each passing moment; as it did so, he seemed to shimmer and fall back down to his previous height and size.

'I don't know what to make of you, lad,' said Culainn. 'You cost me my hound and the lives of many of my men. Yet you fight like nothing I have ever seen. No *human* thing, anyway. And you are true to your word. You have saved Eamhain Mhacha.'

'It is true' replied Setanta. His voice now seemed to be wholly his again, and less unsettling to those who heard it. 'You have lost much since I entered your Fort last night, Forgemaster. For that I would make amends gladly. But I did what I must and feel no regret.'

Conchobar, keeping his eyes on Setanta, leaned his head towards Culainn.

'He bested the Hound?'

'With a hurley stick no less!' replied his old comrade.

Conchobar continued to stare at Setanta for a moment, then back at Culainn with a frown. Suddenly he began to laugh raucously and the Forgemaster joined him.

'Then this impetuous whelp will have to be punished! Setanta! From this moment I put upon you a sacred *geis* to protect these lands, and those of Culainn, and when needed, to bring to bear the power that produced this victory today.'

Then he threw his arms around his foster son and held him tight. He felt sure that he had been waiting for this ever since the arrival of Lugh at Eamhain Mhacha. There was strong Danann magick in the air. It was a day of destiny indeed.

'Your name will be feared, lad, and no mistake.'

'Even more so than that of Culainn's hound, I think,' added Fergus gruffly.

Conchobar chuckled. 'Ha! Nobody will forget the day Culainn appeared and saved Eamhain Mhacha with his new hound!'

Conall Cearnach, who had come to lay his eyes on his friend so strangely transformed during the battle, felt an exultation at Conchobar's words.

'To the Hound of Culainn!' he roared

'To CúChulainn!!'

Then all those assembled on that bloody field began to cheer and add their elated voices to the chant.

'CúChulainn! CúChulainn! CúChulainn!!!'

The name had an undeniable rhythm and power, a life of its own, and it sent a wave of euphoria through the weary and bloodied men.

Setanta looked up at the sky, to the gleaming sun rising ever higher to embrace this portentous day. Then he closed his eyes and gave his thoughts to the source of the power that he still felt thrumming somewhere in his heart.

I thank you great Lugh. I take this geis and swear I will never fail these people.

He opened his eyes again and looked to the hill whence he had come. Even from that distance, his inhumanly keen vision allowed him to make out the distant figure of Emer standing by the dolmen, and he knew the cries of the name CúChulainn were reaching her ears.

As she never failed me.

*****

The early morning light was too feeble yet to penetrate the obscurity at the edge of the woods where a few distraught Fomorians crawled in agony or hobbled blindly to a destination they never would reach alive.

Within that darkness, tingling with malevolent exultation, stood the Morrigan.

The plain beyond the trees before her, with its layer of freshly-felled warriors, was as delicious a sight to her as ever such battlefields had been in the past.

84

Perhaps more so, she mused. For as the ages wore on, these things required increasingly greater effort to bring to fruition; more intricate plotting, prodding and manipulation of kings and fools was necessary to bring about cataclysmic combats of this nature. She would never tire of the moment of reaping, for always, in her remorseless estimation, it was well-earned.

However, now was not the moment to reveal herself to those who now roared their triumph at the defence of their little fort. No, she had far more interesting plans for them, ways in which they could further serve her in their blundering ignorance. Above all, she did not wish for the godling whelp to become aware of her designs just yet. She contented herself with the knowledge that the time would soon come when she would be strong enough to swoop down and gorge herself with impunity. For the time being, it was far more profitable to allow the baying hound-boy to let his killing capacities flourish in the conviction that he was slaying his enemies for the Light.

Nothing could be further from the truth.

The souls of the defeated were rightly hers, but she would steal them with subtlety.

This time.

The Morrigan spread her arms and opened the dark vortex that constituted her true essence, and down upon the battlefield the corpses of the slain began to tremble imperceptibly. Amongst the cheering and congratulation taking place before the gates of Eamhain, none noticed the thin wisps of vital energy that were drawn out from the moribund and the dead alike. Vaporous fingers trailed low across the bloody grass, mixing with the morning mist, until they came to that dark nexus in the forest.

And for those souls commenced a horror beyond all measure.

Part II

The Isle of Shadows

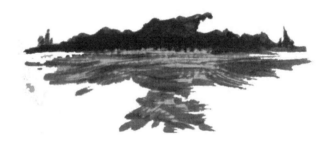

Forgall Manach

It is sometimes said that from sorrow the strongest spirits emerge, through suffering the hardiest characters are born. If this is the case, then never did a stouter heart beat than that of Forgall Manach.

Throughout his life misfortune and tragedy were his constant companions. Some said they were born together as triplets - wherever one was to be found the other two were never far away.

It began, indeed, with his birth - a most traumatic arrival that took the life of his mother Gráinne. His father, the great warrior Celtchar Manach, resented young Forgall for the loss of his wife, and raised him cruelly. Of his unhappy childhood in the plains of Fernmag, I will write no more. Know simply that it produced a man of grit: lean-bodied, tough, and with a constitution of granite.

On coming of age, he left his homeplace and the ageing Celtchar, travelling to Eamhain Mhacha to serve under the newly-crowned King Conchobar. The discipline of military life suited Forgall, and he quickly rose to the rank of general, entrusted with the command of one of Eamhain's twin armies, the Wolf Horde. It was during this period that Forgall found some measure of happiness. He met and married a fair young Eamhain girl, Eibhlín, and they swiftly had four children, three sons and a daughter, Emer.

This happiness was not to last. The grimmest of sorrows fell upon his house and spirited away his loved ones in a manner most awful.

It was said that after losing Eibhlín and his sons, the general closed his heart forever, his battle-scarred features hardening even further to contain the hurt his soul had endured. Only Emer, it seemed, could penetrate his gruff exterior and sometimes draw a smile.

But only sometimes.

Yet in a certain way, Forgall's closed heart was a kindness of sorts, a premonitory defence against the further woes he felt were sure to come.

And come they did...

1.

Silent, Deadly Things

Rain.

It swept across the rolling plain, lending the early morning a blue-grey hue, obscuring the distant hills and the dense copse of trees that broke their low skirting on the horizon. It clung in tiny droplets to the coarse fabric of Forgall Manach's tunic, his great cape and his trim dark beard. He wiped the dew from his bushy eyebrows with a forearm and continued to peer into the murk, looking westward. Ahead of him, becoming fainter and more indistinct as they receded further and further, the army of Connacht was in full retreat. The general smiled.

'Press on, lads! They're scattering like frightened ewes! On, on at them!'

He looked to his left. Fergus MacRoth was surveying the scene with approval. It had been a long night, and a wearying campaign that had taken them well into Lughnasa. And throughout these arduous battles with the westerners, few had fought more fiercely than Fergus. Turning briefly to nod at Forgall, he spoke with tangible relief.

'The day is won.'

Their task here had been an arduous one. When first they arrived at this disputed border territory, more than fifty days ago now, the Connacht forces had taken root, fortifying their positions with impressive efficiency. They had swiftly established a stronghold from which they could strike at Uladh's heartlands and fall back to safety. Using such light and swift-moving tactics, the Connacht soldiers had begun to creep closer and closer to Eamhain Mhacha's key trade routes with the realm of Mumhain in the south. Conchobar knew that it was a matter of time before this artery was severed, isolating and weakening his kingdom. So, he had taken the unusual step of despatching his two most trusted and experienced warriors, Forgall and Fergus, to settle the matter. The king felt that combining the tactical nous of the chiefs of both the Ruddy Boars and the Wolf Horde would finally lead to an end to the impasse.

Early skirmishes were brief and bloody, but necessary in Forgall's eyes, in order to gauge the strength and organisation of his opponents. Having established their weak points, the Red Branch Knights had embarked on a campaign of harrying their enemies day and night, operating in two shifts so that the Connachtmen were afforded no respite. After several weeks of slowly wearing down their resistance – a resistance which impressed Forgall, it had to be said – the men of the west had finally broken. It was Fergus who led the ultimate attack on the wooden outpost, breaking down the very gates with his great axe. He been a sight indeed to behold in his full fury!

Today, though, he looked a tired man. Even now, as he continued to urge his men onward in pursuit of the last fleeing remnants of the invading force, his gait betrayed his exhaustion. His shoulders were more slouched, and his weapon, still streaked with blood, was held mid-haft, as one would carry a spade. He had the look of a man who knew his work was done.

Not so Forgall.

He liked Fergus; he admired him. But he despised his weakness, his *mercy*. Forgall knew it came from the religious devotion to which he was so wedded, and that in Forgall's eyes made him a lesser warrior. Fergus would be content to let the remaining infiltrators slink back across the river Sinann and report back to Medb and Ailill, maybe recounting the strategies that had been used against them here. No, that was something the general would not, *could not* allow.

'No! Follow them in and run them all through. Leave none alive! Let the Uladh hounds bite more from Connacht's flesh!'

Fergus stopped in his tracks, breathed deep and closed his eyes. They had had these disagreements before, and he knew by now that it was useless to protest. In front of the men, anyway. He whispered a silent prayer for the souls of the warriors about to lose their lives, then reluctantly seconded Forgall's command.

'You heard him, men! Into the trees, bloody the soil!'

They watched as the Red Branch warriors raced after the few Connacht stragglers, disappearing into the gloom of the copse of trees. Fergus bent low to clean his axe upon the wet grass. Forgall made his way over to him, and patted him on the shoulder. He could see Fergus's torment.

'I know, Fergus. Unpleasant... but necessary, agree? It will do these young lads good to wet their blades. Come, let us join our brave fighters.'

And slowly, the pair headed toward the copse.

*****

89

Under the canopy of branches, all was still save for the soft tapping of the rain on the upper levels of foliage. A few larger drops filtered through, dripping sporadically onto the leaf and seed-littered floor. The trees were large beeches, and their leaves silently spiralled down from the higher branches to join the mast on the ground.

The band of Uladh warriors Fergus had sent in to finish off their beaten foes - mostly young men, many serving in their first campaign – looked uneasily at each other. There was no trace of the fleeing Connachtmen, no movement, no animals, no birdsong. No signs of life at all.

And yet there was the feeling of cold eyes on them. Watching. Waiting.

They pressed on, deeper and deeper into the dark density of the woods, their sword-tips shaking slightly as they crept. Now they began to peer upwards nervously, the feeling of being tracked – or hunted! – growing stronger with each successive step. But there was nothing, just the dense covering of leaves overhead, shifting in the wind like a green ocean, huge and impassive.

Moments later they came upon a thing that should, *could* not have been.

The advancing warriors stopped dead, the extent of the horror in front of them rooting them to the spot. Ahead of them, piled neatly in a large heap on the ground, lay the remains of the Connacht soldiers, distinguishable only by their shields and swords amid the mound of bloody viscera. If not for the presence of these weapons, what was before them could never have been identified as human. Several of the young warriors, stout of constitution though they were, hunched over to wretch, while the others stood frozen, wondering who, or *what*, could have inflicted such savagery. And so soundlessly, so *quickly*.

And where was it now?

A sudden gust of wind shook the copse violently, releasing a heavy downpour of beech nuts and leaves twirling to the ground. But they were not the only things that descended from the branches. Other things fell, larger things. Silent, deadly things.

Then all was movement in among the trees. All was swirling limbs and flashing steel and piercing howls. And blood. Pain. Terror.

*****

Fergus and Forgall drew closer to the tree-line, the main force of the Eamhain army following slowly behind. The mood was still uneasy between the pair; Forgall could sense the misgivings of the other, though neither had raised the issue of Forgall's order to the young warriors to chase down and wipe out their foes. Somewhat awkwardly, the general attempted to lighten the air with clumsy small-talk.

'I don't know whether it was the hard steel or their thick skulls that did it, but look at that spearhead, dull as be damned.'

Fergus was in the process of mustering a response when his thoughts were interrupted by a pitiful, almost feral scream. Both men had their arms drawn in an instant, but the only figure to move clear of the darkness of the trees was an Uladh warrior.

Or what remained of him.

The young man staggered forward, grievous wounds spurting forth great gouts of crimson. And his eyes! They were wild, haunted, as if they had borne witness to some unspeakable horror. He looked directly at Forgall, yet seemed not to see him. Fergus raced forward to catch the lad before he fell to the grass.

'Sean-Óg! What... What happened?'

The youth slowly turned his head toward Fergus, his breathing pained, his body shaking. He seemed to recognise his old mentor, but as if through a fog. When he finally spoke, the words came slowly and were whispered, so that Fergus had to lean close to hear him.

'From   the trees,' he croaked, 'They fell on us... so fast...'

He began to cough violently, his breathing becoming more and more erratic. Forgall had drawn closer to the stricken young blood.

'Who did this, lad? Who?'

The boy's eyes became glazed, and a shadow cast by the overhead leaves fell across them. He suddenly lurched forward to grasp Forgall by the shoulder, and staring deep into his eyes with a look of endless, bottomless fear,

'Not men... they were... *something else*. Like ghosts... or... beasts!'

Forgall and Fergus had no time to ponder this cryptic statement, for even as they held him, they boy's head was torn open by a projectile, a copper disc which came spinning from the depths of the copse. As the pair of Uladh champions looked on in puzzlement, a full volley of the lethal discs whirred forth from the trees and felled the entire front line of the advancing

Red Knight army. A further volley brought down the second line, with one of the sharp projectiles cutting a deep gash in Forgall's arm. He exchanged a frantic look with Fergus as they huddled behind their shields. These were experienced warriors who were falling like leaves! Cursing his earlier decision, cursing the gods, and this new, terrifying enemy, he called out hoarsely to his troops:

'Retreat. *Retreat!!*'

The Fifth Province

Only rarely do gods err, but when they do, it can be to the detriment of all.

Lugh of the Long Arms, God of the Sun, was no different. In all the tales that have been told of his great deeds and wise judgement, it is my belief that only once did he ever make what we could truly term a mistake. But, as you shall see, that one act would dictate the fates of so many.

Perhaps events would have conspired to the same end whatever he did – evil, it is said, always finds a way. We cannot know such things.

But this one thing we do know – that Lugh did once make an error.

And it would prove to be a grave one.

It all began with Crom Cruach. That hideous, bloated worm had long been one of Lugh's most formidable opponents. The vile Maggot of Time was once a scourge upon the land, drawing evil to him wherever he materialised. As his dark influence began to spread, it fell to Lugh to hunt down and banish Crom Cruach from this fair isle.

But he was unsuccessful.

For each time Lugh engaged the Foul One and thought him vanquished, Crom Cruach would carefully bide his time and eventually reappear in some dark quarter of the land or another. For he was the Temporal Grub, and he would simply retreat into the folds of time and space, hiding there until his strength returned.

And so Lugh employed a different approach to the problem of Crom Cruach – if he could not hunt down the Great Worm, then he would instead leave no place on the land where his evil could take root. Lugh planted Quicken Trees – mystical beings imbued with the essence and goodness of the Dananns – in every place where the Worm sprung forth, steadily driving him further and further away from the people Lugh was sworn to defend. Crom Cruach, vile black creature that he is was forced to recoil from the purity of the Trees, like some scurrying night animal fleeing before a torch.

In this way, Lugh forced Crom Cruach into a desolate and abandoned part of the land, a region known as the Fifth Province. Long had it been shunned and feared by the people of Eirú, for the land there was poor – nothing lived upon it apart from a few mountain sheep, and the fabled Great Elk, of whom it was said that they could survive in any environment such was the strength of their constitution. Moreover, it was thought to be a haunted land, for there was a fortress in that place, a great keep where a dark sorcerer once spun spells. So it was no surprise that Crom Cruach would be drawn to nest in that grim edifice whose name was Coscrach, in the Fifth Province, which was also known as Alba.

What now is the island of Alba was once connected to the rest of the land, lying to the north of Connacht and to the west of Uladh. You will not have seen it on maps, as only the very oldest etchings show Alba in its former position.

And how did it come to be divorced from the land? It is soon told:

Lugh had driven Crom Cruach back into the furthest corner of Alba, the Quicken Trees preventing him from escaping to any other place in the land. He was penned in deep in the shadows of Coscrach, seething with anger at his imprisonment. Yet Lugh was frustrated: his goal was to eradicate the Worm, not trap him, but every time the SunGod ventured out to extinguish this evil for all eternity, the Wicked One vanished into the ether, existing in the space between places – still trapped, but safe from the death-dealing stroke of the Answerer.

Lugh knew that evil draws evil unto itself, that the minds of men were prone to weakness and corruption. It would not be long before the Worm would lure followers to his remote prison and, through them, exercise his dark will.

So Lugh devised another plan. He enlisted the aid of the men of Uladh, his chosen and most trusted people, to dig a great trench, cutting off Alba from the rest of the land. And along the edge of this deep gully a great wooden wall was erected, creating an enormous barricade. All the hardy sheep and Great Elk that dwelled within the province were incarcerated along with the Worm – it was considered a necessary sacrifice.

As Lugh feared, it was not long before the curious and the twisted were found attempting to scale the wall or leap the trench. They were mostly bandits and cutthroats, but the SunGod realised that it would only be a matter of time before someone of true power was drawn to Coscrach, someone Crom Cruach could make use of, perhaps even to the point of attaining his liberty.

It was then that Lugh made his terrible error. Perhaps it was borne of his frustration that Crom Cruach still defied him, or maybe it was out of shame that he had failed in his task. But whatever the reason, he now made a very rash decision, one that he would pay for dearly…

He called upon Mannán Mac Lir, God of the Seas, to fill the trench surrounding Alba with water. Then, climbing aboard his magnificent ship the Sweeper of the Waves, Lugh secured enchanted chains to the rocky north coast of Alba and dragged it out to sea. That mighty ship, driven by the SunGod's very thoughts, rent the entire province away from the rest of the land, breaking it off forever. Lugh dragged the new island far out to sea, then cut loose the lines that bound it and set Alba loose to roam the ocean for eternity – like so much driftwood. He planted a Quicken Tree on the island then, to keep Crom Cruach from escaping in Coscrach, truly believing that the Worm was now contained for all time.

But how could even Lugh have known what Crom Cruach had already done..?

2.

Aifé and the Great Worm

On the isle of Alba, Coscrach castle stood as it ever had, sternly perched upon the cliff edge, frowning into the raging tempest that enveloped the isle that night.

The seaward-facing wall was built flush to the edge of a precarious drop into dark waters. Sinister black seabirds cried wickedly into the night as they battled against the wind and waves. Their loathsome call was delightful to the strange yellow-haired figure peering from a window set low in the craggy cliff wall.

A massive thunderstorm had been battering over the south of the island for some days now and Aifé, the Priestess of All Agonies, was far from perturbed by this.

The sound of the crashing waves was considerable in the low chamber in which she stood contemplating the night seascape. Fires burned upon tall braziers in each of the four corners, illuminating an unnatural cavern whose central space was occupied by a huge, low pan-like cauldron of boiling sea water. Beneath blazed a wide and fierce fire, tended now and then by unspeaking figures wearing crude iron helms that seemed bolted into the very flesh of their collarbones.

In the centre of the pool stood four posts and bound to each one was a struggling man. Their bodies and faces were a patchwork of mutilation; their eyes and mouths were stitched closed by thick thread and careful incisions, leaked a steady flow of redness into the churning water at their scalded feet.

They had been *reconfigured* to experience only pain.

Aifé turned from her reverie and stalked meaningfully towards the pitifully jerking forms. Two of the heavy-helmed attendants flanked the beautiful, ethereal woman and with bowed heads laid down urns to either side of her.

Standing before the pool she reached into the urns and extracted handfuls of some putrid substances upon which she muttered a series of dark phrases before casting them into the steaming pool before her. The bound and bleeding figures began to writhe in even more pain as Aifé's chanting became deeper and louder, an ancient dialect known to very few.

'Father Crom Cruach,' she said finally in the lower Danann tongue. 'If it pleases you, honour me with your glorious presence. I extend a carpet of agony for your arrival: four prime souls from the ranks of Scátach the betrayer. May their suffering grant me a measure of your grace.'

The four former men thrashed about wildly as the water boiled up ever more, the salty liquid biting into their precisely opened wounds, searing the exposed nerve filaments hanging outside their skin, teased out by insidious and precise knife work.

At Aifé's signal her silent acolytes mounted a warped platform of planks traversing the pool, coming up behind the heads of the four victims. The helmed ones bore long, thin knives, which they inserted into holes cut into the back of the men's necks just below the skull. The slender blades were slotted slowly in between the exposed vertebral bones and into the surrounding nerves. Their cries came out only as muffled throat ululations.

Aifé, her eyes now closed, quivered and moaned slightly, moved by the powerful energies drawn from the grotesque spectacle.

The water in the pool swirled vertiginously and after a few moments, glistening white and reddish streams of it rose slowly into the air.

Arcs of lightning began to leap from points between the suspended dripping water columns, becoming more and more frequent, forming the outline of a great coiled shape. Suddenly, with crackling waves of power and an abominable stench from unthinkable realms, the apparition heaved itself fully into existence – a colossal, bloated, pulsating, brown larval entity.

It was as though the great emptiness of the void had taken ghastly, physical form. As though nothingness itself had become something.

Something unspeakable.

Crom Cruach opened its sickening, suckered maw to taste the pain of the sacrificed men and speak to his charge. Its utterances came as a multi-resonant, sibilant sound that was heard equally before and after its true utterance, a bass rumble echoed as a fearful scream. It was as if each syllable was howled by entire populations in direst agony.

To be in Crom's presence was an experience of purest nightmare.

Even the acolytes, enclosed in metal helmets, quivered as they knelt in homage, for Crom Cruach had decided to penetrate and disturb their minds despite their loyal efforts in helping to summon him.

Aifé opened her eyes and looked upon the powerful deity with love in her gaze.

'Crom Cruach, great worm of power. See how those who dare follow the foresaker meet a wretched end,' indicating the hideously tortured men with a gracile hand-motion.

'Behold the lengths that I go to worship you, mighty Father.'

The great worm's head drooped and regarded the prisoners from an uneven row of globular black eyes. Then the horrifying madness of Crom's speech rung through the air.

'Malid, Nemain, Coipre, Niafer. Yessss. Once formidable and noble enemies. It will be most diverting to strip their souls bare and whittle their spirits as you have done their flesh, Aifé my child.'

Aifé merely bowed her head and genuflected, but not too low.

'My lord, my father'

Crom Cruach uncoiled a thick, slobbering tentacle from his quivering mass and extended it around Aifé's waist. The prehensile tip snaked up obscenely along her body to brush and caress her exquisite, fine-boned face.

'It is time, my daughter; you who are the most favoured of my creations. It is time for you to fulfil my designs on this plane. Time for you to repay the life and power that was mine to give, and mine to take away.'

'I am, as ever, your dagger, Eternal One,' she replied, not in the least disturbed by the squirming member probing her face. 'Should you brandish me, the strike will be deadly and true. But I am as nothing without your wielding.'

'This sacrifice is sufficient proof of your worth. For now...

'Narrower and narrower becomes the passage 'twixt this plane and the Aeder Worlds. Fewer and fewer are those who worship and exalt the dark gods. The wars have gone badly for our kind too long. Men have proven worse foes than ever the Dananns were.'

'But yet they are weak, in almost every way my Fath...'

'NOT SO!'

The odious tentacle wrapped itself around Aifé's jaw and tilted it upwards.

'And should you continue to think thus then you too will be swept away, my child. Their strength lies in the very thing you consider their weakness.'

'Pah. They have no connection to the wyrding ways, they have abandoned or forgotten the mysteries it...'

'THAT is what makes them dangerous. We cannot draw strength from the shadows of their wyrdings. The veil becomes more difficult to penetrate. Their abandonment of sorcerous energy is weakening us.'

Aifé did not like the way the conversation was heading; she revelled in being one of only a handful of beings left in this world who wielded the elder magicks. It confirmed her rightful place - far and away above the mortals. Superior.

'You want them to relearn what they have forgotten? Equip our enemy with the means to defeat us?' she said, a note of incredulity escaping with her words.

Crom Cruach twisted and reaching with the slender, extreme end of what could be called his tail, seized Aifé tightly about the waist and hoisted her off the floor.

The mistress of pain gritted her teeth for an instant, then her features relaxed and a euphoric smile emerged on her full, sensuous lips.

'SSSSSSsss... I would gain great sustenance from you, Aifó! But you will provide me with much more before I do.

'Heed me – the futility of our war here grows clear to me. The army of shadow and the army of pain are equally matched.
This endless conflict will never undo the force that binds me to this rock.

'But though I am imprisoned here, our new allies have allowed some of our followers to break free from this place and cause harm upon the mainland. This is pleasing. But I gain no substance from crude death in battle. You, Aifé, must be present to perform the rites of pain so that the agonies of the fallen flow into me, so that I may become whole once more!'

'But what of Scátach?' Aifé asked in a strangled yet sensual voice. 'I dare not leave Alba while she yet breathes. She and her ShadowKin would seize Coscrach in a heartbeat!'

'Yes. First you will bring your disloyal sister before me and I will drain her to a husk. I have waited long enough to absorb a being of power once again.'

'As you have said, great Crom Cruach, our forces are matched. I cannot guarantee a victory.'

Now, however, things had taken a far more attractive turn for Aifé - a chance to finally dispatch her hated sibling. To be forever rid of the arrogant Scátach! Her confidence thus bolstered, she began to stroke Crom Cruach's enlacing tentacular proboscis.

'Have you then some boon to bestow in order to aid me in this, my lord?'

Crom Cruach emitted an appalling sound that might have been a brief, hollow laugh.

'Only your continued life.

'You will work alongside my newest disciple as you carry out my will. And you will listen carefully now to the way things will be...'

Crom Cruach pulled Aifé even closer to his mockery of a head, his many black eyes swivelling madly in suppurating sockets. Aifé could see reflected there her own evilly smiling face, bathed in his weird yellowish glow.

Outside the sea raged and lashed as relentlessly as ever. The dark seabirds wheeled through the air and between the titanic cresting waves. Yet one shape among them was slightly different. The buffeting winds did not affect its course.

The black crow, and the dark spirit within it, rose up into the tormented skies and away, screeching unknowable oaths as dire plans were made in the chamber it departed.

3.

Maps and Legends

In the weeks and months following the Fomorian attack, Eamhain Mhacha had slid into a state of numbed shock. The losses had been high, and many of those injured in battle had not recovered from their wounds. In all, nearly half of the Red Branch army had fallen in or after that grievous conflict, and many of the dead were young men, such as Diarmaid whose father Fiachu also perished during that bitter combat, while many of those who remained were ageing or no longer fit for warfare.

So, a heavy atmosphere hung upon Eamhain; the streets and courtyards were still and sullen. In the air was an unspoken truth that all knew but none dared articulate – *we have lost so very much, and it has left us weaker than we have ever been.*

Through the oppressive streets, Amergin made his way home to his eccentric little hut as night descended. The building was roughly circular, in truth little more than a two-tiered shack. Conchobar had pleaded with him to take up more comfortable quarters closer to the Craobh Ruadh – not to mention a dwelling more fitting to a king's sage and confidante – but the old man would hear none of it; he claimed that his hut was integral to his gifts of prophecy and wisdom, and while none really believed this, it was a convenient excuse that allowed him stay where he was.

As he approached the steps that wound about the hut and led up to its tiny door, he met CúChulainn waiting for him. Amergin smiled warmly, immediately passing some of the bundle of ingredients he was carrying to the younger man.

'Ah, Setan...' He winced. '*CúChulainn*, I should say. Your new name will still take a little getting used to!'

CúChulainn smiled, slightly embarrassed, but the feeling passed quickly; it was not one that troubled him unduly.

'At last!' he mock scolded, sniffing at the package he now found in his arms. 'How can you spend so much time rooting around for scrubs like a piglet? Though if I lived in such a house as this, I too might crave the outdoors.'

Ignoring this, the sage led the way up the rickety steps and into the cluttered hut. Its irregular walls of thatch and wattle contained a chaotic jumble of paraphernalia. Roots, herbs, arcane instruments for tracking the sun, moon and stars, tools for ritual animal evisceration, ancient maps, assorted animal skins, scrolls of parchment and vellum, slates with ogham etchings, jars containing liquids so murky that whatever floated within was quite unidentifiable. CúChulainn regarded the mess with a mixture of horror and amusement as Amergin bustled about, lighting a fire and some wall-mounted torches. The sage directed CúChulainn to put down his package on a cluttered table, then turned to the younger man and fixed his full gaze upon him.

'Excuse the powerful aroma in here, my boy. You'll grow used to it; 'tis the smell of insight... and memory!'

He sprinkled some powder from a small leather satchel into the fire, which released a great plume of noxious smoke and changed the colour of the flames to an eerie turquoise.

'You see: you surround yourself with a potent odour when you fill your mind with lore and then - ' he inhaled deeply. 'When you need to retrieve that knowledge, even many years later, it comes flowing back without effort. *Ahh yes.*'

CúChulainn was covering his mouth and nose from this fresh assault on his senses.

'Indeed. But I still have not found the answers to the questions that beleaguer my mind among the writings and scrolls you gave me, Amergin.

The sage eyed him through the smoke.

'But you have learned much of interest, am I not right?'

'I have... discovered many accounts among the ancient writings, telling of men seized by a blood-lusting fury in battle, to such an extent that they could ignore killing blows whilst convulsing as though possessed. Some called it the *Riastrad.*'

He paused a moment, then shook his head ruefully.

'But I do not think it is so with me. These fighters would need to flagellate themselves to achieve that killing frenzy. I do not require such devices, Amergin. Since the battle against the Fomor pirates, the merest slight may boil my blood, warp my body, and send limbs flying from my blade. I must learn to channel this rage or I cannot truly aspire to be the great leader of men that is hoped of me.'

The worry and frustration on his features were clear enough to Amergin, even in the smoky gloom of his hovel, and he felt for CúChulainn. A ferocious warrior, there was no doubt; destined for greatness, assuredly.

But it was easy to forget that he was sometimes troubled by uncertainty as any youth would be. The sage smiled wanly, though his eyes remained grave.

'You are right. Such records as those I gave you seem the closest to describing your condition, but it is not the same. You told me that the Lugh was with you that morning, that you surrendered your weary body to his power. Perhaps that power was too much for your mortal frame to contain. It may need venting now and again; 'tis just a question of devising ways to ensure that these spasms do not cloud your mind when crucial decisions need to be made.' He placed a hand on his ward's shoulder. 'But do not worry, my boy; together, with patience, we will find a way to best use this gift.'

CúChulainn nodded; he made as if to leave but then stopped, still deep in thought. And as he turned back to Amergin, and was about to speak again, the old man – eyes still shut – pre-empted him.

'There is something else troubling you, is there not? I wonder why it has taken you so long to share it with your old master?'

This did not startle CúChulainn – he had grown used to Amergin's mysterious intuitions.

'It is just a dark flickering, a *shadow* at the edge of my thoughts, and each time I try to grasp it... it is gone! But an evil foreboding remains, and the spectre of it still haunts me.' He frowned, groping for the words to convey the unease he felt

'It is dark, ragged... like a crow.'

Amergin's eyes shot open with a look of urgency that CúChulainn had rarely seen on his sombre features.

'A *crow*?'

'I know not if 'tis real or imagined, but I feel as though I am watched by this creature's malevolence. I have had several unsettling encounters with this mournful bird. I'd swear it was the same one each time! I am beginning, to think it is trying to lure me to my death!' He began to laugh at his own absurdity, but Amergin's expression stilled the urge in his throat.

The old man was silent for a moment, the colours of the fire casting odd shadows across his dark face, making him seem even more ancient and otherworldly. When he spoke again, his voice was low but carried a force that chilled CúChulainn to his very core.

103

'It is well you should beware the crow, CúChulainn. For it is the shape of The Morrigan.'

The word hung in the air for some moments as, from a hidden recess, Amergin produced an ancient piece of bark upon which was crudely daubed a rudimentary image of a crow-like shape. He held up the bark and continued in grave tones.

'The Morrigan - the dark spirit that preys on those who have fallen in battle. Warrior's bane, dread trickster, goddess of death, shade of evil, crone, beauty or wraith, many are the names and guises of the sinister one.'

An ominous, sinking feeling grasped CúChulainn as Amergin spoke this fell warning. It was the dread that comes when a fear that was previously believed merely imagined is confirmed as very real, and more terrifying than had been anticipated. And, for perhaps the first time in his life, CúChulainn felt the stirrings of a deep, mortal terror. When he finally left the sage's hut, his parting words continued to echo in his mind.

'Trust not the crow, my boy. You are a champion of the light, and she is your sworn enemy.'

The sudden chill CúChulainn felt owed nothing to the temperature of the cool and cloudless night.

The Machra Boy-Troop of Eamhain

In other parts of the country the son of a farmer might be expected to take up that noble trade straight from his tender years.

Likewise for the sons of the metalworker, the woodsman or the tanner, who following naturally the paths of their forbearers, consecrated their lives to the perfection of those trades and traditions.

But at Eamhain Mhacha every male was required to take up the sword and the lance and be trained in the arts of warfare as well as learning the craft of his house. This was so that if ever the two great armies of Uladh failed on the field of battle, there would always be the boy-troop – the Machra – who, though they might appear as windy skelps in contrast to a hardened fighting man, would give their last drop of blood and die kicking like demons before the walls of Eamhain would fall.

It was at seven years that the young lads were brought into the Machra. There they learned to hunt, to fight, to wrestle and to play hurling as any youngster of the country might. Except their teachers were Red Branch Knights – harsh, impatient and pitiless – and many were the clouted ears that burned red and the noses that ran with blood.

Through long winter marches in the forests with only a bare sheepskin tunic, and no wrappings on their feet, they learned to suffer; to uncomplainingly endure the bitter cold, lest they earn a belt from the knight and another strip torn from their tunic. To forge their nerve and conquer their fear they would be led far into the woods at night and left there with one burning stick between them and instructions to not try to find their way home until the first ray of Lugh's light. They would be left with nothing to eat for two days until finally there was a contest among them to be the last boy not to be thrown in the river by their fellows, and that boy would eat his fill in the Craobh Ruadh that night and divide up what he couldn't finish among whoever of the others he saw fit.

After another seven years, those lads who did well would be known as The Young Bloods whilst the others would go back to their fathers' trades or, if their father was a warrior, become a chariot driver or messenger.

The Young Bloods would be divided up into packs of friendship and fealty that had been forged during their Machra years, these things happening naturally, and sometimes cruelly.

The Young Bloods would follow one of the two great armies of Uladh into the closer-fought campaigns where they would be the ones baying most lustily for reckless combat – which often led to death, be it glorious or not.

If they lived two years of that exciting, risk-filled life, then they would be accepted into the army proper and they would become Red Branch Knights.

If they had shown proof that they had the necessary presence of mind in battle, then they stood a chance of being selected to join the ranks led by Forgall Manach, the Wolf Horde, and begin to make a name for themselves by carrying out feats, gaining a reputation for their weapons and gathering titles of renown.

Or if he was of the more temperamental nature and could not shake off the feckless war lust of his Young Blood and Machra days, then he would find himself under the heavy fist of Fergus MacRoth and his Ruddy Boars. These were the men more likely to roar into combat throwing caution to the wind and putting the fear of the sidhe into their enemies.

Whichever path they pursued, they would never forget their days in the Boy Troop and their love and passion for Eamhain Mhacha and the Red Branch, which had been pounded into their hearts through arduous trial, and which instilled in them an unbreakable fighting spirit.

4.

River Never the Same

It was high summer, the season the Gaels called *Lughnasa*, and there was much activity by the River Cronn. Fishermen busied themselves from their pirogues, casting lines and hauling in nets at the wider course.

Nearer the banks, children gambolled and tussled with one another, trying to emulate the virile feats of their older siblings who also battled jestingly in front of the young women who either bathed or worked washing garments in the fast flowing waters.

Emer sat among one such group, instructing her charges who alternated their attention from their wicker weaving to occasional glances at the strapping warriors grappling with each other and testing their balance on logs out on the river.

She smiled and reproached them gently now and again to keep their minds on the tressing of reeds into baskets and urns; much needed by the people of Eamhain for a thousand uses and more. But she did not reprimand them too harshly for it was, in truth, a fine sight to see those young lads flexing and vaunting themselves in barely-concealed efforts to catch a winsome female's eye.

Just then a ripple of stifled giggling went through the ranks of her companions and she knew immediately what the source of it would be. She turned to see, with complete lack of surprise, CúChulainn and Conall Ccarnach as they approached the bank where she and the maidens sat working.

These two had the flicker of mischief in their eyes and a cocksure looseness in their gait. *Things are going to get quickly out of hand as usual*, she sighed inwardly. She remembered the last time Setanta, as all had then called him, came to interrupt her lessons at Luglochta Lóga. Things were so very different now; in truth, she had sought him out a number of times, but since his transformation into the champion-in-waiting, this 'Hound' they spoke of, he had been constantly surrounded by the veteran warriors – the inner court or had been locked away with Amergin doing whatever mysterious things they might be doing.

It displeased Emer to think that such a sudden distance could develop between them after what had happened at Fort Culainn. His actions that day had proved his bravery and goodness to her, demonstrated that his arrogance and bluster were only superficial. There was so much more to him than she had ever allowed herself to admit.

107

Conall stopped before reaching the circle of maidens and clapped his hands as he gazed down at a group of young girls (frankly too young for him, Emer thought) swimming under the shadow of a long bough which stretched out over the river. She could hear the playful banter clearly.

'Such a fine day!' Conall exclaimed with hearty enthusiasm, then laid a hand on CúChulainn's shoulder. 'And fitting it is so, for a one-day legendary warrior to enjoy before he tears off to join his first campaign in the west. A pity you won't be with me, CúChulainn; we have dreamed of such a time since we were pups. I wish things were otherwise for you.'

'Aye,' replied CúChulainn, his melodious voice drifting up to where Emer sat, struggling not to show that her ears were pricked for his words. 'Sometimes I regret my oath to protect these lands. Too often I feel that I would be of better use in the thick of it against the armies of Medb and Ailill. Though Culainn has said that he will release me from the *geis* should the Red Branch suffer another defeat such as that we have heard tell of at Brúgh na Boinne.'

'I almost hope we do if that would be the result of it!' blustered Conall.

CúChulainn smiled, and Emer smiled too at the simple beauty of it as much as the reply -

'Perhaps, Conall, it would be unfair on the forces of Connacht to have to deal with the both of us together against them.'

'I suppose. Well, I think it's time now for me to ensure that these young ones here have their fill of this lad to keep them going while I'm gone... ha har!!'

With that Conall whipped off his tunic and belt, and leapt into the water amidst the young women whom he immediately began to splash and harangue. They squealed and yelled and tried to make past him for the river bank, but Conall grabbed one, laughing bawdily. Her frenzied splashing blinded him briefly, and she slipped out of his hands. From the security of the bank, the older maidens, being hardy Gaels, hurled stones and branches at Conall who, with a whoop, dived beneath the water for protection.

CúChulainn shook his head at his friend's merriment and turned to look up at Emer and the others who had briefly stopped their work to regard with disapproval, and perhaps slight excitement, the crude behaviour

going on in the water. A few moments later, he was in front of her, but there was, she felt, something different about his jocular demeanour.

Nonetheless, she was Emer Manach, and she had her own manner.

'And have you come down here to slake the summer thirst for coupling, Setanta, or CúChulainn, as they call you now?' The name sounded foolish to Emer, undignified somehow. And for some reason she could not explain, it frightened her a little.

'Ah well, Emer. I'm not off to war tomorrow. Unlike Conall here, if I did get up to any coupling I would still be stuck around here to face the consequences of it when the season comes ripe.'

The words moved something inside Emer, she wasn't sure what, but as ever Setanta's presence and sayings rendered her uncomfortable and content in equal measure. It was a maddening sensation.

'A strange thing for a warrior to say! Don't all your type yearn for strong sons to carry their name into battle? Many of my father's old fighters rue the strife that kept them from being close to their young in their early years.'

'Old warriors get sentimental in their dotage,' CúChulainn answered smoothly. 'There are plenty of these old veterans to see to the upbringing of youngsters. The wheel turns and there's a time for everything in life. Will you walk a bit with me, Emer, a ways up the river?'

Emer didn't respond but stood, and gave the gourd she was working on to one of her charges. Then she brushed out some folds in her robe, and began walking briskly up the riverside. CúChulainn stepped in beside her.

'A Red Branch Knight's place is on the field when he is young and strong. My own father died at arms before I was born but I do not suffer for his lack of tutelage.'

They walked in silence for a few paces. Emer wondered as to the purpose of CúChulainn's wistful words.

'That is easy for one who has been brought up under the wing of the land's finest minds and fighters to say, CúChulainn. Not all are so fortunate. And...' She stole a wary glance at him before continuing. 'Your father did not die, so don't try and tell me that you lack his attention and guidance.'

CúChulainn stopped and looked curiously at Emer.

'What do you mean by that?'

As they stood there surrounded by the tall reeds, Emer thought back to events at Culainn's fort - and what had happened after.

'My father did not keep from us, the tale of Lugh's arrival at Eamhain Mhacha with his seed in the king's sister, Dechtire,' she said quietly. 'I did not truly believe it until I witnessed your transformation by light on the hill. You are here for a purpose, Setanta. That much is sure.'

CúChulainn, looked down for a moment and sighed heavily.

'At first, I did not believe it myself. I considered the tale some fancy of Amergin's designed to inspire me to greatness. Fergus would merely refer to my father as a warrior without parallel. I had the impression that he always felt unworthy to tell me more. 'It is to Amergin that you should ask such things' he would always say, before clouting me - or attempting to - during training."
CúChulainn smiled boyishly. It was clear that he held Fergus in great affection, and the sincerity of his feelings were written so beautifully upon his face that Emer had to bite her lip.
"But in time I learned my wounds needed only sunlight to heal them. Then, when I called upon his power in that morning battle, it entered me and I knew. But I was left without parents, or any guidance. Amergin says I should be able to hear my father Lugh, but I cannot. There is no...*person* to the power... ach...I don't know what I'm saying or how you could understand it.'

Emer put her hand on CúChulainn's arm, the first time she had touched him since their wild ride from Fort Culainn.

'You will know him one day. My father told me of everything that was foretold about your life that night, CúChulainn - including its *brevity* - so I understand your frustra..'

Emer trailed off as she saw the young warrior's jaw drop. She was suddenly mortified. What had she just done?

Long moments passed while she searched desperately for something to say while CúChulainn stared dumbly at the ground beneath him.

'You... you did not know?'

'Amergin!' he spat. 'Why did he keep this from me?'

CúChulainn whirled angrily around and made to storm back to Eamhain Mhacha, but Emer held fast to his arm.

'Wait! Amergin is a good soul. I don't wish to cause trouble between you. He may not have told you for your own protection.'

'How so? You tell me that I am doomed to a young death - what protection could I need?'

'Maybe, then, for the protection of Eamhain Mhacha. Amergin and Conchobar and the others may have felt that you might not want to spend what little time you have in service to the realm. Perhaps they feared you might turn to a shallow life of mead and debauchery in anger at the SunGod's forecast. Maybe, even now, I have destroyed you with my foolish tongue.'

Despite herself – her pride and her strength – Emer suddenly felt as though she had interfered gravely in matters that went beyond her and had somehow caused irreparable ill. She covered her face with her hands. *Why couldn't she have kept silent?*

CúChulainn looked up at the sun, then slowly down again to stare at Emer. He then took her hands and gently brought them from her face, and held them.

'You... are right. However my elders chose to handle me, I doubt it was for ill. But if I have precious few years in store then I should be thankful of the *geis* that keeps me close to you, Emer, fairest and most wily of champions' daughters. If there is a purpose to all things, then you have already spoken of ours this day.'

The words came ringing clearly to Emer, cutting through a cloud of uncertainty and banishing instantly her feelings of culpability. *Wait! Was he really saying what she thought he was saying? What had she been speaking about? Warriors... absent fathers... raising children...*

CúChulainn cupped her head and looked deeply into Emer's very being, he drew her face close to his.

'It feels... right...' was all she could breathe, too intoxicated by his presence and his words to think clearly.

Then his lips were touching hers and it seemed to her that the warmth of the sun itself was coursing through her body; she felt radiated as her feelings surged and danced like the flame of a torch within her. They embraced passionately then, pulling tightly to each other. Emer felt as if she were drowning in bliss, as his arms encircled her.

The pair sank to their knees among the long rushes. CúChulainn moved his hands up to Emer's face, and she kissed them. Then he moved them down her neck and after a moment she aided his first hesitant efforts to coax the gown away from her smooth, white shoulders.

Suddenly a great flock of black water birds flew up, yawping noisily from behind the rushes. CúChulainn leapt to his feet quickly, his hand instinctively at his blade.

'Show yourself Crow!'

Then brought his hand to his brow.

'But... it cannot be!'

Emer remained on the ground, groaning inwardly with dissatisfaction. She heard then the sounds of thundering hooves.

'What is it, Setanta?'

'Horses. The knights are returned!'

'Father?!' said Emer, as she adjusted her robe and scrambled up to stand beside CúChulainn. Together they watched as the riders passed on their way to Eamhain Mhacha.

'A day of surprises and no mistake' said CúChulainn between his teeth. His vexation stirred the intensity of her feelings, and she seized his head once again and kissed him hard on the lips.

'I'd better see what's happening,' he said, his breath slightly ragged.

'*We'd* better,' corrected Emer.

An electric smile was briefly shared between them, then CúChulainn took her hand and they chased after the charging horses.

*****

By the time they had reached the fort, Forgall and Fergus had not yet begun their audience with King Conchobar.

CúChulainn decided to linger at the back of the hall, hidden from sight, while the general announced his news; tidings which could only be bad given the diminished state of the returning army and the forbidding faces of the hardy veteran warriors.

112

In any case, Forgall Manach, Emer's father, had always been hard work for CúChulainn. The rugged general had never seemed to regard him with much interest when he was a lad in the Machra - never applauding his youthly feats or cheering his triumphant return from a hunt. CúChulainn couldn't have cared less before, but as things stood now with Emer he would have to brace himself for dealings with the taciturn old warhorse.

CúChulainn and Emer noticed the strange hush about the crowded circular room where the king held court. Conchobar had always dealt publicly with his affairs. All were allowed to enter and hear the proclamations and decisions of the Red Branch if they so wished. This openness was both a source of pride for Conchobar and a means to eliminate suspicions of favouritism or dubious politicking. However, CúChulainn knew that in private it was Amergin, Forgall and Fergus that had most direct access to Conchobar's ear.

The newly returned Red Branch Knights stood sullenly around the general who - CúChulainn now saw - was wearing linen tightly bound around a shoulder wound. Things must be grim if Forgall himself had been blemished in combat!

Deerskin curtains twitched as Conchobar and Amergin emerged from a chamber behind the king's chair. The king came forward and stood before his wooden throne while his dark-skinned counsellor raised his staff to signal that Uladh's ruler was ready to give audience.

Forgall came forth and lowered himself heavily to one knee. The king stepped forward swiftly and seized the general by the arm.

'Do not kneel, Forgall. Your bravery and long service in this hall count for something in my presence. Just tell me – how much land have we lost to them?'

With a visible wince, Forgall pulled himself back up straight.

'Lost, Sire? None.'

Conchobar raised an eyebrow, then stepped back to his throne that stood facing the Great Red Branch, and sat.

'Then tell me how it is that the greatest general of the Wolf Horde returns so unexpectedly from the western ventures so shattered?'

Forgall answered without hesitation.

'If you consider, my Lord, the vast quantity of terrain we have wrested from Queen Medb over the last four seasons, then our retreat means that we have lost none of our own land. Merely relinquished our hold on certain parcels of territory that we had lately conquered.'

Emer bristled with pleasure as CúChulainn murmured into her ear from behind. 'A canny one, your father. Removing the sting from bad tidings with guile.'

'The mainstay of the army lingers near Tara,' Forgall continued. 'With orders not to give any more ground, nor move to take any, until I return with my retinue and the advice of the King.'

Conchobar waved a hand dismissively.

'Get to the matter, Forgall Manach. Have the forces of Connacht somehow become mightier than ours overnight?'

'Not so.' Here Forgall glanced quickly at Fergus and his men. 'But among their ranks now lurks a sinister and destructive element. A new kind of enemy. One for every fifty of the normal western men, who are known as... the *Sluagh,* witch warriors named, no doubt, after those vile spirits of legend. Some are men, and some... some are women.'

A murmur of disquiet drifted among the hall at Forgall's strange words.

'Their strikes are quicker than the darting swallow; fiendishly silent in the ambush in open combat they shriek and keen like the *Bean Sidhe* herself, robbing strength from soldier's limbs. Cruel and accurate are their terrible weapons.'

'Though they fight with the Connacht men they will coldly murder their own allies should they flee the battlefield.'

Forgall stared around at the throng of listeners, slicing the air with his hands to convey his tale.

'They danced through us with ease. We were as barley before the scythe. They pursued us to our garrison, picking off our number one by one with strange weapons the likes of which I have never seen...'

For a moment the general trailed off, seeming to close his eyes against a painful memory.

'...fifteen of my finest men, including myself, could only barely subdue even the least of these fell creatures. In the end however, we succeeded in capturing one, for the purpose of gaining some insight into their nature. Behold!'

Forgall made a sign and a man pushed through from the side of the hall with a wooden wheelbarrow upon which a bulky cloth sack was placed. The barrow was upturned and the sack slid to the floor.

Forgall stepped forward and, taking his knife, leaned down and cut open the mud-stained fabric of the sack. Within lay a strange-looking corpse: a gaunt and sinewy form, covered in unfamiliar decorative paint and tattoos, wearing bone adornments totally unlike anything previously seen at Eamhain Mhacha. The left arm was missing at the shoulder and the right hand was gone from the forearm. Four wooden spear shafts still protruded from the chest, broken off from where they were deeply buried. It was clear no risks had been taken in his killing. The most striking aspect of the strange being, however, was the wooden mask that covered its face. The hideously carved helm was inlaid with bone and horn, making for a leering countenance that caused some of those assembled to make warding signs with their hands. The Red Branch Knights stayed impassive at the sight.

'This bastard,' grunted Forgall as he hefted a kick to the side of the dead thing's head. 'Could kill with any part of its body. Of the fifteen of us who ambushed it, only myself and two others survived. And not intact, either.'

Conchobar rose up from his throne

'Has he a face under there?' said Conchobar gruffly.

'Aye I left that on him so all could see the effect of it. Look...'

Forgall dug his fingers roughly into the eye holes of the mask and wrenched it off rudely, slamming the head down hard onto the floor as he did so. Beneath was a wholly human face, though covered also with bizarrely winding tattoos. The expression was curiously peaceful for one who had clearly suffered an atrociously brutal death.

'Forgall,' said Amergin with a stern authority in his voice. 'The mask.'

Forgall handed it to the sage who turned it slowly in his hands, as he began nodded slightly to himself.

'Have you seen its ilk before, Amergin?' asked Conchobar.

'Yes. I fear I have. If I am correct, then it is a most worrying development. For this bears the sigil of Crom Cruach, the foul worm of the Aeder Worlds.'

More than a few in the hall had heard this name in old *seanachaí* tales, whispered fireside stories and snatches of fearful mutterings. The image was always of a great lusty worm, brooding in some hellish realm, waiting for its time to come back into the world and drain all joy and life away into a whirlpool of despair. Crom Cruach. A name not to be uttered lightly.

'Do you suspect Medb and Ailill are in league with this dark god then?'

'Medb, perhaps. I had hoped that it was mere provocation that she named her fortress Cruachán, a flippant and careless gesture to stir up a fearsome reputation. But now I see that things run much further than that. Ailill however, I would not have supposed this of him. But the most curious thing, my king, is that this warrior comes not from the west but from Alba... the Isle of Shadows.'

As these words were spoken, the atmosphere turned deathly quiet. CúChulainn was struck spellbound by the invocation of this place. *The Isle of Shadows:* words that evoked an unnameable dread.

The young warrior gently wrapped a protective arm around Emer's waist and pulled her back to lean against him. He did not know why, but suddenly she felt even dearer to him.

'Then how, Amergin,' said Forgall at last, 'does this fellow come to be fighting alongside the Connacht men?'

For a long moment Amergin did not reply. The tension in the Craobh Ruadh was unbearable; even some of the knights began to cough and shuffle uneasily.

At last the sage spoke.

'I will need to consult the signs to answer this mystery.'

'Do so then!' said Conchobar quickly, the aggravation in his voice unconcealed. 'For now let the hall adjourn. Forgall, rest yourself and your men, we will speak more of this tonight.

'...and someone remove this creature and burn it before its cursed blood seeps into this hallowed earth.'

'As you wish,' said Forgall, who bowed curtly and took his leave. Some of the men wrapped the Sluagh's body up in the sack and heaved it away swiftly.

As CúChulainn watched the wounded general stalk in their direction, his eye was caught by a darkly beautiful woman, of about the same age as

Forgall, who took his arm and spoke with him as he moved along with his men. Emer then came forward and embraced her father tightly. CúChulainn let them speak for a few minutes, watching as Emer was introduced to the woman, then took a steadying breath and joined them.

'Ah if it isn't the lad himself,' declared Forgall wryly as he spotted the young man coming up behind his daughter. '*CúChulainn* they call you now is it, Setanta? I don't know what's happening to Eamhain Mhacha these days. Kill a dog and suddenly you're a hero!'

Possible future father-in-law or not, CúChulainn couldn't help himself whenever a battle-line was drawn.

'Aye... and lose half your army to some painted wenches and you're still a champion.'

Forgall's face twisted in outraged fury, but before he could erupt his clenching jaw was cupped in Emer's hands.

'Father! It was CúChulainn who saved Eamhain Mhacha from the Fomorian invaders. The tale seems unlikely, but it is true - I was there.'

Forgall looked down at the ground for a moment and sighed. Then he glanced to his left and exchanged a brief smile with the raven-haired woman who accompanied him.

'Well I hope it is. The enemies we face now won't be beaten by boastful youths.'

'Come, Forgall,' said the dusky woman, taking him gently by his linen-bound shoulder. 'Bickering will not heal this wound. You can challenge the young man to some contest later, give us women folk some excitement, eh?' she winked and flashed a wild and exotic smile at Emer.

Forgall, his eyes still on CúChulainn, took the woman by the chin.

'Insatiable, this woman!'

Then he took Emer's head in his other hand and smiled with the true tenderness of a father.

'Will I see you later tonight, child?'

Emer nodded and the pair took their leave. CúChulainn followed them all the way with his eyes, then turned slowly back to Emer, starting in surprise to find her staring sternly at him.

'A curious woman. Where did the old man pick her up?'

'Mag is her name. From a captured rebel village, as I understand it. She seems to have caught my father's eye all right. I am glad. He has been without a strong woman to temper him for too long. There has been nothing but war in his heart ever since my own mother was carried off by sickness when I was very young.'

'Well, if she fails to put manners on the old goat, I will!' snorted CúChulainn.

Emer shot him an impatient look, but it melted away as quickly as it came when he threw his arm around her, drew her close and laughed. And indeed they laughed together for a moment, not understanding why, but knowing that, in the shadow of the strange things that day had revealed, their togetherness was precious – and fragile.

Dechtíre's Second Dance with Lugh

Setanta knew of the fragility of such things because of what happened to his mother.

One day when he was still a boy, as he was preparing his spear for a hunting expedition, his mother Dechtíre came up to him and laid ten kisses upon his brow.

Then she told him that, since the sun could not have been any finer, she would go to Luglochta Lóga, the Garden of Lugh, and offer the God of Light her thanks and joy at having brought Setanta into the world.

Then she said 'Take full pleasure in this beautiful day, my precious son, and every day after. For days are short and lives are fleeting. I'm going now to dance with Lugh once more. Never worry for me, for I am the happiest woman who ever walked under this sky.'

He did not know what to make of these words, but he was glad that his mother was so content in life. He went hunting with a lightness in his step.

But when he returned a young maiden, whose name was Athirne, rushed up to him.

She told him that she had wandered down to Luglochta Lóga to gather some of the wild flowers that she knew bloomed there at that time of the year. As she drew near she saw a sight that puzzled her, so she hid behind one of the pine trees that ringed the sacred garden.

She saw Dechtíre cradling the wind in her arms and twirling about gaily. She seemed to be speaking to someone, though Athirne could see nobody else in the garden.

Gradually she noticed a glowing light in Dechtíre's arms. And as she spun faster and faster the light grew steadily more intense until Athirne could see the gleaming shape of a tall figure within it, as if Dechtíre were dancing along with this apparition.

Faster and faster and ever faster she spun and turned with her luminous partner, laughing all the while with unbridled joy.

Finally, when the dance reached its energetic climax, the glowing figure in Dechtíre's arms had grown so bright that she herself was no longer visible. Then suddenly there was an explosion of golden effervescence and where the dancing pair had been there surged into the air dozens of gilded birds who flew around Luglochta Lóga leaving sparkling trails of iridescent light. After a moment the birds came together in a *dizzying, whirling pattern, then flew off with great speed into the blazing sky and were lost to sight.*

Setanta's mother was never again to be seen or heard of at Eamhain Mhacha.

To Setanta's great surprise, as he revealed to me many years afterward, he never felt the need to grieve, because - to use his words - she left in beauty.

5.

Old Wounds

Forgall Manach collapsed wearily onto the rough stool beside his bed and peeled off his tunic. Like everything in the general's life, his quarters were basic and tough. Only utility and strategy mattered to Forgall's harsh mind; comfort was something he rarely allowed himself.

One such rare comfort was the intoxicating woman who now came to him and, laying a basin on the table, took place behind him on the stool, wrapping her firm thighs around his back and pulling him into a tight, exotic embrace.

He had been more used to traditional techniques of love-making, but when he had had encountered Mag, she introduced him to the pleasures of abandon; which he had found far from disagreeable – in their place. And though it could not be said that he hadn't fiercely loved his wife, Eibhlín, it was as a man loves his finest blade, or takes pride in his house. Mag was something else altogether, and she helped him not to dwell on that hollow place in his heart where happy thoughts of Emer's mother once lay.

Mag began to tenderly massage the battle-tautened muscles of Forgall's neck.

'Relax, my Lord, you are as rigid as a stone,' she murmured into his ear.

'You normally like me so,' Forgall replied with a coarse chuckle as he eased himself back against her, delighting in her touch, her strange yet stirring fragrance of pine-wood and cinders.

'Later, great conqueror,' she purred, then began to slowly unwrap the bandage across his shoulder. 'For now, you should loosen and receive healing.'

The habitual harshness returned to the general's voice.

'I might be more at ease if Eamhain were not in such a sorry state. After battling so long and hard for the glory of Uladh, it is disheartening to see how poorly prepared the young warriors seem. Especially in the face of the threat posed by these sluagh creatures. What's happened to the blood here?'

Forgall winced as Mag carefully probed his wound with her fingers and a cloth that had been soaked in some of the medicinal preparations of her folk.

'It was said in my village, Forgall, that a tainted bull can sour many generations.'

'What do you mean by that?'

'Keeping yourself out of the bloodlines can't have been good for the Red Branch. Leaving woodworkers and fisherman to sire the new warriors while the great ones die young on the battlefield, or in your case, are stationed too long, maintained upon it without respite. Often this is the ruination of a kingdom.'

Forgall was silent for a moment. These words were upsetting to him, especially as they might prove true. He thought briefly of Emer who would continue his line, but he had no son. This was not something Forgall had chosen, far from it. He could feel the old rage creeping in behind his temples.

'No,' he said firmly. 'They are not tainted here. This is the hall of legendary warriors, trained as best a man could be in the fighting arts. But they are no match for these... *unnatural* beings that we have seen in the west, and their youthful arrogance will only hasten their journey to the other side.'

'You speak there of CúChulainn, I think, Conchobar's favourite. You believe that, if given command, his foolhardy nature would lead to the fall of Eamhain Mhacha.'

Forgall shook his head firmly, and then had to suppress a groan of pleasure as Mag began once more to massage his upper neck behind the ears, easing away the anger that had been seeping in.

'I would not let that happen. CúChulainn has some skill, but I would rather trust the traditions and strategies that have served the fighting forces of Eamhain so well in the past than to vague prophecies and the meddling of gods. The time of the Old Ones has passed. It is the destiny of men to rule the land now. CúChulainn is merely the last desperate attempt by those ailing powers to regain some measure of control. *Arrghh!* Be careful with those nails, woman!!'

Mag quickly kissed him on the neck and ruffled his short cropped hair.

'Oh I'm so sorry, my mighty warlord!' she said mockingly, but there was more than a little steel in her voice.

'But CúChulainn, yes... I feel you are right. Tainted blood, Forgall. Would you have that for your daughter? For your heirs? Inhuman half-breeds with short, unhappy lives?'

Forgall was strongly troubled by these words, and a pervading sense of imminent desolation which made him unconsciously clench his fists.

'I speak too much of these things with you, woman, when you have me weak and spent as I am now.'

However, feeling that his customary harshness was perhaps unwarranted on this occasion, he reached back one arm and took her hand in his.

'But you are good counsel. I *am* troubled by the fate of my line...'

Mag shifted her weight and lowered Forgall back down on the bed beside her with a skill that elicited an amused laugh from the general.

'What if, my lord...' she said in a playful, yet intriguing voice as she hovered above him. 'What if there could be a way for you to deal with both your woes in a single stroke.'

Forgall laughed again, this time it was with a mixture of bemusement and skepticism.

'What are you now, Mag? A tactician? Will you teach me, of all people, lessons in strategy? Were your people not farmers? Hah!'

'Oh you'd be surprised, Manach; every woman has her wiles. Men are no match for us. If only they knew...'

Forgall laughed heartily at this and dragged the dusky woman down upon him.

'Then I would like to hear such a thing!'

Mag straightened up upon him and laid her hands on his chest. Forgall could see the strength of this one in her eyes then, and despite his amusement at the thought of this rural peasant instructing him in courtly matters, he was mildly intrigued. Perhaps due to his fatigue more than anything, he told himself.

'Then perhaps I will tell it,' said Mag with a coquettish smile and flick of her dark hair. 'But only after a general's taming!'

With that Forgall laughed again and, seizing her arms, yanked her down upon him with authority.

His fatigue would have to wait.

6.

Dread Alliances

On wave-lashed rocks, Aifé and a contingent of her fearsome Sluagh stood between twin braziers. As she gazed out into the darkness of the tumultuous and misty sea, the tall and elaborately-garbed figure beside her turned his masked head to regard his mistress.

'These pirates are rude and base,' it said. The voice had a disturbing whistling aspect to it, sibilant and sharp. 'Even if they turn out to have the spine to meet us here, they are not worthy of joining our cause.'

Aifé did not respond. The figure waited a moment, listening to the crashing waves, then leaned his carved wood-and-bone mask closer to her ear.

'We can take Scátach without their aid, Mistress.'

Aifé did not turn her head, but merely slid her eyes slowly towards the speaker.

'I have no doubts as to the abilities of my pupils, Midac. Worry not on that count,' she murmured, though the other's razor-sharp hearing missed not a syllable over the roaring sea.

'But there are greater circles turning here than you can perceive. The gloom-dwellers are needed to play a larger role than that for which we had previously manipulated them.'

Midac contemplated these words. Manipulation. Great circles in motion. He sensed the arcs of destiny reaching forward to him from glorious (but yet tantalisingly unrealised) futures, and felt invigorated. Along with his twin Nett, he was the longest serving of Aifé's Sluagh - in fact, they were the originals, the true demons. His brother was at this moment leading the mainland forces, while he was solely in command of what he considered an invincible group of fighting beings.

It was good that Aifé's alliance with the repugnant bottom-feeders had afforded Nett and his band transport from Alba. This was the opportunity Midac and his brother had long sought to set their own secret, audacious plans into motion.

Aifé laughed softly then, and Midac wondered for the thousandth time what were the true limits of his mistress's power. What *was* she really?

'Observe, my student, the mists part. They have their ways, the abysmal ones. You'd be wiser not to underestimate them so rashly.'

Midac saw that it was true; the mists were indeed dissipating. Those same unnatural fogs that constantly surrounded Alba, earning it the name the Isle of Shadows. Normally they prevented men or any other creatures that had not been summoned from penetrating to this strange place; but also prevented those odd inhabitants from navigating away from it. These shadows were the work of Scátach, a powerful spell of hiding that had kept all imprisoned here in motionless time...

But lo! Now a hole had appeared in those loathsome mists; Midac had not been there to see it happen when Nett's party had left, and in truth had hardly believed it. It seemed he would have to begrudgingly pay some respect to the sea-filth then. Parting the island's hateful fog was a worthy feat - and a most useful one.

Through the partition, slowly and silently, emerged a mighty black wall of barnacle-encrusted hull, gaining in height as it reared up from the depths. The massive, leaking structure listed and coasted on the roiling waters up to the rocks where the party stood.

Midac was ill at ease before the massive hulk that now loomed threateningly above them, and he glanced warily at his mistress. Aifé simply stretched out her arms before it and smiled, seeming not overawed in the slightest by the spectacle.

After a moment a sickening, and strangely organic sound emanated from the colossal black form that was now protecting them in an eerily silent corner from the shrill winds. It was a vulgar sucking and pumping sound like some great bladder releasing air. Then a leaking, valve-like fissure peeled down the centre of the prow and stretched open, quivering horribly. Other clanking noises echoed up from the bowels beyond, carried by a warm, stinking wind that issued from the detestable opening.

A phalanx of Fomorian guards stood behind the suppurating aperture and, as soon as the breach was large enough, they strode out onto the rocks before Aifé and her followers. Behind them came a larger figure whose dark helmet bore a single mighty horn of some metal that seemed like tarnished gold.

'Welcome, Lord Nardul,' Aifé intoned in her seductive voice, her words resonating and amplified by the mass of strange marine materials and metals that towered over them.

'Your vessel impresses me. You truly are the master of the waves.'

Nardul's answering voice was far less beguiling than Aifé's; to Midac it was a clogged sputtering, and he yearned to sever the unclean throat that produced such ugliness.

'Don't try and soften my ear with your honeyed words, witch!' he belched and with surprising quickness he drew forth a jagged, dagger of sharpened black stone and pointed it at the breast of the yellow-haired woman. 'Be under no illusions. I do not overly like your kind.'

Aifé paid no heed to the blade, and her mocking smile was as luxuriant as ever.

'Yes. Crom Cruach told me of how blindly you played into the tricks of the Dark Crow.'

Nardul was apoplectic at this insinuation. 'Never again!!' he spat, a fine dark spray erupting from his cavernous, fanged mouth.

Again with deceptive speed the Fomor warlord yanked back his arm to drive home his dagger into the sorceress's flesh, but staggered back when he realised he was no longer holding the weapon but instead he grasped, by the legs, a flapping and screeching crow. Nardul was transfixed with confusion and disgust for a moment, then he flung the bird away. It cawed at him; suspended in the air for another instant, then coiled up into itself and fell to the ground – a dagger once more.

By this stage Aifé had her own slender sword drawn and held under Nardul's thick neck, a dark green glow about her eyes. The Fomorian chief's personal bodyguard also found themselves similarly taken by surprise by the incredible celerity of the Sluagh.

'I think, my friend, we should continue to help each other,' she said, the bewitching humour still present in her silky voice.

'I have need of more of your vessels and sea-craft. And you and your kind would do well to learn our ways of stealth and efficiency so that together we might share in the spoils of Crom Cruach's great victory.'

Nardul glared down at her with disdain and revulsion.

'Pah! You offer only words in exchange for our service. The deceit of your kind has cost me enough. Kill me now if you feel capable, for I came here only with a mind to kill you.'

'Words are powerful, Nardul,' replied Aifé, sleekly. 'A word from me and your minions die. And I'm sure that's not what *they* came for.'

Midac admired this turn from his mistress and he enjoyed the uneasy look of betrayal and outrage on the twisted faces of the Fomorian guard.

'But what I offer you is my word of trust. I know that the weapons and information I bestowed upon you in return for the passage of my warriors to the mainland have proven useful to your pirating, for we have found bodies washed up on these rocks bearing wounds from Alban blades. The enchanted kind whose metal does not rust and crumble under the sea's long touch. For all your dominance of the depths, Nardul, you are trapped there. Men have become strong; they are no longer the weaklings you once preyed upon at the shorelines. You cannot defeat me and my Sluagh and you cannot beat the mainlanders. The winding coils of the Great Worm have brought us together this night for a glorious purpose, don't you feel it? All our desires can be met in His great vision. And for you...'

Still smiling, Aifé stepped closer to Nardul and reached up to delicately stroke the golden wrought horn protruding from the front of his helmet.

'A chance for revenge.'

A low growl chundered deeply in Nardul's blubbery throat as he reflected on these words. Midac burned with the desire to slash off his disgraceful head. How dare it hang so close to the sublime beauty of his mistress?

'All military decisions would be mine,' grunted the Fomorian lord finally.

Aifé's smile merely grew more delighted and she lowered her weapon with a dainty flourish, genuflecting very slightly.

'To my castle, then' she said cheerfully. 'Where it is more fitting to discuss such things... my Lord.'

She turned and glided away then, her warriors disappearing soundlessly behind her but not turning their backs on the disgruntled Fomorians.

Nardul glanced around at his guards for a few moments, then scowled and trudged after Aifé who had turned and with graceful gestures was beckoning him to walk alongside her back to her stronghold.

Midac fell in behind Nardul and stayed very close. Though it was to him almost unbearable to be so near such an intolerably hideous creature, he wanted to be the first to drive a knife into that stinking heart if the misshapen brute proved treacherous.

127

The Foul Piracy of the Fomorians

The Fomorians were pirates, and cowardly ones at that. Their craft were bizarre ring-shaped constructions, cobbled together from driftwood, jetsam and, the wreckage of unfortunate ships that passed their way. Buoyed by great sea-beasts, leviathans, their typical strategy was to silently stalk their prey underwater, until they judged the time to be right. Then, the great creatures would inflate their buoyant organs and the entire hideous vessel would rise surrounding the stricken ship. The doomed sailors would suddenly find themselves trapped within a huge ring of barbed battlements and walkways.

Typically the crew were killed immediately or eaten, while the foul pirates stripped the ship down to its frame, added whatever was useful or pleasing to their own vessel, then conveyed the rest back to their undersea realm to further the growth of the submerged city of Fomoria.

But for a long time, these detestable sea-dwellers fared poorly on the surface of the seas, for they were simply not very good pirates. Their limited intelligence prevented them from developing any plan beyond the conquest of the next passing vessel, let alone locating the busiest trade routes that might supply ample prey.

But all that was to change with the exile of Alba.

For the presence of Crom Cruach the Temporal Maggot on that cursed isle generated some very strange phenomena on the seas around it. At a certain radius from the island, there existed a ring of ocean, many miles across, in which time ran differently. Or at least the waters did. In these Slow Waters, as they came to be known, ships made little progress, as if sailing through honey or mud. Everything in the water was slowed, much to the surprise of passing sailors.

Much to their detriment, also.

For the Fomorians were quick to discover this phenomenon, and to avail themselves of the possibilities it offered. To pick off vessels as they crawled agonisingly through the Slow Waters became laughably easy for the pirates, and this sudden increase in easy prey led to an upward turn in their fortunes.

For the next few centuries, the Fomorians prospered, rebuilding their culture and undersea infrastructure with the cannibalised remnants of their victims' ships. Their population increased massively with the abundance of food and resources these new *plunders brought. Their number grew, gradually returning toward the population level of the days of Balor of the Evil Eye, before their decimation at the Second Battle of Moytura.*

Then Lord Nardul came to power, and the foetid ones began to turn their gaze once more toward the land...

As with most things, the origins of many contemporary events – both good and ill – can be traced back to Lugh.

Even the Second Rise of the Fomorian Empire.

7.

Parry and Thrust

CúChulainn nimbly passed his sword from his right hand to his left, then back again. He kept his stance light and flexible, shifting his weight from foot to foot, making ready to spring forward. This was his favourite part of a fight; the moments before the two combatants engaged. He thrived on the tension, the nervous energy that crackled in the air, the battle of minds as each sought to draw some hint of weakness from the other. He feinted forward, then leaned back and twirled his blade with an impressive flourish, his eyes never leaving his opponent – *was that a flicker? A slight twitch of his sword arm?* CúChulainn began to realise that this would be a trickier foe than any he had faced.

His opponent stood stock still throughout CúChulainn's probing. He was far too experienced to give anything away so easily, or be fooled by such tricks. He was a veteran of over forty campaigns. It was said of him that he had slain more men than there are leaves on an oak tree. As for mental jousting – he was every bit as tough psychologically as he was physically. For he was Forgall, first general of the armies of Eamhain, master of the Wolf Horde and father to CúChulainn's beloved Emer.

Without warning, CúChulainn suddenly grew still, both men now motionless as silence descended. Then there was an explosion of movement and noise, as CúChulainn leapt forward with a series of powerful sword thrusts and bellows. Forgall, reading his trajectory perfectly, parried these swipes with little effort, stepping back slightly to gain purchase before responding with a succession of his own blows. CúChulainn, momentarily off-balance, was forced back, and both men returned to their original positions, several feet separating them.

'Come on, boy! Show us some of those much-vaunted skills I've been hearing you boast about!' called Forgall, still as a statue opposite the bouncing, weaving younger man. The general began his own mental prodding, using words rather than actions to destabilise his foe.

CúChulainn did not rise to the bait.

'Forgive me, Forgall, it would not be seemly for me to shame the legendary general of the Red Branch in such a way!'

The older man remained grim-faced.

'I've little to fear from attacks that would barely tax a blind shepherd!' he chided.

'I am forced to move this sluggishly so that your old eyes can even glimpse my skills.' CúChulainn said and his smile broadened for he felt that the barb had successfully found its mark.

Suddenly Forgall feinted forward, luring CúChulainn into overstepping with his return blow. The wily general danced nimbly to the side, before scoring a blow with the flat of his blade across the back of the youngster's shoulders.

'Had I been one of those Sluagh just then you would be dead by now,' taunted Forgall. Picking himself up, CúChulainn was making every effort to seem amused, though he could not hide his annoyance.

'That was but a gnat's sting! I allowed you the blow to spare your blushes!'

He then charged at Forgall with renewed vigour, but the master tactician put the boy's rage to work against him. Forgall made to strike at the head of the onrushing warrior, but instead he dropped to the ground at the last moment, embedding his sword into the earth and rolling to the side. CúChulainn stumbled and tripped over the sword's acute angle to land awkwardly on the ground. In a thrice Forgall was upon him with his dagger to the younger man's throat.

'Headstrong. Rash. Impetuous.'

Forgall's smug remarks were quickly drowned out by a guttural, animal-like growl that rose up from CúChulainn. The sensation took hold of his body rapidly; first his heart began to thump as fiercely as a *bodhrán*, his breathing came in short gasps, his vision grew strange. Then he felt the change in his limbs, the swelling in his muscles, the shifting of his bones. In moments, he was lost to uncontrollable rage, his body contorting with unearthly power. The War-Spasm was upon him, as it had been in the battle with the Fomorians. He rose up, lifting Forgall off him and tossing the general to the ground. Snarling with feral aggression, he hefted up a great table and stood over the father of his beloved, ready to bring down the killing blow.

'Cease, CúChulainn! We've lost enough warriors of late.'

The clear, assured voice of Conchobar rang out in the Craobh Ruadh, causing the silver apples that dangled from the golden branch above his throne to jingle. All in Eamhain knew that, when the apples rang, none should speak until the King had finished his proclamations.

CúChulainn paused for a moment, still panting, before setting the table down, his body gradually returning to normality. He helped Forgall to his feet. The general stood up, wincing slightly as he clutched his bandaged shoulder. Despite the discomfort, he wore a victorious grin. Conchobar continued.

'Well Forgall, what point was it that you wished to make with your little sparring session?'

Forgall sighed, and waving one hand in CúChulainn's direction, he spoke to the court at large.

'So this is our greatest hope - bested by a wounded old warhorse. What chance have we against this new breed of enemy when our greatest are so *undisciplined*? We are fools to put such store in the cryptic half-promises of the old gods.'

This caused some dissent among the court. All knew of Forgall's distrust of the gods, but they had generally assumed that CúChulainn's heroics during the Fomor invasion would have allayed at least some of his fears concerning the mercurial young warrior.

'Is the outlook so grim, Forgall Manach?' asked Conchobar. 'In all the long years of my rule I have never seen you so lacking in hope. It leaves an unsettling shadow over my throne. Is there no remedy to this malady?

Forgall looked down for some moments, allowing the ominous hush in the court to escalate to an almost unbearable level. Then he slowly raised a finger, as if weighing up a thought that had just made itself known to him.

'There is... one possibility. But I fear it involves an undertaking perhaps too *perilous* for any in this court.'

Conchobar sat forward with interest, while CúChulainn, now fully restored to his normal state, listened keenly, his interest piqued (as Forgall knew it would be) by the prospect of a challenge.

Forgall continued: 'I have heard tell of another army, in every respect a match for these Sluagh creatures. They too hail from this... *Isle of Shadows,* and it is told that *they* keep their foul counterparts in check.'

Amergin – perched as usual at Conchobar's shoulder – gazed at Forgall with interest. And suspicion.

'It is also said that those who prove themselves worthy by passing arduous trials may be granted training in skills of warfare far beyond the understanding of natural men.'

The king remained wary, so fresh was the memory of the devastating loss Eamhain had suffered at the hands of the small band of Sluagh.

'What are you saying, Forgall? Form a pact with these devils to aid us against Medb? I won't hear of it! We will live and die fighting as men.'

Forgall had anticipated such scepticism, but continued in a diplomatic tone.

'No, sire. But what if one of our number could be trained in their ways? To teach their martial craft to our own young forces? Perhaps then we could combat this threat on even terms?'

Now Amergin spoke, his ancient, cracked voice barely more than a whisper so that those at the back of the hall had to strain to hear his words clearly.

'I know of what you speak, Forgall, and your plan has some merit. But be warned: their leader, Scátach, does not take on pupils readily. And those who fail the trials pay with their lives. The ShadowKin are not to be trifled with. And I am curious to know how you came to learn of...'

Conchobar interjected, keen to bring matters to resolution. While he trusted Amergin's judgement implicitly, the old sage had such a ponderous way of speaking, always seeming to mull over every point to such an exasperating degree, that sometimes intervention was called for. Forgall's plan had passed the first test – Amergin had not said no. Now to flesh out the details quickly, lest the sage keep them here all night!

'What he says is true. If these ShadowKin, as you call them, can provide us with a means to protect ourselves against the threat from Connacht, then we should give it due consideration.'

Then, by way of placating the old man, he whispered to Amergin: 'You must tell me all you know of these matters.'

The sage, still a little disgruntled, agreed with good grace. 'I will tell you what little knowledge I have gained of the old dark lore, though it seems strange that even soldiers now seem to know of such matters...'

Conchobar glanced uneasily at Forgall, then addressed the court once more.

'Our stock of able men is low enough, Forgall, without sending more off to flounder in the mists or die in bizarre trials. Do you truly think it wise to risk more lives on such a dangerous gambit?'

Forgall was ready for this.

'We need send one only to take on this task. Indeed, the ShadowKin do not train armies but rather lone warriors seeking to perfect long forgotten arts of combat. But... who here could pass these trials?'

Inevitably, CúChulainn was quick to step forward.

'I will take up this task and return with the knowledge needed to strengthen us if I have to squeeze it from each witch in turn.'

A general hubbub of approval greeted this announcement, and brought a smile of pride from Conchobar. Forgall smiled also, and then waved his hands in the air to restore silence.

'No, CúChulainn. Surprising as it may seem, I need you here to captain the Young Bloods I'm sending to the south border garrison. It has rarely been weaker, so thin are our forces.'

'Conall Cearnach is equal to the task; he has proved himself a more than able leader of men. Besides, who else would be sure to overcome these tests but me?'

At this point, Fergus MacRoth spoke forth in his baritone voice.

'The lad has mastered all he could learn from me, 'tis true.'

Forgall considered this for a moment, then looked to his king. Conchobar was frowning, perplexed. Dare they send their greatest hope from their shores, even as their enemies were gathering in strength? Was this too great a risk? He looked to Amergin for guidance.

The druid was thoughtfully stroking his thin white beard but spoke as soon as he noticed the king's regard upon him.

'There is also the problem of the *geis* – CúChulainn is sworn to defend Eamhain, let us not forget – although leaving the kingdom for a short time to enhance his ability to do so *could* be seen as acceptable. After all, we have been charged by Lugh to provide the finest training for the boy. We have hewn the rock as best we could - perhaps now it is time for the stone to be polished.'

Conchobar considered this, then turned to address his foster-son.

'You take on this burden willingly, CúChulainn?'

The young champion closed his eyes, his head cocked to one side as if trying to hear something. Then he opened them, and a steely determination burned brightly within.

'It is the will of the gods that I go. My path leads to this Isle of Shadows, and I will not stray or falter.'

'Very well, then. You had best make ready to leave while the summer seas are calm.'

The court began to disperse, the feeling of trepidation now mingling with some newfound sense of hope. Conchobar and Amergin retired to the king's private chamber, though the sage first stared at Forgall for some time. The general bowed to both king and druid, then walked past CúChulainn, patting him on the shoulder as he went. As he reached the great doors of the Craobh Ruadh, Mag appeared. Taking Forgall by the arm, she led him away into the warm evening.

CúChulainn, meanwhile, was surrounded by well-wishers, all offering advice or blessings for his journey. Through the crowd of bodies, he caught sight of Emer, standing forlornly by the wall of the Great Hall. He smiled hopefully at her, but her austere countenance did not vary. As he made to move towards her, he was waylaid by more well-meaning warriors. Straining to get past, he could only watch as she turned from him and made for the doors, her face like thunder. That sight filled CúChulainn with more dismay than all the talk of voyages to dangerous lands.

*****

Light drizzle clung to the shore, dampening the loose sand and lending a chill to the air. A week had passed since the decision had been made to send CúChulainn to the isle of danger in hope of receiving training from the strange educator Scátach. The plan, when discussed in the safety and comfort of Eamhain Mhacha, had seemed almost sound. But now that he was here, on the verge of departing, a range of feelings occupied CúChulainn's mind.

Amergin had confided much that would be of use to him, should he actually find the mythical Alba. But the sage would reveal nothing of how he came to know so much about the place, only that he had lived on those strange shores long, long ago, and that much might have changed in the meantime.

Conchobar bade him farewell from the gates of Eamhain with the traditional prayers and blessings that accompany a departing hero. It pleased CúChulainn to see the pride with which his foster-father wished him on his way. Forgall, at whose suggestion this journey was being undertaken, was notably absent, citing other matters to which he had to attend.

As the small party of himself, Conall, Fergus and Emer departed the citadel, CúChulainn gazed over at the pine trees that surrounded Luglochta Lóga and wondered how different his life would be when he returned to this place, which he truly loved and would sorely miss should something prevent his return.

So it was with a mixture of exhilaration and sadness that the quartet made the journey to the eastern coast. Fergus and the ever-reliable Conall filled the time with chat and banter, but Emer remained deathly silent throughout, while CúChulainn himself was too preoccupied with his own thoughts to join in with the conversation. Rather, he spent the trip attempting to draw his mount up alongside Laitha, Emer's loyal steed. Emer, though, was having none of it, steadfastly riding on ahead, or else making sure either Conall or Fergus (or both) were between herself and CúChulainn.

Now, as Conall fumbled with the hides covering the currach, loading supplies and checking the integrity of the hull, the Hound of Uladh experienced another feeling which was largely unknown to him - doubt. Was he mad to be setting off on this fool's errand? Would he find this Alba, or drift on the seas forever? Would he come back? And if he did, what would he come back to? Would Connacht lay waste to Eamhain in his absence? Would Emer ever forgive him? Should he stay here with her, send someone else in his place? What was he meant to do?

He looked to Fergus; he was busy tending to the horses. No point asking Conall's advice – he was making his final checks on the currach. And anyway, Conall's advice was reliably unreliable. The safest thing to do, usually, was to ask his opinion on a matter, listen to his counsel, and then strive to do the opposite. That left... Emer. She had positioned herself further along the coast, wrapped in her shawl, her dark hair flowing lightly in the gentle breeze as she stared away toward the horizon. At that moment, CúChulainn thought he had never seen a creature so beautiful and yet so desolate. He would have to talk to her. But not just yet – practical matters first.

Making his way down the beach toward the breakers, he approached Conall with a firm slap on the shoulder.

'There y'are. That will have to do,' his friend offered cheerily.

'She's a fair vessel,' CúChulainn offered, his sense of impending disaster increasing with each look he took at the rickety craft.

'Aye, for being dashed upon the rocks inside! Which is what will surely happen. They say the mists around this cursed isle are impenetrable.'

Ignoring this, CúChulainn only sighed.

'It'll be grand, Conall. The light of Lugh can cut through the densest of mists. And I'm no sluggard as an oarsman.'

The sound of light crunching heralded the arrival of Fergus across the sand and shingle. He arrived with a sneeze, wiped some of the seaspray from his fiery beard and put a huge hand on CúChulainn's shoulder.

'There's little I can tell you about seamanship, lad. But combat I *do* know. I've seen these Sluagh in their fury, and you'd be well advised not to take them lightly. Remember, keep your shield arm high, don't over-reach and you might come back with your head still on your shoulders.'

His wan smile faded into a look that carried great sincerity and care.

'I shall pray to the Gods daily for your safe return. So much depends on you. I trust it is Their will that you succeed in this.'

Then clasping the young man's face in his hands, he added: 'Do come back, lad.'

CúChulainn was deeply touched by this, but even as he nodded and stared back into Fergus's face, his eye drifted over his shoulder to where Emer remained, motionless like a sentinel.

'Go to her now, boy,' said his battle-mentor.

As he began his approach, he was pleasantly surprised to see Emer turn and start to walk in his direction. As she neared, he slowed to a halt, then stretched out his arms for her welcome embrace. Emer strode directly past him and made for the currach.

'Will this riddled log of yours get him out of the bay, let alone to this supposed island of witches and magick, Conall?'

'Well... she's floated more times than she's sunk,' he smiled. Then, after a pause, he added: 'Which would be once. But, eh, she's not the worst auld boat...'

In the face of Emer's icy stare, he made his excuses and hurried off to "help Fergus with the horses". Finally, CúChulainn and Emer were left alone.

137

Unsure of what strategy to adopt, the young warrior took a chance on optimism.

'Tis but a short hop, Emer, and I'm a quick study as you know. It'll be a bare week before I've learned all that they know, and maybe taught them a few tricks of my own, ha?'

'There's little that corpses can learn, no matter how good the teacher,' Emer murmured.

His front of bravado punctured by that, he reached out for her.

'Ah Emer...'

Emer, however, stepped back from his reach, arms folded across her chest. Her words were as sling-stones to his flesh.

'You're setting off to your death, you do know that don't you? I don't know who's the greater fool, my father for dreaming up this insane voyage or *you* for going along with it... Or maybe myself for giving a damn about either of you. This is what happens when all decisions are left to warriors - not a scrap of sense amongst the lot of you.'

CúChulainn let these words hang in the air between them for a few moments before attempting to formulate a response. When it came, it was neither harsh, nor vain. It spoke of his confidence in his mission, his belief in himself, and his love for his land and all her people. As he spoke, he seized Emer's hands, and she was stilled by the power and urgency with which he spoke.

'Have you so little faith in me? Don't you remember the hill? The gods have foretold my destiny, and it's tied to *this soil*. I'm not about to meet my end on some foreign sod! The true task ahead of me lies on this land, so to this land I will return. And when I do, my first task will be to tie my heart to yours.'

For a moment, her face softened, as if the sun's rays had escaped from behind a cloud to illuminate her fair features. Then her eyes seemed to focus on something else, something beyond CúChulainn, and the darkness returned to Emer. Softly, she spoke again, her voice straining as if it were a dam against the tears.

'So I have a great destiny as well. To be CúChulainn's widow.'

At this, she turned from him and was gone, back towards the horses, leaving CúChulainn to his boat. He stood there for a moment, head low, fists clenched. Then he looked up, nodded to himself as if to reassert his determination, and began to push the currach out into the shallow waves.

After wading to waist height, he leapt into the craft as it listed back and forth. Then waving back to the trio on the beach, he called with what good cheer he could muster:

'I won't be long. If I return to find the place plundered, I'll have the pair of yis!

Conall was amused by this, as was CúChulainn's intention.

'Safe passage, ye mad hound!' he called.

As he began to row out into deeper waters, he looked back to try and glimpse Emer one last time. But she had turned her back to the shore. Unseen tears meandered down her pale cheeks, their course quickened by the droplets of mist that clung there.

'Come back to me, you fool,' she whispered.

After some minutes had passed, unable to resist any longer, she turned her head to look for his boat as it receded toward the horizon. But by then, he had already disappeared into the mists, and was gone from her sight.

And Emer wept terribly then.

8.

The Twisted Coils of Crom Cruach

Aifé's yellow hair floated around her head, her skin crackled with energy and her eyes glowed with a fierce greenish light as they always did when Crom Cruach materialised before her.

She had been forced to sacrifice some of her own followers to bring about this apparition - the ones who had failed her recently had served this grisly purpose – but the audience was necessary. She had felt the power of Crom Cruach gnaw at her mind from his unholy dwelling beyond the void, demanding the ritual of invocation, and if Aifé did not satisfy the Great Worm she ran the risk of no longer rejoicing in the power he transferred to her, without which she knew she could not defeat her hated sister, Scátach.

'So, my child' thundered the puissant, writhing mass before her in its malevolently echoing voice. **'By now you must have made your pact with the Deep Ones. Is this not so?'**

'We came to an understanding, Great Crom Cruach,' Aifé replied, her own voice trance-like and distant, her thoughts swirling on the precipice of the all-obliterating abyss that was the dark god's vortex mind.

'You were correct in your estimation of the fools. They do have a glimmer of intelligence, enough at any rate for us to twist to our designs. Everything is ready.'

The slick sounds of lazily-flopping tentacles, and the popping deaths and rebirths of the myriad bubbling eyes were all that passed for a murmur of appreciation from Crom Cruach.

'And what of your deceitful sister and her slovenly followers?'

'Worry not on her subject,' declared Aifé, who - on instant reflection - was delighted to find that behind her words her confidence was genuine. 'They will meet with a fine surprise when they arrive at the Stone of Sorrow, a fine surprise indeed.'

'Vainglorious Aifé!' Crom Cruach bellowed in her head, and Aifé buckled to her knees under the force of his sudden and unpredictable ire. **'Be not so certain that Scátach the Betrayer will hold to her word! I have sensed something strange astir on the mainland of late. Something that moves even now to the Tree, to RathDuille. Something that could throw our carefully laid plans into disarray.**

'A faint spark of light that could become a fiery weapon, something that could even threaten the new age of everlasting darkness towards which we have striven.'

Aifé glanced up from where she knelt, puzzled at the hint of doubt ringing strangely in Crom Cruach's multitude of voices.

'What is this threat, Mighty One? My scryings have revealed nothing to instil such fears.'

The familiar bass-noted background chuckling returned once again to Crom Cruach's echoing speech, and Aifé found herself reassured somewhat by the hateful sound.

'You have some foresight, my daughter, but your vision is miserable next to the long-seeing Crom Cruach, who perceives all happenings throughout time and distance, space and reason.'

Aifé, whose Danann pride made her incapable of remaining too long in a kneeling position no matter who or what commanded it, stood and planted her hands on her hips, a defiant, bitter expression cut into her spectacularly beautiful face.

'Very well then, what do you desire of me, my Lord? What must I do to extinguish this bothersome spark?'

'Ho, ho, ho, ho!!'

Crom's revolting laughter filled every corner and recess of the chamber, and the unfortunate sacrificed ones - whose pain and suffering had created the bridge for this atrocious apparition - rose up, twisting and writhing in dire, silent torment.

'No. This fire may be dangerous, but rather than extinguish it I would sooner steal its burning heart and corrupt it, bend it to my own will, and brandish it to consume those who stand against me. And you, Aifé, you will be my prime instrument in this. You will go to RathDuille and claim this prize in the name of Crom Cruach.'

Aifé was confused by these words. This deviated far from the original scheme that Crom Cruach had previously revealed to her. And further still from her own plans. She disliked this turn of events.

'But my Lord, you know it is impossible to enter that fortress. It is too well guarded by eye and sigil-craft. Scátach would know of my coming long 'ere I arrived to steal this weapon of hers.'

141

'**Know this, young erstwhile of Danú,**' continued Crom dismissively. '**It is of no sword nor lance nor magickal artefact that I speak. But a weapon wrought of blood and muscle, bone and flesh, encasing a fierce light. A weapon in the form of a brash young warrior. A weapon not to be stolen, but seduced. A task for which you... are most ably equipped.**'

In saying this Crom Cruach had sent forth one of his leaking tentacles and it roved up along Aifé's sublime body.

'**As for entering the Fortress of the Tree, my powers will need to wax to their full once more upon this plane to accomplish what you deem impossible. Make ready more worthy sacrifices of suffering. Leave no perversion unventured, no agony unelicited. To do this thing my forces must be at their most hale.**'

Aifé sensed that the audience was over; she felt Crom Cruach receding away even as he spoke these final words, the sacrificed ones that brought him here moved no longer - they had died in an anguish of the purest expression.

'As you wish, my Lord,' she said as the bloated apparition collapsed in upon itself and the final hideous laughter of the Great Worm was terminated. There was a profane sopping exhalation as Crom departed the physical realm.

Aifé turned immediately and harshly addressed the only living witness to her submission.

'Midac! Prepare any prisoners still breathing in the dungeons and send out more patrols - find me some of Scátach's minions. Bring them back alive... and screaming.'

Midac bowed curtly and disappeared up the stairwell leaving Aifé to ponder Crom Cruach's words by the ever-churning Pool of Suffering.

9.

On Strange Seas

There being a complete absence of wind, CúChulainn secured the sail of his tiny vessel and took to the oar. The mist still hung in the air about him, but had begun to thin slightly, just enough that he could make out the looming cliffs and ragged coastline that bordered the horizon to his left. He did not mind the exertion of rowing – in fact, he welcomed the physical distraction, as it would serve to take his mind off the regretful nature of his parting with Emer. Stretching his limbs, flexing his muscles felt good; if only the emotions of women were as easy to control. Or predict!

Quickly settling into a rhythm of movement, his mind drifted back to the conversation he'd had with Amergin before leaving. In the clammy closeness of the sage's hut, he had provided CúChulainn with directions on how to find this elusive island, as well as some general advice on how to stay alive in the midst of danger.

'But how can I be sure to find this island if the mists prevent me from seeing it?'

'As you take to the waters, make certain to keep a steady course with the Cliffs of the Three Sisters at first. Once you pass them, unfurl your sail and let the winds carry you until evening. Once the sun begins to set head towards it, into the west. Through the night, continue west, letting the stars steer you. In the morning, let the sails carry you again in whatever direction they will. Come evening, make for the setting sun again. Do this for three days, and on the third, you will find Alba. Or perhaps it is more correct to say that *it* will find *you.* Stay true to that course and waiver not; do not be alarmed by the Slow Waters, and be careful when you enter the mists that surround the coastline. They conceal treacherous rocks and other perils.'

'How can these directions make any sense? No-one can know what way the winds will blow on each day! Why not simply head west in the first place?'

'Ah, finding the way to the Isle of Shadows is not like travelling from Eamhain to Fort Culainn, lad. It... *moves around.* Some say it was once part of this fair land of ours, but some dark force caused it to break off and cruise the seas in search of prey. Or perhaps it was severed to contain some great evil, set adrift for eternity for the protection of all. Many are the stories of Alba. But you shall see, you shall learn...'

143

'You seem to know so much about it, and the way you speak – have you truly been to this place, Amergin?'

At this, the old man trailed off, muttering something about 'long, long ago' and alluding to some lost past which, perhaps, he did not remember. Or maybe did not want to. And a strange look came into his eyes then, which was filled with regret. And loss. But something else too. Something warm and golden. *Love*?

CúChulainn continued to puzzle on these mysteries as he rowed on through the afternoon. The mists had dispersed now, and to his left, the Cliffs of the Three Sisters were clearly visible, growing smaller now as he had passed beyond them. True to Amergin's directions, he unfurled his sail and waited for the wind, what little wind there was, to steer him. The breeze was gentle, and his progress was agonisingly slow, but he resisted the urge to supplement his speed with rowing – better to conserve strength for the evening and night. Perhaps this was part of Amergin's plan: to allow the headstrong young warrior to practice patience! CúChulainn smiled to himself and settled back into his currach.

By evening, land was no longer to be seen. The wind had strengthened, and was – to CúChulainn's delight – pushing him steadily westward, towards the setting sun. As dusk came, he found himself bathed in orange light as the golden globe of Lugh sank into the horizon. He whispered a prayer of thanksgiving to his father, and asked for Lugh's protection over Eamhain. And Emer.

Through the night, he was able to maintain his course by judging his position relative to the brightest star in the sky, or *Balor's Eye* as the more superstitious of the coastal mariners called it, after the ancient Fomor warlord, he of the Evil Eye. The sky was clear, and the temperature dropped, but huddled in his thick blanket, CúChulainn remained at the tiller, ever-vigilant. So passed the first day.

*****

With the dawn came the rain. Cold, biting rain which seemed to lash the little boat almost horizontally. By this time, tiredness was beginning to take its toll on CúChulainn, so, wrapping himself in some treated sheepskins, he nestled down into the only sheltered part of the currach and tried to sleep.

It was well that he did so, for when he awoke in the afternoon the sky had cleared, and a warming sun began to beat down upon him, but the wind had also changed direction. Now he was being pulled northwards, and if this persisted into the evening, CúChulainn knew, he would have to abandon his sail and row the craft toward the west. For now, all he could do was wait and hope that fortune, and the wind, would favour him.

It was during this long and troubled hiatus that he encountered something strange. He had been idly pondering the nature of clouds when his supernaturally keen senses were assaulted by a foul stench. He immediately lurched over the side of the currach to retch, and as he did so, he was able to discern a great dark shape beneath the waves. His immediate thought was that this was some vast sea creature, perhaps one of the legendary *Ollphéist*. But from what he could make out, the shape of this great mass was too regular to be any form of life. And there was something about the way it moved – its motion was smooth and straight, not darting like a fish or an eel. Had he been given to wild imaginings, he might have even thought that this was some manner of vessel, a boat that moved beneath the waves! But such notions were foolish, and he dismissed them immediately. As the gigantic shadow passed below, heading in the general direction of Eirú, a great wake tipped his tiny boat back and forth, almost capsizing him. He clung on desperately, and was relieved when the currach righted itself as the waves subsided.

He noticed then, far out upon the surf to the right and left of him, a series of black fins pulling through the water. Were they attached to the thing below? It seemed that the foul stench issued from these appendages. As the fins disappeared from view, so too did the sickening smell, and CúChulainn was left to ponder where or when he had encountered such an odour before.

By evening, the wind's direction had not altered, so after carefully consuming a small portion of goat's cheese and fresh water from his satchel, CúChulainn settled back behind the oar once more and faced into a night of rowing. The evening passed without major incident, and though fatigue attempted to distract him, he remained steadfast and true to his task. There was too much resting on the success of his mission to risk the ruin of all for the sake of a few hours of sleep. So on into the night he rowed, heading ever westward and further into the unknown.

*****

The third day was bright and clear, and although he was mortally tired from his night of rowing, he also felt the tingle of anticipation – Amergin had said that the third day would bring him to Alba. Despite this growing excitement CúChulainn knew he needed rest so, after setting his sail once more, he again covered himself in the skins and, huddling under the sheltered part of the boat, he slept the sleep of the weary.

He was awakened by a terrifying scream. Instantly alert, CúChulainn was on his feet and at the prow of the currach in moments, scanning the seas for the origin of the frightful sound. He quickly relaxed when he saw a great sea bird circling low over the waves in wide arcs, but his relief turned to excitement when the implications of this became apparent – land must be near! He scoured the horizon again, and there, off in the distance to the west, a thin, dark smear seemed to almost hover above the farthest waves. The wyrd mists that surround Alba? What else could it be?

He took food and drink again, Amergin's warning ringing in his ears - he would need strength to avoid being dashed on the perilous rocks! He would still have to be careful and limit his portions. Then, checking his rigging once more, he returned to the tiller and watched as the dark smudge at the world's edge drew closer and closer.

After several hours, he met with another unusual phenomenon. The currach had been gliding swiftly across the relatively calm waters when, suddenly, CúChulainn was pitched forward, as if the prow had hit something. His immediate thought was of submerged rocks, but as he raced to the front to check for damage, it became apparent that something far stranger was afoot. There was no evidence of a breach, and nothing could be seen beneath the waves – in fact, the island (if island it was) seemed still too far away for rocks to jut out this far. And, though the wind remained strong, the progress of the currach was now markedly slower, as if passing through thick mud rather than seawater. Baffled, CúChulainn dipped his hand into the water, probing for any change in viscosity. While the texture felt no different to normal water, he found that the droplets falling from his hand seemed to move far slower than was normal; the ripples they made on hitting the surface radiated out in curiously lethargic motion. Amazed, CúChulainn took an oar and smashed the flat paddle onto the surface of the sea. A sizable frill of water rose up gradually, seeming to hang in the air for an unnaturally long time, before lazily gliding back down to the slow-moving waves. CúChulainn even had time to reach for one of his empty gourds and position it underneath one of the falling globules and catch it. Taking it into the boat for closer inspection, he noticed that it did not weigh more than water should, but that tipping the bowl resulted in the contents dripping as slowly as honey or syrup.

Though fascinated by the phenomenon he was nevertheless frustrated by this sudden slowing so he took to the oars once more in an effort to speed his progress. With each mighty heave of his shoulders, it seemed that the tiny boat almost lifted out of the sludgy waters only to land with a lethargic splash. After two hours of such exertion, the boat had passed though the expanse of slowness and returned to normal waters. By this time, a thick bank of mist was now clearly visible, undoubtedly concealing a land mass of some sort. Evening was advancing now, and CúChulainn reasoned that it was crucial he make land before nightfall – navigating rocks in darkness was as dangerous as it was foolish! Safer to drive on through the mist and try to find some bay or inlet.

With a sense of increasing dread, his little craft plunged into the thick, opaque sheet of fog. As he passed through, CúChulainn became aware of great shapes rising up on either side of him, their forms unclear but their size and mass undeniable. Some were low to the water's surface, others towered overhead: rocks, stumps, sea-stacks and other protrusions of deadly stone. At various points he could hear the hull of his currach scrape over some unseen obstacle and he hoped to Lugh that the tough hide would not be breached. Other times, the prow of the boat was shunted left or right as it nudged violently off some protuberance in front. Straining at the tiller, CúChulainn called on all of his might in an effort to steer his vessel to safety, but the further he progressed, the larger the waves seemed to become. Indeed, so precise and unerring was their application of force toward the randomly strewn crags that he began to wonder whether some ill-intentioned force was controlling the surging waters, seeking to dash him against the sharp shards of rock.

Inevitably, the brave currach succumbed to the will of the elements. It was listing to port after being buffeted by a huge breaker when a vicious wave smashed into the starboard side, sending the flimsy wood-and-hide craft sideways into a jagged stump of rock. The hull snapped in half with a decisive crack, and CúChulainn was thrown into the chill waters. He began to swim, but powerful currents sought to drag him below. It felt as though invisible hands clutched at him from beneath, his legs impeded in their every kick, his arms growing heavy. With powerful thrusts, he jerked his way free and began to head in the direction that his instincts told him land must lie.

He could sense that he was nearing a beach; the mists were clearing slightly, and even though it was dusk, he could make out the shadow of mountains. Still struggling against the down-currents, whose treacherous pull was now aided by his own fatigue, he continued to make slow progress toward this new and unwelcoming land. Then, just as a beach of shingle came into view, he felt something, material this time, wrap itself around his leg and pull him violently down. In seconds, his other leg was also entangled, and, opening his eyes as he was dragged below the water, he could see long, thick strands of seaweed wrapping themselves around his thighs, his torso, his arms. Again he was struck by the notion of an intelligence at play, as if these simple sea-plants were possessed of some sinister agency, a desire to keep the secrets of this island from the threat of plunder. With such thoughts did CúChulainn sink towards the sea bed, his body entwined by the powerful ropes of evil vegetation.

His strength failing, his breath spent, he made one final effort to free himself. Remembering that his sword was still attached to his belt, he strained to move his hand to clasp the hilt and release it from the leather scabbard. His first two attempts were thwarted by the seaweed, which even now was coiling itself around his neck in an effort to wring the last air from his lungs. As he struggled in desperation, he began to feel the war-spasm take effect, his muscles swelling as the anger rose in him. This time, however, perhaps due to the cooling effect of the water, he was able to exert more control over it than he had previously. He felt some of the tendrils that were restricting his arms snap, and this was enough to allow him to find the hilt of his sword. Freeing it with a sweeping motion, he sliced through the thick strands that held him in place, the spasm receding even as he did so. He freed himself as swiftly as he could, then thrust upwards for the surface, fully aware that the lack of air was causing his vision to fail, sparkling blotches of light now dancing before his eyes.

With great effort, CúChulainn burst to the surface, gasping to fill his burning lungs. Thrashing about wildly, he spun his head around to regain his bearings. Thankfully, he now found himself closer to land than he had expected, so calling upon what reserves of strength remained in his exhausted limbs he pulled himself onto the beach. Yet even as he staggered away from the waterline, he fancied he spied the odd strand of seaweed break water and whip about – probing, malevolent.

Night had fallen now, and he trudged toward a tree-line, looking for a safe place to sleep. Exploration could begin with the morning's light – the mere approach to this island had nearly claimed his life, and he felt far too weak to tackle the perils of the interior until he had rested. As his eyelids grew heavy, his thoughts returned to Emer, wishing to be in her fair presence again. Sinking into slumber, he almost thought he saw a distant shadow moving within the woods, a huge shape with great horns twisting upwards from its head. But this he attributed to the after-effects of his near drowning; tricks of a tired mind. And the sounds he could have sworn he heard? Ah, surely a memory of sweet Emer calling his name...

But why, then, did the noises sound more like the panting of a great beast? Before this thought fully formed in his mind, sleep finally claimed him.

10.

Stranger Shores

CúChulainn awoke abruptly and, as was his custom, leapt to his feet, his hand clasped to the hilt of his sword. He had always been wary of sleep – it made him feel utterly defenceless and at the mercy of the actions of others. Instantly alert, senses alive, he glanced around; dawn had passed, and much of the morning. Dark cloud hung ominously overhead, yet a strange luminescence existed in the sky, not unlike the false brightness that precedes a heavy snowfall. All was eerily silent save for the soft crash and slide of breakers on the nearby shore, out of sight beyond the bank he had climbed. He looked behind him, and surveyed the small hollow which had served as his bed for the night. Impressed with his own ability to locate such an adequate camp site in complete darkness, having barely survived his arrival, CúChulainn allowed himself a brief smile. Then, the mission returned to his thoughts.

Onward!

His exploration of the Isle began by traversing the expanse of wooded scrubland which bordered the beach. His instincts told him to head inland. He first checked his supply of food, and immediately resolved that he would have to be strict with himself – only his small bag of fruit and bread (strapped securely to his back and bound in protective leather) had survived his landing, for the rest of his provisions had sunk with the currach. Next, he refilled his remaining water gourd from a nearby stream. All necessary preparations finished, he whispered a prayer to Danú for travellers in strange lands then took a deep breath and set off.

He decided to head east, based on the few glimpses of a hazy glow that he imagined was surely the sun struggling to penetrate the dual canopy of cloud and branch. After several hours of trudging through these dark woods, the distances between the trees grew steadily larger, and the soft leaf-carpet was replaced by a parched and coarse terrain. The afternoon was spent making his way across this rough wasteland – populated, sparsely, by creeping plant life and skeletal trees the likes of which he had never encountered before. This scenery continued until the meagre vegetation gradually began to thin, and, as evening drew in, the scrubland wastes gave way to dusty, hardpan desert. As the last of the cover began to dwindle, he suddenly felt a pang of reluctance to move into open ground. Why? Something at the back of his mind, a vague sense of being monitored... There had been times during his trek through the undergrowth that he had imagined hearing sounds. *Voices.* And last night, before falling into sleep, had he not seen a looming horned shape? Or *thought* he had?

He had hoped that, with the clearing of the trees and bushes, he might be afforded a better view of what lay beyond, perhaps spy some manner of landmark that he could make towards. But just as the horizon stretched wide all about him, dusk began to fall, bringing with it an even danker haze which obscured all features ahead of him. Curious shadows occasionally flickered at the edge of his vision as he progressed, but whenever he spun towards them they disappeared only to flicker into existence again behind him. Laughing to himself at the uncanny nature of this island, he pressed on. He walked until night claimed the land, giving him no choice but to stop, for the darkness was complete. He sat down where his last step had fallen, allowed himself two bites of bread, one of fruit and a small drink of water, then settled down to sleep sitting upright, legs crossed, his sword in his lap. Sleep was slow to come, unlike the previous night. He remained squatting motionless for several hours, listening. Now and again, he fancied he could perceive a tiny light (or perhaps an *area of less darkness* was a more apt description) in the distance to one side of him, but as soon as he turned his head to inspect it further, whatever it had been – if it had been there at all – was gone, replaced by the all-encompassing gloom. Such moments came and went. All remained deathly silent.

Or *almost* silent. For CúChulainn had always possessed an extraordinary acuity, not only of hearing and vision, but also taste and smell. And now, hunkering low in the pitch darkness, his ears adjusting to the oppressive din of nothingness, his hearing became more and more attuned. And after an hour of such calibration, sounds did begin to come to him. Not even sounds – *shiftings in the air. Movements of bodies. Breathing.* And then there were the smells. Odours as distinguishable as any sight: sweat. Hair. Leather. And something else, something unexpected – an oily, greasy smell…? The sounds were very distant, the odours weak, and CúChulainn was certain that their source was a considerable distance away. But he was also in no doubt that he was not alone. With this disconcerting thought in mind, the sleep that finally came to him was a fitful one, and thus not particularly restful.

The morning, though still mournfully misty, brought a relatively bright sky, and finally a view of the country ahead. The desert seemed vast and barren, the only features were some strange rock formations visible in the far distance; unnatural-looking spires poked up from the hard ground, but these were close to the horizon, perhaps three days' journey away, so CúChulainn resolved to give them no further thought until they were closer. Far off to his left, which must (he hoped) be north, he could make out a hazy blue line of mountains skirting the horizon. What peaks he could see were jagged, not like the rolling hills and gentle slopes he was familiar with. What a strange and unsettling place this was!

The next three days turned into five, then six and fell into an uneventful routine. By day: walk the desert, encounter nothing, rest little, eat less. By night: sleep upright, remain alert, listen for sounds. The time passed slowly, such that by the third day CúChulainn had begun to grow restless, unused as he was to long periods of inactivity. He was oddly certain that he had already passed through some of the lands he came upon as if he were doubling back on his path, or that the land he had crossed stretched out before him again as he slept each night! It was with some relief, then, that as afternoon slid toward evening, that he came within range of the strange rocky outcroppings he had noticed some days previous and was puzzled that he was only reaching them now. As he drew closer to the nearest of these odd structures, he thought the only things remotely comparable (in shape if not size, since what confronted him now was gigantic) were the tall sea stacks sometimes found off the coast of Uladh, where the waves had burrowed deep into the rock of a cliff to form a cave, then an arch, and finally – when the arch fell – a lonely pillar of rock. But the surface of such seaside formations were often smooth, worn down by erosion and the maritime winds. These desert stacks, as he decided to call them, were far rougher: jagged, bristling with sharp, protruding edges.

Curiosity about what phenomena could have produced such oddities gave way to urgency as a thought suddenly came to him. Evening was fast approaching, and he still had no sense of what lay beyond the desert – but if he was swift, he could scale this tall stack and catch a glimpse of the far distance before the murk of dusk obscured his view. The difficulty of the climb, the risk of falling, the danger of attempting to make his way back down in what would then be pitch darkness – none of these thoughts occurred to CúChulainn as he began his ascent.

His progress was quick and fluid, for the barbed nature of the stack afforded ample hand- and foot-holds (though this advantage was paid for by the many cuts and scrapes that were etched onto his arms and legs). CúChulainn had always enjoyed climbing as a lad, and now his youthful exuberance at scaling the tallest trees in Eamhain Mhacha's orchards returned to him. *So all that climbing was training for this moment,* he thought. *Everything that happens does so to some later end. All part of Danú's plan.* When he judged he had gained sufficient height, he stopped for the first time. Looking down, he estimated that he must be over fifty feet off the ground, but glancing upwards, it seemed clear that he had only gained a third of the total height of the stack. Undeterred, he settled himself upon one tapering ledge and scanned the horizon. His plan had not quite succeeded – while it was not yet dark, the eternally-hidden sun had 'set' more rapidly than he had predicted, so that a grey haze already occluded the most distant parts of the isle. However, he was pleased to discover that he could still see a goodly way ahead.

Off to his left, he could see the desert finally surrendered to wide grassy plains, dotted in places by colonies of thick trees and bush. To his surprise, some livestock seemed to be grazing there: sheep, from the colour, or maybe white cattle. *The inhabitants of this place must eat something,* he reasoned. Far beyond this grassland lay a range of dark hills which rolled back and upward into a ragged range of blue mountains. He could discern the closest of the peaks, which were lofty and impressive, but beyond these nothing was visible. To the right, the desert stretched out further than on the left, eventually changing to rough scrublands. Nothing could be seen beyond this, but he guessed from the dense mist that the coast must lie in that direction.

But it was the view directly ahead that most interested CúChulainn.
 For after a wide expanse which seemed populated by these strange stacks, the desert again gave way to the grassy plains which encroached from the left. The flat plains quickly became more undulating, dipping into a deep river valley. Past this, he could identify another range of mountains, the likely source of the river; but these were lower than the northern range to his left, and somehow more welcoming. Perhaps their soft lines and curves merely reminded him of home. Scanning from left to right again, he watched as the feeble light left the sky and everything changed from dark blue to indigo to black. He could see much from up here, but what could he *not* see? No torches, no campfires, no settlements or dwellings: the island seemed abandoned. For a brief moment, he thought he could perceive a pinprick of yellow light from the homely mountains up ahead of him, but when he strained his eyes to see better, he could detect nothing. A pang of loneliness smote him, a desire to see faces familiar to him, but he scolded himself for such weakness and the moment passed.

Thick darkness had now engulfed everything about him, and so, after dismissing the idea of attempting to see out the night on his narrow ledge, he began his precarious climb down. He found it slightly easier than he had anticipated – one's eyes, it seemed, were unreliable when estimating distances, whereas when only the sense of touch was available a foot-hold was either there or not. In this way, feeling his route downward as a blind man would along an unfamiliar trail, he steadily lowered himself closer to the ground.

To his surprise, he now saw some small dots of light come into being far below him. His immediate assumption was that some luminous insects were the source - but as he drew closer to the ground, he could see that these lights were larger, and erratic. Flames, definitely, but *moving* flames. Increasingly steady in number. Torches! One being lit from the next. As he arched his head to each side, he could now clearly see that a wide circle of torches, carried by unseen bearers, was converging on the base of his stack. By their light, he could see that he was still some twenty feet above the ground, and from a quick count of the torches already ignited, he guessed that between twelve and sixteen adversaries awaited him.

Panic was not a feeling that troubled CúChulainn. As he himself often said when asked, in situations such as this he felt he entered a state of heightened awareness and had access to more rapid decision making. Amergin summed it up best: CúChulainn was able to reap the benefits of all the physical reactions to danger without the troublesome feelings of fear which rendered these bodily changes useless in most men. Now CúChulainn entered into that special state of readiness. Within seconds of identifying the threat before him, he had assessed what options were available to him, evaluated the advantages and disadvantages of each, settled on a course of action and began to prepare himself for the execution of his plan.

By the flickering light from below, he picked out a section of rock close to him which was connected to the body of the stack by a thin junction. Gathering his strength, he sent a powerful leg thrust at this unstable length of stone, sending it tumbling towards the lights. That should disable two or three of them, he though as he leapt towards the opposite side of the circle, drawing his blade as he fell. He landed in a low crouch, sword swinging at the torches as he spun and whirled about. His eyes were still adjusting to the glare from the flames, his movements so swift that his vision was not fully clear as he thrust violently at his foes.

He heard the sharp cracks as his blade splintered the wood of the torches, but to his surprise there was no screams of pain to confirm that his swipes and lunges had met their targets. Confused, he spun to his feet to regard the scene - then all became clear to him. The torches, bound to the hilts of long-handled spears, had been planted into the hard ground, but the bearers were nowhere to be seen. All CúChulainn's improvised attack had managed to do was extinguish several of the flaming brands, leaving the base of the stack in deeper darkness than before.

CúChulainn was nodding appreciatively at the intelligence of this tactic as well as the speed of whomsoever had executed it when he felt the cold point of a blade against his neck. Then a second, a third and suddenly several more. From out of the shadows, into what scant light remained from the few unbroken torches, emerged twelve hooded figures, all clad in black, their swords resting gently against the skin of CúChulainn's throat.

'Move and you are finished,' hissed a low voice from beneath the nearest hood.

'Oh I'll move, my friend, and then you Sluagh will have the misfortune of understanding what fighting mettle CúChulainn is truly made of...'

At this, the hooded speaker inclined his head and laughed softly, the movement allowing his face to become partially visible. CúChulainn was at first horrified at the white, skeletal features which lay beneath the cowl, but closer inspection revealed this to be some form of face-paint, smeared crudely into the semblance of a skull. Now it was the Uladhman's turn to laugh.

'So *that* explains the greasy smell I detected; I had all your other odours placed, but that one eluded me. Do you witches never bathe?'

The hooded figure chuckled again, before drawing closer to CúChulainn's face and drawing back his cowl entirely. While his face was daubed patchily with white, thick black smears of war paint were traced around the eyes and down the hollows of the cheeks. This spectral face with its hard eyes was framed by a tangle of wild, coal-black hair. The iron look in those deep eyes, the total lack of fear or doubt, told CúChulainn that this was a warrior not to be underestimated. When he spoke, his soft tone carried a slight accent that seemed somehow familiar, but CúChulainn could not quite identify it.

'So, you are named for a hound, and you have a nose to match, hmm? Well, you cannot determine all things by scent – for we are not Sluagh, as you seem to think. I am Ferdia, and we have been observing you. Come, our mistress Scátach is waiting.'

Without further explanation, he turned back into the shadows and the other hooded warriors led CúChulainn after him, still under close guard.

*****

King Conchobar had not blindly sent CúChulainn to seek Scátach upon the Isle of Shadows. For there were certain things that Amergin had come to know about this hidden place, and the ways of the mysterious clans who dwelt there.

He had told him that, not far to the north-east, the seas flow strangely around a motionless wall of mist. Behind this dense fog lies Alba, the hidden rock where dwells the eternally battling sisters Scátach and Aifé.

Of pure Danann blood, their powers were apparently matched only by their mutual hatred; for they have been at odds with one another since long before the Gaels had come to inherit this land.

He had said that Aifé is served by the frenzied killers known as the Sluagh. Their already incredible fighting skills, heightened by the sight of blood and suffering in combat, are intensified further by the malevolent power of the evil deity Crom Cruach, to whom they offer the souls of their victims.

Amergin told him that to counter this infernal army, Scátach had surrounded herself with fighters of unimaginable skill and hardiness, named the ShadowKin. Trained by the Dark Lady herself, and nourished by the golden sap of the last Quicken Tree, their bodies become infused with the might of that ancient magickal entity, their minds filled with an intimate knowledge of the long-forgotten fighting techniques of the Tuatha Dé Danann.

With the golden sap burning in their veins, their bodies become the shadows cast by the light of the ChrannGréinne. They strike thrice before a normal man could have but bent back his arm. They can dash at full pelt through a forest without making a sound. Weariness in endeavour, fatigue in battle and fear in the face of death are unknown to them. They are the fearsome protectors of a powerful secret, a prophecy that was soon to reach its fulfilment, so Amergin had said. When CúChulainn had pressed the sage on the nature of the prophecy he had grown quiet, and bade the young champion do his duty in the service of the king.

The Hound of Uladh had thought of Amergin's words often as his captors marched him without stopping for two days and two nights. Although he had been witness to many unusual sights since his arrival, as they travelled onwards, CúChulainn was exposed to the full strangeness of this lost land. Through the desolate Valley of Bones they trekked, where the bleached white skeletons and what seemed like the massive antlers of great creatures lay half buried in the arid sands. Along the Path of Proving, a narrow ledge forced the company to sidle along with their backs pressed hard to the cliff edge, so slender was the walkway. Thence to a broad sweep of land known as the Plain of Ill Fortune.

CúChulainn learned these place names from Ferdia, with whom he had begun to talk as the journey unfolded. He had struck up conversation with the head of his captors in the same easy way that he would with any of his close friends from Eamhain and, to his credit, the painted leader of the ShadowKin, had responded amiably enough. And while he had immediately marked Ferdia as a warrior of some skill – and therefore extremely dangerous - there was something about his confidence and the way he carried himself that appealed to CúChulainn. The ShadowKin clearly respected, or even feared, this man they called captain, leaving no question about his authority. Yet behind all of this, there remained something in those sad, dark eyes of Ferdia's that carried a portent of doom. And so CúChulainn resolved that he liked the hooded warrior, but would remain wary, the way a man can warm to a wild animal that is said to be tamed, though he has not tamed it himself. He was also astute enough to note that, while Ferdia was happy to talk with him about inane matters and the history of the region, he was careful to avoid giving away any information about where they were bound, or why they had sought him out.

'We are now passing through the Fields of Fuilltach,' Ferdia was saying. CúChulainn observed a wide expanse of long, coarse-looking grasses to either side of the raised stone walkway on which they marched; what few trees that dared grow here were stripped of all leaves, and the barks appeared to have been scraped as if attacked by some clawed creature. Elsewhere in the long grass, pieces of metal – armour? – glinted in amongst the swaying blades. There was something about the movement that seemed sentient, intelligent. This made CúChulainn feel anxious, the memory of his experiences at the beach returning to him.

'Here it was,' Ferdia continued, 'that the Legions of Light took up arms to destroy once and for all the scourge of this country, the foul war host of Fuilltach the Malevolent, Lord of Blood. A powerful sorceror was he, his great magick matched only by his hatred for all that is good and righteous. Finally however, after a long and arduous battle, the day seemed won for the League of Light and all that remained was to strike the head from Fuilltach's shoulders. But with one last act of diabolical cruelty he uttered a dark spell, then drew his blade and spilled his own poisonous blood here, tainting the earth forever.

'Then the very grasses of the plain, infused with his dark soul, rose up and consumed all who stood on that evil pasture. Henceforth any man that sets foot into that grim glade is devoured by the Glutton Grasses. The agonised cries of the Army of Light echoed long on this plain, and may sometimes be heard when ill winds blow.'

CúChulainn felt an involuntary shiver as he looked again at the sea of churning grasses. He uttered a silent prayer to Lugh for the noble souls who were lost in this grim place, then walked onwards, taking more care now of his steps lest he stumble into the cursed fields.

Thence the company travelled east, towards the coast. The landscape changed again to rolling downs littered with hump-backed drumlin hills and esker ridges. The constant crossing of these peaks and troughs did not impede the group to any great extent, but it did slow their progress considerably so that, by the end of their fifth day's march, their destination was still not in view. This lack of progress did not sit well with CúChulainn's impatient nature, and as they stopped that evening to make camp, he approached Ferdia uneasily.

'Thus far on our little ramble, I believe I have been a good captive to you and your band. Would you agree?' Ferdia made no reply, merely stared at him and, eventually, made the slightest of nods of affirmation.

156

'And I would even argue that I have made the leagues pass by all the faster, what with my tales and my wit. Your men seem very entertained by me, unused as they must be to any humour with you as captain,' he continued, a gleam in his eye. Ferdia did well to suppress a snort of laughter at this, feigning outrage instead, although the slight stretching of the corners of his mouth belied his bluster.

'What is it you want to say to me, CúChulainn?' he asked curtly, aware now that some of the other ShadowKin had begun to take note of the conversation. 'Speak plainly now.'

'Very well. I merely wish to know whither we are bound, and how soon we are to reach it. Understand, the fate of my people rests with me and the urgent completion of my mission. I dare not tarry too long here.'

Ferdia's features creased into a broad smile, the sort a parent wears when their child expresses a flawed conception of how something works. But when he spoke, his tone was not patronizing; rather it carried the warmth of understanding.

'Of course – you have not yet been told. Do not worry about our speed, or how quickly you can achieve your ends. Time runs differently here. The amount you perhaps feel has passed may not be the case for everyone. And at any rate, we are almost arrived. Tomorrow, or what will feel like it for you, we will reach RathDuille. Now eat and rest. We depart at first glimmer.'

With that he spoke no more, preferring to pull his hood down over his head and fall into what was either sleep or meditation. CúChulainn was left to ponder his strange words as, still under guard, he ate a meagre meal, sharing some of it with his captors.

Then he told a tale of courage and adventure, and sang a song about tearful eyes and lost love and departures on a rocky shore before he finally surrendered to a shallow and dreamless sleep.

11.

Strategies

The sky above Eamhain Mhacha hung white and featureless. The air was still, conditions temperate, and the mood lazy. It was the type of day, thought Conchobar, when it was not unacceptable to be found immersed in activities other than those of a kingly nature. It was on such days as this that he enjoyed some of the simple pleasures that are often denied a chieftain or man of high standing: to walk by a river, catch a fish, or while away some slow hours with a friend.

It was in the last of these activities that he was currently engaged. He had sought out his trusted friend Forgall Manach before noon, and under the ruse of having some pressing matters to discuss, he marched the old warhorse down to a secluded spot near a ford. There, on a felled log, the king had set the *fidcheall* board, the carved wooden figures already in place.

At the sight of this, and the realisation of Conchobar's subterfuge, Forgall had relaxed noticeably, and so the pair had settled into a session of the ancient game of strategy and tactic, as was their long-standing custom. A custom sadly neglected of late, they both admitted, and after much discussion, they finally conceded that the blame for this could be shared equally.

And so, as the game developed, the talk drifted from inane pleasantries and friendly jibes to current events and matters of import, as was the norm. In keeping with his station, it was the king's prerogative to initiate such a line of conversation, and so Conchobar eventually did.

'So. How long is it now since we last saw evidence of Fomorian intrusions in our territories?'

Forgall, instantly registering the change of tone, kept his response light and brief; what the king wanted here was not a tactical report, but honesty and concision.

'A goodly while... Not since a fortnight from *Là Bealtaine.*'

Conchobar smiled, then allowed himself to hope wistfully.

'Perhaps we have dealt them a truly fatal blow this time.'

'I would not mourn the passing of that heinous race,' said Forgall. 'But, didn't Lugh himself once think he had completely vanquished the foul sea-spawn, only for them re-emerge from the depths and bring trouble to our days?'

'True enough,' conceded Conchobar, 'We will keep ever vigilant on the eastern coasts.'

'A wise policy.'

Forgall paused, moved one of his pieces, representing a member of his attacking force surrounding those of the king's, and then continued in a warning tone.

'But we must be equally as heedful of every edge of the board. While we are distracted in our sea-gazings, our worst enemy may move silently behind and push us off the cliff!'

Conchobar nodded.

'Connacht,' he murmured, moving one of his own pieces to counter Forgall's speculative advance. 'Long has the western question needled at my reign. They say Ailill is drawing many tribes under his banner, some from outside of Connacht itself.'

'I well believe it. He strikes me as a great leader,' started Forgall, before quickly adding 'though *misguided* in his vision for the land. Those who have heard his rallying speeches are easily swayed by his well-wrought words of conquest and promises of glory. He gathers men to his cause easily. Much as you once did yourself, MacNeasa.'

'Oh? You admire this king of Connacht in some measure, do you Forgall?'

The old general, spotting the warning signals, proceeded carefully.

'As a warrior, as a leader... perhaps I do. I feel his intent is noble and his heart is true, but it is Queen Medb who holds the reigns of that stallion. Connacht has only grown to be such a threat since that devious woman found her way into Ailill's bed.'

This seemed to arouse Conchobar's interest.

'And who really is this Medb? Never has she presented herself at the Tara Conclave. I find it strange that she would not take the chance to display her might. And how is it she can hold so much power over a man of Ailill's renown? 'Tis unnatural.'

Forgall nodded. It was true that the prophecy of the Liath Fail, the Stone of Destiny, was traditionally reserved to male kings, but all other chieftains

159

and leaders of Eirú, no matter their sex, took pride in displaying their forces at the Great Conclave at Tara. That Medb would snub the ceremony was peculiar.

'Unnatural is right,' he agreed. 'It is whispered that she has knowledge of old dark wyrdings long forgotten. They say she gains counsel from a deviant old hag who some think is her mother, a twisted and mad remnant of the tainted Dananns.'

The king noted the disdain on Forgall's features, well aware that this most practical of generals had no time for the ways of the ancient or mystic. He elected to steer the course of the discussion around to more pragmatic issues.

'What do your spies say of their past, Medb and her lackey? Do we know where these two miscreants hail from, or are they native Connacht stock?'

'Most likely they sprang from some unholy crack in the earth! But no-one knows whence they came, just that they appeared twenty years ago, and their impact on the province's fortune has been profound - it was Medb's first host that defeated Ailill's mother, that honorable warrioress, Mata Mursic, who at least had been content to rule her own realm. How she corrupted the son after, I wouldn't venture to say.'

Forgall grew sullen, attempting to re-immerse himself in the game, spending far too long contemplating his next move.

Conchobar pretended not to notice, continuing with forced levity.

'So: our most pressing threat is nought but the result of what happens when a noble warrior has his heart ensnared by a calculating temptress with her own fell designs of power.'

'How easily is power wrested away from soft-hearted men,' the general replied, to which Conchobar raised an eyebrow, looking the other straight in the eye.

'Well, they say a wild mare will always lead a herd astray,' he said meaningfully. He allowed Forgall to ponder this for some moments, then turned his attention back to the board.

'So tell me, how is this new woman of yours treating you? Mag, is it?'

Forgall clenched his jaw at the realisation of how well-baited he had been by the king. He was in the process of formulating a riposte when the sounds of an approaching horse broke the silence of their tranquil refuge. Turning toward the source of the interruption, Forgall saw the mount heading toward them from a nearby thicket of trees. A breathless warrior leapt from the beast to approach the pair, his nose a bloodied mess.

'That moon-addled vixen daughter of yours, Forgall!' shouted the youth. 'She dares to strike a Red Branch Knight and *humiliate* him in front of his peers! No dowry is worth the weight of shame she would bring as a bride, and the effort it would take to correct her rude manner!

Forgall only sighed.

'Ah... Emer.' But the young man – whom the king identified as Gearóid, a decent young knight of good breeding – had not completed his tirade.

'The arrangement I made with yourself and the lady Mag is no more. Her ways have soured my lust for a wife for now. I'll face dangerous enough foes in battle without having to come home to one in my own hearth.'

At this he brought a hand gingerly up to his ruined nose, wincing painfully at the touch.

'Ack! I am diminished! We will speak no more of this business. Good day to you, General.'

Then, regarding the king as almost an afterthought, he nodded courteously and beat his fist forcefully to his breast before turning on his heel and remounting his horse.

Conchobar looked to Forgall, who was holding his head in his hands and shaking it slowly from side to side. The king decided to suppress his amusement and opted to toy with his general more subtly. Taking on a tone of bemusement, he began:

'Why now, do you think, would young Gearóid O'Neill be bothering your fair daughter when it's widely spoken that she has her heart fixed on our man overseas? You wouldn't be nurturing any hopes of his failure to return and make good on his duty to the girl, and the kingdom, would you Forgall? Indeed, when I look back on it, wasn't it you yourself who concocted the entire venture? Or maybe wild mares have their way in Uludh too, ha?'

Forgall was apoplectic at this.

'What words are these?! I protest! Every action I take is done with the good of Eamhain Mhacha - and my king - in mind.'

He raised a stern finger. 'I *am* the ruler of my household! Furthermore, I have every faith that our champion will return to bolster our defences against the threats to come.'

Conchobar fixed him with a withering stare, the veil of humour quite gone.

'Good, Forgall, it heartens me to hear it. For he *must* return. The Gods have decreed it. And we will trust their judgement on that matter.

'As for ourselves, we must ensure that we remain united and focused on victory. There can be no conflict of interests, General. These times are far too dangerous for our boldest and brightest to be playing frivolous games.'

With that, the king executed a telling move on the fidcheall board, clearing a path for his monarch piece to escape Forgall's besieging forces; he regarded it for a few moments, checking for any possible counter and, finding none, said brightly:

'Do you concede, Forgall?'

The man referred to as the Great Tactician seemed shocked for a moment, and continued to stare ruefully down at his scuppered trap for some time before, at last, raising his eyes to gaze meaningfully at his king.

'I think you had it won some time ago.'

The pair stared at each other deeply for a few long moments then finally Conchobar nodded and the two friends made to leave.

For while it was true that Conchobar MacNeasa enjoyed engaging in the simpler pleasures on a lazy day such as this, it would be wrong to think that he ever allowed his kingly duties to stray far from the forefront of his mind. He never did.

That was what made him a great king.

The Tragedy of Deirdre of the Sorrows

It was true to say that, in his later years, Conchobar MacNeasa was indeed a great king, and a just one.

But 'twas not always so...

Before the time of Great Lugh's coming, and the days of the Hound CúChulainn, before even the arrival of Fergus MacRoth, the young Conchobar fought and crushed many pretenders to his authority. As redoubtable a warrior as he was, he could not be everywhere at once, and so there were two who represented his rule at the head of his second and third armies. For that was Conchobar's way of battle.

Three separate but united armies revolving around Eamhain as the seasons changed, they formed an impenetrable and ever-rotating force. One led by Forgall Manach of the Agile Mind, a group that in time would become known as the Wolf Horde, another by Naoise Uisliú of the Bloody Hands, and that was their name, and Conchobar's own great host that followed the king whenever he personally rode out to crush a stubborn foe. Forgall and Naoise - champions of Uladh, Conchobar's twin blades of elsewhere battle.

But it was not only for his martial skills that Naoise was appreciated; for he was as fair and unblemished a warrior as any have right to be. A fairness that was only too well appreciated by his own king's favourite and promised wife, Deirdre Dall.

Some lament the day they struck each other's eye - but I cannot, for it is well known such pure moments are rare in any life. For, indeed, they loved one another. That is all. That is the simplest of things.

For better or worse.

As they were like brothers, sharing victory and defeat at every moment, Naoise could not keep the contents of his burning heart concealed from Forgall. How tortured Manach was between loyalty to his friend and to his king I know profoundly, for my counsel did he seek, though the names of those in the tale he spun me were false.

I urged prudence, but caution is obliterated in the furnace of the young lover's heart, and soon enough they were discovered.

They were brought then before a speechless king, a man who had never before known betrayal.

Staggered further was Conchobar when he asked his other, supposedly faithful servant Forgall Manach whether he knew of the treachery, and received the reluctant, unavoidable truth.

To regain his standing, the king had to make an example of his two trusted champions. And with my counsel, a means was decided: Naoise was to be put to death for his crimes, and as punishment, it would fall to Forgall to deliver the killing stroke to his friend.

The next day upon the Sapling Hill near Eamhain, Forgall stood, preparing himself to cut the life from his closest companion. A burdensome request, a woeful chore.

But there was no heavier heart in Eamhain that morning than that of poor Deirdre Dall. To witness her lover die was a prospect too terrible to endure. And so, before Forgall could raise his blade, or command be given, she did throw herself in front of Conchobar's chariot as he approached the hill.

Trampled by hooves, crushed under chariot wheel, there she died, that ill-omened girl. Conchobar was so grief-stricken that all thoughts of execution left his mind, and instead he returned to Eamhain with her body, and there mourned for eight days and nights.

Having no more desire for death that morn, Forgall allowed Naoise to leave, and into exile the broken-hearted lover went. It was said that he took his two brothers, Ardán and Ainnle, with him, and that they sailed north, disappearing into the mists of time.

When he emerged from his grief, Conchobar spoke no more of Naoise or revenge, and never again in the remainder of his life did his heart fall prey to a female form, so haunted was he by the ghost of Deirdre Dall.

And in the years that followed, a change came upon the King; the fire of ruthlessness and envy that had so consumed him began steadily to cool, his judgements became more just, and his will, though no less steely, was at least tempered with compassion. So, in a strange way, some measure of good did emerge from the dark events of that terrible day.

But alas for Deirdre. Deirdre of the Sorrows.

12.

RathDuille

CúChulainn opened his eyes to find Ferdia standing over him, the first timid light of Alba's strange dawn dimly illuminating his features with an amethyst glow. CúChulainn found his expression difficult to read – there was something like trepidation there, but also the merest fleck of warmth. As if detecting the other's probing, Ferdia's look changed to one of detachment; he silently beckoned CúChulainn to rise before calling together, with subtle hand signals, the other ShadowKin and commencing their march.

Their progress was swift, aided by the relatively fair weather and good terrain. By the time the hidden sun had seemed to move to its highest point, they had passed through a broad valley and into a flat plain punctuated by great zigzagging clefts. They picked their way around these obstacles and made for a range of low hills which appeared to precede a set of imposing peaks.

Nestling in the heart of these hills, surrounded on three sides by a great chasm, sat an imposing artificial structure. As the band drew closer, CúChulainn could discern the vast size of the castle, for castle it was – sheer walls of stone rose to untold heights, erratic buttresses protruded, chaotic towers and turrets climbed and leaned, and the entire edifice bore signs of decay. And yet, the most remarkable feature of the architecture was not man-made at all – for amid the great rises of piled-stone battlements there grew an enormous tree, a huge trunk of golden-red emerging from the centre of the structure, the great boughs stretching out in all directions. Was it a trick of the design, wondered CúChulainn as he regarded this strange union of nature and human construction, that the enormous branches seemed to be holding the crumbling fortress together?

'There stands RathDuille' announced Ferdia as they drew nearer, 'The Fortress of the Leaves, dwelling place of our Mistress Scátach and garrison of the ShadowKin. In earlier times, the uninitiated were required to complete a test, the Novice's Bridge over the chasm, before they were permitted entry but... we shall enter by the normal way.' He indicated a narrow stone bridge stretching across the deep cleft in the ground, and gingerly led the way towards it. Although he had relaxed slightly after Ferdia's comment about the Novice's Bridge, something still made CúChulainn feel uneasy – a tingle in the air, a sense of anticipation among the other ShadowKin, wherever it came from, he felt he would do well to heed its warning.

Ferdia and the others skipped nimbly over the stone walkway which, as he approached, CúChulainn could see was scarcely wide enough to accommodate his feet if he placed them sideways. Conscious of the ShadowKin observing him from the opposite side, he moved swiftly and with confidence. His concerns were initially allayed – the bridge seemed sturdy beneath his footfalls. He noticed nothing amiss until it was too late – as he approached the halfway point of the crossing, his left foot came down upon a stone slab which, to his surprise, moved laterally away to his left. Lurching forward, he planted his right foot on the next slab which swung away to the right. An undulating motion now gripped the stone slabs up ahead of him, swaying left and right in a rhythmic swinging dance – in one horrifying instant it became clear that the middle part of the bridge consisted of hidden ropes which held the stones in place. Frantically struggling to retain his balance, two thoughts occurred to CúChulainn at once – first, that Ferdia and his men had been able to cross only by stepping on the exact centre of these suspended stones, and second, that the Novice's Bridge was still in use, and he was now upon it!

Trying not to look at the deep precipice below, CúChulainn attempted to propel himself forward again onto the next swaying foothold, barely reaching it with his left foot. He could hear the laughter of the ShadowKin on the far side, the creaking of the ropes that held the mechanism in place, the distant roar of running water at the base of the chasm – but he blocked all of these things out of his mind.

To his surprise, his thoughts instead turned to winter at Eamhain, when the little lake near the forest had frozen solid. He remembered how some of the women folk had taught him how to glide across the ice in his bare feet, switching his weight from foot to foot as the ground seemed to almost slip away from underneath him. The memory for this action now came crashing back into his limbs, and so he shoved himself forward onto his right foot again, just in time to meet the return of the swinging rightward stone. Then, adjusting to the rhythm of the swinging, he leaned back to the left in time to meet the backswing of the leftward slab. Repeating this motion, he swayed forward again and again until he found himself standing once more on solid slabs of rock. The central section of the bridge continued to sway behind him as he strode warily over the final few steps of the walkway. On reaching the other side, he put his hands on his knees and breathed deeply, the shock which he had temporarily postponed finally striking him.

'Apologies for the deception' Ferdia was saying, 'but a test works better when it is unexpected, I think you'll agree.' He smiled broadly. 'You did very well, Hound!'

CúChulainn was about to muster a cutting reply when a movement behind Ferdia caught his eye. From the darkness of the castle entrance, a

166

shrouded figure slid forth, gliding down the steps to join the ShadowKin, all of whom sank to one knee and bowed low. The figure moved gracefully toward CúChulainn, the face obscured by an intricately wrapped headpiece. From its depths, a rasping voice which he assumed from its pitch must be female hissed forth.

'Your passing of the bridge was... *adequate*. I am Scátach. Come.'

Without further utterance, she turned back into the shadows of the fortress. CúChulainn gathered himself and followed.

Ferdia watched him go, a smile still on his lips which faded, however, on overhearing the chatter of two of the departing ShadowKin:

'He did well on the bridge', one was saying, 'I've seen few cross it better.'

'Aye,' the other agreed. 'He may even be a match for the Captain himself!'

Ferdia mulled over the meaning of these words for some moments, then decided that he did not like it.

Not one bit.

*****

CúChulainn followed the mysterious figure into the shadowy dankness of the fortress, down long porticos, through tumbledown chambers and halls. At one point, they passed a doorway revealing a group of training warriors who stopped to look at him with interest. Scátach merely glided on without a word to them. In silence they walked, finally entering into a gigantic central keep. And what CúChulainn beheld there took his breath away.

He stood in the immense cylindrical chamber, his head arched back as he scanned higher and higher. He could appreciate truly now that the entire structure was purposefully constructed around the titanic tree whose upper limbs he had seen on his approach. But his earlier view had given him a false sense of scale, for the huge trunk that now rose in front of him easily dwarfed even the mightiest oaks of the forests of Uladh. And the colour – it seemed almost to glisten a strange golden-red – beautiful, hypnotic and... decidedly familiar. A mighty elder-growth from the Age of Tales whose muscular branches arced out of apertures high up on the structure; these limbs were full and lush and soared up far above the roofless edifice, their dark green leaves rustling moodily in the brisk winds. Arched doorways punctuated the stonework of the towering chamber's walls, revealing further rooms and quarters beyond. Each chamber, hall and room was connected by the branches of the great tree, and the huge,

167

knotted roots, which splayed out across the stone floor like monstrous serpents, had woven back and forth upon themselves into the semblance of a flight of steps.

As Scátach ascended these roots, CúChulainn realised that they led up to the great bole of the tree in which – to his further astonishment – appeared to nestle a curious living throne of sorts, formed of root and bark. It was onto this strange seat that the shrouded one now eased herself, finally turning her head to regard the young warrior now many feet below her. She stared at him in silence for some moments then uttered a single word.

'Speak.'

CúChulainn was still gazing about in wonderment, but at her gruff command he gathered himself and began.

'So this is RathDuille. Never have I set eyes on such a structure as this. Truly this is a place of magick and power and I pay my due respects to its mistress.'

The Uladh champion thumped his fist to his chest and bowed his head briefly.

'Now, time is short and my need great, but before I begin my tale, I must ask – was this fort built around the tree, or did the tree grow into the castle?'

Scátach looked at him blankly, her features all but hidden save for the twinkling of the eyes from underneath her cowl. As she spoke, she reached out a bony hand to caress the tree that seemed almost to pulsate with life around her. When she finally spoke, her voice was harsh and strained, as if she was unused to exercising it.

'Foolish child. Your lack of knowledge depresses me, and bodes ill for your chances of receiving my guidance. The castle is nothing without the tree: RathDuille exists to protect *ChrannGréinne*. As do I. As do all those who I have trained as my ShadowKin. As should any who would wish to do so in future.'

By this time, the group of ShadowKin who had served as CúChulainn's escort had filed into the chamber behind him, while many more had entered from various other routes, including via some of the branches of the giant tree. To his surprise, CúChulainn noted that several had skin of different colour to his own, and that many of the assembled warriors were female. He then quickly scolded himself for having such narrow expectations of so strange a place as this. Scátach was continuing to speak in her rasping way.

168

'And as for *time...*' at this, she emitted a strange sound that must, CúChulainn guessed, be the closest thing she possessed to a laugh, '...you are in the one place where you should not feel oppressed by time. Surely you recall passing through the Slow Waters on your voyage here? Time passes in more than one direction on Alba, sometimes swifter, sometimes slower than it does in your land, so you need not worry on that count for you can neither control nor foresee its humours. The same is true for space – this is a small island, yet you have travelled for many days. You will grow accustomed to these things.'

These cryptic remarks were difficult for CúChulainn to comprehend, so he returned to his original enquiry.

'This... *ChrannGréinne!*' he said, approaching the tree. 'It's not usually the custom to give name to a mere tree. Save one particular kind, a type of tree that legend holds has been lost to the world since the passing of the age of the Dananns...'

'You are not so poorly versed as you would have us believe,' replied Scátach, and she unwrapped a portion of her head-dress. 'You speak of the Quicken Trees, and before you blooms the last of their sacred kind. The sap of this tree runs with the lifeblood of the great gods of the past - it is in itself a warrior of renown. One who has earned his rest, sleeping in forgotten realms... should harm ever come to the *ChrannGréinne*, then all would come to ruin. How eager would the Crooked One be to see it topple.'

What CúChulainn could now see of the bone-white face was creased at the forehead and temples. He could feel power emanate from her as ever more darkness came to her voice and tone. Then she returned her attention to the young stranger before her.

'To become ShadowKin is a solemn undertaking; you are doubtless skilful, but do you have the commitment to become a guardian of the ChrannGréinne?'

'In honesty, I knew of no Quicken Tree when I set forth on this quest. I have been charged with learning your ways that I might return and use this knowledge to help my people protect themselves from a dire threat. I have made an oath to do this thing, and do it I *will*, whatever price I must pay.'

This passionate outburst seemed to please his prospective mistress.

'A noble cause. But the skills of the ShadowKin are not for every haughty mercenary who wishes to impress his king. They are bound to the Tree, and may only be used in protection of it. Some that I have trained departed this isle, it is true, returning to their own lands to accomplish great deeds. Their names are legend. Or *will be* in time. But each of them first spilled their blood in service to the *ChrannGréinne*. It is the way of things. If this is not to your liking, you may leave now with safe passage, for it is I who control the mists. But tell your kinsmen you found nothing on this island save ghosts and shadows. I hold you to this *geis* of silence in exchange for your life.'

At this, CúChulainn reached his hand into his leather pouch.

'My old mentor warned me you might be reluctant, wyrd one. Perhaps you will reconsider when you learn the true nature of the enemy we face.'

He held aloft the carved wooden mask of the Sluagh fighter slain by Forgall, drawing murmurings from the assembled ShadowKin. He tossed it at her feet and turned to leave.

'But if cowardice has crept into the heart of the mighty Scátach and we must face this threat alone, then so be it.'

He had almost reached the entrance, having clambered onto the branch which stretched out from the keep, and as he strode nonchalantly along it towards the portal it traversed Scátach spoke and he felt a shiver of excitement run through the *ChrannGréinne* beneath his feet, as well as himself.

'Where did you come by this foul countenance?' she asked hoarsely. She had stooped to pick up the mask and was now holding it in those claw-like hands.

'This one fell, and not easily, in a battle between my people and the followers of King Ailill and his mysterious concubine, Medb. From Cruachán it came, from the army of Connacht, in the west of my land.'

Scátach now drew back the rest of her head wrappings, revealing her ashen features; the bony angles of her jaw and cheek, the high topknot of hair pulled tight, the black lips and the whiteless eyes! Dark and smouldering, they now danced with fury. For the first time, she looked on CúChulainn directly.

'Cruachán. A name not to my liking; less so if Medb holds sway therein. If this be truth, then matters are grave. We have grown complacent if we have allowed Aifé's evil to spread out from these shores. We have not shadowed their movements as well I had thought.'

Then turning to one of the ShadowKin, an older yet still dashing, warrior with long blond hair traced with silver, she called:

170

'Naoise! Prepare our headstrong newcomer for his training. Once he has taken food, his instruction begins.'

Naoise did so, leading CúChulainn to an adjoining chamber and away from his new mistress. Scátach remained standing, still clutching the gruesome mask of the dead Sluagh. Finally she looked up and bade Ferdia to her side - she did this not with words, but through her will, through the *ChrannGréinne*.

'Anxious, my Mistress?' Ferdia asked softly.

The other slowly nodded.pleasant

'Whatever dark machinations my sisters are contriving, they are now known to Scátach, and by my blood they will fail!'

She flung the hideous mask high into the airy chamber before launching a jagged metal ring from beneath her cloak. The whirling weapon smashed the mask to tiny splinters and then arched through the great chamber, to return to her white, sinewy outstretched hand.

'We must bring forward our plans. We attack before the next moontide. The hour of Aifé's downfall is almost at hand. While breath remains in my body, she will not leave this island to spread the tyranny of her twisted master.'

She gripped Ferdia with a skeletal hand.

'The moment of our destinies draws near!'

*****

Naoise led CúChulainn to a long hall where rations were being apportioned out to a line of ShadowKin. After finally receiving a bowl each of some unknown but sweet-smelling amber substance, the pair seated themselves at one of the long oak tables which ran the length of the cavernous refectory. Some curious comments about 'today's colour' of the meal followed, before a comfortable silence settled upon the two diners.

It was Naoise who finally ventured an utterance of any real import.

'Well played back there. Only an Uladhman would have the gall to try such a risky gamble - most would be dead before they hit the ground for turning their back on the Shadowy One as you did.'

171

He smiled at CúChulainn as the content of his words sank in. Seeing the wry expression on the newcomer's face, he added:

'Have I not placed you rightly?'

'Right enough. Talk scurries along these branches quicker than squirrels, it seems. Aye, I'm a man of Uladh to be sure, and from the sounds of it, you hail from a not too distant corner yourself?'

Naoise seemed to relax, beginning to warm to the younger man.

'Sure, 'tis a hard brogue to shake, no matter how long it might be since you last treaded her soil.'

His expression darkened slightly as he spoke these last words, and a distracted, faraway look seemed to creep into his eyes. CúChulainn noted it, and resolved to quiz his new acquaintance about the matter later, when he knew him better. For now, he pursued another line of questioning.

'So what business brings you here, Naoise? Don't tell me you were sent to save Uladh from certain doom. If you're still sitting here talking to me that can't have gone well! Maybe there's something fancy to keep a man here, forgetting his duties?'

He nodded toward a striking-looking olive-skinned maiden nearby, a female ShadowKin who had arrived in the mess hall with Ferdia.

'The likes of *that* maybe, eh?'

Naoise followed his gaze, registered his meaning and quickly turned back to CúChulainn with an urgent look of warning.

'Keep your glad eye off of that one, CúChulainn,' he whispered. 'For that is Uatach, the very daughter of the Mistress herself. Let not her comeliness haunt your thoughts while you are here; you'll need all your wits when your training begins in earnest. For it is likely that Uatach and Ferdia will be the ones personally taking charge of your initiation.'

CúChulainn regarded the stunning woman a second time. Yes, she was fair of feature, with exotically coiffed blueish-black hair, and she was shapely in an athletic way. But now that he looked more closely, he detected the steel that resided beneath her attractive exterior. And there was something in the line of her jaw, the ferocity of her gaze, that showed she was her mother's daughter, and no mistake.

172

'Say no more, Naoise! I'm not here to hone my skills in that particular art anyway. But, pray tell me, what brings you here at all? You seem sane enough.'

There was a long pause as Naoise appeared to choose the words that would best express himself. He had been enjoying the banter with his countryman, but now CúChulainn noticed that his manner grew curt. When he spoke again, it was in a clipped tempo that carried none of the warmth of his earlier conversation, as if he were reciting lines that he had oft said before.

Perhaps it was to save him from speaking the truth.

'The reason that most find themselves here is either exile... or a thirst for learning the ultimate skills of warfare.'

'Banished from Uladh?' CúChulainn replied. 'Doesn't sound like the work of our noble king. If that's what's holding you here, I'm sure that on my return I could...'

But Naoise cut him off before his offer could even be spoken.

'I'll speak no more of it. I'm ShadowKin now; that is my future and my past.'

As he spoke, Ferdia and Uatach arrived at the table carrying their own rations. As they sat down beside CúChulainn, Naoise continued:

'And now, it seems, *your* future has just arrived. Good luck to ye, Uladhman.'

And with that, he rose and left CúChulainn with his instructors.

'Quare fellow that,' he said brightly. 'Nice enough though. Good food you have here, Ferdia. I won't make much of a shadow if I keep this up!'

Ferdia smiled. 'I told you he was witty, Uatach.' Then to CúChulainn he said: 'Enjoy this feast while you can, for your training will be most strenuous, and will include fasting, abstinence and much misery.'

Even though he could sense the seriousness of Ferdia's statement, and despite Naoise's earlier warning, CúChulainn could not resist the opportunity for a small amount of mischief.

'That's asking a lot, but I won't be too miserable if the fair Uatach here will be observing my exploits.'

173

Scátach's daughter stared at him expressionless.

'Eat up. We begin as soon as the plate is clean.'

Ferdia chuckled, clearly enjoying the utter failure of the cocky Uladhman's attempts to charm the icy Uatach. He watched CúChulainn clear the last spoonfuls from his plate, then leaned forward and whispered confidentially with a mischievous grin of his own:

'I hope you're ready for this!'

*****

In truth, he wasn't.

He had already received the highest martial training that Eriu could offer, of course – no son of Eamhain would be permitted to take up a weapon until he had undergone the rigorous and sometimes harsh tutelage of Fergus. He had covered all the basics of combat, armed and unarmed; he had become skilled with every weapon known in Uladh; he had studied battle strategy and tactics. He considered himself – and he was unashamed to say it, for his deeds fully supported the claim – the most skilful and talented warrior in Uladh at that time. As such, he felt justified in judging himself well-trained in combat.

But what he was to experience over the coming months... That was something else again.

He was used to learning new skills. He was very good at it, and for this reason, he quite enjoyed it. But what he had done in the past was merely to learn and practice a new technique to the point of flawlessness, perfection. Now, under the watchful eyes of Ferdia and Uatach, he began to understand that this was merely the first step on the path to truly *knowing* a skill. Perfection, he came to discover, was merely the starting point, the first faltering steps of an infant; now he would learn to walk, to run, even to fly!

He would be shown a feat once and be ordered to emulate it. Within the hour, he was expected to have mastered it; then to be able to adapt it to suit different situations - within three hours. Next, he would be made to repeat the skill over and over and over, going far beyond the point of reflex in order to reach the stage where the concept resided in his limbs and muscles rather than in his mind. He no longer knew a skill – he *became* it.

'If you have to think of your next action when facing a Sluagh, you will be dead before the thought has formed. Let your *body* react, your mind can follow later,' Ferdia had explained. 'Now... do it again!'

174

Again.

How he grew to hate that word! Every new skill, every action, every minute movement had to be repeated, honed, perfected and repeated again...

And again...

And *again!*

By the end of the first week, he no longer recalled what it felt like not to ache in every muscle. By the end of the second, he had grown to enjoy the feeling. After a month, he began to wonder how he had not been killed in combat years before, so basic and clumsy did his old repertoire appear to him now. Every day brought a new task, a new feat to master and assimilate.

In this way, he learned many secret techniques:

The Feat of the Sword-edge.

The Feat of the Sloped Shield.

The Feat of the Javelin and Rope.

The Feat of the Nine Apples.

The Salmon's Leap

The Sickle Chariot.

And a great many more besides...

At last, after two gruelling months, he had finally mastered the entire array of feats in Scátach's system. He arrived for dawn instruction as usual to find Ferdia and Uatach deep in conversation while he performed his stretches and limbering. When Uatach finally turned to address him – itself a deviation from the norm, as Ferdia had been the principal teacher up to this point – CúChulainn dared to believe (with no little pride) that he had reached the apogee of his education.

'We have concluded that you have learned the Feats well,' she whispered softly, her voice just as unsettling as her mother's.

CúChulainn nodded, hopeful.

'Now you are ready to begin.'

She must have read the puzzlement in his eyes, for she continued:

'You have just learned how to play the basic notes. Now you will be shown how to compose the *music!*'

And so it was that over the following two months, CúChulainn discovered how to combine the many feats into ever more elaborate and exquisite sequences, progressions and improvisations. He produced symphonies of violence.

And as he did so, he began to see that Uatach was right – he had only learned to babble; now he was creating poetry.

By the end of the fourth month, both Ferdia and Uatach knew that there was no more he could learn from them. Although neither of them admitted it to CúChulainn, they had never known a student to progress so rapidly.

And neither was exactly sure how that made them feel.

13.

The Unwalked Path

Ferdia stood staring into the mouth of the pitch dark tunnel and felt no fear.

In fact, he felt nothing at all, and this was what bothered him.

Down there somewhere, at the end of this secret passage deep below the keep of the ancient stronghold that had become his home, lay a destiny and mystery that had consumed him from the first day he had come here to learn from the Mistress.

In the flicker of the light thrown from the torch she held he could see her bone-white face, un-emotive as ever, as she stood alongside him.

'I feel no welcome from this place, I must confess. Should it be otherwise?' he asked, not quite sure he wanted to hear a truthful answer.

Her seemingly always pained and rasping voice rarely carried false encouragement, and it would certainly not do so at such a moment as this.

'You have passed all the tests and you live still. Most of the Kin do not even know of the most secret trials that lead to this, the Unwalked Path. You will need all the skills you have learned, and more. But in the end nothing will see you through if it is not desired.'

Ferdia was not pleased by these words, and glancing back into the gloom he felt a surge of righteous anger swell in him.

'Ferdia MacDamann never lost a battle, nor ran from one' he said tightly.

'I know the measure of myself. If this path can be breached, then there's none better than I to do it.'

So saying, Ferdia strode into the darkness.

After just a few steps he became aware of an unseen movement in the dark ahead, small currents of displaced air and strange, heavy, cracking sounds.

Narrowing his eyes, Ferdia called upon his shadow-sight and in a moment, illuminated in dark blues and purples across his vision, he saw what was moving before him - thick roots were uncurling from the earthen sides of the passageway and probing menacingly, *unnaturally* towards him.

177

But the roots could not touch him, for his speed was too great. He flinched and turned and weaved as he started to race down the tunnel, picking up more and more speed as the roots began to multiply and intensify their efforts to grasp him.

Ferdia leaped and ducked as far as he could and his sword flashed out quickly to reduce here and there the number of questing tendrils.

A moment later and his cloak was pulled from his back, his sword engulfed and claimed by the thick roots. Without hesitation, he abandoned these trappings and concentrated on moving forward. The rewards beyond this tunnel, though he knew not their nature, would surely more than compensate for the loss. A thrill ran through him; he had already passed the point where he had failed on his last attempt, and now he felt he was near the end.

Up ahead he saw a tiny sliver of light in the darkness. Victory!

But just as quickly as it had winked into his sight, it was gone, and the roots surged together to form a solid, impassable wall. Ferdia leaped and hurled himself through a slender fissure before that too was sealed up behind him, propelling himself toward the memory of the light.

Yet there was only darkness beyond the fissure.

He had not made it through to the cavern beyond - the roots held him fast, unable to move but seething in frustration.

His body began to feel pressures working against him, pulsing and pushing him back along his path until finally he was roughly expelled from the tunnel entrance, skidding on his back to land at the Mistress's feet.

'It's impossible!' he spat as he accepted her extended hand and leaped deftly to his feet. 'I move like the whistling wind, but to no avail. Perhaps... you were wrong about me.'

Scátach was silent for a moment, her unfathomable black eyes as hard and uncompromising as ever.

'Perhaps. Or perhaps it is not yet time.'

She glided silently back along the tunnel, her ancient robes billowing in the dusty air.

As the torchlight receded, Ferdia was left in darkness.

14.

Fighting Mettle

High up in a recess hidden behind the gloom and foliage of one of the ChrannGréinne's lesser limbs, Ferdia observed CúChulainn training in the main battle-pen below. The four months that the newcomer had spent here may as well have been a lifetime if one was to judge by the prowess with which he now performed the fighting arts of the ShadowKin. Ferdia was sure he had never seen anyone advance so quickly, but the notion did not swell his heart with a teacher's pride. For truly, there wasn't much teaching to it: one merely had to show him but once the subtle techniques and the Uladhman would be competent within an hour. Inside two hours, he would have improvised his own take on the skill. It would have been frightening, had Ferdia been the sort of man to allow fear into his soul.

The leaves draping down from the branch before him turned from green to a deep gold and rustled softly. Ferdia sensed the Mistress Scátach approaching behind him from the shadows.

'Tell me of the progress of our newcomer; does he take to the skills?' she breathed in her dry, cracked voice.

'Take to them?' Ferdia half-snorted. 'He has stolen them and made them his own! He could teach these arts perhaps better than Uatach or I could now. I'm at a loss, there is little more I can show him.'

'Indeed?'

'It is so.' Ferdia turned to see another figure emerge from the shadows. This was the way of the ShadowKin – silent, secret circulation around RathDuille was natural; conversations in the dark could be joined by a stealthy newcomer at any moment. It was Uatach now who moved to join them.

'He has already achieved in four months what often takes a year for many a ShadowKin to master,' she said. 'His skills are impressive... all save his flapping tongue, which he seems unable to discipline.'

'But his arrogance affects not his performance,' Ferdia interjected, as he turned again to face down Scátach's gaze more steadily than ever before. 'I begin to wonder if he might not be already fit to join us in our offensive against Coscrach.'

Scátach marked a moment's pause to study her captain carefully.

179

'Interesting notion, Ferdia. What say you, daughter?'

'He would bring no disgrace to our host. If he wishes to fight, I would take him into battle with confidence.'

'High praise indeed,' Scátach rasped. 'You must know that I only agreed to his training in return for the useful information he brought here. There is something about his destiny that unsettles me. My instincts would rather have him far from this island than near it. '

Ferdia could sense her gaze bearing into him as she spoke these words.

She neither lies nor speaks the truth, she simply is... unsure?

'I would take a closer look at these sublime skills,' she said at last, then moved forward and began to pick her way nimbly down the widening limb of the ChrannGréinne to the leaf-strewn hard-dirt floor where CúChulainn continued to hone his techniques. Ferdia and Uatach, without hurry or sound, followed her down and took up positions upon a heaving mass of knotted roots to watch what was to come.

The task at that moment was wrestling, but what was going on between the barefooted CúChulainn and the rugged, experienced ShadowKin instructor known as Daimh Mór looked like nothing of the sort. CúChulainn had taken a few welts in his first day under the harsh tutelage meted out by Daimh, and had been surprised at his instructor's impressive repertoire of inventive holds, brutal twists and lung-shattering throws to the floor. The impacts would cripple any man, no matter how stout a constitution, had they not learned the correct way to receive such shocks.

But that was on the first day.

On the second he escaped every hold, reversed each torsion of limb and landed on his feet from any attempted throw that the swarthy ShadowKin could come up with.

Today however, CúChulainn had decided to play, and was simply countering every one of Daimh's clutches with exactly the same manoeuvre but with the leverage turned back against his opponent. Contrary to some of his teachers, after a certain amount of time he couldn't teach this wily ShadowKin anything new, so he merely contented himself to mirroring him. But - of course - he couldn't resist offering the occasional jibe.

'I had thought the dancing lessons would come last and be given by more alluring teachers than yourself, Daimh!'

The comment had the desired effect, for Daimh decided to get one up on his arrogant young foe by countering the elbow and wrist-clutch that CúChulainn had applied to him, but in the opposite direction so that the braggart would be necessarily forced against the spike-lined wall. But the Uladhman was counting on this and, keeping hold solely of the other's wrist, he leaped into the air and over Daimh's swiftly moving body; when he landed again he had gravity and surprise on his side, enough to drag the ShadowKin down to his knees on the hard dirt floor. Daimh was on all fours for not even a second, springing up instantly in a strong fighting pose, but all those watching knew that the damage was done, he had been bested there – CúChulainn could have had his head off in that second had he a sword to hand.

The flippant young warrior smiled at his defeated foe and offered an open-handed shrug, but then quickly noticed that he was being observed, and turned to regard Scátach and the others.

'Ah, it's herself!' he called cheerily. 'Have you come to witness my flourishing abilities?'

Ignoring him, Scátach reached out and inspected a thin shooting branch growing from the bole beside her, carefully caressing the small, emerging gold and green leaves upon it. She then stripped off her long robes, hanging them carefully on a mature branch.

'Nay. I've come to participate.'

To a normal mortal it would have seemed that Scátach had uttered these words at precisely the same instant that her foot crashed into the instinctively raised forearms that had just about shielded CúChulainn's throat. She had streamed across the distance as swift as a demon-thrown lance and toppled the mainlander to lie on the very spot where he had forced Daimh Mór to the ground.

Yet still he defended himself well, she thought, for the intention was that the blow would leave him unable to speak, or at least hoarse for a few days.

CúChulainn's warrior's blood was up already and, regaining his feet, he almost launched himself at his attacker but to her genuine surprise he checked himself and fell back, awaiting her next attack. He had learned much since coming here.

'If it's a fight you're after, I'll give you one,' he said tightly. 'But after your sly opener, don't expect me to hold back.'

Scátach pulled forth two short swords from her belt; she flung one at CúChulainn who grasped it.

181

'That's as I would have it. I'm here to kill you boy. Try to die nobly.'

And she was on him again in the blink of an eye, slicing and hacking from one side to another; to the head, to the legs, at the heart, across the neck. And each time CúChulainn narrowly intercepted the mortal course of these strikes with his own blade, all the time weaving and curving his retreating form in an effort to gain some position from where he might conceivably launch a riposte.

The battle-pen, situated between the crook of two massive roots and the outer stone wall of the castle, was ringed with jutting spikes and several spear shafts were still lodged in the high wooden walls set against the bark of the *ChrannGréinne*. The two combatants began to use them now as they delved deep for every trick of combat.

They rocked back and forth across the hollow, at points Scátach chasing CúChulainn as he hurtled up, somersaulting or rebounding off the very body of the Great Tree in his attempt to get into an attacking position. Higher up they went, exiting the pen, leaping from branches and suspended ropes, thrusting at each other from precarious positions. At one upper branch there hung a weapons rack. CúChulainn grabbed the arms and varied his attack. But she adapted and neutralised each weapon, decapitating the point from a lunged spear, parrying a flung knife from the air, leaping onto a raised shield and scoring a swift cut into the back of CúChulainn's thigh.

The young warrior swiftly reached around the shield to clutch Scátach's heels, preventing her from finishing the back flip she had planned; he then flung both shield and woman down from the high branch into the void.

Whatever her skills, there was little Scátach could do against such a plummeting free fall, and so she rolled the shield under her, curled up behind it and let it take the impact.

Grasping at ropes and branches, CúChulainn raced down the tree to her, but she was back on her feet and swinging her weapon even as

he touched the ground. Hoping for some sign of her being dazed, he tried to get inside Scátach's defences to seize the sword arm or knock her off balance, but in so doing he overreached, and she rolled over his dipping back, simultaneously striking his right wrist with her blade. The sharp blow touched the nerve and CúChulainn's hand spasmed, his weapon dropped, and a second later she had him pinned to the ground with the sharp steel of her sword held roughly under his jaw, her cold hand gripping a tuft of his hair.

Her voice seemed no more strained than usual when she spoke.

'That was reasonable, mortal. But after all I had heard, I must confess to being a little disappointed.'

Despite the tightly held blade causing a red line to open on his throat, Cúchulainn twisted his head back as far as he could to look up at his adversary; he even managed to nod slightly.

'Defeat is always a disappointment. Or so I've heard...'

Scátach scowled, then noticed what he was alluding to. Behind her ear hovered a dagger blade, snatched from her own boot when she had leapt over him; amazingly, it was clenched firm and straight between the toes of CúChulainn's backwards-arched right foot!

Scátach's black lips curled back away from her serrated teeth, then she rolled forward with alarming speed, away from any potential dagger strike. CúChulainn simultaneously pushed himself from the ground to bring his neck clear of his foe's weapon. They collided in so doing, and then went rolling along the floor together, exchanging vicious and cynical blows before untangling and leaping up again in fighting postures. Scátach was deathly still; CúChulainn trembled with furious battle-lust. Ferdia and Uatach exchanged anxious glances at the awesome sight of this unique combat.

'Very well,' said Scátach. 'I concede you would be a passable enough fighter, were it not for that insolent wagging tongue of yours. Fortunately for us all, it is not a necessary appendage for a ShadowKin. Let's have it out!'

She unleashed a lighting-fast sword-attack that arced upwards to the side and around so quickly that the air sang. But instead of parrying CúChulainn spun a full turn inside the woman's step, then clapped one hand around her bony wrist whilst seizing her throat with the other.

'No more words then...' he growled at the hissing Danann, then suddenly his body erupted into a juddering, warped mass of twisting flesh as unnatural power surged through him. With a wild flailing of the mutating limbs, Scátach was thrown clear of his grasp.

Landing, as ever, on her feet, she could not prevent her pitch-black eyes from widening on seeing what he had become. A titanic mass of fluctuating muscle, terrible to behold, his hair stood straight up from his head and flames danced there, one eye had grown large whilst the other had disappeared into his skull. Then he launched himself upon her, a whirling cyclone of brutal force.

The Riastrad! The warped warrior! she breathed to herself.

Scátach had her hands full now. CúChulainn rained down blows at her and was gyrating and spinning so quickly - despite his mass - that she could not get a strike past the rock-hard musculature of his windmilling limbs.

'Uatach! Ferdia! He's lost himself! Help me contain the beast!' she yelled.

The two unsheathed their blades and sprang into action – now the fight became even more outlandish than before. The lithe warriors danced around the bellowing behemoth of what was once CúChulainn - now just a howling vortex of fury - inflicting many minor wounds. But they could not slow him down. One by one he pounded them away from him until eventually Scátach stood alone again against the raging giant. A mighty double-fisted blow was parried but still blasted Scátach through a wooden wall to land heavily in an adjoining chamber. Coming to, she witnessed CúChulainn storming in after her through the hole in the shattered boards. The heat she felt around her told Scátach that she had been propelled into the foundry where several ShadowKin made to approach the creature with their hot-tipped irons, but she waved them back.

CúChulainn made to advance, but he was suddenly held fast as ropes flew out from behind him and wrapped tightly around his neck, his waist and his ankles. Scátach could see the rope-wranglers - Ferdia and Uatach employing yet another ShadowKin discipline - separating behind, dividing their weight and immobilising the colossus.

Scátach wasted no time: screeching words heavy with magick which lent her strength beyond mortal understanding, she took hold of a mighty cauldron of cooling water and hefted it at the misshapen young mainlander. He tried to parry it away but the contents flowed out and covered him from head to toe. Huge clouds of vapour rose up around him and a sibilant hissing joined his mad howlings in the chamber.

'Hold, CúChulainn! Be still, Slaughterhound!' Scátach cried, applying the force of Danann magick behind her words. 'I know what it is that boils your blood and contorts your frame so!'

CúChulainn ceased yelling and faced the bone-white woman who slowly walked towards him with appeasing palms outstretched.

'*And* I can show you how to control the beast that dwells within. To tame this supreme anger and harness it so that it obeys your command rather than keeping you a slave to your rage. Hear my words now! Be still, reclaim your body. Become the master of yourself once again. Your nature is revealed to me now. There is no killing to be done here. I had to put you to the test, to know...'

CúChulainn remained warped, his face crunched and disfigured. Panting heavily, he scrutinized the Mistress of the ShadowKin with one outsized eye as she continued to appeal to him, watching the glowing symbols her hands were tracing in the air before her.

'I have answers to your many unspoken questions. For I have lived long and seen such transformations before. It is clear now your arrival here at this time is no mere chance.'

CúChulainn's body slowly started to shrink down to its normal dimensions, and as it did so, it became apparent that his exertions had taken a toll, for he dropped to his hands and knees. Scátach stepped forward and brought him carefully back to his feet; his wounds did not seem grave.

'Come with me now,' she said softly. 'The answers lie below this place, but we have much to discuss before you attempt to quarry the secrets.'

'Aye, so...' he croaked at last.

Scátach dismissed all around her with a hand signal and began to lead an unsteady CúChulainn away. As she left she shot Ferdia a sad glance.

Her captain turned away with a lowered head and a heavy heart.

Scátach and the Quicken Tree

I did not need CúChulainn to tell me what Scátach had revealed to him that night - for I already knew. Only now can I put down and admit this knowledge, and my heart is infinitely relieved in doing so. The doubts that lingered within me were dispelled. Though my faith in Lugh was strong, I knew of the ancient evils that were ranged against him.

Despite never doubting, it was heartening nonetheless to learn that CúChulainn had impressed Scátach well enough for her to reveal to him her secrets.

Or some of them, at least.

Long before Lugh imprisoned him on the Fifth Province, as the Tuatha Dé Danann were finally leaving this land, the abominable worm Crom Cruach, bringing to bear his accursed powers to bend the flow of time to his will, prevented three Danann children from ascending with their kin. He seized them, and hid them away within the folds of space between normal time. And though their mighty parents scoured the land in desperation, they could not locate where the foul creature had spirited them off to. Finally, they had no choice but to leave this plane at the appointed moment, and with utter sadness and regret they abandoned their children to the void.

Delighted with his new playthings, Crom Cruach secretly raised them as his own on Alba, corrupting their divine souls and searing from their memories all notion of their briefly-led former lives. They would come to call him father and he would slowly feed off their increasing power as they grew to adulthood.

From his hidden place beyond the veil, Crom Cruach watched Lugh Samhildánach's crusade to hunt down those rebellious deities who refused to leave the physical realm, the place from which they - like the Crooked Worm - gained such sustenance and pleasure.

The war was long and destructive, and Lugh waged it alone. The Dark Gods had not gone quietly from the lands and forests, and they would eventually destroy all but one of the magickal Quicken Trees that lived in harmony with the Tuatha Dé Danann. Thankfully the last of the trees, the ChrannGréinne, still grew on Alba, tethering the foul maggot to his island prison. Finally, after long years of battle, it seemed the SunGod's great duty was done and Lugh, wounded and weary, disappeared at last.

Enraged to be held thus against his will, Crom Cruach began to exert his strange temporal influences upon the island in endless attempts to thwart the containing power of the ChrannGréinne. But it was no use; he was a prisoner on the shadowy Isle.

But the scheming evil of Crom Cruach knew no end, and he ceased then to draw force from his three hidden children, allowing them to grow in power while he himself weakened and starved. Then, enfeebled and desperate, he released the elder twins – Aifé, whose beauty was without measure, and Scátach, whose spirit blazed like a star – and bade them destroy the Quicken Tree that sickened him so. Loath to see their father suffer thus, they prepared oils and eldritch spells of immolation, and set out to dispatch the hateful thing.

As they approached the place where the ChrannGréinne stood, Scátach and Aifé argued over who would be the one to set the tree alight. Finally Scátach, knowing her sister's vanity and wishing only to carry out the task well, ceded responsibility, saying to Aifé: 'If the act of killing gives you such pleasure, so be it.'

Aifé took her bow and notched an arrow that burned with sorcerous fire. She took several steps back for a truer aim and gazed triumphantly at her target. As she did so, Scátach heard a faint noise from within the tree, and moved forward to lay her ear upon the golden bark.

In that moment the ChrannGréinne leaped into the mind of the young Danann, and instantly opened the gates to her sealed memories. She suddenly knew then who she really was, what Crom Cruach had done to them - and she gasped.

It was then that Aifé shot her magickally-burning arrow toward the tree. But it would never touch its target for Scátach leaped high to intercept it and with a sweeping blow of her glittering sword sent the arrow hurtling back along its trajectory. Aifé tried to avoid it but the arrow was infused with destructive force and it grazed the delicate perfection of her cheek.

Scátach tried to appeal to her sister, to show her the truths hidden within the ChrannGréinne, to open her eyes to her true heritage. But Aifé, maddened by the irreparable damage to her beauty, cursed her foolish sister and attacked her with all her art and hatred. Scátach defended herself but refused to fight back, all the while trying to reach her twin with words. Finally, a great tearing noise ruptured the air around them and Crom Cruach himself appeared from his realm. Chastising Scátach, he reached forth to take her into himself once more... but at that moment the very roots of the ChrannGréinne surged from the earth and seized Crom Cruach tightly. The two great entities thrashed about in a titanic struggle, but in the end the Temporal Worm retreated from the earthly plane, taking the shrieking Aifé with him to Coscrach, where their anger seethed as they plotted revenge. Soon they began to ensnare passing ships, luring the hapless sailors to the cursed west side of the island, dashing their craft upon the cruel rocks and enslaving them. Training them in the dark arts of combat, Aifé and Crom Cruach began, over the years, to assemble an army, one that would become known as the Sluagh, named after the undead phantoms that still haunted Coscrach from the time of Fuilltach. It was created for one purpose alone – to destroy the ChrannGréinne, thereby allowing the Great Worm to break free of Alba at last.

As for Scátach, she was left alone with the Tree, a life of war and bitterness ahead of her. And it spoke directly to her but once more before falling silent.

The words, she would never reveal, but it spoke of a warrior who would come one day to claim the Weapon of Light which, it was destined, would destroy the greatest of evils. It would guard that weapon until then, and Scátach, in turn, would guard the ChrannGréinne.

Using Danann magick, she built a great defensive fortress around the last Quicken Tree, which she named RathDuille – the Fort of the Leaves – and there she made her home. In time, following the call that came to them in their dreams, adventurous mariners with the requisite strength of soul would find their way to the east of that eerie island, penetrating the eternal mists that surround the coasts. And there they would be trained in combat by Scátach, that they might aid her in the defence of the Tree. Word eventually emerged that a mistress of combat resided there, and hardy souls would soon begin to seek out Alba in search of training under the Dark Lady. Some would learn the secrets of combat and leave the island to pursue their own destinies. But many more would stay, bound to defend the Tree in the shadow of RathDuille. They would become known as the ShadowKin.

And so, the two armies of Alba, the Sluagh of Aifé and the ShadowKin of Scátach, remained locked in battle on that haunted island, their numbers sustained by those who found their way through the mists.

15.

Fairing the Foul

Aifé bathed in the summoning pool under the thousand watchful eyes of Crom Cruach. Her delectable form was attended by servants whose eyes were either sewn shut, gouged out or otherwise mutilated; their former identities long lost even to themselves.

With slow, trance-like motions she lifted a polished blue-green urn and used it to gather some water from the pool. Chanting softly all the while, and with an emerald glow about her eyes, she poured it down upon her hair, her yellow tresses turned to dark brown as the water ran through them. Next she lay down the urn and brought up handfuls of water to her face, which she smoothed and massaged, her head tilted backwards, an expression of ecstasy glimpsed behind her gliding hands.

In doing so, her immaculate features changed subtly, becoming rounder about the jaw and stronger about the brow. As she emerged from the pool her attendants scurried forward to dry her body. They hobbled after her to do so, for she went about her preparations with arch indifference to their efforts.

Suddenly, on a whim, she whirled to face one of those blind servants and addressed it in voice that was not now her own.

'Am I not beautiful?'

The confused lackey stammered an affirmative then hurried away into the shadows.

This inane scene was somehow amusing to Crom Cruach's unfathomable spirit. His unnatural voice echoed throughout the chamber; a laugh both impossibly hollow and hysterical.

Aifé turned her transformed face to the endlessly shifting form above her.

'What a dowdy maid this demi-god has chosen for himself, my Master.'

'**Indeed**,' Crom Cruach agreed. '**I too prefer your natural form, but the deception is necessary for my designs.**'

Aifé uttered a short laugh at the futility of the feelings of vanity that Crom Cruach's words evoked in her. Her father, though prisoner on the Isle, could project his intelligence beyond it; he had spies everywhere on the mainland and it was he who had infused her mind with the shape she had

189

now taken. This was stronger magick than her usual illusions - it had to be, for she knew that her target was canny.

'Of course. It is his loss in any case. But now, to matters - I am ready for the journey, Father. Were the sacrifices to your liking?'

So saying she plucked an ornate incense burner and, taking careful steps in a complicated pattern beneath Crom Cruach's shifting apparition, waved it to and fro, adding thick yellow fumes to the weirdly-lit chamber.

'**Yess**,' Crom Cruach gurgled in contentment. '**They were sufficient to imbue me with the power to accomplish this act. Yet I long for the day when my strength will return to its former magnitude... but come now. It is time. I am your portal. Be swift my daughter for my influence is finite.**'

The heaving mass of the bloated worm reared forward then, and his hideous maw yawned wide open, peeling back in upon itself to create a cavernous opening. His lower mouth touched the floor of the chamber, and Aifé stepped forward.

Beyond her lay a slowly tilting landscape of stars winking in and out of the inky darkness with spots of even greater darkness moving behind, like shapes pushing against a black curtain. It was a cold, dead place and she fought for a moment against a primordial dread of annihilation. She knew to enter this realm was an act contrary to all laws of nature, but she smiled and walked forward into the void.

*****

Upon her chair of meditation, set high up into the bole of the great tree ChrannGréinne, Scátach sat running her whetstone along the length of her sword's blade. She was reflecting over recent events with CúChulainn. By all the old gods, but he was strong! She had never before been bested in combat; the idea itself was unthinkable! Hissing, she quickly rebuked herself for the vanity of dwelling on these churlish thoughts for even an instant, for there were far greater concerns at play. And though there was a certain elation in the possibility she dared now to consider, there was also the sadness of disappointed hope. She had been so certain of Ferdia. He had shown all the qualities of which the Great Tree murmured to her nightly - why did it resist him at that final stage? Through her own divinations she could perceive that destiny was wrapped tightly around him, yet

based on what she had seen these last few weeks with the newcomer... there was no use denying it, the signs were clear.

But the imminent attack on Coscrach was where her immediate concerns should be focused, Scátach reminded herself.

Soon enough, Aifé. Soon it will be your time.

As she pondered these things Scátach pressed her whetstone hard along the edge of her blade and with violent jerks tore sparks free from the metal with each passing, leaving a sharpness there that would split granite. Suddenly, a great cold descended on her and she noticed two things simultaneously: firstly, that all noise had immediately ceased in RathDuille. The murmurs of conversation, the footfalls, the clamour of training or dining - all were cut off as surely as her blade would truncate the screams of a beheaded foe. The second was that the sparks that she had just launched from her sharpening still hung in the air, flickering ever so slightly. She knew then, before even trying that she would not be able to move. But try she did, and anger coursed through her at the confirmation of the complete paralysis that held her body fast. She was frozen and powerless, like every other living thing in RathDuille.

Time itself had been seized and was being held hostage.

Crom! she screamed bitterly in her head.

*****

CúChulainn drove his sword into the misshapen skull of the creature that had brutally attacked Emer. The revolting head of the beast was a multitude of horns, beaks, claws and black feathers. As it squealed in agony and stumbled back CúChulainn realised that, in fact, it was no slavering monster but Forgall Manach he had killed. The general lay dead at his feet, a pool of blood gathering beneath him, but there was something wrong - his body was not really that of a man, but rather an infant with Forgall's head. Emer, terribly wounded, was behind him screaming at him, cursing him, telling him to pick the child up. Confused and frightened, CúChulainn did so and as he peered again at the bloody figure in his arms, it changed once more, into a tentacled, parasitic horror that launched itself at his face.

He woke up with a start. And swore vehemently.

Emer!

What utter madness was that? Was Lugh trying to tell him something through his dreams? No, surely the SunGod did not communicate with such horrific scenes. CúChulainn was certain that there was dark sorcery at play. It was then that he sensed the tinge of wyrdness to his surroundings. The simple cell suddenly felt strange, even for the erratic

Isle of Shadows. But before he had time to speculate on the nature of his feelings his attention was drawn to a further abnormality. The stone wall across from him, just below the small, barred square that afforded some measure of Alba's oddly refracted moonlight, was beginning to ripple as though it were the surface of a pond. The rippling grew more intense and the stone darkened, then disappeared, and CúChulainn seemed to be staring at the starry night sky beyond. A moment later and a shadow emerged from this firmament and when it stepped further into the room CúChulainn gasped in utter stupefaction.

It was Emer.

He leapt up from his bed and stepped towards her, his arms open, shaking his head, searching for some way to grapple with this improbability. Surely it was another dream?

'Shhh. I am here, my sweet Setanta. Be at peace, no ill has befallen me. Save for the constant loneliness I feel since your leaving. How I feared I would never know your tender embrace once again.'

'But how can you...' CúChulainn managed to begin. 'You are not here; this place is too far... You...'

Emer smiled and laid her hands on CúChulainn's cheeks.

'Be not troubled, for this is a dream. And a good one at that. Don't you know that a longing heart can span great distances and turn the mind to its own will? Where else would I be but in your fondest dreams, my love?'

Relief flooded CúChulainn's embattled mind then, and he drew his arms around his heart's desire.

'This dream is to my liking then, fair Emer. For in my darker moments I too had feared I would never again grasp you to me. An unbearable thought.'

With slow but steady steps Emer and CúChulainn drew close to one another as the moon draws the tides and the waves fall upon the rocks.

Seething with desire, CúChulainn took the woman in his arms and to his bed, and with time unmoving around them, proved his burning love to her – convincingly, and more than once.

16.

Rude Awakening

CúChulainn lay in a spent stupor. Behind his closed eyes whirled a world of pleasing shades and colours that soothed his mind. Desirous forms drifted towards him and enlaced themselves around his very soul. He lazed carelessly in this afterglow for an untellable time until he heard Emer's voice and opened his eyes to see the dark hair which lay upon his chest.

'Tell me of the wonders you have seen in this strange place, my love,' she said, the words entering his heart, loosening his will, gently reigning in the swift-charging course of his thoughts.

'Many are the wonders, Emer. And strange to tell,' he responded shaking his own head slightly as he marvelled at his feeling of overwhelming well-being.

'Incredible feats performed, indomitable warriors from strange faraway lands gathered here to learn the ways of Scátach, and if you could see RathDuille! A mysterious castle built around a sacred tree... I can hear it speak to me softly when I sleep...'

'Indeed? How many warriors have you met? As many as at Eamhain?'

'Close to ten hundreds by my reckoning. And each worth ten ordinary soldiers.'

'And what of your new mistress? Does she treat you harshly?'

CúChulainn chuckled lightly at this.

'Scátach? We traded tough blows and words, 'tis true, but she is a powerful soul and a great commander. My gut tells me she will lead us to a famous victory over her enemies on the morrow.'

'*The morrow*?' gasped Emer. 'Your assault on Coscrach is to happen so soon?'

A sudden lance of uncertainty drove its way into CúChulainn's stuporous mind. His natural clarity of thought battled for an instant to illuminate the source of this doubt but the veil of intoxication hung heavily over him and he struggled to identify it.

But then it came. His instinct surged through his blood and roared in his ears. Something was not right.

'Emer... how do you to know the name of that fortress?'

Emer turned languidly around then and slid her face near CúChulainn's, offering a few playful nibbling kisses to his lips. Lips that now remained resolutely shut. Frowning, she sat up and, still straddling him, she lay one hand on his chest and spoke slowly.

'Coscrach? The name is well known to many. And, my love, the day is nigh when all will tremble at its mention. For that is the stronghold of Aifé of the Bloody Tears, the Witch Queen of Alba!'

Under normal circumstances CúChulainn would have been ready to spring into attack, but the lethargic forces around him had instantly become something harder, pinning him down now with violent insistence rather than seductive coaxing. So it was with a will beyond all mortal ken that he managed to bring up his forearms to block the blade that the creature wearing Emer's face drove down upon him. She had slyly taken CúChulainn's own sword from where it lay at the foot of the bed.

The confused warrior only barely managed to lock his forearms in close to the hilt in time to prevent the killing blow, the blade instead cutting shallowly into his right shoulder. The creature straddling him then shook her dark hair and in an instant the colour flowed away revealing the unnatural yellow that was its true hue, and when CúChulainn looked upon her face he no longer saw his beloved Emer but the sensually angular countenance of a woman who he knew instinctually to be of pure Danann stock. She laughed melodiously as she mocked him.

'Oh brave fighting man! Do you have any notion of your weakness? I know so many ways to make you scream. And not always in ecstasy!'

CúChulainn struggled with all of his might to shrug himself out from under her, his confused rage mixed with humiliation. But he found himself still moving too sluggishly to be effective.

Faster than a heartbeat, Aifé seized him by the throat and sprang to her feet upon the bed, dragging the warrior up with her as though he weighed but a feather.

'But such a pretty, weak thing nonetheless,' she exhaled, then drew his face to hers and crushed his lips with a forceful kiss before flinging him down roughly to the stone floor with a snarl of contempt.

As infuriated as he was by the trickery played upon him, CúChulainn still found himself clumsy against the heavy magickal energies weighing down upon him. He hauled himself to his feet nonetheless to face the gloating witch.

'Ecstasy? Don't count on it, creature, I've had better!'

Aifé smiled indulgently at that for a fraction of a second, then snapped open her jaws to unleash an inhuman shriek that warped the very nature of the physical world around them with its fell power.

The shockwave of the cry blasted CúChulainn off his feet and he was sent rebounding off the wooden door behind him, landing in a crumpled heap on the stone floor once again. He had never been hit so hard by anything in his life. Blood pooled under his face from his nose and ears. His ribs and spine still felt as though they were reverberating from the blow. It was pain of a wholly novel kind.

But CúChulainn pulled himself back up, first to his knees, then, with the aid of his hands, to his feet and, eventually, raised his head to face his adversary once again.

'Aaaaah,' said Aifé in mocking praise. 'Such resistance. Such pleasure I'll have in breaking you.'

But her gloating was cut short by another ear-rupturing cry, and CúChulainn's back was sprayed with wood splinters as the door behind him shattered and flew apart.

He saw Aifé's face turn suddenly stark white for a moment, then her eyes blazed with a green light.

'My my, Sister. You must have some strength left in you to move about freely against the grip of Crom Cruach. Though I doubted you myself, Betrayer, our Master still knows the extent of your powers.'

CúChulainn managed to turn and saw Scátach standing at the ruined doorway, her eyes burning with a violet light and her glittering sword held down in front of her.

'Your flesh will bear witness to that strength, Sister,' Scátach rasped grimly. 'You will scream long 'ere you die from the wounds I will inflict, and suffer tenfold for each ShadowKin you have had your depraved way with.'

Aifé's lip curled up slightly.

'*Please*,' she mocked.

Then she emitted another fierce shriek which hit CúChulainn again in the chest and sent him forcefully soaring towards Scátach like a stone from a catapult - but one which didn't find its mark, for the shadowy one ducked under his hurtling form and moved into the room to face her sister.

As CúChulainn passed from the chamber his momentum was abruptly stopped and he hung in mid-air, frozen under the influence of Crom Cruach's time suspension. All he could do was dangle there and watch as the two Dananns launched into a combat which was a frenzied exchange of unimaginable skill. And as he watched he realised he had never seen true fighting before. Physical, magickal, supernatural. Scátach had clearly been holding back during their own battle. He felt suddenly young and foolish and inept, and all he could do was seethe in embarrassed fury and hang in this ridiculous posture.

Inside the room the two forms whirled and clashed, at times projecting themselves at one another from the stone walls whilst trailing energy beams, both luminous green and violet, enmeshed around the figures, searching to trip or hinder the opponent's blows or movements. But the battle was to be brief, for suddenly the wall behind Aifé shuddered and peeled open again and she leaped back towards the stars and inky blackness the opening revealed. Scátach, spinning forward horizontally to avoid a parting salvo of green energy, stabbed at Aifé's heart with her sword, but she was already leagues away from that place and the blade clattered and sparked against the unyielding bare wall.

With Aifé departed, Crom's powerful hold over RathDuille gave way at last and CúChulainn toppled heavily to the floor.

Instantly Scátach was standing over him; she took his arm and yanked him roughly to his feet.

'How much did you tell her?' she growled.

CúChulainn gritted his teeth and shut his eyes in shame.

'Too much.'

Scátach stormed past him then with a hiss of irritation and CúChulainn heard her cries as she began stalking around the fortress shouting orders to the emerging ShadowKin who were now once again able to move.

He staggered into the room and leaned against the wall from where Aifé had materialized. There he hammered his fists in bitter frustration against the uncaring stone.

Sweet Danú, what had he done?

196

17.

The Doom of Clan Manach

Set upon the slanted wattle-and-daub roof of the Craobh Ruadh and encircling the golden shaft of the Red Branch itself, that thrust up from the throne chamber below, were four large barrel-shaped drums. The four young Machra lads, whose job it was to pound these deer-skin tambours, were trained to beat the rhythm of dozens of particular signals. These ancient and revered instruments were used to summon warriors to the meeting chamber whenever King Conchobar desired their presence.

Each veteran knight or important elder had their own beat and would be expected to hurry along without delay to where the Red Branch grew and decisions of the highest importance were made.

At the moment one of those beats echoing around Eamhain told Amergin that the king desired his presence.

His was, of course, the most common drum-beat heard and generally the first in any series.

It had been hammering out for a good while now.

Grumbling, and pulling his cloak around him against the unrelenting autumn rain, the druid hauled closed the door of his hut and tottered down the creaking wooden stair that wound about his curious dwelling.

At the foot of the stairs there stood an equally well-wrapped figure, barring his way.

Amergin's grumbling grew more intense on seeing this potential intruder upon his thoughts, but drawing closer he observed that it was the young Emer Manach who stood shivering in the rain before him.

'Can you spare me a moment, O sage?'

The girl was no doubt still displeased at their sending the boy away on a perilous errand once again. Amergin had not been immune to her acid glances whenever he crossed the young maiden's path. He didn't have time for this right now.

'There are many moments for you to avail yourself of me outside the times of conference, fair Emer. I must keep my mind clear to endure my daily summonings to the king. Especially so in these inauspicious times.'

Emer did not budge from her position at the foot of the stairs.

'My worry will take but a moment to convey, wise master. And I feel this is a matter that may have dire consequences for every person at Eamhain!'

Amergin heard the earnestness in her voice so he sighed and, with a gesture, he invited Emer to walk alongside him then they made their way at a brisk pace towards the Craobh Ruadh.

'Speak quickly, child - the drums of gathering have fallen silent; the king will think me away in the woods.'

Emer seemed to hesitate and said nothing for several steps and so Amergin stopped to allow her time to pose her questions.

'It's this woman, Mag,' she began.'I... suspect her of much. But she is wily... and I have no proof of her ill doings. I...' Emer broke off, shaking her head. Amergin could clearly see the frustration and anxiety of the girl.

'And what deeds or words aroused such harsh suspicions? She speaks not in the court,' remarked the druid.

Emer bit her lip and looked searchingly into Amergin's black eyes.

'Not openly, no. But she makes her will known through the voice of my father. Surely you have seen this yourself?'

Amergin made a carefully noncommittal gesture, then thought about it a little longer and found himself nodding his assent.

'And...' Emer glanced furtively around her before continuing.

'And... I have learned that it was in fact *she* who was behind sending CúChulainn away to his doom! My father had never even heard of this Isle of Shadows 'til she spoke of it, I'm sure of that. She is hungry for power. She is far from a brow-beaten peasant from a razed village. I would advise against giving credence to my father's counsel while she lurks at his shoulder.'

The force of Emer's willful nature coaxed a smile of appreciation from Amergin and he gently traced his thumb across her forehead as though to smooth out the creases caused by her consternation.

'You have your father's keen perception, Emer. Or at least that which I had always known him to possess. At first I too had harboured suspicions about this Mag. Yet... when I think on it now it seems that each time I attempted to scrutinise this unease, my thoughts were led away, distracted by more pressing concerns. Curious how the matter has evaded my full attention until now. Perhaps I am getting old, or perhaps...'

Amergin glanced over at the entrance of the Craobh Ruadh. Then he waved his arms about his head in exaggerated disarray.

'Ack! The squabbling will have commenced inside. If I'm not there to calm the yammerings of the men there will be sourness between the king and myself for a week!'

He took two steps towards the Great Hall, turned quickly and offered a curt bow to the young Manach girl.

'My gratitude, Emer. My mind was a stagnant pool and your words are stones creating ripples. We'll talk again soon.'

Then, muttering audibly to himself and scratching his head, the eccentric old druid trudged into the ever-boisterous atmosphere of the Great Hall of Eamhain Mhacha.

Emer waited several moments then, checking the knife hidden under her cloak, she too entered.

*****

As befitting her standing as daughter to the General of the Red Branch Knights, Emer Manach had the right to sit upon one of the wooden benches that ringed the strategy table of the Craobh Ruadh, where all military decisions were made in the presence of king Conchobar.

Formerly her mother had sat next to her on such occasions as this, but now it was her father's lover Mag who had that honour. Even if matters were not as grim as she and Amergin suspected, this would have rankled Emer somewhat as since her arrival the woman had not ceased trying to meddle in her private affairs. She had even gone as far as taking steps to arrange possible suitors for Emer, knowing full well that she was promised to CúChulainn. Yes, it displeased her to have Mag next to her but she was certain, as she glanced across the chamber to Amergin who nodded gently back in response. For the time being it was the best place for her.

Ah, Setanta, she thought, her heart heavy. *I need your strength, your smile, your arms. Nothing less will do.*

She had, of course, brusquely turned away every advance – fine warriors though they may have been – but it was the simple fact that Mag was making these decisions for her that didn't sit well. Who had she thought she was anyway? She was more or less a foreigner to Uladh. Still, her father was absorbed by her and if Mag brought him happiness, then so be it. But was he happy? He hadn't exactly been himself lately and this convening in the Craobh Ruadh was proof of that. Conchobar was forcefully expressing his discontent to the general in front of the whole fort. There was an overall lack of confidence in the latest strategies of the great tactician Manach.

And Emer kept her eye on Mag.

'I take your point, my king,' Forgall managed to interject at the end of the latest admonishment. 'But matters have changed somewhat since the long mild days of Lughnasa. We must alter our plans as circumstances dictate. If I have learned anything during all my years as your master of war-strategy, it is this.'

'I can't make head nor tail of you of late, Forgall!' Conchobar thundered. 'First you advocate patience and send our mightiest warrior, and dare I say it, challenger to your own position at Eamhain, on some perilous crusade. And yet, now that CúChulainn has gone, a sudden urgency to attack wells up from within you. You stand here advising us to press forward unprepared against the twofold threat of Connacht and their dire new allies when before you claimed our forces could not hope to match their mettle on the fighting field!'

Conchobar leaned forward on his high throne and stared hard at his general.

'What are you at, at all?'

Frowning, Forgall took a deep breath and scratched for a second at his bandaged shoulder before speaking with a dull, expressionless voice.

'I am prepared to concede that sending the boy away was an error on my part. A romantic folly, maybe. But he is only one man at the heel of the hunt, and even if he were to return with these vaunted skills it would simply take too long to train our knights in those arcane ways. It is unfortunate, but as things now lie there is no longer time for such luxuries. Supply boats from Connacht were seen moving along the river Sinann, and according to my scouts they are using this route to bolster a great army gathered secretly near Lough Ramor, a mere day's ride from our borders.'

An anxious murmur rippled through the assembled warriors at this announcement. Suddenly Amergin was on his feet; and, moving toward Forgall, he began to slowly circle the general as he spoke.

'Forgall's words carry much weight in this court on matters of strategy and tactics. However, I fear his grasp of knowledge of the land is slipping. For it would be a fine stallion indeed that would carry a fully-laden siege warrior from Lough Ramor to our battlements in a single day! Furthermore, I am no battle master, but surely there are more favourable places whence a wise enemy might decide to strike at us.'

He paused for a moment to stare deep into Forgall's eyes and, seeing this, Emer became tense with anticipation. At the same time, she could feel Mag stiffening beside her. Amergin continued in his soft-spoken way.

'The armies of Connacht are not yet ready to mount a realistic attack on Eamhain Mhacha. There is time yet...'

He now circled around behind Forgall.

'...is this not so, General?'

Forgall's voice was a strange mixture of burgeoning anger and distracted confusion.

'I know not what you try to imply, Sage, but I....'

The general cut off his own sentence with a cry of pain, for Amergin had swiftly wrenched away the dressing covering Forgall's wound, revealing a long, claw like talon embedded in the flesh; this he tore out without a moment's hesitation and brandished to the court whose gasps and oaths rang out loudly.

Conchobar started to his feet and, from where she sat beside Emer, Mag stood and turned to leave but was confronted with the dagger that Emer had pointed at her breast. The general's daughter smiled and nodded at the other but was disappointed to find not the slightest hint of fear in that darkening face. She merely turned her head to regard Amergin and the scene unfolding before her. The sage was holding aloft the wickedly-curved black claw.

'Behold, Conchobar, it is as I had feared – Forgall's mind was not his own, but tainted by the poison of this claw for the purpose of a dark spirit.'

'What fresh madness is this?' roared Conchobar, livid with fury, causing the golden apples on the silver bough on the wall behind him to jingle and echo.

'Has our great general played us false? Enough! He dies!' Emer could see that Conchobar's battle rage had erupted; there was nothing worse than treachery for a Red Branch Knight. It was the highest transgression and swift death was always deemed the appropriate sentence no matter how close the ties or long-held the friendship.

'Hold! Stay your sword arm, Conchobar!' barked the sage.

Amergin alone had the sway to address the king in this manner, and Conchobar acquiesced but his face remained a mask of disgust and anger.

'The general speaks, now with his own voice I should think,' said Amergin.

He took Forgall by the arm and, with a sweeping gesture of his hand towards the assemblage, urged him to talk.

'I knew my words were... untrue...' he began hesitantly.

'...even as I uttered them. Yet I was powerless to correct them. What was wrong seemed right, in a way I cannot explain. Some... sinister force compelled me to spew forth these lies and half-truths... Oh Forgall, what has become of you?'

He took his head in his hands and sunk to his knees.

'Chide yourself not, Forgall,' said Amergin, a mounting tone of menace in his voice. 'For the blame rests here, in this object of evil. Indeed its presence clouded the minds of many who were near it. To my shame, even I was blinded to its darkness. But no more!!'

Then, with speed that surprised all, Amergin uttered three words in an unknown tongue and hurled the claw into the roaring fire to the left of the chamber. It ignited with an unearthly plume of purplish light and at the same time a hideous scream was heard. Those around the screeching figure of Mag stepped back and watched as she doubled over clutching her hand, trails of bluish-black smoke escaping through her fingers. Emer was too dumbfounded to react; she too merely stared at the strange spectacle.

'So! The succubus is revealed!' shouted Amergin, and began to hold back the curious. 'Who else but *she* has dressed the curiously unhealing wounds of Forgall and has been using this court for her own ends for months now?'

Conchobar had taken up his sword once again and stepped grimly forward to where the cowled form of Mag hunched kneeling on the floor.

'Such treachery before the Red Branch itself! A woeful day for this court – her head will be forfeit!'

Several warriors advanced upon Mag, jostling to deal the killing strike. But a sudden bone-chilling wail completely unmanned them, instantly draining the colour from their faces. They dropped their weapons to the floor and quailed before the form now rising up to challenge them. Those in attendance would tell the tale again and again of the ghastly, twisted thing that rose up from the floor of the Craobh Ruadh that day, even though it was glimpsed for only a few brief moments, and over the years the versions would change or become disputed. But the usual description was of a dread, black spectre with long, curved beak and talons, and an expression of pure hatred apparent upon its loathsome face, if face it could be called.

Emer alone amongst those doughty men managed to keep a grip of her dagger. It seemed that the unspeakable wail was more effective on the menfolk who trembled and turned their heads away from this blasphemous demon. Emer too was petrified, and when the hideous thing swung to face her the instinctive strike she unleashed was feeble and far from its mark. The black creature, indigo smoke trailing its movements, lashed out with the talon of one wing-like arm, stabbing Emer deeply in the abdomen.

'A gift for you before I depart. May you long know grief, my dear!' she heard Mag's voice utter in her head.

Then, with the hateful smoke suffocating those around, the apparition turned and twisted, its shape becoming that of a great crow which immediately took flight and hurtled out of one of the high open apertures of the Craobh Ruadh.

Emer crumpled to the floor, her hands cradling her midriff, her gown stained with blood.

Forgall, now free from the paralyzing effects of the demon crow's presence, ran to where his daughter had collapsed, calling her name in a cry of pure anguish.

'Oh, my child...' he wept, as he cradled her in his arms.

Conchobar hurled his sword to the ground, and turned to speak to Amergin but the sage was already hurrying to where Emer lay and so the king followed him.

'Speak true, Sage!' he said, clapping an arm on Amergin's shoulder. 'Could that have been... *She*? The Dark Maiden of the battlefield, whose name I dare not utter?'

Amergin, kneeling now and reaching in to peer at Emer's wound, turned his wizened head and nodded gravely at the king.

'It was *she*. We have been blind. Let us hope our error is not the ruination of us all.'

203

Conchobar was silent for a moment; he stared furiously at where the dark goddess had flown, then down at the distraught Forgall.

'And what of CúChulainn?' he wondered aloud.

'I fear he may be in great danger,' Amergin answered.

18.

CúChulainn and Ferdia

CúChulainn sat quietly in his crude cell, the modest chamber which had become his home over these past months. So much had happened in recent days that he had scarcely had a moment to fully grasp the gravity of matters. As he etched another mark onto the stone walk, a record of the passage of days – futile, he knew, but an important part of his daily ritual – his thoughts flitted between the curious conversations he'd had with Scátach after their sparring session; to the impostor Aifé's infiltration of his cell, his bed, his... very manhood. These memories were troubling to him, and the feeling was worsened by a sudden sense that, somewhere, the real Emer was in peril. He shook such thoughts from his head and attempted to return to pondering Scátach's words – she had spoken much of prophecy, and destiny, and a great task that would fall to a ShadowKin. His attempts to make sense of her cryptic speech were interrupted, however, by a firm knock on the freshly-repaired door.

'Aye,' he shouted, casting away the sharp flint in frustration, his etching finished. As Ferdia strode in, CúChulainn sighed deeply and dropped his hands to his knees.

'Did you not say we were finished for the day, Ferdia? I am weary and have much on my mind just now.' Indeed, Ferdia noted, the younger man did look exhausted, and certainly the last few days had found him much less exuberant than his trainer had become accustomed to. More than likely it was due to his guilt at having betrayed Scátach's battle plans to the enemy, forcing the Mistress to abandon the attack that had been planned some days back. Nonetheless, this sullen demeanour on the part of the Uladhman had concerned Ferdia who, despite himself, had grown to enjoy the witty banter and outbursts of ridiculous bravado which usually accompanied his tutelage. Still, Ferdia had his own reasons to feel a heaviness of heart, and they were closely tied to the arrival of CúChulainn. But even still, he found he could not help *liking* the man.

'Don't worry, you've more than mastered all the feats already, hard enough as it is for me to believe that you did in so short a time,' he said, taking a seat opposite CúChulainn. 'All bar the Feat of the Nine Apples, which, in truth is of little use in the throes of combat.'

CúChulainn chuckled. 'I never was much good at juggling, unless 'twere the heads of my foes. Why does Scátach make you learn such things?'

'The mistress is... *strange*. And in more than just form. She maintains that each of the Tasks will serve a ShadowKin well one day in combat, but it is up to that warrior himself to decide when and how.'

CúChulainn considered this for some moments.

'I shall endeavour to remember that.' Silence descended, and he could tell by the uneasy stillness of Ferdia that something else, something of importance, was on his mind. He waited, and finally the captain broached the topic that was troubling him.

'She told you then, did she?'

CúChulainn had expected this, sooner or later.

'Of this prophecy business?' he asked, then nodded blankly in the affirmative.

'Aye, I suspected as much,' said Ferdia. 'Speak truly now, CúChulainn! Was this the real reason you came here?'

'Not at all,' he replied softly, 'I knew of no prophecy, no *Quicken Tree*. I told you the truth when first you found me. In many ways I came here to *escape* prophecy, but I suppose Amergin and the rest knew what they were up to.' He laughed ruefully at this.

Ferdia seemed encouraged by this, but his expression – CúChulainn could see, even through the traces of war-paint that had not come off during the day's training – was still troubled.

'I knew nothing of it either when first I came to these shores. Like yourself, when I learned what the Shadowy One could offer I sought only to learn the magnificent skills of legend, but when Scátach got it into her head that I was the one that she has been waiting for all these years... well, everything changed. I too became obsessed with the quest; a renewed vigour came to my heart, the concerns of my former life fell away like the autumn leaves - all that mattered was to fulfil Scátach's dream, to become the great hero foretold.'

His voice had grown excited as the memory of his obsession returned to him, but then he paused, took a deep, shaky breath, and when he continued, his tone was softer, and filled with sadness.

'Now it seems that it is not Ferdia who is destined for this glorious path. Not Ferdia the Deluded but you, my friend, upon whom the honour will fall. I am much fond of you, CúChulainn of the Red Branch, but I cannot say your coming here has not brought great sadness to my heart.'

CúChulainn sighed heavily at this, remained silent for a few moments and then attempted to change this uncomfortable topic. He had grown equally fond of Ferdia over the months of training, and preferred not to be reminded that he himself was the cause of the destruction of his dreams.

'You say you came here to learn the skills of Alba, but skills are not an end unto themselves - what were your motives, what would you have used those skills for if there was no prophecy to claim your mind? Revenge? I think not, you are too noble a man for such low desires. Power? Again, no. You're wise enough to know such glory is fleeting. *Honour*? Yes... Honour. You are a man of honour, Ferdia MacDamann. Is this not so?'

'Honour.' Ferdia smiled as he considered the word. 'I once held such a virtue. A long time ago, in happier days, before some saw fit to strip it from my house. I was drawn here along a... complicated path. Some dire decisions were made - I was young, rash, violent. One day everthing came apart... but I can't remember it all clearly now...'

Ferdia clenched his fists and regarded them. CúChulainn remained silent, allowing the other man the time to scrabble at the door of painful memories, to find his words. He could sense a terrible sorrow and anger there, most of the latter directed inward.

'Perhaps it was the Tree that called me, perhaps it was pure chance. In any case, I ended up here and Scátach gave me new purpose. For many years I thought it was my destiny to learn the ways of the Mistress so that one day I would return to my land and restore honour to my name by leading an army with skills beyond compare, and be held in great esteem once more. My family's commitment in battle would never be questioned again, and I would weigh honour against duty with greater wisdom.

'I have not dwelt on such things in a long time.'

He hung his head, then looked up and stared out the small window towards the sea. Finally he rose, as if to leave, but CúChulainn spoke again and Ferdia paused awhile longer to let his friend finish.

'If I do succeed in breaching the hidden chamber and retrieving the treasures that are said to lie therein, then you should be *glad*, Ferdia. Glad that the burden falls to me, for then you will be free of this long-held obligation and may yet return to your true kin and restore the name of the clan Damann. You should not mourn the loss of being held in thrall to the whims of the Gods and the games they play with men, for those who are marked to become legends are often doomed to an early grave, and I would not like such a fate to befall you 'ere your true purpose be fulfilled.

'For it is the deeds of men - and not the decree of the Gods - that will determine who are truly remembered as legends. And if the name of CúChulainn is to be recalled in ages hence, then my heart tells me that the name of Ferdia will oft be uttered in the same breath. And with equal reverence.'

Ferdia nodded and mustered a faint smile at this new prophecy. He clapped CúChulainn on the shoulder by way of acknowledgement and thanks.

'When are you to make your attempt against the roots of ChrannGréinne?' he asked.

'At first shadowlight. Scátach would dearly desire any advantage we could garner against Coscrach's defences.'

'Yes, and good luck on that score. We'll need everything on our side if we are to defeat Aifé and the Sluagh horde. Coscrach has never been penetrated - we have much to discuss in terms of strategy.'

A little later, Ferdia returned to the Uladhman's cell and produced a sheepskin map over which the pair began to strategise. He seemed more at ease now, more comfortable that he was again dealing with tangible things like battles, tactics and defences. And CúChulainn, for his part, was glad that his words had gone some way toward alleviating his friend's anguish.

19.

Sorrow's Bedside

Following the thwarting of the Morrigan and her subsequent assault, Amergin had commanded that Emer be brought to his hut upon the hillock at Eamhain Mhacha. There he had at hand all the medicines necessary to ease her awful suffering and put her on the path to convalescence.

His druidic knowledge surpassed any in the land; this was known to all. For none had travelled further, nor had wider experience of the ancient ways than he. It was even murmured that he was of Danann blood himself. But even if this were not so, the truth was that there were certain things that he knew and sights that he had seen which would have long ago led most men down the trail of madness. Things that, in view of the events of late and the bitter results of his striving to restore Emer's health, might once again cast their shadow on his life – and also perhaps, on the lives of all those around him.

Forgall, inconsolable, had not left his daughter's bedside since she had been brought here. Even to the point where he hindered somewhat Amergin's ministrations. But the druid was conscious of the mortification that gnawed the general's spirit, and would cast no further harsh judgement upon him. The loss of Conchobar's total trust, and that of many of the Red Branch, was bitter enough and Forgall would have much to do to restore his position.

If ever he did.

Emer slept now and Amergin sat at his rough table surrounded by myriad jars and urns of exotic liquid substances, plant extracts, powders and herbal preparations. In his hands now he carefully manipulated a phial of transparent stone filled with what looked to Forgall like blood mixed with earth and milk.

'Curse these faerie folk and their supernatural ilk,' muttered the weary general - for perhaps the seventeenth time this evening, at Amergin's reckoning. But it turned out he had more to say than usual tonight, which perhaps was a good sign at last. And good signs were rare at Eamhain Mhacha these days.

'Twice now they have ruined this foolish creature Forgall Manach and robbed him of all that he held dear to his heart. Curse them, curse them all to the ends of Eirú...'

Amergin ceased his inspection of the phial and its strange contents, then murmured coarsely before standing and moving past Forgall to inspect Emer's wound once again.

He traced his fingers lightly down the jagged, yellow, bruise-ringed cut which trailed downwards from above the left hip to finish high on the right thigh. Amergin was certain now of the full, sad purport of the insidious wound: revealed and routed, the Morrigan had struck at the very essence of Emer's femininity.

The sage seated himself at the edge of the bed and placed his hand on Forgall's shoulder. He saw the tortured blend of anger and remorse in the general's eyes when the broken man at last turned his head toward him.

'That we were able to tend to her so quickly has allowed me enough time to ensure that her life is not in danger, Forgall.'

Forgall winced and pressed his own hand on Amergin's arm, shaking his gratitude into the druid's flesh.

'Thank you, Amergin. I knew you, at least, wouldn't fail.'

'But...' said the older man, and Forgall stiffened, his face immobile once again.

'...the claws of the Dark One tore deeply into poor Emer, and wrought much destruction. Too much.'

With his other hand Forgall smoothed away some strands of hair from Emer's face with a father's tenderness.

'Speak plainly Amergin. What do you mean?'

The sage regarded him sourly but spoke with infinite compassion.

'The line of Manach ends with Emer. She will never bear children, Forgall.'

And the darkness that descended upon Forgall then was deeper than the wing of any demon-crow that had ever been vomited forth from the foul places of the earth.

Part III

Gods and Mortals

1.

Roots

CúChulainn allowed his eyes to adjust to the darkness of the earthen tunnel into which Scátach had led him, the oppressive gloom illuminated only slightly by the flickering of her torch. Seconds passed, and his gaze refocused to finally allow him to see... nothing. For there was nothing to see here save the rough, root-lined walls on either side and a ceiling too high above his head to even discern.

When his mistress had summoned him from his discussion with Ferdia earlier that evening, he had felt powerful energies emanating towards him from the very walls of RathDuille. Since promising to help him better control his war-spasms and understand his destiny, Scátach had frequently called for him in the middle of the night; he had abandoned trying to guess what mysterious purpose she had for him next: another test? A severe punishment? Expulsion from the ShadowKin? He had never known until the last moment. It was true that she had shown him many valuable techniques for keeping his battle senses keen when the fury overtook his body. Yet this time she had told him in advance that the Greatest Trial was ahead of him, and looking at her now as she moved along with grim purpose in her stride and an inhuman intensity in those hard eyes, he was certain that matters of destiny were about to unfold. He had acquiesced without argument, leaving Ferdia to work out the strategy for the imminent attack. As he did so, he contemplated making a witty comment but decided it was not the moment for mirth. He had smiled to himself then. *I must be learning,* he thought.

Leaving the section of RathDuille reserved for sleeping quarters, Scátach had led him down the main audience chamber and into the depths of the fortress's lower levels. Moving fluidly, she continued on through what appeared to be great storage areas, some long since abandoned, others still housing feed for animals, training equipment, chariots. And weapons. *Oh the weapons*, thought CúChulainn as they walked through chamber upon chamber of swords, lances, spears, slings, shields – an untold variety of piercing, stabbing or otherwise sharp devices whose names he knew not. This served to remind the young warrior that RathDuille was home to more than an academy of combat training – it was the base for what would have been a formidable army on the mainland.

Onwards they went, leaving the armoury for the more dilapidated regions of the castle's bowels. Here, the stonework was eroded in places, and the floor showed signs of neglect. Continuing through this forgotten region, Scátach turned to CúChulainn and finally spoke.

'What lies below will change everything, should you succeed.' Then she had lifted open a distressed wooden trapdoor to reveal a narrow stairway leading down, into darkness.

The same darkness which he now occupied. Calling on his ShadowKin training, he began to attend to his surroundings – visually, even with the ShadowSight - that skill of seeing forms through pitch darkness - there was little to be perceived, so he resorted to his other senses. He detected the smell of dry earth, sap, his own sweat, Scátach's indescribable scent. The feel of uneven ground beneath his feet, of great height above him, of wind on his face. The sound of that same wind, distant dripping water, and a low groaning, like the bass lowing of some unfathomable beast. And there was more – something he discerned through some *other* sense, one he had no name for, but which made his mind drift to thoughts of... magick? He found it hard to describe, yet he knew the feeling well for he had experienced it before: it was the strange tingle he felt whenever he drew near the Red Branch in the Craobh Ruadh. He was a little confused by this, but the feeling also reminded him of his home, and so he drew comfort from it.

His mistress descended after him, carrying a flaming torch which gave some illumination to the dank passageway. She pressed on ahead of him into the gloom at a brisk pace. Finally, she turned to face him. At her back was a portal into another expanse, but unlike the tunnel in which they now stood, the one ahead was not empty. In the torchlight behind Scátach, CúChulainn could see the thick limbs of a thousand powerful roots as they slowly writhed and twisted, like great serpents in ever-tangling coils. This sight awed CúChulainn somewhat, but his mistress paid it no heed. She began to make those facial contortions that signalled that she was about to speak, something which she always appeared uncomfortable doing. Her dry croak echoed in the vaulted tunnel.

'In my many years as custodian of this castle, I have brought the most promising of the ShadowKin to these depths to face the final ordeal. For a long while my hopes rested on Ferdia, but each time he tried, swift and lithe though he was, the roots thwarted him. Perhaps you will have more success... Or perhaps not.'

He felt a quick rush of trepidation at this grim pronouncement, but he quickly dismissed it, and instead focused on the fact that one mystery, at least, had been solved. For that strange tingling he had felt, which was familiar to him from his visits to the Craobh Ruadh, was now clear. His sense of direction had always been strong, and he had correctly reasoned that Scátach's route was taking them directly below the ChrannGréinne – so these roots, which moved as though alive, were undoubtedly those of that magickal Quicken Tree. Yet still he was reluctant to go forward.

213

'Why are you so certain that anything lies beyond?' he asked. 'Surely we could better spend our time making ready for battle?'

'Do not ask how I know,' she barked. 'I know this full well: should you gain access to the cavern beyond, you will find your answers, and our victory over Aifé will be assured.'

She pointed a long, skeletal finger into the dark of the corridor ahead.

'Down this path lies your true destiny, and the real reason for your coming here,' she said. 'It is time for you to challenge the roots of ChrannGréinne. GO!'

CúChulainn weighed these words for some moments, then nodded his head several times – whether to reassure Scátach or himself he could not tell. Then, taking a deep breath, he walked forward, and into the grasp of the roots.

The moment his foot touched the ground on the threshold of the chamber, the roots seemed to react, like blind eels sensing an intruder. CúChulainn stood motionless, evaluating... then, before he could decide, his senses were filled with the signals of frantic motion nearby as the tendrils sprung to life. They whipped and thrashed at him viciously, jostling him back and forth with unnatural force. He was able to use his superior agility to evade a few of the blows, and managed to advance a fair distance through leaps and and rolls but the roots were too many and too swift to escape. Suddenly, a mass of them seized him by his four limbs, stripping him of his sword and leather armour, and lifting him off the ground, one root wrapped tightly around his neck, forcing his head back and forth as if allowing some unseen presence to inspect him.

At the threshold, Scátach heard the sounds of CúChulainn's struggle, lowered her eyes and shook her head slowly. She turned and left the passageway, returning to her throne room above.

There CúChulainn hung for some moments, suspended in the air as the strange roots held him in place. Then, all grew still. Instinctively, he braced himself for the pain to follow, whether due to a new assault from as yet unseen tendrils or the wrenching of his limbs from their sockets. Experience had taught him that a sudden lull was rarely a good sign from an opponent. But on this occasion, he was wrong. Gradually, slivers of pale light began to fall upon his face as cracks started to appear in the wall of roots ahead. With a sound that was more sigh than groan, a passage opened up in the chamber and the roots that had held him fast now nudged him forward, slowly at first, then propelling him smoothly and swiftly across the expanse of the vast chamber and toward its farther end.

214

Onwards they carried him, through an elaborately-carved portal and into the soft, green-tinged light beyond.

He emerged in a vast, wondrous cavern walled by the thick upper edges of the gigantic roots. A stream gushed through it forming a small lake directly beneath the tree, within which several of the roots were immersed. The waters appeared to flow towards a small cave-like opening formed of a latticework of smaller roots, and beyond, close to where the waters fed into the sea, he could discern the prow of partially hidden vessel, a great golden ship. Other metallic artefacts glittered here and there, the light strangely refracted from the rays of the shrouded Alban sun, which - unusually for this isle CúChulainn thought - entered through a high opening to fall on the lake's large central island. Amid the stalagmites, positioned to greet the dawn sun, there sat a great throne hewn of solid rock. Although it faced away from him, he could see that the seat was not empty – a huge figure sat slumped forward. His first instinct was that this was a carving of some great king of old; an ancient ruler of this land. Except that the figure was moving. As he looked closely, CúChulainn could see it shaking slightly, the great head nodding slowly. He was not alone in the chamber.

He approached the island cautiously, skipping nimbly across stones set in the water. As he drew nearer the throne, he could discern terrible wounds on the seated figure – broken spear shafts and other projectile weapons jutted out of the torso and limbs; elsewhere, grievous openings in the flesh were evident – clearly very old, but somehow never healed. CúChulainn witnessed these ghastly injuries with a sense of increasing horror, wishing that the ruined giant in the throne was indeed the statue he had first thought.

He moved in utter silence, as his ShadowKin training had taught him the only sounds were the soft drip of water into the lake and the gentle trickling of the stream. To CúChulainn's surprise, however - and despite his stealthy approach - the mysterious king turned his head towards him as he began to round the throne and regarded the young man with strangely familiar blue eyes. Slowly, a broad smile broke across his weathered features as he painfully breathed two words:

'At last!'

CúChulainn could only stare blankly back as, for the first time, he looked upon the face of his father.

The face of Lugh.

*****

215

Truly stunned beyond words, CúChulainn continued to stare at the gigantic form seated before him. Were he to stand, CúChulainn estimated that the stricken man would be a match for his own height plus maybe a half more. His limbs, scarred and rent though they were, nevertheless looked strong. And his great head, now adorned with silver locks in place of the golden hair of which the old tales spoke, rose from its stoop to inspect the young visitor. The face, with scar-laden brow and straggling beard, looked as though it were hewn of solid granite. But for the eyes. They glowed with purpose.

'Do you know me, warrior?' said Lugh. His voice, though cracked and ancient, un-used for so long, still carried in it a sense of power and authority. The question shook CúChulainn from his stupor, and he answered in a soft, reverent whisper.

'Can it be? I see in your features my own face in years to come, should I live to be ravaged by time... You are...'

'Yes. I am Lugh, Sword of the Dananns. And you are my son, are you not, if the roots have granted you access to this place? You are welcome, Setanta - I have waited a long time for your coming. A long time...'

CúChulainn wrestled with the mixture of emotions that were threatening to overwhelm him. For perhaps the first time in his young life, he felt as though he had no idea what to do, or what to expect.

'I... *am* Setanta,' he said simply, 'though they call me CúChulainn now.'

This seemed to please Lugh. He smiled, and his features began to warm, the stony pall leaving them somewhat.

'CúChulainn? Ah.... yes, I see from your eyes the why of it,' the giant laughed, seeming to enjoy the history he read within the young warrior's gaze.

'They honour you with plaudits for great deeds already, and you are still little more than a boy. I know you have many questions, but our time is short and I have much to tell. In the course of my words, you may find the answers you seek.'

He gestured with his hand, and CúChulainn took a seat on a stump of rock adjacent to Lugh's throne. The SunGod took a long breath, seemed to weigh his words momentarily, as though looking for the starting point of a speech long-rehearsed, and then began.

'You are marked to accomplish great things, my son. All living creatures have a purpose, and yours is a mighty one. You are now the last link between the old ways of myth and the dawning of a new age - the time of the Gaels. You have the virtues of the Tuatha Dé Danann and the noble blood of the kings of men. These have been bequeathed to you so that you might be better armed to tackle the challenges ahead. The time of the old gods is passing, but those of us Ancient Ones who are *Of The Light* knew this was to be the way of things. It was agreed that we should leave this plane, this material world, in the hands of the mortals so that they might forge their own future without our interference. But there are... others. Dark and twisted entities who are not ready to relinquish their hold on mortal affairs. They crave the worship and supplication of their devotees; they do not wish to forego the power they gain from blood-sacrifice and misery. I am sure you have encountered one such darkling already - the Black Wings of Death that have harried you of late?'

CúChulainn nodded.

'The Morrigan. I have felt her pitting her dark will against me.'

'She is the greatest of my enemies. And there were others like her, be aware. I perceived this threat long ago, and sought to counter it. But... I could not. Not by any means of combat or strategy known to me. I was close to despair, my son.'

Lugh gritted his teeth and shook his head slowly, an expression that was part regret and part disbelief wrote itself on that noble face. But when he looked up again at CúChulainn, a fire suddenly blazed once again in his eyes.

'Eventually, however, I was granted permission to contrive a bold gambit, to bestow men a new weapon against the final throes of the Dark Gods. *You* are that weapon. Part Danann, part man, it falls to you to vanquish these craven spirits. Here, under the last Quicken Tree, you will find the implements that will aid you in this war. I pass them to you now, for my strength is almost spent, my time almost passed.'

As CúChulainn attempted to process all this, his eye was drawn again to the horrific wounds that scarred his father's body.

'What ill befell you? Each gash alone looks grave enough to kill a man.'

'Before your birth,' Lugh continued, 'I smote down many a vengeful phantom with righteous blows, and did battle with the multitude of the armies of dread. For long years I hewed them, in countless secret campaigns, out of sight of man. And, oh, I believed I was glorious as I stood alone against the hordes! Perhaps such foolhardiness was borne of some paternal urge to ease your task a measure.'

217

He looked down at his injuries.

'It appears my many battles have taken too great a toll on this corporeal form. Soon I will rejoin the others of my kind in the arms of Danú. I have tarried here for you by drawing strength from the ChrannGréinne, waiting, hoping that your path would lead you here. And now here you stand. My time is almost come.'

But this prospect so distressed CúChulainn – he had only just found his father, to lose him again so soon would be a cruel fate.

'*Why* must you depart?' he said angrily. 'Could we not stand *together* against these daemons? Fighting shoulder to shoulder, we could defeat god and man alike!'

Lugh only smiled sadly.

'Alas, my son, I am pierced and poisoned by cruel weapons and terrible magick – this outer form can contain me no more. But even were I fit to carry on, it is no longer my war to wage. It must be *men* that drive these devils from the land and claim their own inheritance. My kind must die and yours awake.'

These words were painful to CúChulainn, yet in his heart, he knew the truth in them. He lamented the fact that this knowledge did nothing to lessen the anguish.

'If that is how it must be, so be it' he agreed sadly. 'But how am I to conquer such powerful spirits? I know nothing of magick! And how am I to find them?'

'Only two now remain with the power to truly cause harm. One has already found you, that foul crow. Defeating her will be your greatest challenge, for she is as one with Death. I pray that you will find a way to destroy her, since I could not. The other lurks here on Alba, growing stronger with every day that passes.'

A sickening realisation washed over CúChulainn at this.

'This other, is it Aifé who has power to alter time and appearance, and move through solid stone?'

'Not her, but the master she serves: Crom Cruach, the Temporal Worm of the Aeder Worlds. Long have I yearned to hack his lecherous coils. Aifé is a disciple of Crom Cruach. She is one of three Danann children, abducted by the baleful maggot when the bulk of our number departed from this material plane. He planned to raise the three as his daughters, as his generals, to usher in an age of worship to himself: an all-conquering empire under the banner of the worm. The soil itself would turn red with the blood of sacrifice. Pain, suffering, anguish – these things are most pleasing to Crom Cruach. But I and ChrannGréinne learned of his scheme and managed to reclaim one of the three from his thrall and return her to the Light. She betrayed Crom Cruach and her sisters, and joined me in battle against them. For years I have prevented the followers of Crom Cruach from spreading their evil beyond this island, while the redeemed one guarded my resting place. But now as my strength diminishes, the tentacles of Crom Cruach reach for the mainland.'

'Scátach is the one you rescued,' exclaimed CúChulainn, his mind racing. 'Aifé, her sister and nemesis, resides in Coscrach. What of the third?'

'The third, the vilest and most powerful, left this isle to weave her dark arts elsewhere. You will come to know her before long, I fear. But there are dangers closer to home to contend with. And our time draws to a close. You must take my sword, Freagartach, the Answerer, the finest blade ever forged, sharp enough to cut the wind and dealer of wounds that no healer could tend.'

From the left side of his throne, he lifted a beautiful, adorned scabbard of silver and gold, festooned with a multitude of precious stones, and passed it to his son.

'But you would be wise to use it sparingly, my boy. For the blade is under a dark spell, put upon it by Balor himself,' Lugh said softly.

'When I struck him down at the Second Battle of Moytura, he of the Evil Eye sent forth his dying curse; desiring that I become as bloodthirsty and wicked as he. But I managed to deflect the hex upon the edge of the holy blade of Freagartach, and thus its malignancy was attenuated.

This did not completely expunge the evil, however, for now the wielder of that weapon bears a lesser curse: the more he uses it, the more he takes an unhealthy delight in slaughter. He becomes inseparable from the sword, and yearns more and more to viciously cut apart his foes.'

CúChulainn removed the sword from the exquisite sheath and beheld with amazement how a blue-grey light, like the glow around a Samhain's moon, could be seen running finely along its cutting edge.

Next, Lugh turned to his right side to reach for another gift. It was wrapped in a crimson cloak, and when the giant folded back the garment, CúChulainn could see an embossed golden plaque fixed above a series of interlocking square plates, held fast by thick bands of smooth leather.

Upon the breastplate he could see three swans engraved in great detail, a kind of soulfulness visible in their eyes.

'This is the armour of Mannán Mac Lir, *Salodor*, which no weapon could ever pierce. It will be unto your body like a living skin of gold, moving to protect you where needed, but also taming and focussing your war-frenzy.

CúChulainn took the bundle and, kneeling, laid it reverently before him.

'All else in this place belongs to you now: my helm, cloak and shield, the ship that brought me here, the *Sweeper of the Waves*, whose course is set by thought, and sails just as fast. Now she will obey only you. And finally this...'

He pointed now to a trough of steaming water beside the running stream.

'This is my spear, *Areadbhar*, which for you will now be known as the *Gae Bolga*, for its name and story are different for every arm that wields it.

'It is the most fearsome of shafts to man or god: when cast in anger, it can pierce the chests of a hundred warriors. The cool water quells its tempestuous spirit, much like your own. You must call to it – but in so doing you must release me from this ruined form.'

He brought himself to his feet shakily, his movements clearly causing him much pain. CúChulainn reached to help him up, but Lugh waved him away, leaning on the arm of his rough throne as he slowly straightened himself.

'Let the shaft pass through this body and into your hand.'

Filled with utter horror, CúChulainn protested, his voice breaking.

'Father... *I cannot do this*! Why must I strike you down? Are these wounds not grave enough to send you from this realm? Can your passing not be peaceful?'

Lugh shook his head sadly.

'Alas no, my son. Death is the game of the Morrigan. If I were to die of wounds dealt in hatred, then that foul crow would feast on my spirit. No, I would rob her of that victory. For if I die by a compassionate hand, of a stroke dealt out of love, then she can have no claim on my soul. Forgive me that I ask this of you, my son. One day, you will understand.'

CúChulainn nodded grimly, rivulets of tears streaking down his cheeks. He mustered himself, and spoke forth in a strong voice.

220

'My brave father, I would that our time could have been longer, that we could have drawn swords together... Perhaps in the next world. What is the word of summoning?'

Lugh staggered forward a pace to stand facing his son. The rays of the morning sun fell on him then, catching him in such a way that he appeared to radiate light. He smiled.

'Our time together is eternal, my son. You will make me proud... the word is... *stróic.*'

CúChulainn smiled sadly back at his father, the SunGod, Lugh Samhildánach, Lugh of the Long Arms. He knew this was how it must be, though his very heart yearned to leap from his chest, screaming '*No*'. But to know such agony and to do one's duty despite it – that is what makes a hero.

If he was anything, CúChulainn was that.

'*Stróic!*' he shouted through the tears and the pain. It was a word of the Old Language. It meant to rend or tear.

An ornately wrought yet barbarous-looking throwing spear leapt forth from the boiling waters, nine hateful spines on its killing head, their metal tips glowing red hot. It spun in mid-air sending flecks of boiling water flying, and an unholy screech, like a sword scraping granite, could be heard from it. The cry reached its paroxysm as it hurtled through the body of Lugh and into the waiting hand of his son. The glowing amber liquid of the SunGod's earthly blood was quickly absorbed into the spear. The face of Lugh glowed with relief and light began to radiate from each of his wounds. Soon the luminescence became too great for CúChulainn to gaze upon, growing stronger and brighter until it dispersed in a blinding explosion, whose light travelled up through the roots of the Quicken Tree and thence through the trunk and branches above. When the flaring glow faded, the body of Lugh was gone.

The leaves of the Quicken Tree gleamed brilliant gold for a moment, then faded, withered, and softly began to fall.

Scátach was addressing her warriors in her throne room when the tree began to die. Murmuring grew from the ShadowKin, but Scátach simply looked up and sighed sadly, placing her hand on the trunk of the tree.

In the chamber below, CúChulainn was bowed on one knee, a fist pressed against his forehead, his face wet with tears. He remained thus for a moment, then looked down to the sword: the Answerer. A feeling of bitter determination seized him; he rose to his feet, picked up the sword and swung it with force at the now empty throne of Lugh – it sliced through, strewing molten fragments across the floor. CúChulainn inspected the blade – there was not a mark on its edge. His eyes narrowed, and he turned his gaze to the entrance to the cavern, now guarded only by dead roots.

*****

In a copse near Eamhain Mhacha, Amergin the Sage knelt in some bushes, his bronze sickle in hand, stooping to collect some deadly nightshade. He paused, becoming aware of something strange. A soft groan, as if a mournful lamentation, seemed to emanate from the trees around him. The druid closed his eyes for a moment as if to perceive something distant. Then he rose with a look of concern on his face, and hurried back to the citadel.

2.

Dawn on Alba

Aifé stood upon the balcony window of Coscrach castle. The first pale rays of morning light were struggling to penetrate the eternal mists surrounding Alba, as they did every morning - and the witch smiled.

The broiling dark fog clouds were particularly thick this dawn, for the island was at its most unnatural state due to the convergences of potent magicks welling up from within, below, around, and also *towards* it from other dimensions. Aifé felt the confluence of dangerous powers around her, but it merely served to delight and arouse her all the more.

Her eyes ignited with an eldritch green as she opened her connection to the unseen eddies of the gathering sídhe magick.

There, pulsating sharply out beyond the shifting mists, was the cold presence of Scátach. Aifé raised her hand and softly brushed her cheek. As she did, so dropped for an instant her illusory magick and the wicked scar became visible. She traced the long, raised blemish with the back of her hand and cursed her sister with all her being.

At the same place where she perceived Scátach's hated presence, she felt the fading vestiges of the force of the Quicken Tree, ChrannGréinne. Its pulsation had grown steadily weaker as the ages passed, but recently she felt the Tree's energy diminish considerably. She was sure: its existence would soon be terminated. She smiled at the irony of it; those very mists created by Scátach to shroud the island kept Lugh's sunlight from the Quicken Tree, condemning it to a slow, and now imminent, death. What an utter fool her sister was!

Nearer to her, she felt the power of Crom Cruach and exulted that it was she who profited most from the Crooked One's strength - *she* who was the favoured child, the most trusted ally to the most powerful entity who still had influence on this plane.

And yet even he, she mused, *does not realise the degree to which I am in control of all that is passing now, and all that will come to pass!*

Aifé could not have felt happier. All her efforts were soon to bear fruit. How she would revel in these richly deserved rewards!

A tremor of excitement running through her, she turned and quickly descended down into the chamber behind, where her gaudily-attired captain, Midac, stood patiently waiting.

'The day we have long awaited has dawned, Midac,' she said with elated satisfaction. 'A new era of dominance for those of us loyal to the Great Worm; He whose coils grow tight around the weak jowls of our enemies. Long will he loll in their blood and rejoice in their suffering... and generous will be the rewards for his beloved disciples: we, the enforcers of His reign, Oh Midac...'

She seized the feathered bone-and-wood mask that hid Midac's face and pulled his head forward very close to her blazing eyes. The dark green glow illuminated and rendered even eerier the demonically-carved features.

'Providing my orders are carried out *unfailingly*,' she hissed urgently. 'There can be no mistakes!'

'There will be none, so the Worm consume me,' Midac answered in a hollow, toneless voice.

Aifé smiled, satisfied with what she saw in her fearsome captain. She released her grasp and began to pace around him.

'Are my elite warriors well prepared for the last confrontation with Scátach and her rabble?'

'They are in position, my mistress. And as for Scátach - hah, the Betrayer will find in her adversaries skills the likes of which I am sure she has never before encountered on the battlefield.'

The dark humour Aifé detected in Midac's assessments amused her in turn. She could feel the pleasures of victory already brewing within her twisted heart.

'Go now, Midac, and join your faithful brethren. I have blood-work to attend to.'

When Midac had bowed deeply and silently left the chamber, Aifé began to mutter low incantations as she approached the table whereupon lay her full array of silver implements of torture. There was a collection of glittering blades, vices, skewers, pins and abominable scraping tools inlaid with curses etched in ogham and other more ancient runes.

'Loathsome Scátach,' she murmured, her hands lovingly hefting and weighing her favourites from among the assorted instruments.

'You should not have abandoned your kin, my sister. You will not know the ecstasy of Crom Cruach's glory today, but instead find only humiliation and despair. And your ultimate, miserable end.'

Finally selecting an incredibly sharp hooked rod and triple-bladed scalpel, Aifé turned her attentions then to the bound and gagged men dangling and squirming upside down from the chamber's rafters.

*****

The sombre eyes of a thousand ShadowKin were riveted upon the golden-armoured figure standing beside the Mistress on the Covenant Rock. The ogham inscriptions on this great megalith that stood before RathDuille were the sacred signs of the pact each of them had entered into on becoming ShadowKin. A hallowed vow to obey the will of the Mistress in exchange for tutelage in the forgotten Danann fighting arts, and the right to partake of the golden sap of the last Quicken Tree. This numinous elixir melded those skills to their souls and raised their bodies to levels of physical magnificence normal mortals could only dream of, or dread, depending on which end of the sword they found themselves.

This assemblage of redoubtable, magickally-transformed warriors, who had for many unnaturally-slowed decades honed their skills, gazed up now at the one who had so quickly won the respect of the fiercest martial being they had ever known. He stood before them clad in the armour and bearing the holy weapons of Lugh Samhildánach himself. So attired in Lugh's metal and crimson cloak, but with the war-paint of the ShadowKin colouring his face - he resembled a true Danann. The perfect avatar of a god they never knew had been living beneath them for so many years.

Their eyes held him with silence and reverence, which was met by CúChulainn with equal respect.

Ferdia and Uatach appeared from the throng of warriors and, climbing the steps carved into the rock, came to join the Mistress and the man who had defied - and overcome - the challenge of the roots.

CúChulainn turned and regarded Scátach, whose gaze was fixed on the battlements of RathDuille, where the now-colourless upper branches and leaves of the ChrannGréinne hung wanly across the stone, all vitality lost, the ancient, powerful magick evaporated.

Had she known my fulfilment of this task, this thing she had awaited so eagerly, would lead to the tree's destruction?

CúChulainn, taking stock of the unfathomable woman, thought the answer was no. For there was, he perceived, a new dimension of sadness to her austerity.

Nevertheless, he felt sure that Lugh's strategy was true and wise. He took forth The Answerer and pointed it down at the assembled ShadowKin.

'A mighty force,' he said, addressing Scátach and the two new arrivals. 'I would that Uladh's army were so skilled. Never have I seen such a collection of highly accomplished warriors. But tell me, is Aifé's host just as great?'

Scátach remained silent, her unblinking gaze still upon the lifeless Quicken Tree.

It was her daughter Uatach who finally answered.

'Neither side has advantage of number. Victory shall come to us simply because our cause is not one of depravity. They fight for love of suffering, we fight to end it.'

CúChulainn nodded at this, then once more indicated the preparations below.

'I see no chariots. They are the backbone of a fighting force. The battle will take place on an open plain, as I understand it. How will we counter the enemy should they pit chariots against us?'

He turned to the ShadowKin Captain.

'Today we have something much better than mere chariots,' Ferdia said. Peering over to where the ShadowKin captain indicated, CúChulainn's sight quickly picked out a trail leading from the darkness between the trees. A herd of huge beasts was emerging.

'Behold, my friend. A sight surely forgotten on Eirú - The Great Battle Elk of Alba!" said Ferdia proudly, then explained to CúChulainn what he was seeing.

Twice as tall as a man and crowned with antlers wide as a chariot, these mighty creatures roamed the island at will and were possessed of a strength and vigour that made all ordinary beasts of burden seem risible. Hunted to extinction on the mainland, the last Elk had migrated to Alba, scraping an existence on its windswept pastures. When Lugh separated Alba from Eirú many generations ago, the creatures had been safe, but were forced to share their island prison with Crom Cruach.
It was only the ShadowKin who knew the ways of communing with these awesome stags, and who could mount them safely, charging into battle with a complement of four riders. Two would sit either side of its flank on a specially constructed leather saddle, lances and long pikes at the ready. Two more would be perched upon either antler, a dizzying platform from

where they could launch slings and javelins. But they did not ride the elk, for these majestic creatures were untameable. They would only take part in these eternal wars against Aifé, whom they hated, for a few weeks after the time of breeding, after which they would return to their own mysterious existence. CúChulainn was sure that Lugh must have planned that time to coincide with the final attack on Coscrach.

At the sight of these awesome creatures, a sudden jolt of recognition shook the Ulaghman's mind. That distinctive shape, the huge mass with those enormous antlers... *that* was what he had seen as he fell asleep on the shore after his arrival. They must monitor the coasts for new arrivals, and inform the ShadowKin when newcomers wash up. That must be how Ferdia and his troop had known of his presence, and had come to intercept him.

As the battle elk walked among the army, the ShadowKin genuflected before them. Then, with the aid of a handful of pelt, they leaped deftly into their respective positions upon the great beasts.

'Still worried, CúChulainn?' Ferdia asked sardonically.

At this the Uladhman laughed heartily.

'Only for our enemies!'

The others smiled, all save Scátach, who then took forth her glimmering blade and waved some exotic sigils that took visible form, glowing violet in the air. Seconds later something unheard of occurred, and the assembled ShadowKin gasped at it. The sun broke through the eternal mists of Alba and illuminated those standing upon the Covenant Rock. Then Scátach turned to CúChulainn, whose golden armour blazed brightly under those rare rays, and nodded curtly to him before leaping from the rock to land perfectly upon the antlers of the finest, most noble of all the battle elk: this was Garracht, the Elk-Lord.

The beast turned slowly around so that Scátach could face her mounted army.

'Look to the Tree, my ShadowKin!' she rasped, and her voice carried on the windless morning air.

'ChrannGréinne has passed and needs our protection no more! Our long-held duty on this isle will come to conclusion today. Here begins the reckoning. We have but one more task 'ere our purpose be met. When all is done this day your lives are your own once more, and you may live them as you will.

'But not until Aifé draws her last breath.

'As we march for the first time with the sun at our backs, our shadow will fall on Coscrach, and from that shadow we will stab forth the righteous intent of our blades!

'Feel not sorrow for our enemies for they have long since been consumed by the Feculant One, and clean death is the only kindness to be shown them.

'Today, let the shadows drop and burn now with the power of the Quickensap that is in you, and with such fury that the hated Crom Cruach will at last know fear!

'We will send him screaming back into the darkness!!'

At this the whole host of RathDuille raised their weapons and roared one single word, accompanied by the thunderous bellowing of the battle elk.

'*SCÁTACH*!!!'

And none were unaware that the beams of Lugh's light remained upon the Covenant Rock, reflecting brightly from CúChulainn's golden armour.

*****

Rivulets of blood coursed down along the pure whiteness of Aifé's perfect arm, pooling up and dripping from her elbow.

She paid no heed and with her cruel, thin blade continued to carve an intricate pattern upon the naked flesh of the bound victim, whose groans, struggling to escape his sewn lips, produced only a pitiful, dull drone.

'Do you wonder why I cut this flesh so?' she enquired in her silky, seductive voice.

'It may seem to you no more than wanton cruelty, I know, but the process is far more complex than you can imagine. Each incision, every twist of the blade, the slightest flick of my hand must be carefully and precisely carried out.

'My carvings are not random; nor is it idle or morbid fascination which guides my hand. For the flesh is a lock, and my artistry is the key. Every flash of agony, every muffled scream, each time the threshold of excruciation is breached – all this cements the foundations of the bridge between our world and the domain of my Master, my Father. Each drop of blood joins the river of anguish that flows beneath.'

From his inverted position, Aifé's weakly struggling victim could see his lifeblood flowing into the unnaturally troubled pool below him. He wondered why he hadn't been allowed to die; *oh how he so dearly wished to die.* He felt so pathetic: he, a ShadowKin warrior of RathDuille, reduced to this...

Aifé seized him roughly by the hair.

'Wallow not in despair, my handsome fool. One fortunate individual will have the honour of being the keystone for that bridge. The one who suffers even more than all the others...'

She wrenched his head around so that he could view his brothers who were similarly hung and rent, slowly bleeding their vital forces into the pool. Blood which had been infused with the energy of the sap of the ChrannGréinne, was now being used for this wretched end? The shame was unbearable. He tried to shut his eyes to it, but Aifé had long since sliced away his lids.

'...and achieves greater enlightenment,' she continued. 'Yes, we are most grateful to you.'

Aifé kissed the hapless warrior, his head feebly trying to turn away from it, then stepped back and flashed her blade across his face and neck.

'There!'

Satisfied, she snapped her fingers and one of her obsequious attendants hobbled over and, head low, offered fresh linen upon which Aifé cleaned away the blood from her arms and face.

'A triumph. One of my best to date.'

A loud belch emanated from one dark corner of the chamber, and a guttural voice followed.

'You sick witch.'

Nardul grunted, then bit into the severed human head that he grasped in his huge webbed fist. His large teeth crunched easily through the skull and, having spat out the pieces, he then used his other hand to scoop out and devour the brain matter inside.

'Savage,' retorted Aifé in disgust. 'You should be thankful that I allowed you to witness these sacred rites.'

229

Nardul growled, impatience in his voice. He hurled away the empty skull.

'I have no more time for your perverted games. My boys are eager for battle, let us away.'

Aifé's eyes blazed with their dark green luminescence as they always did when she called upon her powers of illusion. Her bloody robes blurred into a fabulous white armour, clean and exquisitely decorated.

The Fomorian lord wondered then what the real Aifé must look like underneath all her sorcerous glamours.

'Very well, Nardul,' she said.

'The time draws close, and the weapon of surprise is ours to wield.'

*****

Scátach led the great battle host of RathDuille, mounted upon their mighty elk, to crest the final hill that separated Aifé's territory from the disputed central lands.

Before them, perched at the very edge of the cliffs, loomed Coscrach Castle, that nexus of sorcereous energy constructed in ages past by Fuilltach the Lord of Blood, later home and prison to the cardinal evil of Crom Cruach.

But immediately in front of the army stood a steep slope leading up to a grassy plateau that stretched up to the forbidding castle's gates. And to the right of this innocent-looking pastoral land rose a bizarre rock formation that resembled a weeping figure – this was the Stone of Sorrow.

Just outside the shadow of the Stone, Aifé's army of Sluagh was in plain sight. They stood high above in their white armour, brilliant in the rays of the noon sun which persisted through the hole Scátach had pierced in Alba's mists and that she seemed to be able to move about the sky at her whim, sending the light ahead of her army as a dire warning to her sister. They ambled about slowly and quietly, seemingly unworried about the arrival of Scátach's army. And to the consternation of the ShadowKin force, Aifé's host appeared to outnumber them three times over!

All were silent as they took in the gravity of the situation and calculated their chances of victory. In the end it was Ferdia who spoke first.

'Many a man there. But we have our elk, and with careful steps we can grind them down... But still...'

He looked over at Scátach. The Mistress had barely spoken during the march on Coscrach and had left the talk of strategy to Ferdia, Uatach and CúChulainn. And despite her vociferous and rousing battle speech, Ferdia knew she was perplexed, and he didn't like that at all.

'Curious,' said Uatach. 'Has Aifé grown so arrogant that she supplies her army with neither horse nor chariot, or any other device to defend themselves? Their numbers are substantial, but it won't be enough.'

CúChulainn leapt from his mount and stalked a few steps ahead of the line.

'Perhaps it is a challenge of honour. Maybe we should meet them on foot. I still warrant they will be no match - Lugh's strength is now mine: I could kill hundreds alone!'

'*No!*' shouted Scátach, and all in the battle host turned to hear her.

'We will meet them with all our strength! Aifé is without honour and no trickery will save her now. Abandon thoughts of mercy. Hew them down! Rain havoc upon their heads!!'

No further encouragement was needed. The bellows of the elk and the cries of the thousand most skilful fighters that ever lived shattered the air as they galloped up the slope to bring down dreadful woe on the Sluagh army of Coscrach.

3.

Lambs to Slaughter

To any of the folk of Eamhain Mhacha, the ramshackle hut of Amergin the sage was a fearful place, full of potions, strange artefacts and texts only he himself could read. Any who lived in the vicinity of this crude dwelling learned quickly to ignore the odd smells or occasional explosions that emanated from under its crooked roof.

Today, the quaint shanty played host to one of the most arcane of all the ancient sage's arts – divination. Under the flickering candle-light, Amergin peered closely into the entrails of a dead goose. He had incanted a prayer for the unfortunate creature before sacrificing it, and now the information it yielded would ensure the taking of its life was not in vain.

With trembling hands, he moved parts of the offal back and forth, muttering quietly to himself as he did so. He had felt most uneasy since that morning, when he had been gripped by a feeling of sudden foreboding, as if he had been propelled to the edge of a deep precipice and left to teeter above the void; the sickening feeling in the depths of his stomach had not left him since. This was why he felt compelled to consult the entrails and attempt to read the future from them. This was why he was certain the forecast would be a bad one.

The initial signs were unclear, ambiguous – as they always were. Something about danger, something suggesting conflict, death and... *deception.* These were not revelations to the sage; they lived in dangerous times, where conflict and death were as common as dawn and dusk. But deception – he cared not for the way it seemed entwined with the other elements.

He considered for a moment, then swiftly began to drag pieces of intestine from the carcass of the fowl onto an ancient map of Alba, moving the bloody sections of tissue around with his knife. Some moved fluidly around on the slickness of the intestinal gore, others stuck in certain locations, snagging the rough material of the map and settling where they would. As the signs became clearer, Amergin continued in this ritualistic gesturing, until a dawning horror caused him to slow, then stop.

And the knife dropped from his shaking hand.

'But, if *they* are not... then where are...?'

The answer to this unfinished question presented itself to the sage, and it was the one he most feared. He ran from his hut, uttering the desperate plea of a man who has glimpsed impending terrors that surpassed all human reckoning.

'Lugh save us!'

*****

The ShadowKin army charged onward across the battle plain, a thunder of hooves shaking the very earth as they bore down upon the Sluagh forces. At the forefront of the advancing charge, Scátach – still perched nimbly among the antlers of Garracht – peered closely at the defending army, her sense of concern and uncertainty beginning to grow. No defensive formations in the centre. No cover on the flanks. No apparent organisation. No *discipline*. They were now only a dozen yards from the front line, and yet some Sluagh seemed to be *looking the other way*!

Something was wrong, *very* wrong!

*****

In Conchobar's private chambers, the king and Forgall were discussing Emer's health. They had made a habit of such chats since her tragic assault, and had he not been consumed by feelings of guilt for Emer, Forgall might have been glad of the fact that his old friend's trust in him had not been too badly dented by the whole affair with Mag. In fact, it was Conchobar's intention to convey this very message; now that the evil crow's manipulations had been revealed, his compassion for his friend far outweighed his anger at how his court had been compromised.

Many of these discussions had been grim, particularly in the early days following the realisation of the extent of Emer's wounds. Fearing Forgall would never emerge from the pit of despair, Conchobar had offered what little hope and encouragement he could. Of late, though, things had been more positive – Emer had awoken, and in recent days she had even begun to walk around for a few hours. Progress was slow but encouraging. So it seemed she would recover, if... diminished.

Forgall was speaking.

'Aye, her strength returns to her. She is redoubtable.'

'As is her father,' smiled Conchobar, relieved to see some small good cheer return to his general. 'She is a warrior, that one. And as strong as you, I'd warrant.'

233

'Nay, stronger,' said Forgall, then adding ruefully 'And a sight wiser...'

He looked into Conchobar's eyes briefly, then allowed his own gaze to drop to the floor.

'I was a fool,' he whispered.

Conchobar rose and put a hand on his friend's shoulder. He was weighing up some words of comfort when the curtain of the chamber was flung open by Amergin, his eyes blazing with urgency. Forgall leapt protectively across his king, blade drawn, but the sage paid him no heed, his attention fixed solely on Conchobar.

'*Deception! Sorcery! Betrayal!* Hear me now, King of Uladh! I have seen doom approach from afar, a great storm comes to topple the Red Branch! We must move to meet it, or be broken against its fury!'

His proclamation delivered, and still failing to acknowledge the presence of the general, Amergin hurried away, shouting further warnings as he receded into the distance.

The king and his general stood in perplexed silence for some moments. Then, with the barest flicker of a smile, Conchobar said:

'You heard the madman, Forgall. General, rouse the knights! Battle calls us once more.'

'So she does,' replied Forgall Manach, happier to be engaged in a more familiar task.

'And we shall answer.'

*****

The foremost elk-riders broke upon the Sluagh front line like a furious tidal wave crashing down upon jagged white rocks. They ploughed into the stationary defenders with ease, cutting a swathe through their number. The mounted ShadowKin hurled spears and other weaponry upon the vast Sluagh horde, swinging from the sides of their huge mounts to deal killing blows of stunning precision.

After the initial rush, the ShadowKin immediately noticed something amiss. The Sluagh were strangely inactive in defending themselves or mounting any sort of counter-attack; rather they seemed to wander blindly into the mass of blades and projectiles. Elsewhere, many of them seemed to flee in groups like startled animals.

234

CúChulainn and Ferdia had leapt to the ground, their respective elk-mounts continuing on across the battlefield, wreaking havoc and destruction with antler and hoof. Uatach and Naoise soon joined them, opting to engage the enemy in close combat while the cavalry charge regrouped. Ferdia was first to reach a retreating Sluagh, leaping high into the air to descend with a powerful killing stroke to the man's neck. But to his astonishment, his blade passed straight through the shoulder and torso of his enemy, leaving no trace apart from a strange shimmering effect, like a mirage, around the upper body of the warrior. The creature continued its escape, running off in a peculiar, jerky motion.

The nearby ShadowKin had witnessed this, and were equally perplexed.

'What devilry is afoot here?' shouted Naoise. 'Take the legs from them, lads, there's magick at play! We'll not be lured to a trap – it ends here!'

Heeding this call, the ShadowKin then launched a volley of projectile weapons – spears, discs, barbed javelins – at the lower regions of the scattering army. Several were taken down by the razor-sharp objects that bored into their legs. They all fell as one. They all emitted the same strange sound:

The fretful bleating of a dying beast.

Confusion stilled the ShadowKin for a moment. Uatach was the first to shake free from its grasp, rushing over to the nearest fallen corpse. Turning over the white-clad warrior, it shimmered for a moment, then its true form was revealed – a bloodied sheep carcass. The other slain Sluagh were now also revealed as such. The whole of the battle plain seemed to undulate briefly as the illusion was lifted, and the full carnage of livestock was unveiled.

*****

Elsewhere, Aifé opened her eyes. It had taken considerable force of will to maintain the illusion over so great an area and for such a duration. But it had succeeded. She inhaled deeply, the wind jostling her vivid yellow tresses, and allowed herself a slight smile.

*****

Having re-mounted their elk once more, CúChulainn and the others now surveyed the strange sight of the battlefield - the plain was strewn with the bloodied carcasses of dead sheep, while flocks of living ones fled in many directions. Not a single Sluagh – alive or dead – was to be seen. Scátach rode up alongside CúChulainn, the enormous girth of Garracht easily dwarfing his own gigantic elk-mount. He spoke darkly to his Mistress.

'The veil is lifted – another illusion of your sister's making.'

'Perhaps her numbers have been exaggerated,' ventured Ferdia, 'our scouts may have been similarly deceived in their estimations.'

Uatach was struggling to conceal her anger at the artifice. She wanted Sluagh blood, and she would have it yet this day!

'The coward seeks to delay us,' she spat, 'knowing her weaker numbers might better withstand us in her fort rather than meet us in open battle. She means to ultimately draw us on to Coscrach; this false host was perhaps for us to weary ourselves upon before attacking the walls that even now they are fortifying.'

Scátach finally spoke, her dry, rasping voice was calmer than that of her daughter, though CúChulainn thought he could detect a note of irritation, perhaps with herself for not seeing through the phantasm sooner.

'This trickery is not wholly unexpected – nothing is what it seems with Aifé. Onward to Coscrach – if she wishes to cower within the walls of her castle, then it shall become her tomb.'

She roused the mounted warriors to regroup themselves then turned to march on the sheer walls of Coscrach Castle. As they moved off, CúChulainn shot a final glance back at the massacre of sheep, and thought of the livestock farmers of Eamhain, and what they would have made of the scene.

'What a waste.'

Runes and Sigils

As I inscribe these words I am conscious of a painful thought: that there is no longer, to my knowledge, anyone living in this land who can understand what it is marked down on these skins.

For it was far away from this place that I received my instruction in this way of writing, and though ogham markings are well understood and used by the local druids, these other arts have yet to find their way to Eirú.

But alas, I fear that by the time this does happen my works will have long since deteriorated or be scattered or otherwise destroyed.

So be it. And perhaps it is little harm after all.

For this has ever been a land of oral tradition and so I will do as the druids of the thorn have always done - endeavour to pass these tales through the ages upon the lips of the seanchaí and other sage minds or tellers.

So that something of the wonder of our times survive into the future, even though my dreams tell me that it will be an age that will have scant time - or desire - to reflect upon a past so strange, so shrouded in uncertain mists and unlikelihood.

But if the language I use to note these events appears as little more than senseless scribbling to the people of Eirú, those same folk are, of course, not without their own means of record.

For there are notches and lines etched upon stones - which may survive - and into wood - which may not - that could indeed conceivably bear witness down the generations to the names of great chieftains, mighty fighters and incredible events.

Though again, there is no certainty that there will always exist those capable of understanding and relating the meaning of the ogham inscriptions.

However, there are other secret runes, sigils, patterns and symbols that I almost hope will not survive to fall into the careless hands of the disloyal or ill-learned man of a new and innocent epoch.

These are the arcane and closely-guarded signs through which the Tuatha Dé Danann channeled and focused their magickal energies.

Sigils of hiding that could keep your fort or your army concealed from your enemy's eyes. Or those of finding that could lead a druid to places of destiny or enlightenment of the future. There are signs that can put a glamour on things to make them seem as another, and many are the symbols of binding and summoning and holding others to their word.

There are runes infused with great power when forged upon a weapon so that their complex patterns can be traced into visible existence upon the very airs, causing queer and unnatural effects on what we consider the material world.

Very few are those now who have the power to wield such dangerously potent symbols, and we'd nearly be better off if there were none at all.

It would indeed be thus, I think, if it were up to me to decide such things.

4.

Shadowfall

The blackwood doors to Coscrach finally splintered and came apart under the tremendous battering attacks of the great fighting elk of RathDuille.

It was Garracht, Scátach's own fearsome mount, who was first to charge through into the courtyard. He bucked his head wildly left and right, searching with nigh-unbreakable antlers to tear asunder any Sluagh defenders foolish enough to attack.

But none came.

A third of the ShadowKin army then poured into the courtyard and dashed around, searching for enemies while the battle-elk charged about with furious intent.

CúChulainn felt a certain tightness in his stomach, aware of an unwholesome tang in the air, and a silence that bespoke of nothing but ill-tidings. Inside the courtyard the strange island mist seemed to have settled and concentrated, creating trails of thick, green-tinged vapour.

He looked across at Scátach; the winds upon the cliff had swept the cowl away from her stern, pale face which was now creased with uncertainty.

The mighty Danann woman stepped up onto the antlers of her mount and turned to address those now entering behind.

'Scour along the inner walls. Be wary of the ramparts,' she commanded.

Then, having leapt to the cobbled ground, she signalled to CúChulainn and Ferdia to descend from their elk and follow her to where, flanked by braziers lending that unnatural green light to the obscuring mists, lay the dark entrance to the inner keep.

Uatach, Naoise and several of the ShadowKin joined them and, following in the wary steps of their Mistress, they entered the hostile darkness of Aifé's lair.

CúChulainn and Ferdia took up position just behind Scátach, their muscles tense and weapons thrust steadily before them.

Immediately CúChulainn felt the invisible traces of misery wafting towards him from the gloom.

The echoes of screams and of suffering seemed to linger on the chill wind that gusted from unseen spaces directly ahead.

They advanced cautiously into the murk.

A shrill cry rent the still air above and to the right of the group. CúChulainn's night-keen vision just about made out the silhouette of a Sluagh descending from above, twin swords flashing about in its hands.

The plummeting attacker was instantly beset by a volley of projectiles cast by the unflinching ShadowKin.

But the bronze and copper discs passed through the body to clang against the stone wall somewhere in the darkness behind. The ghostly form of the Sluagh disappeared leaving trails of magickal light swirling around the trio of bats who careened off into the upper reaches of the keep.

'Be on your guard,' rasped Scátach. 'There are yet more phantoms here for us to contend with.' She raised a chalk-white hand and designed a number of sigils whose magickal luminesence did not hang in the air as before but were promptly snuffed out like a candle by the dark forces natural to Coscrach.

'Follow me. Aifé will most likely be spinning her spells from the Chamber of Pain.'

So saying she hurried off towards the deepest darkness. CúChulainn and the others followed without hesitation.

Scátach was a dim shape moving along beside him, but CúChulainn could feel the pounding strength of her presence within him. Since his meeting with Lugh he felt a deep, true kinship with the Shadowy One. He drew pride also in the newfound knowledge that he was of her people in a way that none here, bar Uatach, could claim to be. Danann blood ran through each of their hearts, and this thought made CúChulainn feel less alone in a world that he now began to perceive as the battleground for a war between gods and mortals.

Yet he had not spent countless years with her as had Ferdia and the others, so he was keen not to provoke their rancour by giving the impression that he had superseded all of them in their Mistress's eyes.

They came then to a yawning archway illuminated either side by more of the eerie, green-burning torches. The path was clear. Yet Scátach hesitated before this portal. She dropped to one knee and, with closed eyes, muttered some incantations.

CúChulainn turned to Ferdia and whispered.

'A barren plain, an empty castle, naught but spectres to resist us – with each step I take in this place my gut fills me with warning.'

'And justly so,' responded the ShadowKin captain. 'But we must put our trust in the Mistress. She knows of such things, and will not lead us awry.'

Scátach regained her feet quickly and, without a word, dashed through the archway and down the steps which emerged from the dark below.

'Come, you may yet get to test that shiny new blade of yours!' said Ferdia as he, CúChulainn and the others raced down after the ghostly shape of the Mistress.

The stairwell terminated in a wide, open chamber which was dominated by a pool of crimson water fed by four trenches cut into the stone. The air was tangy; an odour of rust and old blood mixed with the scent of the sea hung heavily in the dismal obscurity.

Suddenly a cry of anguish prompted the group to drop into defensive stances, weapons aimed and searching the recesses of the chamber for attackers. But it had been one among them who had cried out – Naoise. He was running along one of the slim rock bridges that quartered the central pool where, sagging upon barbed posts, hung four horribly disfigured bodies.

Some of the other ShadowKin gasped at the sight as they approached. The corpses were torn and opened in ways that seemed unconceivable, ways that were also designed, in their elaborate execution, to prolong excruciation to a horrendous degree. And yet... insanely, they seemed to be alive. Muffled moaning sounds emanated from their tightly sewn lips, and the shapes of their eyeballs could be seen moving beneath the stitched lids. One man no longer had eyes at all. Their delicately-exposed organs quivered and steamed, leaked and pulsated.

Naoise had taken the mutilated head of one these unfortunates in his hands and stood still, muttering, his forehead pressed to that of the suffering man.

'His brothers, Ainnle and Ardan,' said Ferdia, aghast. 'And old Sciabar, and Fintan too. Incredible fighters. Some of our best. Indomitable spirits, mighty souls. It pains me to see this but increases my desire to drive my spear into Aifé's corrupt heart!'

'We must release them from such pain!' cried Naoise as he took his knife and made to cut his brothers down, but the complex fashion by which their skin, muscles and tendons were pulled and wound around the holding post forced the blond warrior to hesitate with his blade.

'Be cautious, Naoise,' said Scátach. 'The magick wrought from their bodies is thick and potent... this was surely for a great summoning... yet I do not sense the residue of an apparition...' She trailed off, rubbing her sharp chin in consternation.

Her uncertainty discouraged the ShadowKin, whose eyes were all upon her.

Naoise cried out in despair once more as he realised that all he was doing was increasing his brother's agony.

'What can be done, Mistress?' he implored.

Scátach did not take another step, but rather bent forward hesitantly to inspect the grotesque display.

'Stitching closed the eyes, the mouths, the ears... so that no agony can escape... holds the torment in their bodies, in reserve. Fixed by the sigils that have been made through the entwining of their flesh... Aifé's art has achieved its apogee...'

CúChulainn had had enough of both this trickery and the group's hesitation; he stepped forward onto the stone bridge and drew The Answerer from its scabbard.

'Wait, Slaughterhound!' Scátach shrieked.

But it was too late.

Incandescent haloes of energy exploded into existence around the four sacrificial bodies which began jerking in silent agony. Phosphorescent flames burned away the stitches upon their lips and their screams at last curled out, echoing around the chamber.

Arcs of energy surged forth from each of the flaring bodies and struck CúChulainn from all four sides. He cried out in shock and pain as the energy raced across his body, burning brightly upon his Danann armour. His helm, his sword and the Gae Bolga strapped to his back were equally wrapped in filaments of frenzied, feeding lightning.

He found to his horror that could not move except to shudder against the unwholesome current running through him, siphoning his vital life-force upwards into the air of the chamber.

Dimly, against the pain and the loud crackling noises, he could see Scátach and the others leaping to safety and readying their weapons to attack something that seemed to be forming above him, something being traced into the air by the wildly whipping lines of energy searing out of his body.

'It is the Worm!!' yelled Scátach.

CúChulainn managed to arch back his neck to witness the massive, bloated form of Crom Cruach force its way into existence above him. He realised that the energies pouring from both he and Lugh's magickal weapons were aiding this manifestation. Somehow lending power and solidity to the primordial form. What an imbecile he had been to blunder into such a trap!

The ShadowKin had, by this time, already loosed many projectiles at the tentacled apparition before them, but neither disc nor lance, spear nor throwing knife had any effect upon it; each exploded in a ball of sparks or melted away at mere contact with the slick, shimmering hide of the deity.

Crom Cruach's cruel laughter joined the screams of the four tortured men that had served as both bait and energy conduits for this breach between the worlds, and with his squirming tentacles he seized six ShadowKin with ease.

The warriors were immediately sapped of their life energies as the tentacles wrapped about them and entered into their bodies, sluicing away their vital forces in an instant, then flinging away the dried husks to quickly scrabble across the floor and grab the next screaming victim.

Terror and confusion reigned, but CúChulainn could not move, and was growing ever weaker as Crom Cruach swelled with power.

'You fools!' echoed the myriad voices of the Crooked Worm.

Scátach rallied the remaining warriors, running horizontally across the wall of the chamber to avoid a searching tentacle, then flipping over it and cutting off its tip with her glittering blade.

'Ahh, Scátach. Welcome back, my treacherous child,' Crom Cruach jeered. **'I have longed for your return. And to bring such tribute with you befits your last act of service. Your Danann weapon can scratch through to my earthly form of course, but your flock is not so fortunate. I thank you for this offering, my wayward daughter!'**

Many more ShadowKin rushed into the chamber to join the fray and, before Scátach could warn them to stay away, the bulbous, multi-eyed mass that served as Crom Cruach's head nodded and the great doors of the chamber slammed shut behind the newcomers, sealing them in with the now fully-formed god.

'What can we do, Mistress? Our blows are useless, can we even flee?' called Ferdia, panic barely suppressed in his voice.

And even the brief moment he took to pose the question almost cost him his life, for a tentacle had reached out and taken hold of him, but he shrugged out of his cloak and tumbled away. Daimh Mór, the hardy instructor, was not so fortunate, and Ferdia saw the man being seized, his body becoming rapidly aged by Crom Cruach's touch, transforming in the blink of an eye from robust warrior to old man to withered skeleton, then finally to dust which fell about the tentacle and was absorbed into it.

'**Ahh, a succulent morsel**,' Crom Cruach crowed. '**But come now, Scátach. Embrace your father and I will not feast on your suffering overlong.**'

Crom Cruach's larger tentacles split into finer ones in order to increase the chances of grasping her, but Scátach managed to repel his advances with the mastery of her sword, her blade whirring around and winnowing away the searching members as soon as they emerged. Seeing that only the Mistress could do any damage, Ferdia and Uatach abandoned their futile attacks for the moment and with skilful feints and lunges, concentrated on luring away some of the seeking feelers in order to give Scátach room to breathe.

It was just enough. Leaping and wheeling over several swipes of the tentacles, she ran straight through the pool, and though the coruscating energies inside flashed and struck at her violently, she made it through and from the opposite wall she propelled herself landing upon Crom Cruach's back. She raced along the serpentine spine and quickly came to what passed for his head. There she plunged her silver blade into the flesh and quickly tore it away. The tentacles below took some time to stretch up to clutch at her, giving her some scant moments to use her long, talon-like nails to carve powerful sigils into the very brain of the creature.

She leaped away as quickly as she could, but was batted in mid-air and struck the far wall, before falling to the stone floor.

CúChulainn saw Scátach crash heavily to the ground but was amazed when she sprang instantly to her feet once again.

'The binding spell I tore into him will last but a moment, for he will regenerate against the wound!' she called. 'Ferdia! Uatach! The suffering is his gateway, the source of his power! End it, end it now! *Break the connection!'*

Indeed, the tentacles nearest the pool were wavering as Crom Cruach struggled to heal the spell dug into his brain matter, and so Ferdia leaped over them and struck away the mutilated head of one of the bound ShadowKin. Immediately, the corresponding beam of energy gripping CúChulainn disappeared.

'That's it!' cried Uatach and she leapt in, driving her spear into the heart of Ainnle, killing him as cleanly and painlessly as she could.

Another beam cut out, but Crom Cruach had regained control of himself and the tentacles multiplied and reached out for the ShadowKin once again. Ferdia and Uatach were forced flee the pool, leaping and ducking away to safety.

Scátach bore in nevertheless, and jumping high she landed atop a sacrificial pole and took off the head of Sciabar, leaving only Ardan to be mercifully dispatched. But the tentacles were too thick around the pool, and one thin member wrapped around her heel even as she tried to leap from the post to safety. She was slammed hard to the ground and then quickly dragged skywards to the level of Crom Cruach's head where she dangled upside-down before his slavering maw.

'Know, my rebellious child, that all your years spent fomenting plans beneath the cursed Tree could only ever have come to naught. And thus they have,' mocked the multitude of voices.

Below her, Ferdia, Uatach and Naoise sought desperately to find an opening, a chance to bring an end to Ardan's suffering. But it was no use – Crom Cruach had tightened his thickest tentacles about the post upon which Ardan was tied, covering the hideously-suffering ShadowKin from sight. Their weapons were either blunted against the pulsating mass or blazed into shards of burning metal.

High above, Crom Cruach continued his victorious proclamations, all the while whirling Scátach by her ankle so that she could not twist around to her advantage.

'I alone peer through the weft of time itself: it is a dimension that holds no mystery for Crom Cruach. I saw that you would deliver Lugh's whelp for me to devour as clearly as I see you before me now: pathetically helpless, weak and predictable. Even more so than your sisters.'

Scátach grasped one of the nearby flailing tentacles, and with that leverage somehow managed to bring her knees up so that she could hack away the appendage that held her ankle. She dropped through the air and Crom Cruach grasped out at her yet again as she fell. Several of his feelers were slashed away by her flashing blade, but he put all of his effort to it and seized her once again before she could reach the floor, this time carefully holding her fast around the wrist of her sword arm.

Below, in those precious, hard-won seconds, CúChulainn - enfeebled by the sole shimmering umbilicus that drained his life-force into Crom Cruach – launched himself roaring in pain and fury at the mass of alien flesh covering Ardan. The Answerer, Danann blade that it was, cut away the protecting tentacles, and CúChulainn collapsed to his knees in the pool once again. But Naoise seized the opportunity and with his feet upon CúChulainn's shoulders, he leaped towards the hole in the quickly reforming tentacles and, with great sadness, he drove his blade into his brother's briefly exposed head, ending his supreme agony with the gift of death.

The countless choral voices of Crom Cruach screamed in the heads of every living creature upon the island. The bridge of suffering destroyed, the darkling god was brought fully into the natural plane of existence.

'He is in *our* world now! Cut him to pieces!!' screamed Scátach from above, and Crom's terrible howling grew more shrill as his flesh was ripped and torn by the now effective blades of the ShadowKin.

Ferdia, Uatach and Naoise added their own feverish battle cries to the cacophony in the chamber as they hacked great gibbets of flesh- from the newly vulnerable and awkward mass.

*****

Aifé's eyes snapped open in the dimly glowing chamber, awakening from her trance. Something was amiss.

'My master's plain waivers,' she said. 'Scátach is more resourceful than we imagined.'

Nardul, who had been speaking with his war counsellors, turned to regard her, suspicious as ever.

'Will she trouble us?' he grunted.

'No,' Aifé replied, her voice like steel. 'I will deal with my sister; my powers are still formidable in my own castle.'

Her eyes began to glow, filling the dark chamber with unearthly green light.

*****

Crom Cruach's hideous symphony of voices resonated around the Chamber of Pain, launching invectives at the dancing figures who were tearing apart his freshly-materialised flesh.

'Think not that you have conquered, Danann-spawn!!' they howled. **'I have taken enough pure force from the boy to yet breach the worldly walls. You will feed and replenish me for thousands of years to come!'**

Still holding Scátach tight with his intact upper tentacles, Crom Cruach began to collapse in upon himself, to shrink away towards a rapidly growing disc of blueish energy that appeared halfway up the height of the chamber.

'He's trying to flee...' CúChulainn forced himself to yell in spite of his utter fatigue. 'Ferdia...'

Ferdia did not have to be told; already he was running full pelt at an angle along the stone wall and, just as the laughing mass that was what remained of Crom Cruach was disappearing into the scintillating breach between worlds, he leapt and landed amongst the retreating tentacles. In less than a second, he cut away those limbs, then he and the freed Scátach tumbled to the ground below.

A tremendous noise, an awful sucking of air and moisture, crushed flesh and compressed bone accompanied Crom Cruach's disappearance from this plane of reality, his final threats hurled at CúChulainn.

'Your efforts are in vain, whelp of Lugh! The Age of the Worm has already begun!!'

The dazzling blue disc then dropped to the centre of the blood-red waters of the pool, sending up a plume of sea-water and plasma.

CúChulainn spat into the water, then leaning heavily upon the Answerer lowered himself to one knee; he felt a fatigue unlike anything he had ever experienced before. He was truly drained in the most literal sense.

But from the corner of his eye he saw a white shape moving towards Ferdia where he lay stunned upon the stone floor.

Aifé!

He knew not from where she had emerged, but he saw the Danann witch advance now upon the downed captain, drawing from her white robes a long, serrated dagger.

Too weak to cry out, CúChulainn dug deeply into his final reserves of energy and grasped the Gae Bolga from its sheath upon his back. He invoked the word of power and launched the deadly demon-spear towards Aifé who now had one arm extended towards the dazed Ferdia.

The Gae Bolga screeched across the air and sliced through the white-clad figure, embedding itself in the stone wall behind, a steaming string of viscera hanging from its shaft.

Aifé turned to face CúChulainn and the other ShadowKin, her hands moving to the patch of red spreading outward from the centre of her white gown, an expression of utmost shock on her beautiful face, and then she smiled.

Suddenly the white of her robes turned to black, her bloodied arms became paler, thinner, her mane of golden hair melted away and the lines of her face hardened into the severe visage of Scátach.

Ferdia, flecked with her blood, gasped, then leaped up to support his stumbling mistress.

'*Areadbhar,* the lance of Lugh...' she whispered to him. '...a fine weapon to fall by. Alas, none can withstand its piercing... *none.*'

CúChulainn and the surviving ShadowKin, along with those others who flooded into the chamber now that Crom Cruach's sealing spells were no more, rushed forward to gather around their faltering leader.

Ferdia laid Scátach gently to the floor and Uatach knelt beside her and cradled her head. But the Mistress reached out to CúChulainn and, swearing vehemently in a sorrow-cracked voice, he took her hands in his.

'Mistress!! What have I done? Curse Aifé and her mind-bending!'

Dark blood began to trickle from the corner of Scátach's mouth but she gazed about her, her white-less eyes as unfathomable as ever.

'...ShadowKin, I salute you. I have trained you as best I could and regret that I will not join you in the conflicts ahead... For great will they be...

'The evil of Aifé and the Worm must be purged from this world! This... this is my last decree. I know not where my sister hides, but I charge you with her destruction... and... the Slaughterhound will lead you in this!'

Scátach then, to the amazement of all, actually managed to pull herself up to a sitting position and put one arm around Uatach's neck. There was great insistence in her voice: and it was clear that she was using the very last of her superhuman force to speak.

'Do not condemn him, for the ploys of Aifé are to blame. He will lead you to greatness. He is the answer, my daughter. Carry forth the legacy of Scátach, so long hidden... in the shadows.'

Then she turned to Ferdia and her head fell against his shoulder. He took her face in his hands and struggled against the urge to weep. He knew it would not be fitting.

'Ferdia...' she uttered, '...my champion for so long, forgive me the mistakes of my hope. Greatness is ahead, on you and your deeds will much depend.'

Finally Scátach turned her head to face CúChulainn and her ShadowKin again.

'The darkness comes... for me. I fear it not.... for I know it well...'

And then she died.

*****

Aifé emerged from the dim interior of the Monitor to stand on a viewing platform perched high upon the rear of the Fomorian flagship.

Feeling dizzy with pleasure and triumph, yet weak from the exertion of her final illusion from such a distance, she had to grip the barnacle-encrusted railing for fear of shrieking with unseemly joy in front of Nardul and his counsellors.

She gazed back at where the wakes of the other leviathans of the attack fleet began to break up, back to the distant island of Alba where the spirit of her bitterest enemy was fading out of existence.

'It is done,' she intoned, then turned to face Nardul. 'A great shadow is lifted from my heart. There is nothing left to thwart us.'

Nardul stood nodding for a moment, then moved to the viewing platform to join Aifé. He removed his great golden-horned helm and gingerly touched with one webbed claw the painful stump where once his Horn of Prestige had grown. He knew it would only truly grow back if he succeeded in amassing great victories so that he might psychically absorb the euphoria of triumph that would emanate from his grateful people.

249

'You have had your revenge on your sister – now, at last, comes the moment of Nardul's vengeance upon Conchobar. Land filth!' he growled into the whistling wind.

The Fomorian vessels acknowledged his oath with a deep bass rumbling that sent all nearby sea life darting away or scuttling under rocks for safety. Then their enormous muscles flexed and churned the sea, eager to bring the master to his glorious destiny.

On the horizon ahead of them, the strip of land that was the coast of Uladh, grew steadily thicker as the Fomorian fleet approached.

5.

Despair

Uatach could not bear her mother to lie in that evil chamber where Aifé had lately spun her depraved magick. She lifted the slender body in her arms and headed towards the heavy doors to seek cleaner air.

But after only a few steps streams of smoke unfurled from Scátach's body and in moments she had completely disintegrated into clouds of greyish vapour which rose into the darkness of the vaults overhead, where a dim resonance could be heard, almost like a distant laughing voice...

Empty-handed and bewildered, only one sharp, grief-stricken word betrayed her.

'*Mother...!*'

CúChulainn meanwhile had called the Gae Bolga to him once again, though it filled him with disgust to hold the weapon. The indomitable spear, which he had received from his father with such pride, was tainted even now. Twice he had used it and twice it had killed someone close to him.

There was no blood on it however, even that had disappeared. For the greedy spear was eternally clean, always lapping up the sweet red wine of victorious violence.

At the sight of her dissolution, his heart lurched sickeningly. *My guilt will be eternal* thought CúChulainn, with absolute certainty.

He looked around him at the devastation he had wrought by his presence here. Uatach, in her desolation and loss. Naoise, who was cutting free the mutilated bodies of his brothers. Ferdia, and others, grasping at their wounds. Hollowed out shreds of skin that had once been proud ShadowKin warriors littered the floor.

Unsteadily, he approached Uatach. He dared not put a hand to her shoulder but spoke as softly as he could, even though he half hoped she would strike him, punish him for his stupidity and failure.

'My father... Lugh... his body too disappeared. I... I think, maybe... they go back to the Danann realms, when they die.'

Nothing.

'Uatach, I...'

Finally Uatach looked over her shoulder at him. There was not sorrow but the same harshness as ever on her face. CúChulainn could see a flinty beauty there, and a limitless resolve. He esteemed himself weaker than she at this moment and felt ashamed.

'Save your words, Uladhman,' she said. 'Just be equal to my mother's faith in you. Or I will take that hateful spear of yours and cut you into ribbons. Do you hear me?'

CúChulainn winced and nodded.

'I hear you well, Uatach. I will.'

Ferdia appeared beside them then. He had quickly taken the reports of those ShadowKin that had been searching the rest of the castle.
He too spoke tightly, but as captain he refused to sully Scatach's memory by allowing all strategy to fall apart in the face of grief.

'The barracks are empty, not a soul to be found. As is the eastern wing, it seems. Another ploy to draw us out perhaps. So that they might plunder RathDuille in our absence. We should hasten back.'

CúChulainn breathed in deeply and composed himself, seeking the power of Lugh but not finding it, fighting against a rising panic that was so foreign to his nature.

'But what would be left there to plunder, Ferdia, save a withered stump - ChrannGréinne is no more,' he said, hating the despair he heard in his own words. 'It seems this conflict has become a senseless war. What can either side gain from such destruction?'

Uatach spun around and rasped spittle into CúChulainn's face as she spoke.

'No struggle against Aifé's evil is senseless! Our enemies do not know of the Great Tree's passing! But whatever way the branches lead, we must find that cursed sorceress and destroy her – that was my mother's dying wish. This we will do! And I hold you all to it!'

'But where is the Sluagh army?' Ferdia demanded. 'From our vantage point at the Stone of Sorrow earlier we would have seen the traces of a horde on the move, even disguised as livestock or other phantom forms. No force of such number could have skulked by us.'

'Unless...' mused CúChulainn. 'Unless they slithered along the coast, staying close to the cliffs. They could pass unseen on the seas behind the mists and attack without warning!'

'Then, in any case, we must return to the fortress!' cried Ferdia.

'We will defeat them on familiar soil. Away, ShadowKin!'

But after they had climbed the stairwell from the chamber, they found their way out blocked by two ShadowKin warriors emerging from the floor via a hidden staircase carved into the rock that seemed to lead even further down.

'My Captain!' cried one of them on spotting Ferdia and the others. 'We have searched the lower levels of the castle – no Sluagh. But we found their vessels moored in underground caverns that give to the sea. All empty - none have taken to the waves, it seems.'

Ferdia was perplexed. 'There is no sense to it,' he mused.

'No boats are at sea, 'tis true, my brothers!' called a voice high off above them. There, the group spotted another ShadowKin at a hidden recess high in the wall, and quickly their eyes made out the hidden footholds built into the stonework leading up to that passage.

'But there is something ill afloat on the waves and drifting away from Alba – come to the ramparts and look!'

Ferdia led the way, leaping without hesitation towards the wall and, instantly finding the footholds, scurried up and entered the concealed corridor.

Uatach and CúChulainn followed suit - though the Uladhman was far slower, still drained as he was by Crom Cruach's poisonous magick and the weight of shame that clung to his soul.

The narrow passage brought them to a balcony overlooking the turbulent seas around Alba.

There below them, a fair distance from the plunging cliffs but too large for even the mists to obscure them completely, slowly drifted numerous great dark masses of various size. Hell-formed lumps, horrible to look upon, they churned the waters behind them with broad strokes of massive paddle-like appendages; yet their backs were hybrid constructs of ancient wooden scaffolding and some horn-like carapace.

'What is this?' Ferdia gasped at last. 'Are they beast or craft?'

CúChulainn had not believed it possible that his heart could become any colder, yet this sight managed the feat. The normal lilt to his voice was dead when he spoke.

'So now, finally the mists draw back on Aifé's greatest illusion –this war with Scátach was only the beginning, her sights are set beyond these shores.'

He laughed bitterly.

Uatach seized him roughly by the shoulders and shook him.

'This war was no illusion, mainlander! Too many noble ShadowKin met their end in this struggle for you to diminish it so!'

With a snarl of anger, CúChulainn grabbed Uatach's forearms.

'It is not a question of their valour, Uatach! But of our knowledge of Aifé's designs. I see it now. This cursed rock was but a stepping stone for her, the ultimate prize lies beyond this Isle of Shadows!'

He indicated with a sweep of one arm the steadily disappearing shapes behind the roiling mists.

'It is *my* home that is now imperilled – she seeks to conquer the mainland, and has formed a pact with sea-demons to achieve that end. My old mentor Amergin described such things to me. Those are Fomorian warships, I have faced their masters before in battle, they are filled with death and woe.'

CúChulainn saw Uatach suddenly stiffen. His words held terrible portent to be sure, yet he felt he there was something else going on behind those jet-black eyes. Some recognition? There was no time to mull upon what it might be for Naoise - who had been forced to accept that there was no time to bury his brothers - now spoke.

'Then the outlook is grim. For even were we to take their boats and give chase at once, it would come to nothing: the inhabitants of this island are only capable of navigating close to the shore; otherwise they flounder in the mists.'

'The shrouding curse of Scátach is eternal,' agreed Uatach, her head bowed and her voice low. 'It is a *Mallachtmór* – an overcurse - even with her gone, the fog will remain.'

'I would swear that those sea creatures know the moods of the strange waters,' Ferdia added. 'Aifé had clearly been planning her escape from the island with her new allies for a long time. We have been fools of the highest order.'

CúChulainn shook his head as a measure of courage seemed to come back to him.

'My friends, if I can still call you thus, Eamhain Mhacha has not the numbers to repel such an invasion. If any of you have the heart to carry out Scátach's final *geis*, then I beseech you to come with me - let us take those boats and follow the enemy while we can still see her vessels. Keeping a close eye upon them, we can guide ourselves through the mists! Have you come so far only to not join battle one final time against the Sluagh who have so sorely mocked us all with this cowardly trap?'

The ShadowKin kept their habitual silence, but their gazes finally fell upon Ferdia.

'All of us lust to bring vengeance down upon Aifé,' said he, defiantly. 'We are not afraid to follow her no matter where she might flee. We will hound and destroy her, and all those who surround her, or die in the attempt. For remaining here is meaningless now that the ChrannGréinne is no more and the Mistress has passed.'

CúChulainn nodded and addressed the group as one. 'I am undeserving of your help, but Eamhain Mhacha is not. You would be doing a great thing, o noble ShadowKin.'

'Keep your gratitude, pray rather that Lugh grants us some favour in our plight. A kind wind or a smooth crossing would be welcome,' said Ferdia brusquely. 'But to be honest, by the time we join battle, I fear the outcome will already be decided. Look the warships are barely visible. *Ar aghaidh!* Let us make haste then, to the docks below and get this madness underway.'

Uatach glared one final time at CúChulainn, then she, Naoise and the others disappeared quickly back down the passage, as silent and swift as ghosts.

Despite his words, Ferdia was the last to leave. He hesitated at the passage entrance, turned and noticed that CúChulainn was still staring out to sea, his hands upon his head. Ferdia came to stand beside him.

'We'll make it somehow. And the ShadowKin will avenge your dead,' he said quietly. 'Take a moment now, my friend, and pray to Danú for your dear ones. Mourn their fate now, get it over and done with, for we will have no use for a grief-broken warrior when the wrath of the ShadowKin unfurls. Mourn briefly, then join us below, and we will become vengeance!'

Ferdia punched CúChulainn with decent force on the shoulder, then hurried away down the passage leaving him alone for a few moments.

He would not mourn them, he thought grimly. No, to give in to despair now would be to betray every oath he had made both to the Red Branch and to the memory of Scátach. So resolved, he turned and headed to join the others.

But a terrible voice from behind suddenly stopped him in his tracks, the soul-raking sound of it cut a colder dread into his heart than anything he had ever felt before. It was a voice composed of pain and smoke and... death.

'Your hope is false. You do not truly feel it. Admit your fear, boy!'

CúChulainn, to his horror, looked down to see his hand tremble as he placed it on the hilt of the Answerer. He was *afraid!* What was happening to him?!

'Lugh would be mortified at your lack of mettle... had you not eviscerated him. That you even had the courage to carry out the act came as a surprise to me.'

Fighting against a terror he could not explain, and being utterly unaccustomed to fear of any kind, CúChulainn forced his mind to remember the face of Lugh; to remember Amergin's words of warning; to remember also the Red Branch, his home, and Emer.

Emer!

Anger rose up at last and submerged the fear. Without further thought he spun and unsheathed the Danann sword in one movement, then plunged its long blade through the dark figure standing before him.

It was Mag. But at the same time it was not. The features were similar but the lack of humanity upon that face was as terrifying as it was total.

The raven-haired, wild-faced woman started slightly at the shock of the impact, then a small sneer curled her black lips. It was surely meant to be a smile but CúChulainn felt that such a face could never truly express good humour.

Then the fell woman, whose night-black cloak seemed to float about her with an unearthly life of its own, took three steps back to stand at the parapet. The Answerer was thus no longer planted in her breast, and its blade was shining and unbloodied.

256

She slowly drew her clawed hands up to indicate the point where CúChulainn had struck, and where no wound lay. *'All who draw close to CúChulainn meet with impalement before long! Were I mortal, I would be wary of your friendship!'*

'I know you, Morrigan, Crone of the Battlefield!' CúChulainn shouted. His rage was mounting, and he was glad of that. 'Come to mock me now? It falls on deaf ears!'

He raised the Answerer once again but hesitated to strike when he saw the complete lack of concern on the woman's profoundly cruel face. She shook her head then.

'Did Lugh not tell you how many times he struck at me with his weapons in the past? How long it took him to realise that it was all in vain?' Then she leaned closer to him, tiny wisps of smoke escaping her mouth and nostrils as she spoke softly, menacingly. *'I AM the Death that comes in war, and all those who leave by that door come to my hearth.'*

CúChulainn wanted nothing more than to unleash his fury upon the creature, but he knew her words were true. She was the harvester of souls on the battlefield; what fear could she have of violence and death when it was the very thing that nourished her?

'The witch has tricked even you, Morrigan' he scoffed finally. 'For there was no battle today, no carrion souls for your craven beak to peck at!'

With that he decided to leave, for he understood that she was delaying him here for her own evil designs and it was foolishness to listen to her duplicitous words any longer.

'I only needed one from this place,' she replied as CúChulainn sheathed his sword and made to leave.

Then the Morrigan spread out her clawed hands and between them CúChulainn could see a vortex of swiftly moving wisps begin to coalesce and take shape.

He looked closer, then a strangled cry of horror escaped him. The whirling shapes came together and formed the face of Scátach. Though CúChulainn could not hear her, she seemed to be roaring, a prisoner in some nightmarish black landscape. She was the very figure of despair.

Then the Morrigan clasped her long fingers together and the harrowing image was gone.

'You horror. You unspeakable abhorrence,' said CúChulainn through gritted teeth. 'You are all in league together! I promise that I will find a way to kill each of you!!'

An expression of deeply insincere hurt contrived to show itself upon the Morrigan's human mask.

'Think you so badly of me?' she crooned. *'I do what I must to exist, like all things. It is my lot to embrace those lost on the battle plains. To rescue the fallen from the darkness and pain of oblivion. I create life from their untimely passing! There is no misery or malice to be found in my bosom. And yet my name is spoken in tones of dread. You know me not, boy!'*

'The Morrigan seeks pity! How the gods must laugh!' scoffed CúChulainn. 'I have neither the time nor the desire to be convinced of your false virtue!'

'Then let me demonstrate it, so that you may judge my nature for yourself.'

'Do not seek to delay me with your lies, crow. I must make haste!'

CúChulainn snorted with disgust, then turned to leave. But the Morrigan's billowing form was already standing in the passage. He was not surprised that she could displace herself thus, but he flinched nonetheless at the unnaturalness of it.

'The lateness of the hour matters not; you are already far behind in the game,' the Death Goddess continued. *'And you still do not see the one hope that might turn the tide in your favour.'*

She cackled softly and shook her head as she pronounced these puzzling words.

CúChulainn was a maelstrom of emotions as he peered at that unfathomable face. Disturbing but absorbing in its aberrant, false perfection.

'Speak on, hateful one. What hope should I harbour?' he said suspiciously.

'Look to you your sword, your armour,' answered the Morrigan.

'The treasures of Lugh are yours. But you did not bear all of his gifts into battle this day. For I know them all and have seen their splendour. Where lies the Sweeper of the Waves?'

CúChulainn looked at her askance for a moment, then grunted in derision.

'Humph! Too far from here to aid us in our plight.'

258

The Morrigan shook her head ever so slightly and clicked some odd reproachful noises.

'Strange. For Lugh, distance was of no concern. For that vessel is not bound to the laws of sea or wind, nor steered by oar or rudder, nor propelled by sail. She cuts her path as fleet as the thought that commands her.

'Think on it, son of Lugh.'

The Morrigan spread out her arms under the undulating cloak, her features blurring into a black smog that fumed and twisted for a moment before shattering into ashen fragments that were quickly lifted into the air by the sea breeze. Higher up, the cinders flowed together again, taking the shape of the crow once more. A shape that, with a single hoarse cry, flew off in the direction of the long-vanished Fomorian fleet.

CúChulainn swore under his breath at the fleeing black speck as it was quickly lost to view in the mists of Alba.

Coming to this island was a grave mistake.

A mistake made by his father all those many years ago, and now repeated by himself.

'Little good will come of all this,' said he to the indifferent seas that he suddenly hated so much.

Then he closed his eyes and sent his thoughts racing across the forsaken isle.

*****

Down in the dank cavern below Coscrach, Ferdia was shouting orders to the ShadowKin as they moved with their usual agility across the sturdy boats they had found moored below the castle.

The vessels were empty and seemed to have been used infrequently. Unsurprising, given the difficulty of navigation to and from an isle where, once arrived, those seeking to learn from the great Danann sisters could seldom leave and certainly never without facing the prospect of a pointless death amongst the rocks and mists. These rugged boats were used either for fishing between the coves or transporting the Sluagh to coastal drop-off points for raids against RathDuille. They were not built for open sea, and so Ferdia had ordered that the cumbersome masts and sails be improved, lengthened and broadened. But he was beginning to see the futility of this command for, only a few among the ShadowKin could claim to be expert mariners.

'We have scarcely the time to go chopping down trees to fit out these tubs!' he raged.

Uatach leaped across the rotten planks of a dilapidated jetty, landing in a cat-like crouch beside him.

'We have no choice, Ferdia. It would be folly to try and navigate in these boats as they are now. We must make them ready or the crossing will surely fail,' she said sternly.

'Eamhain Mhacha will fall then,' Ferdia replied, and Uatach heard that his words were indeed tinged with true grief.

Uatach was silent for a moment; then she threw back her head and unleashed an ear-splitting cry, primal in its lust for bloody vengeance.

'Aifé will NOT escape us!!'

Ferdia looked at her and saw her desperation. Saw that her only fear was for the shame that would consume her soul and mind should she be denied her chance to avenge the Mistress.

He knew this because it was also his own sole fear. But a sudden rushing noise filled the cavern, preventing Ferdia from falling prey to despair.

The thunderous sound scattered the ShadowKin from their perches upon the boats and masts. The silent warriors slid back behind the rocks of the cavern to await whatever bore down on them from the strange seas.

One of those Fomorian monstrosities come back to trap them, perhaps?

A huge wave blasted its way into the cavern, jostling the moored boats about like mere driftwood. Ferdia and Uatach leapt deftly up the rocks to the stairwell leading back to the castle and stared down in astonishment at the golden prow of the finest looking ship they had ever seen - or could ever imagine –filling the grotto's entrance.

It was broad and long and the very timbers seemed to pulsate with vitality. The golden prow that looked down upon them was worked into the shape of a beautiful maiden with long flowing hair upon which were inset various enormous jewels exquisitely cut into the shape of sea shells and leaping fish.

Upon its great sail was painted a radiant circle in the most vivid reds and yellows, pierced by a flaming lance.

Suddenly a shape fell from the battlements of the castle above, and as the ShadowKin eyes tracked a human silhouette sliding down through the gilded fabric of the sail, CúChulainn slipped into view, then fell the last few feet to the deck of the superb vessel.

He strode to the side of the breathtakingly-crafted ship and Ferdia and the Shadowkin could see by his stance that his pride and confidence were flourishing anew.

CúChulainn's booming voice echoed about the dripping cavern.

'Prepare your wrath, ShadowKin! Hope comes from unexpected quarters.'

The Geis

I have recorded at other times the dangerous power of the sigils and runes that held fast and channeled the power of the Tuatha Dé Danann.

And if I have said that most of these have been long forgotten to men, it is not true that their power is never brought to bear by the Gaels from time to time.

For there are rituals and rites and customs known and used by the warriors and other instructed peoples of this land that have their origin in Danann magick.

You may have heard tell of the spancel hoop, or even seen one about the country.

These curious bands of oak wood are bent after a very ancient manner which corresponds to a potent rite of binding; a rite that compels intended adversary to take up the challenge of single combat.

All warriors of the Red Branch have learned the complex way to bend and weave the lengths of tough wood together, all the while fixing the image of the foe in their head and letting their anger and fighting spirit run through their hearts and hands.

And the man the spancel hoop was made for, coming across it, knows by enchantment straight away who put it there for him and why. And in his mind he sees when and where the challenge must take place.

And he must honour it, and fight.

For if he does not, sickness will be in his blood and in his seed, and no children will come from him save stunted and blackened unlovely things, sorrowful to look at and only good for drowning.

Another known way of binding a man to an act is the geis.

Most men know the signs to be made with the hands crossed one over the other, palms held outward so that the fingers throw a mesh and the well-spring of Síle na gCíoc is formed by the oval under it.

This done, by the invoking of that word 'geis' - so deeply soaked in elder magick - one might hold another to a soul bond. And if it is a just bond both will know it, for into their hearts and heads will leap the truth of the thing, along with the smallest details of the sacred engagement and the length and conditions of its fulfillment.

But few know truly that the form made by the splayed fingers - in conjunction with the utterance of the heavy word and the force of the bitter thoughts - unlocks one of the most potent Danann sigils that was ever instructed to the Gaels, back when that luminous race and our own gaily shared the land and complemented one another with our weaknesses and strengths.

And as with the spancel hoop, woe to he who becomes a geis-breaker - though the precise form of that woe is not always the same.

Misfortune arrives in any case, and it more often than not has to do with the nature of the bond and how far against it the breaker has transgressed.

In this way, a geis-breaker held to keeping a secret who later tells it outright may choke on his tongue and die. Yet if he reveals the secret through sly hints and games, it might only be that his worst shames end up brought out to the light for all to see.

Or the geis-banished man who enters back into the territory straight away might find himself crippled in an accident. Or should he even come back a day or two before the appointed duration of his exile is up, countless other unhappy events could blight his life in those parts until he meet a miserable and meaningless death with five hundred regrets on each of his dying breaths.

Yes, a geis is a serious thing, and a breaker leaves joy forever behind him.

6.

The Cliffs of Dún Sobairce

The sun shone intermittently through a cloudy sky upon the stoic cliffs of Dún Sobairce. A strong, bitter wind blew inland, fretting at the coarse marram grass and scrub with idle mischief, while lower down, overlooked by the tall cliffs, the broad strand stretched out along the coast. Gulls wheeled overhead as soft breakers announced their arrival with a hiss, dampening the sand with their advance then retreating as if admonished by the land.

From this high vantage point, Conchobar MacNeasa looked to left and right, the arms of the bay reaching out to either side in a vast crescent. Flanked by his closest and most trusted counsel – Amergin, Forgall, Fergus – he surveyed the massed ranks of the Red Branch Knights as they busied themselves down near the beaches. They had embarked on the two-day march to the coast, hauling along their tents, provisions and weaponry. They had travelled swiftly and with few breaks, but not at a reckless pace – for their king knew that the bulk of their strength would be needed in the days to come. So now, below the cliffs, they made their hurried preparations and readied their defences for the battle that would determine the fate of this land.

A battle that would surely claim the lives of so many of them.

How young they all look, thought Conchobar as he regarded his army. *How many will never leave this place?* He tried to banish this thought from his mind, and turned instead to Amergin, who was making shrill bird calls with his lips and staring at the sky. In moments, the distant form of a great sea-hawk glided into view, swooping majestically down to perch on the sage's outstretched forearm. It sidled up towards the old man's shoulder as he leaned his head close to the bird's beak. A succession of clicking chirrups followed, Amergin nodding in perfect comprehension.

To most, such an exchange might have seemed bizarre, but Conchobar had been in comparable situations many times with the mysterious old man. In fact, the inner-circle of the Craobh Ruadh had a phrase for such occasions: '*Amergin's ways are his own, and not for us to ponder*'. It provided no explanation for his uncanny abilities, but seemed to put them at ease nonetheless, as if an admission of shared bafflement somehow made it less threatening. To the king, though, Amergin's powers were a constant source of reassurance: this strange mystic was an enigma, certainly. But he was *his* enigma.

'What news from the waves, Amergin?' he said, nodding toward the hawk. 'Does yon familiar of yours confirm your dread suspicions?'

The old man nodded gravely. 'The sea, it seems, presents nothing to the keen eyes of *Seabhac* here. At least not yet. But they are coming.'

Fergus was unconvinced.

'We have had much magick pitted against us of late. Could this be more trickery from vague and dark forces?'

It was not that he doubted Amergin – none did, for it was well known that the sage possessed the *imbas forasnai*, the Light of Foresight, which permits the holder an unnatural knowledge of the future. Rather it was Fergus's natural optimism that made him cling to any chance that the prediction of imminent doom might somehow be misguided. That was one of the great contradictions about Fergus MacRoth – although he was as stout a warrior as ever wore the bark of the Red Branch, he always retained a hope that conflict might somehow be avoided.

'Could your reading of the portents be confounded in such a manner?' asked Conchobar. Fergus, it seemed, was not the only one clinging to that hope. 'After all, the presence of the Battle Crow in our court eluded even your notice for long enough.'

'I admit to my failure on that score. My blindness was unforgivable,' replied Amergin, his shame over that whole episode clear to see in the apologetic glance he darted toward Forgall. 'But by all the virtues of the Dananns, I believe I have not erred in this matter. There can be no doubt: a great shoal of evil spews forth from Alba. And it is intent on our destruction. They will soon be here.'

At this, he dropped his head, eyes closed. It was clear that he had no more to say, and a dour silence lingered between the four men on the cliff.

Forgall was the one to break it.

'So speaks Amergin! And we'd do well to heed his words.'

'What's this?' said Fergus with genuine surprise. 'Forgall begins to hold with the wyrding ways? Have recent events shaken you to your core?'

Conchobar winced slightly on hearing this – Fergus had many excellent qualities, as a warrior and as a man. But tact had never been among them, and nor had knowing the appropriate time to deliver a friendly jibe. He shook his head ruefully and prepared to step in between the two before blows were exchanged.

But they never came. For the general's response, when it arrived, was delivered in low, soft tones which somehow carried more menace that any torrent of shouting possibly could. His eyes blazing, his shoulders tense and knotted, fists clenched, he spoke with the voice of anguish, of regret, and of a fury barely held in check. A fury that would soon be unleashed - but at a target of Forgall's own choosing; not at a friend whose mouth acted faster than his brain.

'My distaste for the ethereals remains strong. Nothing but ruin comes from their works,' he said, spitting on the ground as if to purge his mouth of the very mention of the gods.

'But never has the sage given unwise council so long as I have been in service to the Branch. And so long as I am general, I will take stock of his advice. We will camp here and await whatever demons the night throws forth. See to the men.'

Fergus, who had understood his mistake as soon as Forgall's choleric gaze had fallen upon him, opted for simple obedience rather than attempted apology. To the relief of all, it was the right choice.

'Aye, general,' he said quietly, and turned to walk down the line of warriors stretching from the cliffs to the sandy beaches. His gruff commands could be heard as he receded into the distance: 'Set up a watch! Let's have our sharpest eyes on the waters. I want to know if so much as a sprat breaks wave. And be sharpening those blades, men - for who knows what class of flesh will rise up for the severing!'

Conchobar, very much relieved, called after him:

'Good man, Fergus! Get your blood up, lads! Come the battle, any foot on this shore that's not attached to an Uladhman, I want quickly parted from its owner. I am in no mood for an invasion this weather.'

This was greeted with a cheer from the men and a hearty laugh from Fergus. Good humour restored, he drew closer to Forgall - Amergin had departed muttering to his hawk - leaving the two old friends alone.

'Don't mind your man,' he said softly to Forgall, his hand on the general's shoulder. 'His words are born of ignorance of your tribulations.'

Forgall said nothing; he remained motionless, staring silently out to sea as if his gaze could burn holes into the horizon. Conchobar went on, though carefully.

'Perhaps if you spoke more of such things, then your dealings with others would be less tense. It's been nearly fifteen years, my friend.'

These words hung uncomfortably in the air for some moments, until Forgall finally spoke. But unlike his earlier response to Fergus, this time his voice was unsteady, quavering, on the verge of breaking.

'A wound cannot begin to heal until the blade has been withdrawn,' was all he trusted himself to say. He looked at the ground, his expression dark, then walked slowly off in the direction of his troops.

Conchobar watched him depart, his own heart heavy for the grief that so wracked his friend's. Alone now, he sat on the ground and stared bleakly at the horizon once again from the high, rocky cliffs of Dún Sobairce.

7.

Fighting Words

Night had fallen upon King Conchobar's camp. The same night that, somewhere on that ill-spoken island to which his bravest champion had been sent, would precede the tragic calamity forged between supple thighs and cruel deception.

But those things would take place far from the men of Eamhain's notice. Their thoughts were dominated by the bitter, gnashing wind they felt hurtling up from the glacial late-autumn sea, whose clamourous waves throbbed and waxed upon the arms of rocky piers and sea stacks that seemed to venture, hesitantly, out to the unknown marine realms like reluctant sentinels.

The bands of men had raised shelters made from deer and sheepskins pulled across bent lengths of wood to shield their meagre flames from the squall. Huddled about twenty spluttering fires with their furs and fleeces pulled tightly around them, they sharpened their weapons and quaffed a fortified battle-mead prepared to Amergin's special recipe; designed to give light but restorative sleep and – importantly - no head of stone the next day. It wouldn't be their poison of choice, but it was heady enough to do the job of preserving their will to fight against the sapping cold and relentless drizzle.

One such band was Na Giorraí h'Óige, a particularly hardy group of lads, fresh from the Machra, under the leadership of Conall Cearnach. The young Red Branch Knight had gained great respect since his heroics against the Fomorians at the gates of Eamhain Mhacha, and had been charged with taking on the most wayward young fighters, the sort who found it hard to take orders. Fergus had recommended this, the thinking being that, since there was no skull thicker than Conall Cearnach's, it would be well to let the young hot bloods try to measure their grit against someone who warmed himself by the same kind of timber.

In this way not only would they learn a bit of common soldier's respect, but Conall would also get his first true taste of leadership and hopefully ripen into a wise, as well as brave, champion.

'This is it, boys,' said Cearnach to the fidgeting and rudely-jostling band of youths. He tapped his sword agitatedly across his knees as he spoke. 'It may seem all quiet out there now, but I can feel it in me gut. There's a battle on the way alright, a bloody big one! You've all seen some action down at the garrison, some good scraps. And two hefty Connacht bands taken down last month at the border. We won't forget that. I know you're good, and you know it too.

'But *this!*' – he whipped up his already legendary cudgel *Lamhtapaidh* and pointed out towards the crashing waves that had now turned a forbidding cobalt.

'This will be something else again. Make me proud, lads. I want Na Giorraí h'Óige to be a name said with reverence after this fight!'

There was a curt bawdy cheer from most of the young fighters, but not all were paying full attention. Half were more interested in swigging their brew or bickering amongst themselves as they tried to cook up chunks of rabbit on the stuttering fire. One lanky individual with his brown hair shorn close on either side of his head stood up and, knocking back his mead, belched loudly before flinging the earthen cup out to where the sea sighed into the deepening night.

Conall had known from the start when he took over this group of rapscallions that Niall would be the hardest to keep in line. The lad had already earned two sizeable welts and a broken finger from Conall for standing up to him, but he was either too stupid to understand his place or completely impervious to the fear of physical punishment.

'Ah, Cearnach, I don't think there's anything out there at all save mackerel and a damn *cowld* wind!' he scoffed, jutting his lower lip out at his superior. 'The auld sage has lost it in his dotage. Bringing us all the way out here! The only enemy we'll face in this place is a savage dose!'

He roared the last part, which raised some uncouth chuckling from some of the other Giorraí and irritated Conall. Perhaps, in part, because it was the kind of thing he might have said himself not too long ago.

'Ah, this is a load and a half of dung for an evening; we'd be better off back home and giving it to these witch *hoors* like real men! Our auld lads should be ashamed of themselves!' the petulant youngster slurred on.

'Shut your hole, Niall!' roared Conall, leaping to his feet with his weapon held firmly at his side. 'You've yet to even face one of those curs! Didn't it take myself and a score of others to subdue that one we found amongst the Connachta boys of Sliabh Fuait? And half of those brave lads are below the sod tonight.'

'Ah that's you, Conall,' said Niall in a slow, jeering tone. 'If one of those things ever came face to face with me, it wouldn't be long about getting a few soft ones of that!' he held up a brutal-looking mace that still had shreds of pulped rabbit flesh and fur stuck to it.

More guttural laughter from the troop. Conall felt put out by this bravado.

'Oh the big man, is it Niall?' he said as he stalked over and butted his chest against the taller Uladh boy.

'Big enough!' said Niall and, digging his heels in, tried to push back against his troop leader, just with his chest and forehead. Both men's arms were down at their sides, having dropped their respective weapons to the ground: the traditional opening ritual when squaring-up.

'Aye, big enough! Maybe big enough to lead Na Giorraí h'Óige, even. Sure aren't you only in charge since *himself* went off rambling?'

Conall felt a brief moment of shame, but it had nothing to do with the comparison between himself and CúChulainn. It was more that he was aware of the anger surging up within him, and that he could not now master this whelp's challenge with wise words, leader-like poise or noble authority.

 No. He was just going to have to batter the nose off Niall.

 Again.

Damn it, he swore inwardly, then clenched his fists and gave in to rage.

'Ho, Conall!' a strong voice cut in from somewhere in the darkness, and all heads turned to make out the speaker approaching the fire.

It was the General, Forgall Manach.

'Your young hares seem eager enough for the fight. But be sure there is enough discipline there to harness that fire when the time comes.'

With his hands on his hips the veteran war-dog quickly surveyed the group.

'Remember boys, every battle is your last... until it's over.'

'Oh there's fire!' answered Conall loudly, though he wasn't yet sure if he was relieved or annoyed at the General's arrival. He simply felt full of nervous energy.

'Don't be fooled by the rough cut of them, Forgall. They're a sharp enough outfit when stuck in the thick of it. Sure, young Niall here was just showing us now how he would face down his attackers even if his two arms had been chopped off! Hardy lads, I'm telling ye! That right, Niall?'

The lanky warrior smacked Conall on the arm, then snatched up his mace from the ground and shook it at Forgall.

'Right enough! Just show us the enemy, General, and we'll pull hard on them! Hahooo!'

Na Giorraí h'Óige cheered and whooped at this causing Conall to wince just a little. But he saw that Forgall took the scene with good humour and was glad that another difficult situation was resolved without needing to rattle some teeth and risk having them losing a bit of spirit.

'Well. That'll do for a start,' said Forgall, half-smiling. 'But put your heads down now and sleep, those who are not on watch.' He stepped further into the firelight and clapped a heavy hand on Conall's shoulder.

'I'm proud to fight alongside you once more, Conall Cearnach, staunch cleaver of heads!'

Then the general turned and bade them all goodnight and went on his way around the camp. Niall scratched his roughly shorn head awkwardly for a moment then took his place without another word.

Conall went about the group, clapping them on the shoulders, cajoling them and promising that they would see the fight of their lives very soon. Then he went and sat beside Niall and spoke quietly with him, letting his appreciation for the fire of the younger lad be seen by the others.

They began to settle down, chewing their lumps of charred rabbit, and now and then glancing up at their leader with earnest looks of pride, and respect.

Good, thought Conall.

*****

Upon a heather-strewn bluff higher up from the fire of Na Giorraí h'Óige, and affording a broader view of the empty dark horizon of the sea, Forgall came at last to the command camp.

He beat his right fist twice upon his left breast as he approached the two knights sitting around a small fire set up outside the tall bull-skin tent. They jumped up quickly and returned the gesture.

Forgall grasped each man on the shoulder and, nodding appreciatively, gently pushed both to sit back down then entered the tent.

271

He could not yet begin to express - even to himself - how grateful he was that the warriors still respected him despite his recent shame. Despite his being, manipulated like the lowest piece on a fidcheall board. He shook his head firmly, refusing to allow his personal feelings of humiliation and lust for vengeance against the faerie folk, dim his qualities as a battle-strategist.

Inside he saw King Conchobar seated before a cauldron set upon a wooden rack and surrounded by his most revered inner-circle of Craobh Ruadh warriors.

Forgall took his place between the king and Fergus MacRoth, snatching up a heavy fur and throwing it over his shoulders. Then he took the cup of mead offered to him from a young Machra lad whom he surmised from the spiked crest of fiery red hair was surely one of Fergus's many offspring.

'Anything stirring?' asked Conchobar then.

Forgall finished his drink in one draught, then held out the cup to be refilled.

'The only thing that's stirring is the blood of the men. They grow restless. Fear and impatience are a lethal mix,' he answered.

Fergus spluttered some mead from his mouth in an unruly spray.

'Fear!' he cried and shoved away the youth who had moved forward with a rag to mop up the mead from his tunic. 'How it ails me to hear that such a thing resides in the hearts of those who serve the Red Branch! Time was when even the slightest runt among us wouldn't baulk at the prospect of facing down a whole army, and he but sky-clad with only a twig to defend himself and his skull throbbing from the head pangs of yesternight's mead!'

A murmur of agreement drifted around the tent.

'That was before these phantoms, spirits and faeries returned to interfere with our affairs,' said Forgall bitterly. 'I long for those simpler times, Fergus. When battle was waged between men on equal terms – all this deception and sorcery sicken me to the core. You've seen the things I've seen, MacRoth. Those devils that dropped from the trees like poisoned leaves on our heads. *We* ourselves have not the skills to stand against them, less so these young bloods.

'That's where the fear comes from. Those young lads out there can sense our hesitation.

'They can feel that our usual mettle has been lacking since that day. You know it, all of you. Even those that won't admit it, but mutter their secret prayers into their tankards, as if that will do any good.'

Fergus's brow could be seen to knit with annoyance above the rim of the cup of mead that he was now emptying. Forgall, meanwhile, had stood up.

'Be it here on this beach or when Connacht finally attacks, we will be hard pressed to prevail. Any gods that still endure are malevolent; they will not rest until all that we have struggled to achieve has been washed away on a tide of violence.'

Fergus could take no more and was on his feet at that, stabbing his finger at Forgall as he stormed. Conchobar merely leaned back and shook his head slowly.

'Lugh still endures!' cried Fergus. 'And is more than a match for these rogue deities! He will not abandon his people. Recall, Forgall, it was the men of Uladh who answered His call and fought at His shoulder against the many waves of filth who bedeviled this land in the elder days.'

In full flight now, he turned and spoke with his massive arms wide to the tent at large.

'It is because of the valour of our forefathers that He continues to keep His watchful eye on our fortunes. His arm pulls on every sword slash, his vision guides each spear launched.

He is still with us to be sure, and continues to repay that ancient debt. Going so far even to gift us with his miraculous son, a god in mortal skin,'

He snorted then and looked admonishingly at Forgall.

'A gift we have seen fit to squander in our hour of need.'

Forgall sat down again heavily; his head bowed and he seemed to be seething quietly, struggling against the desire to defend his warrior's pride and the restraints of his internal shame.

'We cannot dwell on our handling of the Hound,' pronounced Conchobar, placing a calming hand on Forgall's shoulder. 'All of us are guilty of being led astray on that matter. Let us have no more of it; Lugh will look after him as he will the rest of us. Now let us implore his presence in our ranks and in our hearts, for whatever fate awaits us.'

273

Conchobar bowed his head and, seeing this, most of the others did similarly, Fergus going further by taking out his axe, kissing it and falling to his knees dramatically.

'Bah!' grunted Forgall after a few moments of silence, then got up and left the tent, noisily kicking aside cups and shields on his way.

The warriors tried, unsuccessfully, to ignore his departure. After a few more moments of silence, Fergus finished his prayer, kissed his axe-head anew, then pushed himself to his feet and stared over to the tent flap through which Forgall had left.

'Do not rile him further, MacRoth,' said Conchobar. 'I want no more discord in the camp tonight.'

'Nor I,' Fergus answered roughly, then stormed out into the wind regardless.

*****

Fergus looked up to the sky for a moment to get his night eyes back, then gazed about and soon spotted Forgall. The general was some feet away from the tent with his back to it, standing perilously close to the edge of a long rock slung out over the inky blackness of the churning sea.

He cursed the biting wind and, pulling his sheepskin cloak around this neck, made his way over to the brooding figure. Fergus noticed the other man's head tilting slightly as he approached - a sign of alertness. Whatever might be said about him, you still couldn't easily sneak up on Forgall Manach.

Fergus was no man for preamble, and because it was well known that he never lied, he never had to try hard to convince people. His delivery might be coarse, but he always spoke true.

'My words were harsh, Forgall Manach,' he said, simply. ''Twas no fault of yours, the business with the crow. Even Amergin himself could not scry her nature. That's probably why the old coot has been in his tent praying all day - doing penance.'

Forgall had not turned around; he merely continued to stare out at the sea.

'In truth,' continued Fergus. 'She had us all duped and there is nothing to be done about it. But why do you turn your back on our ancient ways? There's little enough of the old confidence among the troops without their own general scorning their beliefs! There's no need for it, Forgall!'

274

The general slowly turned regarding Fergus with an expression of at once pity and disgust.

'*Need*?! Fergus, there is no *need* for need. Can you not see this?

'This is meant to be the time of the Gaels. *Our* time. Why should we be slaves to need? To gods? To vague prophecies that none can interpret?

'Long have I served Eamhain Mhacha; my beard has grown grey and my face deeply scored in her service. You would think that the gods would favour me for such loyalty, but no!

'What reward was I granted for my vigours save to return weary from the field to find my home in flames, my family all but wiped out. A wife, Fergus, and three sons, fine-limbed and proud. All brought low and butchered by creatures of the sídhe - I don't know what to call them, fell spirits, demons. They were not from this world and their cruelties I cannot describe to you.'

He rounded on Fergus, his voice breaking as he recountd this long repressed memory.

'Where were the gods then, Fergus? *Tell me!*

'My Emer alone was spared, though for what sick purpose I shudder to imagine. I am unable and unwilling to fathom the workings of these inhuman minds. But I tracked them to their lair – what an abominable mound of evil it was - and when I wrought my revenge and took back my girl I did it alone, with no help from the gods.

'It was *my* revenge, Fergus. I slew them not in the name of Lugh that day. As I struck them down I called the names of my lost wife and sons that they might know who they took from me, and why their own deaths would be so slow, so agonising.

'I had no need of Lugh that day, Fergus. Nor any day since. My need for gods is buried in that grassy tomb.

'And I am the stronger without it, without *them*, as would we all be!'

Forgall finished, his hands shaking from emotion and memory, his panting mingled with the howling of the indifferent wind. Fergus was staggered at these words.

'How can it be that I have not before heard this tale of sorrow? Had I been aware of it, my tongue would never have been so barbed against you!'

'No songs were sung nor tales wrought of those events, and nor do I wish there to be,' said Forgall quietly. 'Nor have I ever told this to my daughter, letting her believe that illness carried off her mother and brothers before their time. Mercifully, she was too young to remember. No, these wounds are my own and not for drunken recounting around campfires.'

Fergus stepped forward and took his old friend and battle-companion by the shoulders.

'I do not have the words to salve the wounds in your heart. And I don't know what course I would have followed had these things befallen me in your place. But I pray that your faith may be restored to you on the battlefield.'

Forgall half smiled and shook his head sadly.

'Pray then Fergus, if you have a need to...'

Forgall then disengaged himself from Fergus; not roughly, but firmly, then went walking off into the night along the stony shore.

Fergus watched him quizzically for a time, then sighed heavily. After a few moments, he turned back to the command tent, stopped, thought better of it and headed to his personal shelter to pray or to sleep... he wasn't sure yet.

*****

With the customary pre-battle reveling over, the veteran Red Branch Knights drifted out of the command tent to find their own covered chariots or hastily erected shelters for the night. Short was the carousing this time for if indeed they were to face the full contingent of the redoubtable Sluagh, then Conchobar wanted the men to be at their very best. He fervently hoped that Amergin's brew, concocted to sharpen reflexes and quash fear, would aid them in this.

The king got to his feet and chased out Muirgin, the young MacRoth boy, who was preparing the king's weaponry for the morn, polishing and placing them upon a rough wooden stand. When the lad was gone and he was alone he went over to the stand and took up his broad iron sword, *Gan Trua,* the Merciless. Then he too exited the smoky warmth of the tent.

He surveyed the campfires of his army below him. Dotted about the rocky landscape were banded together groups of young bloods, older warriors, proven Red Branch Knights and some with ten or fewer battles but not yet veteran, some woodworkers, horse handlers and chariot crafters. They all tended to form groups according to type, age or friendship, but were utterly united as Uladhmen, as defenders of Eamhain, the Craobh Ruadh, and all that she stood for.

And her king.

Conchobar couldn't have felt prouder despite his uneasiness in the wake of all the strange recent events and the vagueness of Amergin's fears.

In any case, it was time for him to offer up his battle prayer. He would dedicate it to the people of Eamhain, for his heart burned with his love for them at that moment.

He crouched down to one knee and struck Gan Trua into the ground before him, then pressed his forehead to its hilt.

'Sleep, men of Uladh,' he began.

'Though dire danger be at hand,
And shadows creep across the land,
Though darkness looms from o'er the foam,
And death approaches hearth and home.
Take heart from dreams of battles won,
Of villains slain and brave deeds done,
Of summer days in warm embraces,
Of your children's tender faces.

Then rise, men of Uladh!

Rise up to greet the rays of dawn,
With javelin poised and long-sword drawn,
And shield raised and dagger ready,
Sling-stone hard and spear-point steady.
With hearts of stone and blood of fire,
Strike your foe with thunderous ire,
Slash and stab and beat and crush them,
Into the great abyss push them.

And when the day is won once more,
And fields are red with blood and gore.
With Uladh's lands again defended,
Battle won and combat ended.
Then may you fall again to sleep,
And all the spoils of victory reap.
Your valour shall endure so long,
Another verse in Glory's Song.'

8.

Havoc and the Hackles

Conchobar was deep in the throes of battle. He swung Gan Trua about him and the limbs of demons flew in all directions. Blood and screams splashed together and he sang along with them, joyful to be defending his land and his people. But the euphoria swiftly disappeared. He noticed that he was hopelessly outnumbered. The bodies of his enemies were pressing so densely around him that they blocked out the sun; but worst of all, a persistent shrill cry was offending his ears. What was this horrible mockery of a laugh? He dreaded that it was The Morrigan, that the foul battle-crow had come to take him at last. He was sickened that she had penetrated the very Craobh Ruadh.

That horrible keening laugh....

Then he opened his eyes and the battle receded away to wherever nightmares dwelt.

But the unwholesome mocking cries continued. Conchobar pulled himself stiffly to his feet and left his tent. The morning was cold and it was late, he had slept deeper than he would have wished.

Getting old, getting soft, he cursed to himself.

Once outside he immediately gazed skywards, towards the shrill, jeering sounds that had roused him, and was greeted by the sight of hundreds, maybe even thousands, of seagulls as far as the eye could see.

They turned and dipped in complex patterns, filling the air with their raucous calls and their gleaming white plumage. They swept low over the waters and moiled together high in the air. Conchobar winced from their wicked cries, then spotted Amergin and Forgall at the cliff line looking down at the preparations that were now underway on the beach below.

Still seething that he had not roused himself at dawn, he trudged up to where the two men stood speaking and pointing to the cliffs to either side, and to the sea.

Forgall, turned to greet the king before he was within twenty paces of them. Even against the cacophony that was shattering the very skies above, the general was aware of all things around him.

'My lack of fondness for birds grows ever deeper,' Forgall said, without humour.

278

'What a villainous din this morn!' growled Conchobar. 'Is this to be some herald of doom, Amergin?'

When Amergin turned, Conchobar saw a strange, worrisome regard in those dark eyes,. A look that, as he spoke, seemed to fix upon something beyond this world.

'It is troubling to my eyes,' he said. 'This is not the first time I have witnessed such a thing. Direct your gaze not at the sky but towards the sea, for the real threat lurks below the waves.'

Amergin turned his back on the king to stare out at the seemingly innocent waters stretched out before them.

'The struggle will soon be upon us, and it will be hard fought,' Amergin added.

Conchobar stepped up beside him and scanned the horizon for himself.

'You say battle is at our door, yet still no sail nor ship breaks the sea line. Nevertheless, if your guess is true and the Fomorian threat returns, we will welcome them with the points of our spears, lances and javelins as they crawl onto our beaches. We shall be more than a match for them, for their limbs will surely ache from the effort of their journey.'

Forgall also stepped closer to the edge of the cliff then so that the three men made a single line of defiance against the uncertain terrors of the future. His right hand worried the hilt strap of his saw-toothed long sword, Nithach the Wounder, as he spoke.

'And I will gladly ease their suffering; their long swim will end in hot pain and much peeling of flesh by metal.'

'*Caution!*' cried Amergin suddenly, his voice rippling with an authority that genuinely startled the other two men.

'When the squamous ones embark on a long journey from the deep, they tax not their own limbs but those of the great beasts they long ago ensnared. Defeating them on land was a mighty deed, for they are cruel fighters. But on the waves and along the shore the task will be doubly gruelling. And I assure you, they will not be weary from travel.'

Conchobar saw that Forgall was shaking his head.

279

'If the odds are so stacked in their favour, why then are we rushing to meet them here? Why not on a solid battle plain as before, where the advantage will be with us?'

'No, Amergin is right,' the king interjected. 'I see the sense of it at last. If we defeat them at the door of their domain, where they are proud and strong, it will be crippling and fatal to their kind. If we rout them here, then by the grace of Lugh, they may bedevil us no more.'

It was clear that Forgall was still somewhat uneasy with the strategy, but he said no more for Fergus MacRoth was clambering up towards them from the beach.

'Are the Hackles ready?' said the general when the burly champion had joined them.

Fergus nodded, his face was flushed and he couldn't keep still as the thirst for battle was hard upon him. It always boded well for Eamhain when the indomitable MacRoth was in this state.

'All we are lacking is a foe. And the sooner the better, *Heaven's Call* burns in my hand,' Fergus said, clutching the handle of his fearsome battle axe.

'Fear not, Fergus,' said Amergin, as he slowly raised an arm and pointed out to sea. 'For now is the time for havoc. Send forth the signal.'

Out in the distance, just beyond the furthest rocky stacks, the men could make out a wild whipping of spray as the far waves began to churn violently. The hysterical squawking of the seabirds overhead intensified and the men had to force themselves, out of pride, not to cover their ears but instead frown and draw their weapons. Then an ominous rumbling joined the hideous chorus from above. This menacing sound soon became a concert of long moans that seemed too animal to come from the sea, yet too unwholesome to be of this world.

It was then that the leviathans emerged into view and Uladh hearts stopped beating.

At first it seemed the seas were draining away and that submerged towns were being revealed. Domes and spires, towers and buttresses slid up into the air. But the earth upon which they were planted soon became visible too – a pulsating green mire, bedecked with countless barnacles and other marine parasites.

The men could now see that there were twelve vaguely ring-shaped monstrosities. They appeared to be floating hill forts - much like Eamhain

Mhacha herself had she been taken and re-shaped by some maniacal demon.

As they bore towards the beach, Conchobar could see the huge arms, three to either side, thrashing the waves imperiously, powering the things along. And bobbing up intermittently between the waves were colossal wedge-shaped green mounds upon which titanic yellow discs – the creatures' eyes – glared balefully towards the beach.

Whilst Conchobar, Forgall and even Amergin stared in awe, Fergus had taken off at a stumbling, sliding run back down the beach and began shouting at the carpenters and artisans who had been finishing the preparations below.

'Raise them up!! Raise the Hackles!!! Raise the Hackles of Uladh!!' he bellowed.

The knights and warriors dropped what they were doing and rushed to the shoreline, scrabbling in the sand. As the seconds passed they were quickly joined by the rest of the army, who were now pelting down the slope from the camp onto the beach in answer to Fergus's shouts - commands that were all but drowned out by the terrible rumbling coming from the giant sea creatures.

Forgall had slapped himself out of his shock and was making his way down to the beach himself. Now was the time to see if the defences that he had hurriedly designed to counter the threat would be of any use.

On his arrival, the men were hefting thick ropes up from the sands and dragging them over their shoulders. They drove their feet into the sand and slowly heaved free the mighty structure that they had spent the last two days hewing and binding together from the nearby forest's trees. Then a drove of oxen were herded forward and the ropes were attached to their yolks. The handlers skilfully had them turned around again and the beasts, heading inland, pulled the sharpened stakes fully into position upon the beach. The men of Eamhain ran forward to rope down these massive lances which, secured to a wooden frame and platform, projected out at a fierce angle, menacing the oncoming sea monsters.

Conall Cearnach was to be heard among the throng, bawling his young pack into the best imitation of order he could manage.

'C'mon lads, let's get them up there now! We'll skewer these hell-fish before they despoil our beautiful shores!'

Upon the platform, behind the lengthy spikes of the Hackles of Uladh, the Red Branch Knights brandished their weapons and roared defiance at the hideous masses which now seemed to be slowing their approach. Forgall's plan had given them confidence - some hardy souls even walked precariously out along the sharpened poles themselves to taunt the Fomorian flotilla.

Conchobar and Amergin had come down to the beach too, and mounted the platform.

'Behold the leviathans,' said the druid to the king. 'Mighty creatures held in thrall by the cruel shepherds of the seas; enslaved and forced to propel the foul crafts of their masters. Each one full to the gills with a host of enemies.'

Conchobar pulled contemplatively on his beard as he sized up the nightmarish vessels.

'Impressive alright, but how do they hope to land now that Forgall's Hackles are up? We can hold them here for as long as needs be. They can't get up the cliffs. And a ship that lives can surely die. Those bloated beasts are easy targets for our javelins now. We will send them bleeding to the sea floor!'

Just then Conchobar's eye roved across an artificial structure above the head of the largest and most impressive looking Leviathan. Upon this balcony he saw a familiar, brutish figure gesticulating angrily down at the beach defences.

'Nardul!' he said, then removed from the weapon-harness strung across his back the grisly artefact that he had won from the Fomorian leader at their last encounter.

He held the severed Horn of Prestige aloft and saw that Nardul had noticed, for the Fomorian lord slowly dropped his arms and became still.

Conchobar weighed the Horn in his hand with some satisfaction, and as he brandished it he roared out to Nardul, hoping that the wind would carry his words.

'When last you dared challenge me, I took your pride! Come ashore again and I will remove the ugly head from which it grew!'

He could see that the Fomorian warlord was suitably enraged, though his bellows were somewhat drowned by the droning of the Leviathans and the infernal cackling of the gulls.

But then he saw Nardul turn and speak to another figure beside him, a tall, slender character, gaudily dressed in reds and purples and seemingly wearing a long, feathered mask of some sort.

'Amergin,' said Conchobar uneasily. 'I don't like the look of that other one. It would seem the unholy alliance of which you foretold is a reality. The Sluagh and the Fomorians have forged a pact against us.'

'It's worse than that, King Conchobar,' replied Amergin. 'Aifé herself comes down upon us, which means that... all must be lost on Alba.'

Conchobar looked quizzically at Amergin, and saw the sage close his eyes and falter, clearly overcome. It irritated the king that Amergin dispensed his knowledge so leanly - so *cryptically* - even in the throes of warfare. But he had never let him down before and so he would not press him further despite his eagerness to understand the situation.

In any case, today victory is my only concern, he thought grimly.

Still peering across at the lead Fomor vessel, he saw the brightly-garbed figure nod to Nardul, then hop onto the edge of the balcony and with some curious, elaborate wooden arc, unleash a thin, flat projectile.

Conchobar saw it silently hit home upon the young Giorraí h'Óige warrior who was balanced insolently on one of the wooden stakes. The cleanly-cut tip of the young lad's spear fell off into the water. Then there came two larger splashes when his head, then his body, followed.

Before any Uladhman could react, scores of Sluagh emerged along the pitching ramparts high on the Leviathans' backs. They began sending volley after volley of bronze discs, which embedded themselves unerringly, even at such great range, into the skulls of any exposed Red Branch Knights.

The Eamhain soldiers scattered for cover behind the spikes, and hefted up wooden boards to protect their lines, but they had already taken significant losses. Some began to hurl spears back at the Sluagh, but they were either easily avoided or lacked power upon reaching their targets due to the pitching and rolling of the vessels and the higher ground enjoyed by the enemy.

Fergus MacRoth was running along behind the platform shouting orders.

'Forget the slingers and throwers! Puncture the beasts! Aim at the creatures and sink them! We can fight the blackguards at close quarters on dry land, but *sink those ships!*' he bellowed.

Responding, the warriors began to aim their lances and spears at the huge blubbery sac-like organs that were visible just below the line of the lowest waves lapping against the leviathans' hides. These delicate parts would normally never be exposed as the creatures would crouch down upon themselves after a beach landing, thus protecting their flotation sacs. But here, stuck halfway between the shallows and the shore, they were in an unusual position of vulnerability.

Forgall's plan, conceived in accordance with the cryptic advice from Amergin about what horrors the sea promised them, seemed to be proving crucial.

Many spears then struck deeply into the soft parts, and hissing blasts could be heard escaping from the ruptured swim bladders. The creatures groaned mightily in pain and they began to heave awkwardly in the shallow waters, mercifully putting the Sluagh off their aim.

'That's it!' cried Forgall, who had been directing a detachment of artisans below the platform who were working on extending some of the lower stakes underneath the beasts. 'If we can force them to roll over onto their bellies we'll have a chance at least!'

But such hope was quickly abated when one of the sea monstrosities opened up its enormous baleen mouth and spewed forth a stream of bilious green corruption over the platform.

The enormous gouts of foul-smelling liquid splashed upon the heads of several warriors and their screams were terrible as the acidic substance burned away hair, flesh and bone within seconds. Bodies slid convulsing to the floor, their heads completely dissolved away.

The other leviathans opened up lethal salvos of their own; the very wood of the Hackles began to crumble apart under the corrosive effect of their defensive juices.

Conchobar and Amergin narrowly avoided obliteration themselves, with the king throwing up his bronze shield at the last moment over their heads to deflect the deadly spray - and even that fine metal began to bubble and steam.

'Our men are being destroyed!' he cried. 'The artifice failed, Amergin! We can't defend these sands; we must head back up the cliffs and rally the troops, or perish.'

Amergin grasped the king's shoulder then, for - from their crouching position beneath the liquefying shelter of the Hackles - he glimpsed something through a crack forming in the decomposing wall. Something in the distance.

'There are yet more surprises from the sea, Conchobar! Look to the horizon!' said he.

Conchobar shuffled about on his knees and squinted through the crack.

'What can this be? Does Mannán himself join the battle in our aid? Little would surpise me today!'

'You are not far off, good king! His home is in peril, and so the Hound returns!'

*****

At the bow of the Sweeper of the Waves, CúChulainn surveyed the scene before him. He was forced to shield his eyes from the tremendous white walls of water that were thrown up to either side by the sheer speed and power of the vessel as it cut through the seas. But even through the haze caused by their incredible velocity, he could make out the plight of his kinsmen. The formidable attack ships of the Fomorian fleet had them penned in along the coast, and from this remove he could faintly pick out the scattered Red Branch warriors as they cowered behind the Hackles. The situation looked grim.

He turned to look behind him; Ferdia and Uatach stood at his side, calmly evaluating, strategising, weighing options. Their gaze carried a steely keenncos only matched by their swords. Further behind them, Naoise and several other ShadowKin were organising the small group of warriors who had crowded onto the deck of the Sweeper. Their main task was to keep the other shipmates restrained and in check – for the Great Elk had also been taken on board. Still under the command of mighty Garracht, they shuffled their hooves and thrashed their heads, but for the most part they remained still and calm. Like the other warriors aboard the Sweeper, they were eagerly waiting to engage the enemy.

The rest of the ShadowKin army were not actually aboard the Sweeper of the Waves, but *behind* it. They crouched huddled in the dozen or so Sluagh craft – liberated from the cavern under Coscrach - which were tethered to the stern of the boat, clinging on tightly as their smaller vessels bounced and skimmed after the SunGod's ship at break-neck speed. Some were tilted to almost right angles as they surfed the enormous wake generated by the Sweeper, but no hands had yet been lost to the sea, and now the entire ShadowKin army – complete with elk mounts – were driving ever closer to the shore.

Ferdia stepped forward to address CúChulainn. His face was bleak.

285

'Your people are beset, my friend. Aifé's forces have the upper hand. I'll warrant they did not expect the might of the leviathans, nor the artfulness of the Sluagh.'

'Perhaps not,' the Uladhman replied, his eyes never leaving the approaching shore. '...but their presence here proves that Conchobar anticipated the attack. I am heartened that they were not taken by surprise and instead have come to meet the foe head on.'

Ferdia nodded and pointed to the defences.

'See how they keep at a distance and pick your men off from the shallows. It will not be long before they are overrun.'

CúChulainn took a final look at the scene, the positions of the Fomorian ships, the rocks, the disintegrating wooden defences. Then he turned to Ferdia, his decision made, and spoke urgently.

'Then we have little time. Un-tether the fleet! And bid them keep back for now.'

He watched as Ferdia, Uatach and Naoise raced to the stern of the ship and swiftly severed the ropes that bound the satellite craft to the Sweeper. Once these were cut loose, their instructions were called to them.

This done, Naoise made off to see to the elk, while Uatach and Ferdia returned to the prow. CúChulainn nodded back to them.

'You'd be as well to catch a-hold of something - I wish to make a small wave...'

Understanding his meaning and the wild look of mischief in his eyes, the pair immediately secured themselves to the elaborately adorned ship, and held tight. CúChulainn closed his eyes, grasped the carved figurehead that represented a female Danann whom CúChulainn suspected was Fand, the daughter of Mannán Mac Lir, and stretched out his thoughts to make the enormous ship come about.

*****

Lord Nardul was pleased. He was overseeing the final advance toward the shore from his position on the viewing balcony of his personal attack ship, the Monitor. High above the battle, he looked down to see cohort after cohort of Fomorian leaping from the sides of their vessels, driving the defenders further back from the beach into the coarse grass of the dunes and beyond. Their line was broken; they were beginning to scatter and would be easy to pick off, and, he grudgingly conceded, the Sluagh were, for their part, proving impressive in the field as well. He had harboured great reluctance about this alliance with the witch, but it seemed his doubts were unfounded. Victory would soon be theirs, and once established on the land again, it would not be difficult, with the aide of his Deepwatch, to kill Aifé and enslave her warriors. He smiled his ghastly smile.

However his reverie was broken by a curious sound behind him. He turned to look from the far side of the balcony to the open seas beyond. In the brief moment before he was engulfed by water, he glimpsed a sight he could scarcely comprehend: a large, golden ship, cutting through the waves at phenomenal speed, moving parallel to the shoreline. In the following instant, there was nothing but noise, foam and confusion as the gigantic wall of roaring water generated by the Sweeper smashed against the stern of the Monitor and every other Fomor vessel down the length of the coast. All were pitched violently forward, pushed up high by the rising tide only to lurch down onto the jagged rocks, the piercing Hackles or the rough, unforgiving shingle of the beach. Several Fomor ships were crushed, others ran aground, and many had their leviathans impaled on the wooden defences.

Deep in the bowels of the Monitor, Aifé was flung forward from her meditation and sent sprawling across the moist floor. She arose with a whispered curse, regained her poise and summoned Midac.

All along the shoreline, the men of Eamhain had been driven further back toward the dunes. Those nearest the sea had been caught in the breaker and washed back up the beach. Those who were further away from the waterline – Conchobar and his fellows included – merely received a thorough soaking. An unfortunate few found themselves crushed between the towering Fomor vessels and the land, or worse, the Hackles. Now, having witnessed the devastating effect the wave had had on the Fomorian fleet, they advanced on their enemies once more, surging toward the ruined craft like a second tidal onslaught – but one that originated inland. They bore down on Fomor and Sluagh even as they scrambled from the wreckage, a second wave every bit as deadly as the first - froth and spray replaced by fist and steel.

Meanwhile, the Sweeper of the Waves had cut back upon itself; as the ship approached the rocky headland that formed the northern extent of the bay, CúChulainn mentally dragged its course seaward once more to veer around in a wide arc, finally pointing back towards the shore to form a figure-six path. When it hit its own wake, it was thrust upwards, high into the air. Ferdia and Uatach roared as they struggled to cling on, the great elk bellowed, but CúChulainn remained still and silent, his sole focus bent on steering the vessel. The Sweeper came crashing down to rest in the central ring of the Fomorian flagship.

Stability slowly returned; the Sweeper's violent rocking gradually subsiding as the floodwaters settled. Ferdia helped Uatach back to her feet then made off to check on the others in the hold below decks. CúChulainn remained motionless for some moments more, waiting until the ship had come completely to rest. At last he turned to face the others, who were now emerging to take up a position on deck. He looked around, past port and starboard, to see where they had emerged. He registered their position – at the very centre of the ring-shaped craft, within leaping distance of the internal battlements – with delight. He drew his weapons – the glimmering Answerer, the fearsome Gae Bolga – and smiled at the ShadowKin army before him.

'Well! That worked out nicely. Now, my brothers and sisters of Rathduille – *let us purge this place!!*'

*****

Out in the deeper waters, the rest of the ShadowKin fleet had waited for the violent backwash from the tidal wave to quell. Now, with calmer waters before them, the call went out to advance on the land. The oars were brought forth – and the ShadowKin began to row with dogged purpose. They glided inexorably toward the land, descending on the failing Sluagh-Fomor alliance like a dark cloud. One that was to rain down death.

*****

Halfway up the cliffs, Amergin observed the strange panorama before him. He had retreated to this position as soon as he had noticed the gigantic crest of spray that had heralded CúChulainn's arrival, leaving Conchobar, who had stubbornly refused to retreat, behind at the Hackles.

There was much to see out in the bay ahead of him: the shattered Fomor fleet, impaled on the defences – natural and man-made – of the coast; the resurgent Uladh army, hacking and slashing at the invaders as a man would chop briar from his path; the mysterious ShadowKin fleet, whose identity was not yet clear to him given that the craft bore the insignia of the Sluagh, yet their occupants were clearly moving to attack both Fomor and Worm-worshipper alike. Yes, much to see, much to ponder.

However, it was not long before the sage's experienced eyes became fixed on one point on the battlefield. He gazed in wonder toward the direction of the beached Monitor, and the shimmering, golden ship that bobbed gently within its vile walls. The ship with the sails that bore the symbol of the sun.

'The Sweeper of the Waves,' he mused. 'So, you found him then...'

9.

Second Winds

Lord Nardul had been pitched from the prow of the Monitor when the tremendous blast created by the Sweeper of the Waves had struck. To his horror, the supreme commander of the Fomorian race was almost impaled upon the accursed sharpened wooden poles the humans had erected to defend their land.

Yet even though his reception upon the rocky shallows was hard and his right arm had been ripped open at the shoulder as he hurtled past a splintered spike - he was still alive.

He sank slowly, paralysed for a few shocked moments; injured, and furious beyond measure.

But alive.

He had no idea what had just happened. He couldn't even begin to fathom how, from his position of total control at the bridge of his flagship and bearing down at last upon his hated enemy, he had ended up ignominiously dethroned and bleeding his brackish blood into a seaweed-strewn rock pool.

Nardul howled in disbelief, gusting foam and hate into the water around his hideous face. He would not go down this way!

The war-master scrabbled along the slippery rock in front of him and, having at last found decent purchase, hauled his massive form into the air of Uladh once more.

And there before him he spied his old nemesis.

Conchobar had his back to Nardul, and he waded through dazed Fomorian pirates, chopping them down where they stood and beheading any that tried to stagger to their feet.

Instantly the pain in his arm disappeared and Nardul was filled with a giddy joy at having his despised enemy presented so fortuitously - and so vulnerably - before him.

He wrenched off his thick seaweed cloak and unsheathed the wickedly-crafted sword, Doomwave; a black weapon made from a hard enchanted material from the time of Balor. Then he tossed aside his ceremonial belt and scabbard and stalked after his prey who, oblivious, battled an injured Deepwatch between the hull of the stricken Monitor and the smashed spears of their crude wooden defences.

Nardul's sense of honour would not have been bothered in the least if he struck Conchobar down with a coward's blow from behind, and so he raised Doomwave high above his gruesome head. Nonetheless, he wanted the human to know who it was that smote the life from him, so he bellowed out his name as he brought the long, heavy sword down upon Conchobar's head.

Yet the king was far from slow, and this moment of vanity cost Nardul the stealthy kill. Conchobar half-turned instantly, dropping back on his left knee and bringing his sword protectively up at a horizontal angle across his head and shoulders.

Their blades clashed forcibly.

Nardul pressed heavily down with all his body-weight and the strength of his broad arms, trying to force the cutting edge of his sword over the top of the blocking blade. But Conchobar pushed up from his knee with great effort, and with their heads inches apart they roared pure aggression at one another.

'You have something of mine!' spat Nardul then, and he jutted his head forward, trying to pierce Conchobar's eyes with the golden horn of his helmet.

'All I have for you is woe!' the king snarled in reply and shuffled quickly around to the right, half upon his knees, to open up for a strike at the Fomorian's ribs.

Nardul blocked it without difficulty and then they began to lay into one another in earnest with their fiercest blows.

*****

In the heart of the central ring of the Monitor CúChulainn, Ferdia and Uatach fought with a fury and dexterity that caught the dazed Fomorians aboard the flagship completely off guard, and led to many a crewman's head spinning off wildly into the air. The Sluagh were quicker to react to the calamity however - at the moment of impact, they had used their great agility to cling to the battlements built upon the leviathan's carapace.

Several of the bone-masked fighters spotted the whirlwind of fury that was CúChulainn and, without a word exchanged, divided their number in half. The first group launched various projectiles at the Uladh warrior which were duly deflected or dodged, but only just. A moment later the second group flew down upon him with jagged blades and spears audibly rending the air.

CúChulainn rejoiced that *Salodor*, the armour of Lugh, was adjusting itself so well to the battle-spasm he could feel coursing through his body. The overlapping golden plates held together by the thick, smooth leather straps slid across his flexing and bulging muscles, keeping in check the more encumbering corporal fluctuations that might diminish his speed. The contractions of the armour diverted and channelled the flow of kinetic energy into areas more propitious to a successful strike. He could now truly profit from the tremendous power that he could call upon in the midst of frenetic combat.

Accordingly, he had leapt into the air to meet the descending Sluagh, knocking aside or cutting the shafts of their weapons as he rose and applying fatal wounds to the back of their heads as he twisted in the air and fell back on top of them, dispensing death more swiftly and grievously than he had ever done.

Upon witnessing this feat, Ferdia, Uatach and the other ShadowKin were heartened and sped along the listing inner wall of the Monitor's ramparts. They used the curved structure to propel themselves from novel angles at the floundering Fomorians or to gain the upper hand in duels against the hated Sluagh.

Scátach's army had a slight advantage in this arena for they had spent many months and years - decades even in some cases - battling one another across the branches and lumpy protrusions of Chrainngreinne which might shift or sway under careless feet.

But the Sluagh also possessed incredible agility, having trained along the niches of the ramparts of Coscrach, or upon the precarious cliffs which tumbled down before it. Thus they fought with assurance and vigour, however much the motion underfoot was not to their liking.

CúChulainn spotted Naoise and more ShadowKin, leaping into the Monitor from a crooked tower upon a leviathan-vessel that had been wrecked alongside the larger craft. Having already dispatched all those aboard, they were coming now to the flagship to add their strength, and began battling the invaders from seemingly impossible angles and footholds.

The son of Lugh now drew forth the *Gae Bolga* from its enchanted harness and flung it hard. The weapon flew through five bodies potitioned around the central ring, then returned to his steady grasp, the blood upon it - both Sluagh and Fomorian - already almost completely absorbed into the ever-thirsty spear.

291

At last, he was using this legendary weapon to kill his enemies rather than those he loved.

Suddenly with his heightened senses he noticed, beneath the clashing of metal and the piercing cries of combat, an ominous, constant rumble from somewhere down below.

All the while fending off attackers and ducking the lethal flights of razor-sharp discs, he made his way to an orifice-like aperture towards the back of the creature-ship where he felt sure the unsettling noise had its origin.

Uatach appeared in the field of vision to his right. The slender ShadowKin woman had landed upon a supporting strut of the Monitor's carapace and - from the look of the black blood dripping from her twin short swords, *Nightfall* and *Nightcurse*, her flight to this perch had terminated a lethal somersault over unfortunate Fomorian heads.

'I sense Aifé's wyrdings,' she said icily, and her gaze went to the dark, quivering opening.

'Come, Uatach!' said CúChulainn. 'Into the belly of the beast we will go, and make Aifé pay sorely where we find her.'

'Agreed. But her death belongs to me.'

CúChulainn nodded and Uatach scuttled down nimbly to join the mainlander, then together they stalked into the interior of the Monitor.

*****

The darkness was total, and the throbbing noise grew louder as they advanced. Suddenly combat was upon them, a mass of hulking warriors surging towards them in the pitch black. The Fomorians were accustomed to living far from the light of the sun, against normal foes that would have given them an insurmountable edge in this environment, but CúChulainn's and Uatach's senses were extremely acute, and further enhanced by the ShadowSight taught by Scátach. This allowed them to transform the footfalls and rushing of agitated air that they heard and felt into distinct images before them – images which they cut down without mercy.

The Fomorian floatsmen, the caste who tended to the Leviathan beasts, rushed forth to meet them next; they fought with trident and net and tried to ensnare and stab the life out of the intruders.

But the Answerer spun about CúChulainn as he strode unwaveringly forward, and his attackers fell apart bleeding and squealing before him. Uatach pivoted and danced and cut fatal arcs into the air around her, with her double blades snapping trident handles and hacking off any webbed hands that sought to throw a net or knife. CúChulainn marvelled at her fighting style as she moved steadily through her barely-visible foes. He saw Scátach's teachings in her art but there was something different to it with Uatach. The gestures were slower and more deliberate, eminently cunning and efficient. She never moved needlessly and each step or motion had a clear – and deadly – purpose. She ducked and stabbed, she twisted and hacked, she jumped and slashed. Every evasion coincided with an attack and she never recoiled - always going resolutely forward towards her goal. It was magnificent to watch. She reminded CúChulainn of something or someone... but he couldn't afford to dwell on who or what just now.

Presently their enemies were no more and they proceeded through another archway.

In the next chamber, which stank abominably of putrescence, the heavy, thrumming noise could be felt under their feet.

'There! The steersman!' said CúChulainn, pointing with his sword to a place high up on a strange coral structure that resembled six large cylinders plunging through the floor. Seated high-up upon the tapering cylinders was a grotesquely fat Fomorian creature whose blubbery arms were alternately being dipped into polyp-like growths that surmounted the rim of each coral pillar. His movements were agitated; clearly his manipulations were no longer having the desired effect since the crash. His face on either side was horribly distended by membranous air sacs that were inflated now to their maximum as he puffed into a valve-like mouthpiece growing out of the panel before him.

'That sound he makes with the horn. It augurs nothing good to my mind,' CúChulainn said grimly.

Uatach needed no further encouragement. With the points of her blades and feet she scaled the crenulated cylinders and came up before the flustered steersman.

His globular eyes bulged a little wider in fright at her presence but he only blew harder into the pipes.

The rumbling sound spluttered and choked out a moment or two afterwards when she sliced his flabby neck and booted the misshapen head off its shoulders to land with a soft plop somewhere in the dank of the steering chamber.

293

'Onward' urged CúChulainn when Uatach had leaped down once again. But the next portal they crossed led to a clammy, sinuous corridor that mounted and brought them up and out onto the deck again. And battle.

*****

Conchobar staggered back once again from the force of Nardul's blows. The long, heavy, irregularly-barbed sword of the Fomorian warlord had reduced the king's already acid-scarred copper shield to a mangled plate. Conchobar found it unwieldy now and flung it at his foe, then turned and hauled himself up onto some higher rocks – seeking advantage; Nardul was simply too large, too powerful and his wounds only seemed to stoke his vengeful rage.

The Fomorian leader contemptuously swatted Conchobar's crumpled shield aside.

'Are you wishing that you had killed me when you had the chance, runt?' he gargled.

Conchobar took a defensive stance with the point of *Gan Trua* held out towards his advancing enemy.

'Look around you, sea-scum! Your unholy alliance has failed. You are already finished - don't embarrass yourself further. Present your neck to me now for the death strike and I will give you an honourable cut!'

This goading had the desired effect for Nardul abandoned all caution as he scrambled up the rocks and thrust himself straight forward towards the Uladh king. Conchobar dropped his shoulder and leaned to the left, aiming some considerable cuts into his enemy's ribs. Nardul tried to catch the king with the spikes that grew from the black armour at his elbow, but Conchobar was already behind him and had hopped back down the rocks to the warlord's former location.

He drew back into his goading, defensive stance again and chuckled at Nardul, beckoning at him with the tip of *Gan Trua* to descend the rocks and rejoin the fight.

Nardul narrowed his blood-red eyes and gazed at Conchobar with purest hatred.

He howled and raised Doomwave above his head, but he nonetheless came down the rocks a sight more carefully than he had ascended them.

10.

Turning Points

There comes a moment in every battle when a great many things – the course of the conflict, the outcome of the engagement, countless lives – hang precariously in the balance. Every warrior knows the moment when it arrives: it is a feeling, a sensation in their very soul that the weight of history now bears down upon them. An implicit knowledge that their next action will have a significant impact on the future, for better or ill; that their next decision could prove to be the triumph or ruination of all.

The rise of Fomoria signalled the arrival of that moment in the Battle of Dún Sobairce.

It began with a profound, threatening rumble, a thrumming pulse that drummed in the ears of every creature - man, beast and demi-god alike – who stood on or near that contested shoreline. Gradually, in the open seas out beyond the line of the Fomorian and Sluagh vessels, the waters began to bubble and churn as the sound gathered force and became a deafening roar. Then, at distant points across the expanse, great, jagged spires began to rise above the waterline, slowly revealing huge, twisting towers as they reached skyward. As they protruded further, great domes followed, vast, coral-encrusted structures, linked by strange gangways and passages. The seawaters gushed down from these bizarre buildings as they pushed further upwards from the sea floor, revealing mighty walls, ramparts and defences. To the horror of the men of Eamhain, it soon became apparent that these structures were, in fact, *all connected*, all linked – what had risen from the depths before them was one gigantic city, the hideous underwater fortress of Fomoria.

Finally, the roaring ceased – the only sound was the steady hiss of the waters as they continued to issue down from the newly-surfaced citadel. The waves crashed roughly against the artificial shore, and now the true structure of the fortress was revealed – a monstrous hybrid of natural rock and coral growth, supplemented by assorted parts of ruined and plundered vessels. Embedded into the walls and domes could be seen evidence of many a hapless fleet – boats and ships of exotic design from far-off unknown realms that had fallen foul of these pirates of the deep over the centuries. And distributed all around the periphery of this vast floating horror, the source of its buoyancy, were not dozens but *scores* of giant leviathan creatures, their great, sac-like bulk inflated almost to bursting, the ghastly home of the Fomorians supported on their backs.

Every combatant froze for a moment as the full implication of this event sank in. For the forces of Uladh and the ShadowKin, a pang of trepidation arose, a feeling that was dispelled with varying levels of rapidity and success. Amongst the Fomorian and Sluagh warriors, the sight of the floating city was greeted with cheers and croaky howls of encouragement, their weakening resolve now galvanised beyond measure.

Next, a forbidding horn sounded from beyond the high walls of Fomoria, and this was followed by a grating, mechanical clanking of rust and seaweed clogged wheels and pulleys as mammoth gates were opened all along the expanse of the fortress. Waters gushed out from these portals, followed swiftly by a most horrifying sight, as dozens of huge, darting serpents – *Ollphéist* of legend – shot forth into the seas, each bearing a Fomor rider. They made directly for the conflict, slithering between vessels, picking off ShadowKin, Red Branch and Sluagh alike, consuming the lucky ones whole, the unlucky with one or more bites of their savage, dagger-like fangs.

Every warrior on the battlefield felt these events in his very soul; they knew with complete certainty that the moment – the turning point – had arrived.

*****

Ferdia and CúChulainn felt it.

As they continued to carve and stab their way through a cohort of Fomor attackers, they found themselves fighting back to back. A brief respite ensued in which their adversaries waited, acutely aware that by driving them together, the threat posed by their quarry had now increased dramatically. Ferdia nodded towards the sea-battle that now raged across the waves – the Ollphéist were darting around the periphery of the shore and between the hulls of the Fomorian ships, casually devouring the hapless or distracted with savage efficiency.

'This is no good!' he said fiercely, then called across to the Sweeper of the Waves, where Naoise was felling Fomorians with broad strokes. 'Naoise!' he shouted above the chaos of sound that enveloped everything, 'Yon serpent riders could colour things sourly. Set Garracht and his kin on them!'

Naoise nodded then shouted an order to another ShadowKin below decks. A creaking, a rumble of hooves on wooden boards, then dozens of giant elk, led by the magnificent Garracht, came out from the hold and leapt over the side of the Sweeper onto the ramparts of the Monitor, cleared that crude wall and plunged down into the sea. They made at once for the writhing Ollphéist as they continued to attack the Red Branch and ShadowKin warriors, gouging at the serpent's tender bellies with their great antlers and, in the shallows, trampling them with their hooves.

296

CúChulainn observed this with surprise.

'I never knew the elk could swim?!'

'Ah yeah,' said Ferdia absently. 'Are we ready to go again?'

'We may as well,' replied CúChulainn with icy determination. Then, with a mighty unified roar, the two friends delved back into the Fomors.

*****

Fergus and Forgall felt it.

They were on the beach, surrounded by Sluagh and Fomor, and beginning to struggle in their attempts to drive the invaders back from gaining a solid hold on dry land.

'There's a fair number of them, Forgall, and who knows how many more on that city,' panted Fergus. 'Killing them is close to tiring me out. And now we have the Ollphéist to deal with on top of it all!'

He smashed another Fomor skull with his great axe, then spat on the corpse.

'You may be right, Fergus,' Forgall shouted back. 'If I don't get to speak to you later, I ask you to forgive my earlier hard remarks.'

A trio of Fomorians fell apart in a heap of bloodied, crushed limbs as Conall forced his way through to join the two wearying fighters

'Put away that melancholy now, auld lads!' he grinned. 'That sounds like dying-talk!'

He raced over to a Sluagh warrior - a particularly menacing-looking one – as he disembarked from a ship. Conall charged directly at him, raining blows down relentlessly on the witch warrior's bone-white armour, eventually shattering its elaborate mask. Driving his foe to the ground, the young warrior thrust kick after kick and strike after strike down until, through sheer enthusiasm, the Sluagh succumbed

'Would you look at that!' laughed Fergus, a mixture of amusement and awe in his voice.

'There's plenty of life left in the Young Hares anyway!' smiled Forgall Manach.

Fergus nodded. 'And maybe in the old dogs as well, ha?'

They exchanged an almost demented grin of complicity, one that could only ever be born from the shared experience of countless fierce combats, then each drew a deep breath and engaged the enemy with newfound vigour.

*****

Amergin felt it.

He had watched the rise of the Fomor city from his vantage point atop the cliffs. The sight had filled him with many emotions - with untold horror; with fear for the fate of the Red Branch army and his friends... and with something else. There was another feeling there, one he was only dimly aware of, but an emotion he could not ignore once he had identified it. *Pity*. He felt such a powerful ache of compassion, but for what? He scanned the scene for a clue, certain that this was vitally important. He looked from the shore to the seas, the wounded Fomor attack ships to Fomoria itself and back to the Hackles again. His gaze finally came to rest on a point at the shore, by the great wooden spikes of the defences. A curious idea struck him then and he began to climb down to the beach.

Weaving his way through the coarse marram grass of the dunes, avoiding the projectiles of the conflict that now and again sent up fountains of sand where they hit, he slowly approached a point where a Fomor vessel had foundered on the shoreline. Two of the great leviathans had been impaled on the thick spikes of the hackles, their sides torn open to reveal layers of blubber now stained pink with their own blood. A deep moaning emanated from the dying creatures, a sad, mournful lowing, and Amergin was surprised to find his face dampened with tears. He drew close to the nearest of the leviathans, avoiding the great, paddle-like flippers, and leaned close to what he discerned must be the head. He lplaced his ear against the beast's scaly hide and listened...

*****

Aifé felt it.

From her position ensconced within a hidden chamber of the Monitor, she felt the tingle of destiny. She had been meditating here for the duration of the battle thus far, stretching out with her *second sight*, discerning the ebb and flow of the conflict, sensing the ascendancy as it fluctuated between one side and the other. And now, at this moment, she felt the gravity of the hour. Surely the advantage was with her Sluagh-Fomor alliance.

And yet she felt somehow uneasy.

298

Midac appeared like a ghost, his taut body a shock of bright dyes and garish war-paint, in the dimness at the entrance to the chamber.

'What is happening?' she snapped at him. She liked Midac, he was a powerful creature and the lynchpin of her forces, but she also knew that her displeasure helped to keep him focused and deadly.

'The ShadowKin have somehow followed us. But Fomoria has been raised; their number cannot hold out against us for long. I will do all I can to hasten our victory.'

'See that you do, Midac. Crom Cruach grows impatient.'

The slightest, involuntary movement of her hand toward her abdomen at the mention of her master's name. Did Midac see it? Did he notice it before he turned heel and departed?

She knew not, but she closed her eyes again and stretched out with her senses. In her mind's eye she followed the general as he stormed back onto the deck of the Monitor, as he encountered a heavily muscled ShadowKin, and mercilessly rent him asunder. She felt the anger in his spirit, the chilling clarity of his intention.

And this pleased her.

*****

Conchobar felt it.

Still locked in single combat with Nardul, balanced precariously atop a craggy rock face with the towering prow of a scuppered Fomor vessel above and the shallows of the coast far below, he felt the turning point as it arrived, heralded by the rise of Fomoria.

Nardul, it seemed, felt it also, for he hesitated one fraction of an instant at the sight of his foul home raised above the waves, and in that moment, Conchobar inflicted a powerful strike to the Fomor warlord's shoulder. Nardul bellowed in pain, remembering with self-disgust his shame the last time Conchobar had exploited a distraction like that, then launched himself at the Uladh king, driving him down onto the jagged rocks beneath him. Winded and overpowered, Conchobar could only gasp for air as the hulking Fomorian kicked *Gan Trua* from his hand, sending it spiralling from the rocks down to the sandy shore below. Punch after sickening punch rained down on Conchobar's head as Nardul vented his full fury on his adversary until, judging the king sufficiently weakened, he reached down to reclaim his severed horn from its place around Conchobar's neck.

Then, seizing that neck, Nardul lifted the limp human into the air with his other arm before driving the horn deep into Conchobar's gut.

'Here is your trophy, weakling. Enjoy it one last time before I take back what is mine!' he laughed horribly as he twisted the cruel spike to left and right, drawing groans of agony from his enemy.

'And know, as you die miserably, that your lands and kingdom are now mine. Mine!'

He retracted the horn and released his grip, allowing Conchobar to slump to the ground. Nardul, triumphant, reached for his sword.

*****

Naoise felt it.

The ShadowKin and former Uladh champion felled another rash Fomor warrior with precise and deadly blows, then stepped back and looked again at the fearsome sight on the horizon – the sprawling Fomor capital, spewing new Ollphéist from its belly to join the fray, fresh Fomor warriors leaping from the battlements to bolster their beleaguered comrades. He was a veteran of many battles, and he had seen this moment come and go many times before. He knew it for what it was – the instant when matters were darkest, hopes lowest. And he knew what was required now: stout heart, strong arm and no hesitation. He hoped that such wisdom as this had been imparted to the younger warriors on the field this day.

He looked around him - he was aboard the uppermost deck of the Monitor; a debris of bodies and limbs strewn all about. He had leapt from the Sweeper of the Waves onto the nearest battlement, and thence he and the handful of ShadowKin who followed him had set about decimating the remnants of the crew, gouging and slicing their way through the ranks of Fomor raiders and mariners, steadily working their way up the decks toward the upper viewing platforms. This task almost complete, his thoughts turned to his next move, in full knowledge that his decision may prove crucial.

He looked around again; to his left, the unholy sight of Fomoria blighting the horizon, to the right, the coast and the battle for control of it. Overhead - the spiralling motion and incessant shrieking of thousands of gulls. Below, in the lee of the Fomor ship, two figures in combat on the rocks. The larger one clearly in the ascendancy, casually circling his fallen opponent, his enormous black sword poised for the killing stroke. The defeated party, Naoise discerned, was human; he struggled to regain his feet, as if determined to meet his end with some honour. From his garb and stature, he was Red Branch, and as he raised his head to face his death, Naoise was stunned to recognise the figure as Conchobar Mac Neasa.

Countless emotions swirled within Naoise as he witnessed the king of Uladh, the man who had banished him and his brothers all those years ago, about to lose his life. The man who had exiled them to Alba, whence Ainnle's and Ardan's bones would never return. The man who had denied him poor Deirdre, his love that no longer lived. He thought of her eyes, the touch of her skin, the smell of her hair. And for a moment the sorrow of her loss began to well up in his heart once more.

This is the moment, he reminded himself.

Stout heart.

In less than a second, his decision was made.

Strong arm.

Nardul raised Doomwave above his head as Naoise tightened his grip upon his own faithful sword, *Luithech.*

No hesitation.

Screaming an oath to his brothers and his lost love, Naoise leapt headlong over the prow and toward the rocks below.

*****

Every one of these figures – and many more un-named but no less important combatants besides – felt the arrival of that pivotal moment on the battlefield that day. Each one responded to it in a different way: some with anger, some with calm. Some with courage, some with compassion. Some with despair, some with resolve.

Every one of them knew the importance of their next actions. And though each called upon a different aspect of their own character to dictate what form this action should take, all those engaged in that terrible battle harboured the same fearful question in the deepest recesses of their hearts.

Will it be enough?

301

11.

Sea-Change

Conchobar was willing to accept that his life was over.

War and strife had always been the dominant elements of that life, and from the moment he could lift a sword he had been fighting for both his life and recognition under the cruel blows of his foster father and battle masters. His every waking day had been an unbroken series of trials and challenges to arrive upon the throne of Eamhain Mhacha. Bloodshed and combat filled his mind as he slept each night, and death walked ever beside him.

So when it came down to it, dying - he didn't mind.

Nevertheless, he felt irritation and disappointment at going down in defeat to this particular foe.

Ignoring the agony that wracked his exhausted and grievously-wounded body, he painfully raised his neck, for he would face his moment of extinction head-on and with open eyes.

There upon that sloping rock that jutted out over the sea, Nardul loomed above him like a mountain: blocking the light, blocking his future. Conchobar truly understood then that he was about to die upon his knees before the Fomorian warlord, and the thought of such a death revolted him at the deepest level of his warrior's soul.

In outrage he sought the strength to stand, but there was none. He managed nonetheless to raise his arms in an attempt to grasp or somehow attack his killer, as a cry of raw defiance and hate exploded from deep in his chest.

Nardul howled in triumph, and seizing a fistful of Conchobar's hair in his left hand, he raised his accursed sword with his right. For the barest glimmer of an instant the king saw a blurred shadow hurtle past behind that wicked blade.

And then... Conchobar saw no more.

For suddenly his eyes were filled with dark blood, his face drenched with the cold, filthy liquid that *Gan Trua* had spilled so many times that day.

He spluttered instinctively and, with the back of his leather gauntlet, he hastily wiped away the foul fluid just in time to see Nardul stagger back on jittering legs. The Fomorian warlord coughed out three or four coarse words in his black tongue. Then a portion of the upper half of his massive body, along a diagonal line that ran from his right shoulder to his left hip, peeled off from the trunk and tumbled down into the waters below the rocky precipice on which the two rulers had fought.

The evil sword that had almost ended Conchobar's life clattered to the rocks a second before Nardul's truncated carcass collapsed, convulsing in front of him.

A splashing down in the waters below and to the right of him caught the king's attention. He turned to behold a warrior hauling himself onto the rocks.

Once he was on his feet the figure turned and Conchobar could see the fine, handsome features and long blond hair of the man who had surely saved his life by leaping from the leviathan wreck far above and striking down his arch-foe with extreme precision.

A heroic deed and no mistake, he thought.

Then he recognised the warrior for who he was and gasped.

Naoise held Conchobar's gaze for a long moment, then slowly knelt down and grasped a handful of sandy earth which he touched first to his forehead then to his heart. When he again looked up to meet Conchobar's weary eyes, the king nodded solemnly to him and raised his own hand shakily to his breast.

Then he closed his eyes and inclined his head in respect.

When he opened them again, Naoise was already moving away, his back to him, wading out to some of the nearby floating craft to rejoin the battle that continued there. All along the coast, the battle still raged, and the dreadful cacophony of rugged combat mingled with the creaking of the lurching leviathan wrecks, the hateful horns emanating from Fomoria, the squeals of the *Ollphéist* as they writhed upon battle-elk antlers, the shrieks of the Sluagh and the stentorian roars of the Deepwatch as they engaged the ShadowKin and Red Branch defenders on blood-slick rock or heaving sea-beast's back.

And above all of this, the discordant screeching of the thousands of seagulls overhead.

*****

303

But Amergin had closed his mind to all of this pandemonium. He concentrated on the feelings coming to him through the hands he had placed upon the oily hide of the leviathan, through the vibrations he felt emanating from some deep throat that rippled all through the great fleshy head of the suffering creature.

He felt, and he understood. For it was an age-old story. One too often repeated already in the world's history and would, he was sure, be repeated multiple times in the long years that lay ahead.

It was the sad tale of the forcible destruction of innocence and liberty. Of oppression, domination and exploitation. And the final notes were the most painful: that of an all-too-late realisation, and regret.

Amergin had heard this story many times before, from many different peoples in many different places – so he knew the words that were needed. When the old druid spoke to his hawk she heeded him, and so did the boar in the forest, and the rabbit in the field. Sometimes even the trees near Eamhain Mhacha took his sage counsel.

This was his most eminent gift.

He leaned close then to a bleeding, conical orifice protruding from the side of that massive head and whispered into it.

He spoke to a dying heart and told it that its last beat need not be fettered, that redemption was always possible, however late.

Always.

The leviathan heard these words.

When the revolt began it went almost completely unnoticed in the tumult of battle.

The huge, mussel-encrusted eyelids of the beast slowly began to open, wider and wider. Then suddenly they shut tightly and another massive shiver rippled along under its flesh, the tremor rattling also through Amergin's body.

The titanic paddle appendages, with which it had once driven itself so proudly through the seas, began to oscillate wildly in the waters, shaking with the expenditure of its final reserves of life-force. Then the leviathan jerked that enormous head into the heavens, the tremendous displacement of mass hurling Amergin away into the sea, and it unleashed a roar that cracked the very skies apart.

Those of the Fomorian race stopped in mid-combat and quailed at the sound. It was a blast of fury that seemed to target their souls in particular, and it rooted them to the spot.

ShadowKin and Red Branch warriors, however, paid little heed and struck down their paralysed foes without hesitation.

Moments later other thunderous roars joined the first, emanating from those leviathans wrecked upon the Hackles of Uladh who now too condensed their dying moments into one final detonating cry of refusal, of rebellion.

Amergin surfaced from the agitated waters and, though winded, immediately ducked beneath the waves once again to avoid Garracht, the great battle elk of Scátach, who thundered past him through the waves.

On emerging once again he saw the mighty beast charging through the surf towards an *Ollphéist* with the firm intention of gutting it upon his already gibbet-draped antlers. But Garracht pulled up suddenly before an unexpected sight - the targeted serpent bucked and trashed about viciously, causing the Fomorian rider to lose grip upon the fins that ran across the creature's head. The *Ollphéist*, seemingly affected by the mournful braying of the leviathans, whipped the startled rider into the air before snapping up and catching him in its jaws. A second later and the Fomorian disappeared down its gullet.

The skewered leviathans on the beach heaved themselves painfully from the Hackles, ensuring the fatality of their injuries, and began to trample every Fomorian in sight while more and more *Ollphéist* shrugged off their jockeys and devoured them.

This defection slowly rippled out all across the battlefield, until finally it reached Fomoria itself.

Chaos began to rip the city apart in the most literal sense, for its battlements and very structure resided upon the harnessed backs of scores of massive creatures. Beings that were revolting against their cruel masters at last, breaking free from the shackles that held them together. Even where bound together by chains, they tore and pulled and the agony of it only made their roars all the more dreadful.

Within the marine city, the Fomor beast-keepers were sucked into valves and then projected at velocity from the animal's bodies far out to sea or were seared by the acids spewed from voluntarily exploding organs. Viewed from the exterior the entire structure of the floating city shook and pitched sideways as the beasts that were for so many years its foundation stones began to break free.

The sundry pieces of the city, those strange and weirdly-crafted hulls, prows and walls from myriad ancient or lost civilizations, crashed into the sea, sending up walls of foaming spray.

Fomoria was sinking. Disappearing forever.

The men present that day bore witness to the shoal of tremendous beasts and serpents making their way to the open sea, and soon enough they too disappeared out of sight and living memory.

The hordes of Fomorians who spilled out of the falling pieces of the city who were not impaled on the antlers of the battle elk, devoured by sea-serpents, or skewered by spears launched from the ships of the ShadowKin fleet, took their chances swimming out into the depths or made towards the rocky shore, where they were quickly cut down by the Uladh defenders.

In the tumult, one Sluagh captain, whose bone mask had been blackened by fire for effect, called to her contingent and they broke away from their combat to follow their leader, leaping from one piece of sinking wreckage to another until they came to an area of shore away from the main theatre of action. There they headed to meet a larger band of similarly shipwrecked Sluagh who looked upon the captain with a mixture of uncertainty and expectation when she landed among them.

Several Fomorians who had avoided the multiple dangers in their hazardous and panicked swim to shore staggered up at that moment towards the group of Sluagh before the leader could pronounce her new orders in light of the catastrophe.

'It's a rout!' the first Fomorian garbled in terror. 'You must aid us, our city has come apart! They are wiping us out!'

The Sluagh captain put a calming hand on the creature's shoulder.

'Let me assist you then.'

She drove her sword through the sea dweller's heart and pushed the body away in disgust. It landed with a wet thud before the other oncoming Fomorians who could only gape at it in utter dismay.
The Sluagh captain turned back to her witch warriors.

'All is chaos,' she announced. 'Leave the Fomorians to their doom. We were unwise to put faith in their abilities. We must to Cruachán Ai in the west to rejoin Nett and our brethren.'

'What of the Mistress?' inquired another.

The female leader, whose name was Charr, reflected for a fraction of an instant.

'I was on the Monitor. Her quarters were empty. She has abandoned us, or is dead. Either way we gain nothing from lingering here. Summon the others with the Call of the *Bean Sídhe*, then away with us before Scátach's rabble and the mainlanders finish off the rest of the sea-scum.'

At this command, the eerie warriors emitted a shrill scream in unison, and all across the beach the various Sluagh who were still engaged in combat ceased immediately and disappeared across the dunes. The Uladh heroes were too tired to give chase for long, and soon sagged to the ground when they realised that the enemy had been routed.

They had done it. They had broken them.

*****

CúChulainn had returned with Ferdia to the wreckage of the Monitor. Both men and Uatach had leapt from one Fomorian ship to the next and scoured them for their target to no avail. Finally they had decided to battle their way back to the flagship once again, just in case the now familiar trickery of the Danann woman had led them astray.

Along the way Uatach had spied Amergin struggling in the shallows and, without fully understanding why, she leapt into the water and swam to aid the old man, briefly leaving CúChulainn and Ferdia to continue on.

'Where is she?' swore Ferdia on emerging from another fruitless search of the cracked interior of the flagship. 'Scátach's soul will not rest while the witch yet lives.'

CúChulainn glanced uneasily at the ShadowKin captain. His own bitter knowledge of the current state of Scátach's soul was not something he felt he could share with Ferdia.

He gazed down at the battle-strewn beach before him. The blood-stained rocks, the smashed stakes, the jumbled wreckage of animal flesh and fractured vessel hulls.

He saw also the ongoing slaughter of the Fomors and the retreating Sluagh and knew that, no matter what else, this day was won and his home was safe.

Emer would be safe.

His heart soared.

His sharp eyes roved over the battlefield, across the faces of the living and the fallen alike. He spied Uatach helping Amergin ashore, the old man seemed tired but hale enough; CúChulainn had no idea what he had been doing in the water.

'Getting in the way, no doubt!' he chuckled to himself.

But his burgeoning good humour evaporated when he spotted a group of men huddled around a fallen figure upon the rocks.

Conchobar!

There was a dreadful wound in his side and there seemed to be some kind of green malignance issuing from it.

But when he also saw the Fomorian leader's sword lying nearby, and what was surely a part of the huge carcass of Nardul, his concern for his foster father was balanced by the pride he felt towards him for having vanquished such a terrible foe.

He spotted Fergus MacRoth, still battling away with his contingent of warriors against some desperate Deepwatch, and not much further off, Forgall Manach.

Forgall. How had things developed here with the general while he had been on Alba?

His eye roamed up about the rocks further inland to where the Uladhmen must have made their camp. Had Emer come along too? He doubted it, for though her bravery could not be faulted her father would have been vigourously against such a thing.

CúChulainn was curiously both relieved and disappointed to not spy her anywhere.

As long as she's safe, he thought to himself again.

Just then his gaze was drawn to a slender warrior - too bloodied to identify from which camp he hailed - who was ambling his way across the furthest rocks.

CúChulainn found the behaviour of this man troubling, and he tracked him for a few moments more.

The figure walked between two large rocks as a shard of sunlight penetrated the thick clouds, falling upon him as he emerged from the other side.

And for a fraction of a second his true shape was revealed, the illusion momentarily dispelled by the unexpected flicker of the sun: a beautiful yellow-haired woman in an immaculate white gown, walking imperiously away from the chaos of Dún Sobairce.

Aifé.

CúChulainn did not allow himself further hesitation; he reached back and seized the Gae Bolga.

'The light of Lugh has picked her out!' he cried 'Now we have you. For Scátach!'

He pulled back the deadly spear with his right arm, and with his outstretched left he pointed with two fingers at his oblivious but distant target.

'Stró...'

CúChulainn did not get to finish even that one simple word, for the air was blasted out of his lungs and he was pitched forward over the splintered railing of the Monitor to the knife-edged rocks below.

The Sluagh general, Midac, had emerged from a hidden recess behind him, and in one blindingly fast motion had both seized the haft of CúChulainn's spear and struck him with a tremendous spinning kick.

CúChulainn's fall was awkward. The unexpected, jarring blow from behind had snapped his neck back so that he was completely disorientated during his plunge onto the rocks. He could not right himself in time nor adjust for the impact, but the armour of Lugh reacted faster, the plates shifted and pulled themselves across his body as he fell, reinforcing the areas where he was most likely to hit the rocks.

He was nonetheless senseless in the seconds following his landing.

Midac had already spun around and flung the Gae Bolga at Ferdia, who had been facing out to sea, searching for the target that CúChulainn had pointed out.

But the Danann weapon would not be used in this way and, tracing a path of flames through the air, it disappeared in an explosion of fire and blood before it reached the ShadowKin captain.

Both men were amazed by this for a heartbeat, then Midac leapt and spun into the air, vaulting over the side of the ship. In so doing he unleashed two bronze disks at Ferdia which were only narrowly turned away on the ShadowKin's blade.

Midac had not leapt blindly. He had grasped one of the long rope-like entanglements of leathery sea-vegetation that bound the sections of the Monitor together and were now hanging loosely from the hull. With this he rappelled quickly down to where CúChulainn lay.

Releasing the sinewy vine he fell the last few feet with his bone-handled short-spear held over his head to deliver a killing strike.

The blade of the weapon clashed against the golden armour upon CúChulainn's knees for he had rolled over at the last second and drawn up his legs to block the piercing trajectory of the Sluagh weapon.

Midac's masked head loomed over him. The feathered helm was carved into a hideous representation of the *Bean Sidhe*, the evil keening spirit that turned blood to ice with her mournful, death-summoning call.

Fittingly, the warrior behind the mask spoke in a bizarrely-accented voice, devoid of any humanity.

'The Mistress had me take a *geis* to end your life, mainlander. You must know then that this will surely happen. You may struggle if you desire, I care not.'

CúChulainn cursed inwardly as his eyes flicked up involuntarily past the horrible mask for it was enough to alert his enemy to the danger represented by Ferdia, who had followed Midac down by the same method, sword and dagger in hand. The Sluagh ducked and somersaulted, parrying Ferdia's strikes with spear and dagger.

It was not the first time that Ferdia had faced Midac. Every time they had fought in the past, however, circumstances had dictated that the combat arrive at a stalemate, a tactical retreat by one force or the other, or the demand of strategy had cut short their encounters. This time he knew that his most prized foe was committed to a fight to the death, for he had heard the word '*geis*'.

Ferdia exulted in the moment and called upon all the skill that Scátach had imparted to him. He would show Midac that the ways of his Mistress were superior to those of the Sluagh; that the island of Alba had always belonged to Scátach, not Aifé.

On a personal level, he just plain hated Midac!

Breathtaking combat ensued then between them, but Midac was careful to retreat and draw Ferdia further and further away from where CúChulainn lay, in order to avoid any chance that the fallen warrior could regain his senses and join the battle.

He turned and sped hopping across the rocks that protruded out into the sea, stopping now and again to deflect the bronze discs that Ferdia sent after him.

The ShadowKin captain followed Midac out onto the perilous sea stacks, hurling his projectiles until finally both warriors engaged in close combat upon a slippery rock. Exchanging a long period of parries and swipes that could not be tracked by mortal eyes - hopping over each other's weapons, spinning and dodging, stabbing and striking in a lethal dance.

It was Midac who broke it off, for he spotted CúChulainn bounding towards them along the rocks in his golden armour, the Answerer twirling in his hand. It was clear to Ferdia that Midac hadn't expected CúChulainn to be fighting fit again so quickly, for his opponent began searching for an escape route.

But there was none and CúChulainn was closing, so Midac leapt further and further out to sea where the rock formations became narrower and narrower until they were but slender poles of stone which were battered incessantly by the crashing waves.

CúChulainn and Ferdia followed him out until the combatants squared off with each man standing perilously upon one of three wave-lashed pinnacles.

Midac emitted a bone-wilting scream and unleashed his final throwing-discs at CúChulainn and Ferdia. Sparks danced along the edge of the Answerer as CúChulainn deflected those destined for him whilst Ferdia, holding on with one arm and one leg, slipped down the side of his rock to avoid those aimed his way. Then with his free hand he reached into his belt-pouch to fire off his own last bronze projectile.

311

The angle was unexpected, novel, and it caught the Sluagh directly in his masked face, smashing one whole side clean off.

Midac, though clearly shocked, wasted little time; he ripped off the splintered remains of the elaborate mask for the buckled edges were obscuring his vision. Some of the skin underneath came off in the process. He then tossed the mask angrily into the raging sea.

The scarred, broken-nosed and ritually-marked face beneath scowled bitterly at his foes.

'It was a fair plan, but a cowardly one, Midac,' called Ferdia. 'And despite all Aifé's deception and scheming, it has come to nothing. All is lost for Coscrach.'

Then his voice took a darker tinge.

'We won't be taking you prisoner.'

Midac said nothing; he wiped the blood from his ruined nose and palmed it along the blade of his weapon.

Then he nodded at Ferdia and CúChulainn, and the three men gripped their sword handles and tightened the muscles in their legs and backs. This would be the moment.

All three men launched themselves in unison from their precarious rocky pedestals, the air between the thrashing waves becoming a blur of colour, sparking blades and blood.

Midac landed skilfully on the tapering rock vacated by CúChulainn, then instantly spun around on one foot to face his foes once again.

CúChulainn landed at Midac's former position, but heavily and with a gasp.

Ferdia had also leapt for the pillar that had been Midac's, but he did not quite complete his landing; with CúChulainn's already occupied, there was little space for two warriors on the one stump. Ferdia rebounded off the side of the stack and disappeared into the spraying surf, his body leaving a bloody streak upon the barnacled stone.

CúChulainn heaved himself to his feet and gripped his side in pain. The Sluagh had struck quickly enough to find his mark before even *Salodor* had shifted its plates in anticipation of the strike. Expertly finding the gap before it was closed by the panels of gold, he had thrust his spear deep into the Uladhman's ribs.

He looked across and beheld Midac, who was staring intently at the prone form of Ferdia as it floated to the surface. The Sluagh warrior lifted his arm to fling his long dagger at the unconscious man, but then he stopped and clutched his midriff.

He glanced down in puzzlement to find it drenched in crimson, saw the huge gash The Answerer had ripped across his torso. With one hand Midac scrambled around frantically deep inside the wound then pulled out the slender dagger that Ferdia had swiftly lodged within.

He stared at the blood-slicked ShadowKin weapon in wonder for a moment, then the poisons upon it reached his head; he thought of his twin, Nett, their secret schemes, his impossibly long life of sadistic violence... then his body failed and tumbled into the slapping waves.

The last thing Midac saw, before the waters claimed him, was the smiling face of Ferdia, his war-paint all but washed off, as the ShadowKin captain clambered back up onto the stack to rejoin CúChulainn.

And as he sank, he found himself unable to tell which pain was more exquisite, the hideous, gaping wound to his torso, or the cruel triumph in that smile of Ferdia's.

And so, in perplexity, Midac died.

12.

And the Victors Did Feast...

The Battle of Dún Sobairce was over.

The triumphant men of Uladh looked around to drink in the scene of their great victory.

Along the length of that bitterly won coastline, where not long before all had been chaos and motion, things were now almost still. The waves lapped against the shore, the waters and foam stained crimson and black from the blood of the fallen. Debris and bodies floated and knocked against the jagged rocks, against what remained of the Hackles, against the sinking wrecks of the Fomorian warships. Beached leviathans moaned softly, thrashed their paddles and breathed their last. On the red shore, groups of warriors moved to rescue their injured fellows or, far more commonly, to retrieve their dead. Everywhere the seas ebbed, there bobbed the corpses of the lost; Fomor and Uladhman, ShadowKin and Sluagh, *Ollphéist* and elk, all united now forever in that unhappy group of *Those That Fell* at Dún Sobairce.

The flotsam and jetsam of war.

All would have been silent were it not for the gulls. They had heralded the arrival of the Fomor fleet, and still now they soared and screeched, swooping low over the dead and worrying the living. Again and again they spun and they swooped and they called, until finally...

They stopped. All of them. At exactly the same moment.

The silence descended like a hammer, instantly alerting the surviving combatants on the shoreline and drawing their attention skyward. Something was afoot here – what new threat was this?

Then, before the wearied eyes of Amergin, CúChulainn, Ferdia and the others, a bizarre metamorphosis took place. For the plumage of the gulls now began to grow dark, as if black ink were issuing outwards from the very skin of the birds. The white and grey which had caught the afternoon sunlight were in an instant replaced by sleek, oily black feathers, the yellow beaks and orange legs similarly mutated into rough, black skin as each one of the seabirds that filled the sky transformed into a crow.

Then the noise returned.

314

But now the call of the gulls was replaced by a low, hoarse croaking, a guttural, hacking call which, when amplified by the thousands, became a spine-chilling cacophony.

The great dark mass of crows hovered like a low storm cloud bearing malice. For a moment, the briefest of moments, they converged into what appeared to resemble a face. A dread female face, smiling, framed by raven hair.

CúChulainn recognised the likeness immediately, felt his stomach lurch at the sight of the Morrigan's hated semblance, and then the awful reality of what was happening occurred to him. For even as he looked on, the dark cloud shifted and mutated again, changing from the image of that mocking face to a swirling funnel, a cylindrical vortex. It dipped closer to the sea, and before the horrified gaze of the onlookers, something began to happen to the bodies that floated on the waves. Wisps of spectral light, strange, shimmering coils of pure energy left the bodies of the dead and were sucked howling into the swirling black infinity. As it moved onto the shingle of the beach, the same dreadful phenomenon was repeated, but not just with the departed. For the souls were also sucked out of the dying, the wounded. Many brave warriors that may well have survived with proper care were taken in this way, their spirits torn from their bodies to the dire sound of the caterwauling of crows.

And thus did the Morrigan feast.

The monstrous phenomenon continued, until finally there were no more souls to devour, and the awful funnel dissipated, the crows fled and daylight returned to the coast. Only then did true silence descend upon the battlefield. The waves lapped once more against the shore, the wind began to pick up, but otherwise all was still.

The victorious men of Uladh looked again on the scene, and did not feel quite as triumphant as they had moments before.

*****

Down on the beach, pockets of men were searching among the wreckage for survivors, or scouring the brush for their friends. It was in this way that Forgall and Fergus happened upon Conall Cearnach, half trapped beneath the hull of a ruptured craft, but fit and hale. All along the shoreline they saw ShadowKin coming ashore, some on foot, others riding Great Elk, some still in the craft that had dragged them across the waves from Alba. Many emerged arm in arm with Uladh warriors, each helping the other to dry land. They exchanged praise and spoke of each other's

315

heroism in the fray. Bonds had been made, it seemed. Fergus remarked as much to Conall and Forgall.

The trio then made their way further along the coast where they came across Amergin; to their dismay, the sage appeared to be hunched over the motionless body of Conchobar. Fearing the worst, they raced across the sands to their king's side.

'Say it's not so, Amergin!' panted Fergus as they drew near to the old man, but the sage turned to them with a broad smile.

'Fear not, he is with us. In pain, certainly, and in need of much healing, but not even the fell crow could drag his soul from his body – his spirit is too strong, even wounded thus!'

The pride in Amergin's words was tangible, and it filled the others with wonder. On hearing Fergus's voice, Conchobar stirred, opened his eyes and beckoned Amergin to aid him as he slowly rose to his feet to address his champions. He paused a long time, as if at a loss for exactly the right words for such a moment. His wound was clearly terrible – that was plain to the king from the reactions of those around him. So he decided to give it no credence. In this way Conchobar MacNeasa had always survived his battle injuries – by simply refusing that they had any effect on him. Eventually he smiled, the appropriate expression found at last.

'My friends!' he said simply. 'It is good to see you alive.'

Emotion welled in all of them then, most of all young Conall, who was visibly moved. It fell to Forgall to restore decorum to the situation, the old general feeling he should return the focus to matters at hand before sentiment led them all to behave in ways unbefitting of warriors.

'What bizarre wonders we have seen this day,' he said, 'And yet the men of Eamhain have stood firm against the dark tide, though we have lost many...'

'Indeed.' said Conchobar, sounding pained. He looked across at the arriving ShadowKin and their elk as they continued to emerge from the waves. 'The seas have brought ruin and salvation on the same wave today. Who are these sinister and unlikely faces who came to our aid riding gigantic steeds?'

It was CúChulainn who answered, as he trudged his way over the wet sand towards his king, half carrying an unknown wounded warrior.

'These men and women are none other than the ShadowKin, finest pupils of Scátach of Alba, servants of Lugh and champions of virtue. And this...'

316

he said, indicating the black-clad man at his shoulder 'is Ferdia, their leader.'

Conchobar yearned to embrace his foster son, but it would be unseemly and his injury prevented him from doing so in any case.

He contented himself with the explosion of quiet joy he felt inside.

Ferdia, his proud face visible now that the sea had washed away his war-paint, walked a few steps closer to the king unsupported, then bowed low and planted his sword into the sand.

'Conchobar of Uladh!' he intoned with reverence.

'We are indebted to you, Ferdia of Alba,' smiled Conchobar, 'and to your warriors.'

'I am told by your champion that you have lately been troubled by the disciples of Aifé,' said Ferdia, rising. 'My kin and I have dedicated our lives to their destruction - should you ask it, you will have our help in ridding the land of this scourge.'

'Then I would ask it, openly and without shame,' replied Conchobar. 'Join us and you will be welcome in the Craobh Ruadh.'

Ferdia turned to the assembled ShadowKin, who had begun to converge around their captain.

'It is clear that the evil of Aifé and her bloated master has spread beyond Alba,' he shouted. 'We are charged by the memory of the Shadow Mistress with cleansing their kind from any place such darkness might take hold. What say you?'

They roared their approval. Then, each one of them, starting with Uatach, walked slowly toward Conchobar, the Uladh warriors parting to allow them through. One by one they raised their swords to the king, bowed and stood aside. They were welcomed into the Uladh fold with rousing words, the union of two armies consecrated by the crimson waves.

Conchobar's eye fell on Ferdia, whose gaze was fixed on a small boat not far from the shore. It was one of the craft taken from beneath Aifé's fortress, and in it stood Naoise, accompanied by several ShadowKin who were personally loyal to him, staring dourly at the ceremony that was taking place before him.

'He will not set foot on this land,' said Conchobar, stepping forward to the shoreline with the help of Amergin.

317

Ferdia was surprised. 'How comes the king to know of Naoise, son of Uisliú?'

'"Tis a tale too long in the telling, and not one for a victorious day such as this. Sufficient to know that his destiny lies not in these lands,' said the king mysteriously, turning away to leave Ferdia watching the boat as Naoise nodded briefly to his former captain, then sailed off south down the coast behind the cliffs, and disappeared.

Conchobar, in the meantime, had made his way over to CúChulainn, who was regaling Conall and Fergus with this adventures.

'CúChulainn my lad!' the king broke in, 'You swore you'd return with skills, 'tis true... but to bring back an entire army! Well!'

'Aye, well... they'd have been going to waste,' beamed CúChulainn. 'And they're not the worst fighters you'll see.'

There was much laughter then, and clasping of arms, and occasional embraces between those who assumed they would not see each other, or the dawn, again. And the stories began anew: of combat, of triumph, of near-death, of valour. Stories that would be told again and again, down through the generations. And if some were embellished over the years, well... what harm?

As the two armies continued to mingle and swap anecdotes of bravery, CúChulainn spied Forgall some distance away near the cliffs. Breaking clear of the crowd, he made his way over to the old warhorse.

'General! I was gladdened to see Uladh's fangs so sharpened and ready for this vicious threat. Our defences are in good hands with instincts such as yours.'

Forgall shifted about uncomfortably, not meeting CúChulainn's gaze nor sharing his cheer.

'"Tis Amergin who is accountable for our timeliness here. I merely fought as best I could,' he growled.

'I see...' the young champion replied, a little puzzled. Then, in an attempt to lighten the tone, he said 'And tell me of Emer. Is she well?'

Forgall's face darkened further.

'Speak not to me now, CúChulainn, the day may be won but my mood is dark. Go, enjoy the victory.'

He made to turn and walk away, but CúChulainn seized him by the arm, drew his face close to Forgall's and said, in a stern growl of his own, 'Tell me now that she is well, Forgall!'

The general looked him in the eyes, unwavering and hard as flint.

'She lives. And for that we are thankful, though her life and future would be the richer were it not for the blindness of this old fool. But at least she lives.'

He shook his arm free and walked away toward the cliffs, leaving CúChulainn to puzzle over his strange remarks.

Finally, reluctantly, he returned to the beach, where the survivors of the two armies were still revelling in their victory, although their joy was diluted by a sense of unease at the strange apparition in the skies that had followed the battle. They stayed there as evening turned to dusk, and campfires were lit along the shore. Then feasting was done and there was no small amount of drinking. As the stars emerged in a cloudless sky, they told tales of heroes and battle, and sang songs of love and magick and myth, and made laments for the fallen, whose fate none but CúChulainn truly knew. For all those who were present at Dún Sobairce would carry with him a dark shade on his thoughts, a vague feeling of disquiet when talk turned to death in battle.

But for those hours at least they put such things aside and the untameable fighting spirit of the Red Branch Knights burned bright within them as they relished such a success against what seemed for so long overwhelming odds. So they talked and revelled long into the night and beyond, until the dawn crept grey-blue along the rim of the horizon. And still they celebrated.

They celebrated their victory.

They celebrated their survival.

They celebrated life.

Epilogue

As the Battle of Dún Sobairce passed into legend, so the armies of Eamhain Mhacha and the ShadowKin of Scátach became one under the flag of the Red Branch. The two armies met in the great hall Craobh Ruadh under the Lughstave itself, and there did Conchobar and Ferdia repeat solemn words and vow loyalty to the acclamation of all present.

To my great gladness, my skills as a healer allowed Emer Manach to recover from her ordeal with the Morrigan. Though she was depleted as a woman, she was to realise her heart's desire: she became CúChulainn's bride on the feast of Lugh, and this was pleasing to Him, for it was a day blessed with glorious sunlight. On that joyful afternoon, as they stood in a circle of standing stones, they were bound to each other with a ceremonial tether by Morann the Judge. This was to be CúChulainn's brief moment of true happiness in a life most troubled, though most great.

But though this was a time of rejoicing and celebration, the enemies of Uladh were also gathering power, and the dread designs of Queen Medb in Connacht were beginning to quicken. For - unbeknownst to any in Eamhain - the Sluagh horde had fled west. There, at the gates of the vast and imposing castle at Cruachán Ai, they were warmly met. And just as two armies merged under the eyes of Lugh in Eamhain, so too did the forces of Connacht and the Sluagh of Alba unite under the cool gaze of Medb and Ailill.

There were yet other dark agents afoot which sought to bring tribulation to all the Gaels who dwelt in the land. The Ancient Ones would not easily surrender their legacy to the peoples of this dawning age. Least of all Aífe and the dark secret that now grew in her swollen womb.

For there would be great struggles in store for the Hound of Uladh and the followers of Eamhain, great deeds to be done and battles to be fought. Tragedy, joy, victory and sorrow.

For all that had happened thus far was to herald the beginning of what was to become known as An Sraith Ultach, the Uladh Cycle. And what was to become of CúChulainn and the Red Branch Heroes in these tales?

It is soon told…

CúChulainn will return in

Book II

Seeds of Ruin

Pronunciation Glossary:

Aeder (Ay-der)
Faerie realm of spirits and demons.

Aifé (Ee-fe)
Mistress of Pain, sorceress of the race of the Tuatha De Danann. Sister to Scátach and Medb.

Ailill (Al-eel)
King of Connacht.

Ainnle (Ann-leh)
ShadowKin warrior. Brother to Naoise and Ardán Uisliú.

Amergin (Ammer-jinn)
Druid and wise counselor to King Conchobar.

An Cú (On Koo)
Enchanted guardian hound protecting Fort Culainn.

Ardán (Ar-dawn)
ShadowKin warrior. Brother to Naoise and Ainnle Uisliú.

Areadbhur (Arr-ay-ad-var)
Demon spear of Lugh; also known as *An Gae Bolga*.

Bealtaine (Byowl-tennah)
Day marking the beginning of summer.

Brúgh na Boinne (Broo na Boy-nah)

Important site of tombs and standing stones.

Calad Bolg (Kallad Bulg)
Mighty enchanted battle axe belonging to Fergus Mac Roth; also known as *Heaven's Call.*

Camán (Kam-awn)
Stick used for the sport of hurling.

Celtchar Manach (Kelt-car Mann-ack)
Legendary hero and Forgall Manach's father.

ChrannGréinne (Krann Gray-nyah)
'The Tree of the Sun' - last of the magickal Quicken Trees, growing in the centre of RathDuille.

Coirpe (Quir-peh)
ShadowKin warrior captured by the Sluagh.

Conchobar (Kon-co-var or Kon-co-bar)
King of Uladh, foster father to CúChulainn and brother to Dechtíre.

Connacht (Konn-act)
Western region of Eriu.

Conall Cearnach (Konn-al Kerr-nuck)
Young blood warrior of Eamhain Mhacha.

Coscrach (Kus-krack)
Fortress of Aifé and the Sluagh on Alba.

Crannóg (Krann-ogue)
Wooden dwelling structure, usually built over lakes or rivers.

Craobh Ruadh (Krayve Roo-ah)
Great Hall of Eamhain Mhacha where the Red Branch grows.

Crom Cruach (Krom Kru-ack)
Evil deity known as the Crooked Worm who feeds on human suffering.

Cruachán Ai (Kroo-akawn Eye)
The fortress of Medb and Ailill of Connacht on the Plain of Ai.

CúChulainn (Koo-hull-in or Koo-kull-in)
'The Hound of Culainn' - ceremonial title bestowed upon Setanta,
son of the solar deity Lugh, young blood warrior of Eamhain Mhacha.

Culainn (Kullen)
Leader of Fort Culainn, a boisterous auxillary settlement of veteran
soldiers, armourers and artisans. Known as the Forgemaster.

Currach (Kurr-ack)
Small boat.

Daimh Mór (Dawve Moor)
ShadowKin Warrior/Instructor.

Danú (Danoo)
Goddess, over-mother of the Celtic pantheon.

Dechtíre (Deck-teerah)
King Conchobar's sister, mother to CúChulainn.

Deirdre (Dear-drah)
Naoise's lover, bethrothed to Conchobar.

Diarmaid (Dear-mid)
Young blood warrior of Eamhain Mhacha.

Donagh MacLabhrás (Dunnah Mack-low {rhyming with cow)-rawce)
Apprentice bard at Eamhain Mhacha.

Dún Sobairce (Doon Sub-ar-keh)
Coastal cliffs in the north of Uladh.

Eamhain Mhacha (Owan Waka)
Seat of King Conchobar's power in Uladh. Home to the Red Branch Knights.

Eibhlín (Ev-leen or Eye-leen)
Wife of Forgall Manach, deceased.

Emer Manach (Ee-mer Mann-ack)
Daughter to Forgall Manach, beloved of CúChulainn.

Eochu (Uck-hoo)
Eldest son of Fachtna Fatach, previous king of Uladh.

Eochaid (Uck-idd)
Veteran Red Branch Knight.

Eochaind Salbruide (Uck-ind Sal-brooda)
An Uladh chieftain defeated by Fachtna Fatach.

Eriú (Ay-roo)
The country in which the story takes place.

Fachtna Fatach (Facktnah Fattak)
Previous king of Uladh before Conchobar.

Feidlech (Feed-leck)
Second son of Fachtna Fatach, jealous of his brother.

Fergus (Fer-guss)
Loyal Red Branch knight and commander of the Ruddy Boars.

Fiachu (Fee-ah-koo)
Red Branch Knight, father to Diarmaid.

Fidcheall (Fi-hill)
Ancient strategic board game.

Firbholg (Fear-bullg)
Ancient race of misshapen, mysterious and powerful giants.

Forgall Manach (Four-gal Man-awk)
General of the Red Branch Knights and Wolf Horde; master tactician.

Freagartach (Frag-ar-tok)
Magickal sword of Lugh, also known as *the Answerer*.

Fréamh (Fray-av)
Horse given to CúChulainn as he rode out to Fort Culainn.

Fuilltach (Fwill-tack)
Malevolent sorcerer, former master of Coscrach.

Gan Trua (Gonn Tru-ah)
Conchobar's broadsword, meaning 'without pity'.

Garracht (Garr-ockt)
The Prime Stag of the great battle elk of Alba.

Gae Bolga (Gaye Bulgah)
Demon spear of Lugh, also known as *Areadbhar*.
Gearóid (Gar-oydge)
Red Branch Knight. Unsuccessful suitor of Emer.

Geis (Gesh)
Sacred magickal oath, the breaking of which brings dire consequences.

Giorraí h'Óige (Gyur-ee Hoe-iggah)
'The Young Hares' - fighting group of the more wayward young warriors
of Eamhain Mhacha.

Gráinne (Grawn-yah)
Forgall Manach's mother, wife to Celtchar Manach.

Imbas Forasnai (Im-bash Fur-a-snee)
The gift of foresight; clairvoyance or soothsaying ability.

Imbolc (Imm-bulk)
Day marking the beginning of Spring.

Laegire (Layg-ah-rah)

Master charioteer at Eamhain Mhacha.

Lá (Law)
Day.

Laighin (Lie-an)
Eastern province of Eriú.

Laitha (Lay-thah)
Emer's faithful horse.

Lámhtapaidh (Lawve Topp-ah)
'Quick Hand' - Conall Cearnach's long-handled cudgel.

Lugh Samhildánach (Lug or Loo Sawill-dawn-ack)
'Lugh of the Many Deeds' - Sun god of the Tuatha De Danann, father to CúChulainn; also known as *Lugh of the Long Arms*.

Lughnusu (Loo naεεa)
Day marking the beginning of the harvest season; feast day of Lugh.

Luglochta Lóga (Lug-lockta Low-aga)
Peaceful gardens of reflection at Eamhain Mhacha; named after Lugh.

Luithech (Loo-theck)
Naoise Uisliú's sword.

Machra (Mack-rah)
The boy troop of Eamhain Mhacha. Future Red Branch Knights.

Mallachtmór (Mall-ackt Moor)

An 'overcurse', a powerful spell whose effects remain even after the death of the caster.

Malid (Mal-eed)
ShadowKin warrior captured on Alba and absorbed by the Crom Cruach.

Mannán Mac Lir (Man-awn Mack Leer)
Water deity of the Tuatha De Danann.

Medb (Mayve)
Queen of Connacht. Younger sister to Aifé and Scàtach.

Morann (More-awn)
Druid and judge respected throughout the land and bearer of the Collar of Truth.

Muirgin (Mwur-gwin)
Fergus Mac Roth's youngest son.

Muirthemne (Moor-thaym-nyah)
Great plain of Uladh, sight of major battles.

Mumhain (Moo-an)
Southern province of Uladh.

Naoise (Nee-sha)
ShadowKin warrior and former champion of Uladh; brother to Ainnle and Ardán.

Niafer (Nee-a-fer)

ShadowKin warrior captured and Alba and feasted upon by the Crom Cruach.

Niall (Nye-all)
A rowdy young blood warrior; member of na Giorraí h'Óige.

Nemain (Nem-ayn)
ShadowKin warrior destroyed by the Crom Cruach.

Ness Fian (Ness Fee-an)
King Conchobar's mother.

Nithach (Nitt-ack)
Forgall Manach's sword; known as *The Wounder.*

Ogham (Oh-am)
Celtic alphabet traditionally carved as horizontal or diagonal strokes on standing stones.

Ollphéist (Ullah-faysht)
Hideous sea serpents. Used as mounts by the Fomorians.

Ramhar (Row {rhyming with cow} –ar)
A portly traveling bard that was actually Lugh in disguise; literally meaning 'rotund' or 'fat'.

RathDuille (Wrath Dwillah)
'Fort of the Leaves' - Scátach's fortress on Alba.

Saidbh (Sigh-ve)
One of Emer's friends at Eamhain.

Samhain (Sow-wan)
Day marking the end of the harvest season.

Scátach (Skaw-tok)
Leader of the ShadowKin and Mistress of RathDuille. Sister to Aifé and Medb.

Sciabar (Skee-a-bar)
Another ShadowKin Warrior captured and tortured by Aifé and the Crom Cruach.

Seanchaí (Shanna-kee)
Storyteller.

Sencha (Sen-sha)
Poet at Eamhain Mhacha.

Sídhe (Sheed)
Faerie mounds that can be a dwelling place for demons, a prison or a portal to the Aeder worlds.

Síle na gCíoc (Sheelah nah Gee-ock)
Mysterious Goddess revered by the Firbholg.

Sinann (Shin-an)
Great river of Eriú running north to south.

Sliabh Fuait (Shleeve Foo-itch)
Site of a battle between Uladh and Connacht forces where Conall and a group of knights only barely defeated a single Sluagh.

Sloitar (Slitter)
Hard, small ball used in the game of hurling.

Sluagh (Sloo-ah)
Mysterious masked fighters loyal to Aifé, their combat skills bolstered by the power of Crom Cruach.

Stróic (Strow-ick)
'Rend' - Word of invocation to unleash the *Gae Bolga*.

Tuatha Dé Danann (Too-aha Day Dannin)
Race of immortal beings with seemingly god-like powers; former occupants of the land of Eriú.

Uatach (Oo-tok)
Scátach's daughter.

Uludh (Uhlla)
The north eastern province of Eriú, homeland of CúChulainn.

Uisliú (Oo-ish-loo)
A proud family of Red Branch Knights, including Naoise, Ainnle and Ardán.

Printed in Poland
by Amazon Fulfillment
Poland Sp. z o.o., Wrocław